Notes on an Execution

ALSO BY DANYA KUKAFKA

Girl in Snow

Notes
on an
Execution

A Novel

Danya Kukafka

HARPER LARGE PRINT

An Imprint of HarperCollins*Publishers*

NOTES ON AN EXECUTION. Copyright © 2022 by Danya Kukafka. All rights reserved. Printed in the United States of America. No part of this book may be used or reproduced in any manner whatsoever without written permission except in the case of brief quotations embodied in critical articles and reviews. For information, address HarperCollins Publishers, 195 Broadway, New York, NY 10007.

HarperCollins books may be purchased for educational, business, or sales promotional use. For information, please e-mail the Special Markets Department at SPsales@harpercollins.com.

FIRST HARPER LARGE PRINT EDITION

ISBN: 978-0-06-321139-1

Library of Congress Cataloging-in-Publication Data is available upon request.

22 23 24 25 26 LSC 10 9 8 7 6 5 4 3 2 1

For Dana Murphy

I am awake in the place where women die.

—JENNY HOLZER (1993)

Notes on an Execution

12 Hours

You are a fingerprint.

When you open your eyes on the last day of your life, you see your own thumb. In the jaundiced prison light, the lines on the pad of your thumb look like a dried-out riverbed, like sand washed into twirling patterns by water, once there and now gone.

The nail is too long. You remember that old childhood myth—how after you die, your nails keep growing until they curl around your bones.

•

Inmate, state your name and number.

Ansel Packer, you call out. 999631.

You roll over in your cot. The ceiling forms its

usual picture, a pattern of water stains. If you tilt your head just right, the damp patch near the corner blooms in the shape of an elephant. Today is the day, you think, to the fleck of lumped paint that forms the elephant's trunk. Today is the day. The elephant smiles like it knows a desperate secret. You have spent many hours replicating this exact expression, matching the elephant on the ceiling grin for grin— today, it comes genuine. You and the elephant smile at each other until the fact of this morning blooms into an excited understanding, until you both look like maniacs.

You swing your legs over the edge of the bed, heave your body from the mattress. You pull on your prison-issue shoes, black slippers that leave an inch for your feet to slide around. You run water from the metal faucet over your toothbrush, squeeze out a gritty trail of toothpaste powder, then wet your hair in front of the small mirror, in which the glass is not actually glass, instead a pitted, scarring aluminum that would not shatter if it broke. In it, your reflection is blurry and warped. You bite each of your fingernails over the sink, one by one, ripping off the white carefully, evenly, until they are uniformly and raggedly short.

The countdown is often the hardest part, the chaplain told you, when he visited last night. Usually you like the chaplain, a balding man hunched with something like shame. The chaplain is new to Polunsky Unit—his face is soft and malleable, wide open, like you could reach right in. The chaplain spoke about forgiveness and relieving the burden, and accepting what we cannot change. Then, the question.

Your witness, the chaplain said through the visitation window. Is she coming?

You pictured the letter on your shelf, in that cramped little cell. The cream envelope, beckoning. The chaplain watched you with a stark sort of pity—you have always believed that pity is the most offensive of feelings. Pity is destruction wearing a mask of sympathy. Pity strips you bare. Pity shrinks.

She's coming, you said. Then: You have something in your teeth. You watched the man's hand rush anxious to his mouth.

In truth, you have not given much thought to tonight. It is too abstract, too easy to bend. The rumors on 12 Building are never worth listening to—one guy came back, pardoned only ten minutes before the injection, already strapped onto the gurney, and said he'd been tortured for hours, bamboo stuck up his fingernails like he was a hero in an action movie. Another inmate claimed they gave him donuts. You prefer not to wonder. It's okay to be afraid, the chaplain said. But you are not afraid. Instead, you feel a nauseous sense of marvel—lately, you dream you are flying through clear blue sky, soaring over wide swaths of crop circles. Your ears pop with altitude.

•

The wristwatch you inherited back on C-Pod is set five minutes ahead. You like to be prepared. It claims you have eleven hours, twenty-three minutes left.

They have promised it won't hurt. They have promised you won't feel anything at all. There was a psychiatrist once, who sat across from you in the visitation room in a crisp suit and expensive glasses. She told you things you have always suspected and cannot forget, things you wish you had never heard spoken aloud. By your usual calculations, the psychiatrist's face should have given you more—usually, you can gauge the proper level of sad or sorry this way. But the psychiatrist was blank, purposefully so, and you hated her for this. What do you feel? she asked. The question was pointless. Feeling held so little currency. So you shrugged and told the truth: I don't know. Nothing.

By 6:07 a.m., your supplies are arranged.

You mixed the paints last night—Froggy taught you how, back on C-Pod. You used the spine of a heavy book to crush down a set of colored pencils, then mixed the powder with a pot of Vaseline from commissary. You soaked three Popsicle sticks in water, saved from the ice cream bars you traded dozens of ramen noodle flavor packets to afford, and worked the wood until it frayed, fanning like the bristles of a paintbrush.

Now, you set up on the floor by the door of your cell. You are careful to ensure that the edge of your cardboard canvas nestles directly inside the strip of light that beams in from the hall. You ignore the breakfast tray on the floor, untouched since it was served at 3:00 a.m., the gravy filmed over, canned fruit already swarming with carpenter ants. It is April, but it feels like July; the heaters often run in the summer, and the pat of butter has melted to a little pool of fat.

You are allowed a single electronic device—you have chosen a radio. You reach for the knob, a screech of static noise. The men in the surrounding cells often holler their requests, R&B or classic rock, but they know what will happen today. They do not protest when you tune to your favorite station. Classical. The symphony is sudden and shocking, filling every corner of the concrete space. Symphony in F Major. You adjust to the existence of sound, settle it in.

What are you painting? Shawna asked once, as she slid your lunch tray through the slot in the door. She tilted her head to squint at your canvas.

A lake, you told her. A place I used to love.

She was not Shawna then, not yet—she was still Officer Billings, with her hair pulled back in its tight low bun, uniform pants scrunched around the bulge of her hip. She was not Shawna until six weeks later, when she pressed her flattened palm up to your window. You recognized the look in Shawna's eyes from other girls in different lives. A startle. She reminded you of Jenny—it was something in her wanting, so vulnerable and unruly. Tell me your name, Officer, you asked, and she flushed a harsh red. Shawna. You repeated it, reverent like a prayer. You imagined the nervous leap of her pulse, fluttering blue-veined from her thin white neck, and you became something bigger, a new version of yourself already stretching across your face. Shawna smiled, revealing the gap between her teeth. Sheepish, mawing.

When Shawna had gone, Jackson hooted his approval from the next cell over, teasing belligerent. You unraveled the fraying strings from your bedsheets, tied a miniature Snickers bar to the end, and shot it under Jackson's door to shut him up.

You tried to paint something different, for Shawna. You found a photo of a rose, tucked into one of the philosophy textbooks you requested from the library. You mixed the colors perfectly, but the petals wouldn't sit right. The rose was a blur of searing red, the angles all wrong, and you threw the whole thing away before Shawna could see. The next time she unlocked your cell to walk you down the long gray hall for a shower, it was like Shawna knew—she reached for the metal of your handcuffs and pressed her thumb to the inside of your wrist, testing. The officer on your other side breathed heavily through his nose, oblivious, as you shuddered. It had been so long since you'd felt anything other than gruff arms pulling you through cages, the cool ridges of a plastic fork, the boring pleasure of your own hand in the dark. It was electric, the thrill of Shawna's touch.

Since then, you have perfected the exchange.

Notes, tucked beneath lunch trays. Moments, stolen

between your cell and the recreation cage. Just last week, Shawna slipped a treasure through the slot in your cell door: a little black hairpin, the kind that peppered her slick bun.

Now, you dip the Popsicle stick into a smear of blue while you wait for her footsteps. Your canvas is arranged patiently at the edge of the door, corners aligned. This morning, Shawna will have an answer. Yes or no. After your conversation yesterday, it could go either way. You are good at ignoring doubt, at focusing instead on anticipation, which feels like a physical creature resting in your lap. A new symphony begins, quiet at first, before tightening and deepening—you linger in the rush of cello, thinking how things tend to accelerate, building on themselves, leading always to some spectacular crescendo.

•

You study the form while you paint. Offender Property Inventory. No matter Shawna's answer, you will have to pack. Three red mesh bags lie at the foot of your cot—they will transfer your most essential belongings to the Walls Unit, where you'll have another few hours with your earthly possessions before everything is taken away. You stuff them lazily full of the things you have hoarded these past seven years at Polunsky: the Funyuns and the hot sauce and the extra tubes of toothpaste. All meaningless now. You will leave it all to Froggy back on C-Pod—the only inmate ever to beat you in a game of chess.

You will leave your Theory here. All five notebooks. What happens to the Theory will depend on Shawna's answer.

And still, there is the matter of the letter. There is the matter of the photograph.

You have vowed not to read it again. You have mostly memorized it anyway. But Shawna is late. So when you are certain your hands are dry and clean, you stagger to your feet, reach to the top shelf, and pull the envelope down.

Blue Harrison's letter is short, concise. A single sheet of notebook paper. She has printed your address in slanting script: Ansel Packer, P.U., 12 Bldg, A-Pod, Death Row. A long sigh. You place the envelope gently on your pillow, before moving aside a stack of books to find the photograph, taped and hidden between the shelf and the wall.

This is your favorite part of your cell, partially because it never gets searched and partially because of the graffiti. You have been in this cell on A-Pod since you got your official date, and sometime before that, another inmate etched the words painstakingly into the concrete: We Are All Rabid. You smile every time you see it—it is so bizarre, so nonsensical, so unlike the other prison graffiti (mostly scripture and genitalia). There is a quiet truth to it that you would almost call hilarious, given the context.

You peel the tape from the corner of the photograph, careful not to rip. You sit on the bed, holding the photograph and the letter in your lap. Yes, you think. We Are All Rabid.

•

Until the letter from Blue Harrison arrived a few weeks ago, the photo was the only thing you kept for yourself. Back before the sentencing—when your lawyer still believed in the coerced confession—she offered you a favor. It took a few phone calls, but eventually she had the photograph mailed from the sheriff's office in Tupper Lake.

In the photo, the Blue House looks small. Shabby. The camera's angle cuts out the shutters on the left side, but you remember how they bloomed with hydrangea. It would be easy to look at the photograph and see only a house, bright blue, paint peeling. The signs of the restaurant are subtle. A flag waves from the porch: OPEN. The gravel driveway has been plowed to create a makeshift parking lot for customers. The curtains look plain white from the outside, but you know that inside they are checkered with little red squares. You remember the smell. French fries, Lysol, apple pie. How the kitchen doors clanged. Steam, broken glass. On the day the photo was taken, the sky was tinged with rain. Looking, you can almost smell the sharp tang of sulfur.

Your favorite part of the photograph is the upstairs window. The curtain is split just slightly open, and if you look closely, you can see the shadow of a single arm, shoulder to elbow. The bare arm of a teenage girl. You like to imagine what she was doing at the exact moment the photo was taken—she must have been standing near her bedroom door, talking to someone or looking in the mirror.

She signed the letter Blue. Her real name is Beatrice, but she was never Beatrice to you or anyone who knew her then. She was always Blue: Blue, with her hair braided and flung over one shoulder. Blue, in that Tupper Lake Track & Field sweatshirt, sleeves stretched anxious at the wrists. When you remember

Blue Harrison, and your time in the Blue House, you recall how she could never walk by the surface of a window without glancing nervous at her own reflection.

You do not know what the feeling is, when you look at the photograph. It cannot be love, because you have been tested—you don't laugh at the right moments or flinch at the wrong ones. There are statistics. Something about emotional recognition, sympathy, pain. You don't understand the kind of love you read about in books, and you like movies mostly for the study of them, the mastery of faces twisting into other faces. Anyway, no matter what they say you are capable of—it cannot be love, that would be neurologically impossible—looking at the photograph of the Blue House brings you there. To the place where the shrieking stops. The quiet is delicious, a gasping relief.

•

An echo, finally, from the long hall. The familiar shuffle of Shawna's footsteps.

You drop back to the floor, resume a stilted motion with your paintbrush: you are dotting the grass with tiny flowers, blooming red. You try to focus on the pinpoint bristle, the waxy smell of crushed pencil.

Inmate, state your name and number.

Shawna's voice sounds always on the verge of collapse—today, an officer will come by every fifteen minutes to check that you are still breathing. You do not dare look up from your painting, though you know she will be wearing that same naked face, her desire plain and unhidden, mixed now with excitement, or maybe sadness, depending on her answer.

There are things Shawna loves about you, but none of them have much to do with you. It is your position that enthralls her—your power caged while she holds the literal key. Shawna is the type of woman who does not break rules. She turns dutifully away while the male officers perform their strip searches, before every shower and every recreation hour. You spend twenty-two hours a day in this six-by-nine cell, where you cannot physically see another human being, and Shawna knows this. She is the type of woman who reads romance novels with hulking men on their covers. You can smell her laundry detergent, the egg salad sandwich she brings from home for lunch. Shawna loves you because you cannot get much closer, for the fact of the steel door between you, promising both passion and safety. In this sense, she is nothing like Jenny. Jenny was always prodding, trying to see inside. Tell me what you're feeling, Jenny would say. Give me your whole. But Shawna revels in the distance, the intoxicating unknown that sits always between two people. And now, she perches at the edge of the gap. It takes every ounce of self-control not to look up and confirm what you know: Shawna belongs to you.

Ansel Packer, you repeat calmly. 999631.

Shawna's uniform creaks as she bends to tie her shoe. The camera in the corner of your cell does not reach to the hall, and your painting is positioned perfectly. It comes in the slightest flash of white, nearly nonexistent: the flicker of paper, as Shawna's note slips beneath the crack in your door, hiding seamlessly under the edge of your canvas.

•

Shawna believes in your innocence.

You could never do that, she whispered once, paused outside your cell on a long evening shift, shadows razoring across her cheeks. You could never.

She knows, of course, what they call you on 12 Building.

The Girly Killer.

The newspaper article was generous with the details: it ran after your first appeal, spreading the nickname across 12 Building like wildfire. The writer had lumped them all together, as though they were intentional, related. The Girls. The article used that word, the one you hate. Serial is something different—a label meant for men unlike you.

You could never. Shawna is certain, though you have never once claimed this for yourself. You prefer to let her talk in circles, to let the outrage take over: this is immeasurably easier than the questions. Do you feel bad? Are you sorry? You are never quite sure what this means. You feel bad, sure. More accurately, you wish you were not here. You don't see how guilt helps anyone, but it has been the question for years now, all through your trial and your many fruitless appeals. Are you capable? they ask. Are you physically capable of feeling empathy?

You tuck Shawna's note into the waistband of your pants and gaze up at the elephant on the ceiling.

The elephant has a psychopath smile, alive in one moment, just an impression in the next. The whole question is absurd, nearly lunatic—there is no line you cross over, no alarm you set off, no scale to weigh. The question, you have finally deduced, is not really about empathy. The question is how you can possibly be human.

And yet. You lift your thumb to the light, examine it close. In that same fingerprint, it is inarguable and insistent: the faint, mouse-like tick of your own pulse.

•

There is the story you know about yourself. There is the story everyone knows. As you pull Shawna's note from your waistband, you wonder how that story became so distorted—how only your weakest moments matter now, how they expanded to devour everything else.

You hunch over, so the camera placed in the corner of your cell cannot catch the note. There, in Shawna's trembly handwriting. Three words:

I did it.

Hope rushes in, a blinding white. It sears through

every inch of you as the world cracks open, bleeds. You have eleven hours and sixteen minutes left, or maybe, with Shawna's promise, you have a lifetime.

•

There must have been a time, a reporter said to you once. A time before you were like this.

If there ever was a time, you would like to remember it.

Lavender
1973

If there was a before, it began with Lavender.
She was seventeen years old. She knew what it meant, to bring life into the world. The gravity. She knew that love could swaddle you tight, and also bruise. But until the time came, Lavender did not understand what it meant to walk away from a thing she'd grown from her own insides.

•

"Tell me a story," Lavender gasped, between contractions.

She was splayed out in the barn, on a blanket propped against a stack of hay. Johnny crouched over her with a lantern, his breath curling white in the frigid late-winter air.

"The baby," Lavender said. "Tell me about the baby."

It was becoming increasingly clear that the baby might actually kill her. Every contraction proved how horribly unprepared they were—despite all Johnny's bravado and the passages he quoted from the medical textbooks his grandfather had left, neither of them knew much about childbirth. The books hadn't mentioned this. The blood, apocalyptic. The pain, white-hot and sweat-soaked.

"He'll grow up to be president," Johnny said. "He'll be a king."

Lavender groaned. She could feel the baby's head tearing at her skin, a grapefruit, half exited.

"You don't know it's a boy," she panted. "Besides, there's no such thing as kings anymore."

She pushed until the walls of the barn went crimson. Her body felt full of glass shards—a jagged, inner twisting. When the next contraction came, Lavender sank into it, her throat breaking into a guttural scream.

"He'll be good," Johnny said. "He'll be brave, and smart, and powerful. I can see his head, Lav, you have to keep pushing."

Blackout. Her whole self converged into one shattering wound. The shriek came then, a mewling cry. Johnny was covered in gore up to his elbows, and Lavender watched as he picked up the gardening shears he'd sterilized with alcohol, then used them to cut the umbilical cord. Seconds later, Lavender was holding it. Her child. Slick with afterbirth, foamy around the head, the baby was a tangle of furious limbs. In the lantern's glow, his eyes were nearly black. He did not look like a baby, Lavender thought. Little purple alien.

Johnny slumped beside her in the hay, panting.

"Look," he rasped. "Look at what we made, my girl."

The feeling hit Lavender just in time: a love so consuming, it felt more like panic. The sensation was followed immediately by a nauseous, tidal guilt. Because Lavender knew, from the second she saw the baby, that she did not want this kind of love. It was too much. Too hungry. But it had been growing inside her all these months, and now it had fingers, toes. It was gulping oxygen.

Johnny wiped the baby down with a towel and positioned him firmly against Lavender's nipple. As she peered down at the scrunched and flaking bundle, Lavender was thankful for the dark of the barn, the sweaty damp of her face—Johnny hated when she cried. Lavender placed a palm on the ball of the baby's head, those initial traitorous thoughts already laced with regret. She drowned the feeling with assurances, murmured against the baby's slippery skin. *I will love you like the ocean loves the sand.*

They named the baby Ansel, after Johnny's grandfather.

•

Here were the things Johnny had promised:

Quiet. Open skies. A whole house at their disposal, a garden of Lavender's own. No school, no disappointed teachers. No rules at all. A life where no one was ever watching—they were alone in the farmhouse, completely alone, the nearest neighbor ten miles away. Sometimes, when Johnny went out hunting, Lavender stood on the back deck and screamed as loudly as she could, screamed until her voice went hoarse, to see if someone would come running. No one ever did.

Just a year earlier, Lavender had been a normal sixteen. It was 1972, and she'd spent her days sleeping through math class then history class then English

NOTES ON AN EXECUTION · 23

class, cackling with her friend Julie as they smoked pilfered cigarettes by the gym door. She met Johnny Packer at the tavern, when they snuck in one Friday. He was older, handsome. *Like a young John Wayne*, Julie had giggled, the first time Johnny showed up after school in his pickup truck. Lavender loved Johnny's scraggly hair, his rotation of flannel shirts, his heavy work boots. Johnny's hands were always filthy from the farm, but Lavender loved how he smelled. Like grease and sunshine.

The last time Lavender saw her mother, she'd been slumped at the folding card table, a cigarette dangling from her mouth. Her mother had attempted a house-wife's beehive—it was flat, lopsided, like a drooping balloon.

You go right ahead, Lavender's mother had said. *Drop out of school, move to that ratty farm.*

A sick, satisfied smile.

Just you wait, honey. Men are wolves, and some wolves are patient.

Lavender had swiped her mother's antique locket from the dresser on her way out. The locket was a circle of rusty metal with an empty nameplate inside. It had adorned the center of her mother's broken jewelry box for as long as she could remember—the only proof that Lavender's mother was capable of treasuring something.

It was true that living on the farm had not been quite what Lavender had imagined. She'd moved in six months after meeting Johnny; before that, Johnny had lived alone with his grandfather. Johnny's mother had passed away and his father had left, and he never spoke of either of them. Old Ansel had been a war veteran with a grizzled voice who made Johnny perform chores for every meal as a child. Old Ansel coughed, and he coughed, until he died, a few weeks after Lavender arrived. They buried him in the yard beneath the spruce; Lavender didn't like to walk over the spot, still humped with dirt. She'd learned to milk the goat, to wring the chickens' necks before she plucked and disemboweled them. She tended to the garden, which was ten times the size of the small patch she'd kept behind her mother's trailer—it was always threatening to outgrow her. She had given up regular showers, too difficult with the outdoor spigot, and her hair had become permanently tangled.

Johnny did the hunting. He purified their water. Fixed up the house. Some nights, he'd call Lavender in from a long day in the yard—she would find him standing by the door with his pants unzipped, engorged and waiting with a sneer on his face. Those nights, he threw her against the wall. With her cheek slammed hard on the splintering oak, Johnny's hunger growling into her neck, she would revel in the essence of it. His thrusting need. Those calloused hands, exalting her. *My girl, my girl.* Lavender did not know if she thrilled with Johnny's hardness or the fact that she could gentle it.

•

They did not have diapers, so Lavender wrapped a clean rag around Ansel's waist and knotted it at the legs. She swaddled him tight in one of the barn blankets, then stood to limp after Johnny.

She hiked barefoot back up to the house. Dizzy. She'd been in so much pain, she did not remember the trip to the barn, only that Johnny had carried her, and now she didn't have shoes—the late-winter air was biting cold, and Lavender held Ansel to her chest as he spluttered. She guessed it was near midnight.

The farmhouse sat at the top of a hill. Even in the dark it looked lopsided, leaning precariously to the left. The house was a constant work in progress. Johnny's grandfather had left them with the burst pipes, the leaking roof, the missing windowpanes. Usually, Lavender didn't mind. It was worth it for the moments she stood alone on the deck, overlooking the wide expanse of field. The rolling grass shone silver in the mornings, orange in the evenings, and across the pasture, she could see the gnashing peaks of the Adirondack Mountains. The farmhouse sat just outside Essex, New York, an hour's drive from Canada. On a clear day she liked to squint into the bright, imagining an invisible line where the distance turned into another country entirely. The thought was exotic, enchanting. Lavender had never left New York State.

"Will you make a fire?" she asked, when they were inside. The house was frigid, the previous night's cold ash sitting gusty in the wood stove.

"It's late," Johnny said. "Aren't you tired?"

It wasn't worth the argument. Lavender struggled up the stairs, where she sponged the blood from her legs with a washcloth and changed her clothes. None of her old clothes fit anymore: the bell-bottom corduroys she'd thrifted with Julie sat in a box with her best collared blouses, too tight for her bulging stomach. By the time she climbed into bed, wearing one of Johnny's old T-shirts, he was already asleep, and Ansel was fussing in a bundle on her pillow. Lavender's neck crackled with dried sweat, and she dozed upright with the baby in her arms, anxious, half dreaming.

By morning, Ansel's rag had soaked through and Lavender could feel the slick of diarrhea running down her deflating belly. When Johnny woke to the smell, he jolted—Ansel started to cry, a shrieking upset.

Johnny stood, fumbling for an old T-shirt, which he threw onto the bed just out of Lavender's reach.

"If you can hold him for a second—" Lavender said.

The look Johnny gave her then. The frustration did not belong on his face—it was the kind of ugly that must have originated inside Lavender herself. *I'm sorry*, Lavender wanted to say, though she did not know what for. As she listened to Johnny's footsteps creak down the stairs, Lavender pressed her lips to the screaming baby's forehead. This was how it always went, wasn't it? All those women who'd come before her, in caves and tents and covered wagons. It was a wonder how she'd never given much thought to the ancient, timeless fact. Motherhood was, by nature, a thing you did alone.

Here were the things Johnny had loved once: The mole on the back of Lavender's neck, which he used to kiss before they fell asleep. The bones in her fingers, so small he swore he could feel each one. How Lavender's teeth overlapped in the front—*snaggle*, he called her, teasing.

Now, Johnny did not see her teeth. Instead, the scratches on her face from Ansel's tiny nails.

"For God's sake," he said, as Ansel screamed. "Can't you make him stop?"

Johnny sat at the pockmarked table, using Ansel's pudgy fingers to trace cartoon animals into the left-over fat on his dinner plate. *Dog*, Johnny explained, his voice croaking tender. *Chicken.* Ansel's face was blobby, uncomprehending—when the baby inevitably started whining, Johnny passed him back to Lavender and stood for his evening cigar. Alone again, as Ansel's fingers streaked grease across her shirt, Lavender tried to hold the scene at the front of her consciousness. How Johnny had gazed at his son for those brief, perfect minutes, like he wanted to impart himself on the child. Like DNA was not enough. With the baby in his lap, cooing and affectionate, Johnny looked like the man Lavender had met in the tavern so long ago. She could still hear Julie's voice, misty and beer-soured.

I bet he's soft on the inside, Julie had whispered. *I bet you could take a bite right out of him.*

•

By the time Ansel could sit up on his own, Lavender could not recall the contours of Julie's face—only eyelashes, and a sly, sneaky grin. Fraying jeans and a choker necklace, nicotine and homemade lip balm. Julie's voice, humming the Supremes. *What about California?* Julie had asked, betrayed, when Lavender announced she'd be moving to the farmhouse. *What about the protests? It won't be the same without you.* Lavender remembered Julie's silhouette through the window of the departing bus, a homemade sign tucked somewhere by her feet. *End The War In Vietnam!* Julie had waved as the Greyhound groaned away, and Lavender had not wondered—had not even questioned—whether a choice was a thing that could ravage.

•

Dear Julie.

Lavender composed the letters in her head, because she didn't have an address or any way to get to the post office. She didn't know how to drive, and Johnny only used the truck once a month, alone, to go to the store. The farm needed so much work, he said—why would she need to go into town? Johnny would sulk as he unloaded the cans of food, muttering in a voice that belonged to his grandfather. *Expensive, keeping the two of you.*

•

Dear Julie.

Tell me about California.

I think of you often—I imagine you are on a beach somewhere, browning in the sun. Things are fine here. Ansel is five months old now. He has the strangest gaze, like he's looking right through you. Anyway, I hope the weather's nice there. Someday, when Ansel is old enough, we'll come find you. He's a good baby, you'll like him. We'll all sit in the sand.

Dear Julie. Ansel is eight months today. He's so chunky, the rolls in his legs look like baking dough. He has two teeth now, spaced out on the bottom, like separate little jutting bones.

I keep thinking about summer, when we hiked to the edge of the property, where the raspberries grow wild. Johnny fed the berries right into Ansel's mouth, and Ansel's hands stained red with the juice. They looked like a postcard of a happy family, and I felt so outside of myself, watching them play. Like a bird perched on a distant branch. Or one of Johnny's rabbits, strung up by the legs.

Dear Julie. I know, I know. It's been a while. Spring again now. Ansel is walking, getting into everything. He sliced his arm on some construction equipment in the yard, and of course it got infected. He had a fever, but Johnny said no hospital. You know I don't believe in God or anything, but it's the closest I've come to praying. Summer will be here soon—you know how it goes. I don't even remember the last few weeks. It's like I slept right through them.

Dear Julie. Did you ever learn to drive? I know we promised we'd do it together. We should have, when we had the chance. I haven't left the property since Ansel was born—he's almost two years old now, can you believe that?

Johnny took Ansel hunting in the forest yesterday. I told him Ansel was too young. When they came back, Ansel had these purple splotches up his arms.

You should have seen the shape of those bruises, Julie. Like fingers.

•

It started small like that. Trivial, easy to ignore. A grunt from Johnny's throat, an angry slammed door—a grip of the wrist, a flick on the ear. A palm, playfully smacking her cheek.

•

By the time Lavender looked up, Ansel was three years old. They had lived their days and nights in a long, repetitive procession, time sucked into the lonely vacuum of the farmhouse.

It was dead summer, a sweaty afternoon, when Ansel walked into the forest. Lavender was on her knees in the garden. When she stood from the dying dahlias to find the yard empty, the sun was high in the sky. She had no idea how long Ansel had been gone.

Ansel was not a pretty child, or even a cute one. His forehead was massive, and his eyes bulged too big. Lately, he'd been playing tricks on Lavender. Hiding the spatula while she was cooking, filling her water glass up in the toilet. But this was different. He had never gone alone beyond the edge of the field.

The panic came in a flood. Lavender stood at the tree line, calling Ansel's name until her voice rasped.

Upstairs, Johnny was napping. He grumbled when Lavender rolled him over.

"What?"

"It's Ansel," she said, panting. "He ran into the woods. You have to find him, Johnny."

"Calm down," Johnny said, his breath sour.

"He's three years old." Lavender hated the alarm in her own voice, how it shrilled her. "He's all alone in the forest."

"Why don't you go?"

Johnny's erection poked through the slit in his boxer shorts. A warning.

"You know the woods," she said. "And you're faster."

"What'll you give me for it?" he asked.

He was joking, she thought. Grinning now. His hand moved down, into the elastic seam of his shorts.

"That's not funny, Johnny. It's not funny."

"Am I laughing?"

He touched himself, rhythmic, smiling. Lavender couldn't help it—the tears were lodged in her throat, thick and painful. When she began to cry, Johnny's hand stopped. His smile melted down into a grimace.

"Fine," Lavender said. "But you promise, after, you'll find him?"

She climbed on top. Tears fled salty into her mouth as she shimmied out of her linen pants. As she pressed Johnny inside, she pictured her baby, toppling scared into a stream. She pictured water, filling his tiny lungs. A vulture, hovering. A steep ravine. Lavender pumped up and down, numb—by the time Johnny wilted inside her, the sneer on his face had transformed him entirely.

I don't think you can ever see the whole of another person, Julie used to say. As Johnny shoved her off, limp and heaving furious, Lavender studied the disdain. The moon of his face, revealing its cratered underside.

•

Afternoon bled into evening as Lavender paced the yard, hysteria blooming. Johnny had stormed out—to search, she hoped—and she hugged her knees to her chest on the bottom step of the porch, rocking anxious. By the time Lavender heard the rustling from the forest, night had fallen, and her worry had hardened, crystallizing into an urgent, profound dread.

"Mama?"

It was Ansel, crouched in the twilight at the edge of the forest. His feet were filthy, a ring of dirt caked around his mouth. Lavender rushed him, her eyes adjusting: he was covered in crimson, and he smelled like rust. Blood. She patted him frantically down, felt each of his child bones for a break.

The blood, it appeared, was coming from his hand. In his fist, Ansel clutched a chipmunk with no head. It looked, in shadow, like a mutilated stuffed animal, a decapitated doll. It didn't seem to bother him—just another forgotten toy.

A scream built in Lavender's throat, but she was too exhausted to let it out. She scooped Ansel onto her hip and hiked back up to the house, shuffling him into the outdoor shower. Bugs flew in clouds around the single bulb, while Lavender ran the mottled sponge over Ansel's toes; she kissed each one in apology as the freezing water pounded.

"Come on," she whispered, as she toweled him off. "Let's get you something to eat."

When she turned on the kitchen light, Lavender's body felt like a funnel, her relief draining slowly away.

The house was quiet. Johnny had gone. But while Lavender had been pacing the perimeter of the property, he had taken a trip to the shed. His grandfather's dusty old locks had been pulled from storage and fitted to the pantry door. Johnny had locked all the canned food away, locked the refrigerator, drilled a hole in the cabinet above the sink just to fit a lock over the dry pasta and the peanut butter.

Lavender could hear his words, an echo parroting constantly in her ear: *You and that boy need to learn to earn your keep.* Never mind the long afternoons she spent in the garden, trying to bring the tomato plants to fruit. Never mind the mornings she passed with Ansel, teaching him words from the leather-bound dictionary. Never mind the evenings she spent scraping grime from Johnny's old hunting boots. Johnny had made himself clear: his job was to provide. Lavender could not parse exactly what her job had become, but clearly, she was failing to do it.

Okay, Lavender thought, as she surveyed the locked food. Her head, a scramble. Okay. They would eat in the morning.

She did not dare sleep in her own bed that night. She could not face him—she did not know what she might find. Instead, she curled up with Ansel on the hard floor in the extra bedroom, on top of the old blanket from the barn. *Hungry*, Ansel babbled into the night, as Johnny's footsteps finally thunked up the stairs. When Ansel began to shiver from the hunger, Lavender took off the bathrobe she'd been wearing since the shower and wrapped it around him. Naked on the floor, breasts bared to the window, Lavender caught the glint of her mother's locket, shining in reflection—the only thing she owned for herself. Gently, she unclasped it. She threaded it around Ansel's neck.

"This is yours now," Lavender said. "It will always keep you safe."

Her voice quavered, but the words themselves seemed to lull the boy to sleep.

Lavender waited until the house was completely still before she crept downstairs and pulled one of Johnny's jackets from the front closet. Until that point, her worry had been negligible. Johnny had never done something like this—had only gripped her wrists a little too hard, shoved her aside on his way up the stairs. The locked food was a promise and a threat, spurred by her inability to do the most basic thing: the mothering.

The pickup truck loomed near the edge of the field. Lavender waded barefoot through the tall damp grass. The night was so dark. No moon. She felt faint, withered. She hadn't eaten since breakfast. The key fit easily into the lock on the door; it opened with a whining creak.

Lavender settled in the driver's seat.

It was irresistible: the almost. She almost put the keys in the ignition. She almost drove through the night, until she found the ocean. But the sight of the stick shift pushed the truth over Lavender, even more devastating now that she'd made it this far. She didn't know how to drive. She didn't know if the car had gas, and she wouldn't know how to fill it either way. She wasn't even wearing a shirt, and she couldn't get a shirt without going into the room where Johnny slept. It was so desperate, too much. She could never.

Lavender bent over the steering wheel and let the sob overtake her. She cried for Ansel, for the chipmunk, for her own grumbling stomach. She cried for the things she had wanted, which she couldn't even picture anymore. It was like she'd held her own desire too long in the palm of her hand and it was now just an object, devoid of meaning, useless and taking up space.

•

She woke the next morning to the smell of sizzling bacon.

Lavender was alone on Ansel's bedroom floor, the blanket tangled at her feet, sun streaming through the window in sharp, doughy rays. She slipped into the bathrobe, discarded in a heap, and padded downstairs.

Johnny stood over the stove like always. That familiar hulking self. Lavender knew his body so well, it was like she had become a part of it—she felt silly now, remembering her thoughts of the highway. Johnny stretched a plate toward her. A pile of steaming eggs and two strips of the crunchy bacon they froze for special occasions. A quick glance told her: the cabinets had been locked again, the extra food cleared and tucked away.

Ansel sat at the table, happily gulping a glass of milk.

"Please," Johnny said. Soft now. "Eat, my love."

Lavender could no longer remember what Johnny had promised, but she recognized the sound of it. She let Johnny twist his fingers in her hair. She let him kiss the ridge of her hip. She let him whisper *I'm sorry I'm sorry* until the words sounded like a completely different language.

While Johnny napped, Lavender sat with Ansel in the rocking chair. The chain of the locket had left a faint green smudge around Ansel's neck, and her fear dipped in a momentary panic at the resemblance to a bruise. They pulled all the books from the shelves—technical manuals and maps of the Philippines, Japan, Vietnam—until they found it. A cartographer's map of the Adirondacks. Lavender jiggled Ansel in her lap, spread the paper over their legs.

"We are here," Lavender whispered. She traced Ansel's hand down the highway. Farmhouse to town to the edge of the page.

It was a specific violence, the white of her underwear. Four weeks late, then six: Lavender prayed for a spot of blood. Every morning, her body betrayed her, morphing slowly without her permission. She vomited into the crusty bowl of the toilet, the terror rising up with her insides—swelling tidal, petrified.

Dear Julie.

Do you remember how we loved the Manson girls? How we followed the trials like a television show? I dream about those girls now, how they reached that bloody end. I wonder if Susan Atkins ever felt like this. If there was a whispering voice in the dark of her head, saying: *Go*.

It's growing, Julie. I can't stop it.

•

Lavender found a burlap sack in the barn. Inside, she placed one meager can of corn—she'd stolen it when Johnny's back was turned, a lump beneath her shirt, heart hammering with the recklessness. She stuck an old winter coat in the sack, and though it was too small for Ansel, it would keep him warm if necessary. Last, she added the rusty kitchen knife that had fallen behind the sink. She shoved the sack in the back of the closet in Ansel's room, where Johnny would never look.

That night, Johnny snored like always and Lavender placed a hand on her stomach, which felt swollen, alien. She thought of the bag in the closet, beaming its promise. When she'd told Johnny about the baby, bracing for explosion, he had only smiled. *Our little family.* Bile, rising treacherous in her throat.

Lavender grew. As she expanded, she took up residence in the rocking chair by the back door—she sat first thing in the morning and often only moved for bathroom breaks. Her brain was a sieve, no longer hers. The new baby ate her thoughts as they came, and Lavender was just the shell, the zombie vessel.

Ansel crouched constantly at Lavender's feet. He squished bugs between his fingers and presented them like gifts. He cracked acorns with his baby teeth and gave her the splintered halves. Johnny disappeared for days at a time, and Ansel fetched Lavender the cans of soup Johnny left on the counter. Their rations. They'd take turns licking the cold spoon. When Johnny returned, his mood was snarling—Lavender thought of the bag in the closet, the jacket, the knife. She had grown too big to walk up the stairs.

•

Dear Julie.

I wonder about choices. How we resent them, and how we regret them—even as we watch them grow.

•

The contractions started early. A shooting pain, in the cold husk of dawn. Lavender begged: *No barn. Let's just do it here.*

Johnny rolled out a blanket next to the rocking chair. He and Ansel stood over Lavender while she shrieked and bled and pushed. It was different this time—like she was not inside her own body, like the pain had consumed her and she was only there to spectate. Halfway through, Ansel flung himself over Lavender, his sticky palm pressed to her forehead with worry, and Lavender felt a primal bursting that brought her briefly back into herself: a swell of love so powerful and doomed, she was not sure she'd live through it.

After, there was calm.

Lavender wished the floor would open beneath her, pull her into a different life. She was certain that her soul had exited her body along with the baby's head, fingers, toenails. As Johnny passed the bundle to Ansel and tried to rouse her from the floor, it occurred to Lavender that reincarnation was in fact a last resort: there were other lives, in this very world. California. She turned the word over in her mind, a sweet sucking candy that disintegrated on her tongue.

She could not look at either of her sick, sniffling children. Ansel, with his strange monster face. The new baby, a bundle of warm skin that she couldn't bear to touch without feeling like she'd catch some disease.

What disease, she didn't know. But it would trap her here.

Lavender sank into the hardwood. She wished to be a speck of dust on the ceiling.

Weeks passed, and the new baby did not have a name. One month melted into two. *Baby Packer*, Ansel would coo, as he played with the bundle on the floor by the fireplace. A little song he'd made up, tuneless and lilting. *Baby Packer eat, Baby Packer sleep. Brother loves you, Baby Packer. Brother loves you.*

Johnny made the occasional show of tenderness, a halfhearted attempt to bring her back to life. He rubbed Lavender's feet, crouched at the end of the mattress. He cleaned her wounds with a sponge, ran a hairbrush through her tangles. She stayed nestled in bed while Johnny brought the baby in to nurse—the rest of the time, Baby Packer squirmed under Ansel's watchful four-year-old eye.

For the few minutes a day that Lavender held the baby, she wondered how he had gotten here, whether it was possible that this sweet suckling thing even belonged to her. With Ansel, she'd felt the same way, but her love had been so new and fierce. Now, she feared she had used it all up.

"Take him," she monotoned, once the baby finished feeding. "I don't want him here."

Johnny's frustration was hardening. Lavender could feel it, building up in his chest like molten lava. The horror only made her sicker. Numb. She had been subsisting on a single can of corn or beans per day, the hunger pangs like background static. *More when you start contributing again,* Johnny promised idly, his voice turned sour with disgust and frustration, repeating the words that had become a fixation. *You have to learn to earn your keep.*

So by the time Johnny stood over the bed, brimming with indignation, Lavender was so weak and brainless, she could not bring herself to care. Lavender looked up at the mass of him, seething, enraged, and tried to conjure the Johnny in the field with the raspberries. It wasn't that he'd been replaced by this grizzly stranger, more that he'd evolved. Grown into his own shadow.

"Get up," Johnny said.

"I can't," Lavender told him.

"Get the fuck up, Lavender." His voice itched, curdled. "You have to get up right now."

"I can't," she said again.

Lavender felt like she'd willingly asked for what came next. Like the plot had already been written out for her, and all she had to do was live it. She realized she had been waiting months for this. The locked food, the little bruises—warnings she had registered but not heeded.

Before Johnny lunged, she expected some nightmare version of him, a person she'd never seen. But no. In the milliseconds before the blow, Lavender looked at the same rugged man she had always known, and she thought, with a clarity that bordered on sympathy: *You could have been anything, Johnny. You could have been anything but this.*

A fistful of hair, yanked from the scalp. A scream, pleading, as Lavender's aching bones slammed against the floor. The wound between her legs, open now, searing. Johnny's steel-toed boot, rearing back like a horse, landing square in her stomach. The shock, a glittered red.

When the sound came from the door, Lavender saw double: the stuttering form of Ansel's silhouette. He held the baby like Lavender had taught him, one arm beneath the head. Blurred, he looked too young—pants-less and chicken-legged—to be holding an infant. Ansel and the baby were both crying, panicked, but when Lavender reached for them, her whole body smarted, a series of wounds she had not yet cataloged, her mouth a sandy pool of blood and grit.

"Ansel," Lavender croaked. No sound came out. "Go."

Time slowed.

"No," she tried to scream. "Johnny, please—"

It was too quick. Too thoughtless. With one massive hand, Johnny yanked Ansel's head back and slammed it with a crack against the wooden doorframe.

After, the silence.

It rang in Lavender's ears, punctuated only by Johnny's heavy, labored breaths. Even the baby had stopped crying, surprised. The room was incredibly still. Lavender watched from the floor, stunned, as the realization seemed to wash over Johnny. His giant body trembled with bewilderment as he backed out of the bedroom. They listened as he stormed down the stairs, slammed the back screen door. Ansel blinked slowly, dazed.

Lavender dragged herself across the hardwood. A slugging creak. When she reached her children, she gathered them in her arms and wept.

Johnny did not come back that night. Lavender huddled in the bed with the boys, vigilant and alert. She nursed the baby until he fell asleep—when Ansel withered hungry, Lavender shook her head in apology. Not enough milk. Ansel peered up at her with spindly wet lashes, the hollows around his eye sockets like those of a frightened little ghost.

•

At the first light of dawn, Lavender slid from the bed. The bruises across her legs and stomach were already purpling—both boys were asleep on the old mattress, breathing steadily. The wound on Ansel's head had swollen, protruding to the size of a golf ball.

Lavender creaked open the window, stuck her face into the morning. The breeze was a gasp on her cheeks, the dewy air like a new kind of promise. Beyond, the fields were a morning yellow. Beyond, beyond. Beyond was a place Lavender could hardly remember. Beyond this room, beyond this house, there were mothers who cooked pot roast for their children. There were little boys who watched cartoons on Saturday mornings, innocent and unafraid. Buttered popcorn at the movie theater, boxed cereal, real toothpaste. There were televisions and newspapers and radios, schools and bars and coffee shops. Before she moved to the farmhouse, a man had landed on the moon—for all she knew, there could be a whole city up there by now.

Johnny stayed away until noon. Twigs in his hair. He'd slept in the forest. The look on his face made him so much smaller, like a completely different Johnny, slumped and ashamed. His entire body was a beg, curled desperate for forgiveness.

Lavender could not fathom forgiveness. But she would do this one thing—for the blue sunrise, that tantalizing beyond. For the world outside, which she was starting to fear her children would never see.

"Please," Lavender said. She bared her teeth so Johnny could see the chip he'd left in her canine. "Take me for a drive."

•

Lavender put on real clothes for the first time in months. She combed her hair, splashed water on her puffy cheeks, and tied a sweater around her waist, the soft wool knit she'd spent all winter making.

"Are we going to the barn?" Ansel asked, as Lavender slipped on her nicest shoes, penny loafers, untouched since her school days. Johnny was already waiting in the car. It had taken surprisingly little to convince him: a pointed gaze at the marks up her thighs, plus the reassurance that the boys would be fine for an hour or two. Lavender did not have a plan. But she could not see a way forward that was not also out.

"Daddy and I are going on a trip," Lavender said. "We'll be back soon."

Ansel stretched his arms out from the floor, and she picked him up. He was getting too big to sit on her hip, but the weight was familiar, like she'd been carrying it a long time. The bump on his head bulged like a fist, and Lavender resisted the urge to touch it. She kissed the hair around it, then squatted over the baby. Wrapped in one of Johnny's jackets by the fireplace, Baby Packer squirmed and babbled; they'd been playing with a set of old spoons, and his spastic palms were stained black from the polish. Lavender pressed her nose to the baby's scalp, breathing in his sweet, tangy musk.

"Ansel," Lavender said, pressing both her hands to his cheeks. "Can I trust you to take care of your brother?"

Ansel nodded.

"If he cries, where do we take him?"

"To the rocking chair."

"Good," Lavender said. Choking now. "Smart boy."

It was time. Lavender's decisions did not feel like decisions—more like flakes of ash, settled on her shoulders. The moment was not hers to judge. She could hear the grumble of the truck's engine at the edge of the field, Johnny's looming presence, constant and menacing.

Lavender could not bear even one more glance. Somewhere deep and full of denial, Lavender knew the last time she saw her children had already passed—she could not withstand their questioning eyes, their rosebud mouths, the little fingernails she'd grown from nothing. So she didn't look. With her back turned, Lavender stepped into the day.

"Be good," she said, and she shut the door.

•

Lavender had not left the farmhouse property in over five years. At first, the isolation had been a gift, the wilderness like an antidote to the chemical misery of her mother's trailer—Lavender couldn't pinpoint the turn, the moment the farmhouse had become her captor.

Now, the universe was unfolding through the wind-shield, both familiar and alien, gas stations bustling with energy, fast-food restaurants puffing the deliri-ous scent of beef. With one arm stuck out the window, the wind chopping and whirling in her ears, Lavender almost forgot the wreck of her life. She had to count on her fingers to remember that she was twenty-one years old—her friends from school would have jobs by now, husbands, children. Lavender realized she did not know who the current president was; she had com-pletely missed the election of '76. Speeding at ten over the limit, Lavender was hungry. But also, she was free. She was away from her children, and it felt intoxicat-ing; she was light-headed, giddy.

"South," Lavender said, when Johnny asked where she wanted to go. Shame radiated off him, and he drove in silence. The steering wheel seemed so trivial, minia-ture in Johnny's hands—they were going at least eighty miles an hour. She could have done it, veered them into oncoming traffic, or fast into the ditch on the side of the highway. Vaguely, this had been the idea. But the air smelled so fresh, the radio was humming, and it was a surprise when Lavender realized that she did not want to die.

They stopped for gas outside Albany, two hours from home and halfway down New York State. Lavender smiled as Johnny pulled the truck into the station, picturing the hundreds of miles between him and her boys.

"What's so funny?" Johnny said, still sheepish.

"Nothing," Lavender told him. "Bathroom."

As Johnny clicked the door open, she studied the hair that trailed up the back of his neck. The knot of his spine, the breadth of his shoulders, the divot of tenderness between his ear and his skull. The difference, she thought, was as small as that. A patch of vulnerable skin. She wished that patch was the entirety of Johnny—it would have been so much easier, if he had just been good.

Lavender swiped quarters from the dashboard as Johnny pumped the gas. She walked toward the store, her heart jumping to a pattering beat. When the bell on the convenience store door dinged her entrance, Lavender realized that this was the most alone she'd been since she was sixteen years old.

The cashier, an older woman, eyed Lavender suspiciously. Rows of snack food lined the walls in bright colors. In the very back of the store, between the soda fountain and a freezer of ice cream, there was a pay phone.

This was it. Lavender's pulse thudded in her temples. Her chance.

Lavender wished for time. She wanted to sit and think this through, to consider what she'd be giving up. But through the grimy window, Johnny was jiggling the gas pump, and she could still feel the raised lump of goose egg on the back of Ansel's head, throbbing phantom beneath her palm. Time did not belong to her. Nothing did.

"Nine-one-one, what's your emergency?"

Lavender forced herself to stare at the label on a bag of potato chips as she gave the address for the farmhouse.

"Ma'am, you're going to have to speak a little more clearly."

"A four-year-old and an infant. You need to get there, before Johnny comes back. He's hurt them, you'll see. We're two hours away. Please, before he gets back."

She was crying now, tears rolling onto the plastic. She repeated the address, twice for good measure.

"Dispatching now, ma'am. Stay on the line. Are you the mother? We need to know—"

Out the window, Johnny craned his neck. Lavender panicked and hung up the phone.

The clerk behind the counter was watching intently. She was maybe sixty, with frizzy gray hair, a stained polo shirt, nails bitten down to raw red circles. She glanced from Johnny to Lavender to the phone, useless on its cord. She lifted a finger and pointed past the bathroom, where the door to a supply closet was propped open.

Lavender nodded her gratitude. She ran through it.

There was no light in the supply closet. Cleaning supplies were stacked onto towering shelves, looming in the inch-long strip of yellow that came in under the door. Lavender leaned up against the metal, breathless with the shock of what she'd done—the woman on the other side propped something up against the lock, trapping her in. The fear raced, urgent. The fear had lived inside her so long, it had distilled into a new force entirely. It jumped, acidic, fresh and electrifying.

Lavender pressed the back of her head to the door, listening. It was too thick. She could hear nothing. She let her hands slow their shaking and tried to recall the voice on the phone.

The dispatcher had sounded so controlled. So confident. Lavender imagined people in suits swarming into the farmhouse, speaking in professional, adult voices. They would find Ansel and the baby, wrap them both in big warm blankets. They would feed them something other than canned beans. She pictured a woman in a police uniform and a tight bun picking up the baby, so much stronger and more capable than Lavender had ever been.

In the pounding, waiting dark, Lavender breathed in bleach and dust and vinegar. In a box on a low shelf, she found dozens of individually wrapped chocolate cakes, the kind of neat, processed squares she had not seen since her childhood. Despite it all, her stomach gurgled. Lavender began to sob as she unwrapped one little cake, then another, shoving them whole into her mouth—the dough globbed, perfect in her throat, as she choked them systematically down. Surrounded by crinkling plastic wrappers, her fingers sticky with excess, Lavender wondered if she'd made the greatest mistake of her life. Maybe. But through her doubt, there was something else, a glimmer of solidity she could hold on to. She had always heard that there was nothing more powerful than a mother's love. For the first time since she became a mother, Lavender believed it.

•

The woman at the gas station unlocked Lavender's supply closet, and blinding light flooded in. Her name was Minnie, she said, as she helped Lavender off the floor. Lavender squinted into the bright rows of candy, gum, cigarettes.

"I told him you called the cops," Minnie said, handing Lavender a cup of coffee. She did not comment on the cake wrappers, the smear of chocolate across Lavender's cheek. It was night now, moths swarming the lights around the empty gas pumps. "I never even let him inside. He spent a long time storming around the pumps, yelling and such. Kicked the hell out of his own car. But he left eventually."

"Which way did he drive?" Lavender asked. Her head throbbed, but the first sip of coffee was brilliant, bitter on her tongue.

Minnie pointed south. Downstate, away from home.

Later, Lavender would track down the number for social services. She would call and call and call, begging for information, until finally the receptionist took pity on her and confirmed: The boys were in the foster system. Their father had not come searching.

That night, Lavender slept sitting up in the storage room, an iron paper towel rod clutched in her hand like a gun.

She found it when she reached for her sweater—a cold lump in the breast pocket. It was the locket she'd given to Ansel, curled up regretful. She'd unclasped it from his neck the last time she'd given him a bath and pocketed it thoughtlessly. *This will keep you safe,* she had told him. It seemed unbearably cruel, that she could bestow such a promise then accidentally steal it away. The truth felt swollen in the dark of the closet. No little trinket—and no amount of love—could keep anyone safe.

•

In the morning, Minnie gave Lavender a steaming egg sandwich, a twenty-dollar bill, and a ride to the bus stop.

"You go, honey," Minnie said, as Lavender slid from the car. "You get as far away as you can."

Huddled on the bench, Lavender wondered where Ansel was then. She hoped that someone had given him real clothes—he'd spent his entire life waddling around in men's underwear, pinned at the hips. She pictured him in a clean set of pajamas, a plate of juicy meat heaped before him. She'd forgotten to tell the police about the little bag she'd packed, with the corn and the knife and the winter coat. But now she was glad for it. How pathetic, the tiny things on which she'd placed so much hope.

Dear Julie, Lavender thought, as she boarded the

first of many buses. The shaking fear in her chest was tinged with something else now. A pulsing in the glands beneath her teeth. It was not freedom—too wrecked for that—but it was close.

Dear Julie.

Wait up. I'm coming for you.

•

When Lavender finally reached the ocean, it smelled exactly how she'd hoped.

It had taken her weeks to get to San Diego. She'd hitchhiked, stolen wallets, begged on corners for bus fare. When she came across a hunting knife, lost in a sewer outside Minneapolis, Lavender recalled how Johnny used to gut a deer, anus to diaphragm. She spent four days in the passenger seat of a beer delivery truck, her hand never leaving the hilt of that knife, tucked into the waistband of her jeans.

Now, Lavender kicked off her shoes, let the board-walk warm her blistered feet. It smelled like hot dogs, seaweed, car exhaust. The beach was crowded with families, lounging and playing, running through the surf. Lavender left behind the plastic bag of things she'd acquired (toothbrush, comb, cigarettes) and stumbled onto the burning sand.

The water was frigid, delicious. Lavender splashed it on her face, let the salty cold trickle into her mouth. She stripped off her clothes right there on the bustling beach and stood in her bra and underwear, ankle-deep.

The guilt was with her, always. Sometimes it suffocated, like a pillow held over her face in the night, and sometimes it stabbed. She'd been having the same nightmare for weeks—Ansel was digging in the yard beneath the spruce where they'd buried Johnny's grandfather, though it wasn't Johnny's grandfather beneath the soil. It was Lavender herself. *Look, Mama,* he'd say, holding her own stiff gray hand up from the dirt. *Look what I found.*

When Lavender was awake, the guilt mostly simmered, a low boil, steady discomfort. Her breasts were a constant reminder, still heavy with milk. But she couldn't deny it: there was also a clean, gulping relief. The joy of her own solitude, the long hours alone in her chest. The fear, ebbing bit by bit from her bloodstream.

Lavender did not know where she would go next. It didn't matter. She closed her eyes to the sun, as the water took her knees, thighs, hips, ribs—then sucked in a lungful of air. Before she surrendered to the freezing tug, Lavender thought of her children.

She had created two living beings. Eventually, they would be people. Lavender hoped that the mystery of their futures held exactly this: gritty sand, goose-bumped arms, waves breaking over their freckled shoulders. She remembered the bedroom window in the farmhouse, that tease of a breeze. They had it now. If nothing else, Lavender had given them the gift of possibility. Her boys could touch it with their hands, the wide expanse of the world.

Someday, Lavender hoped, her children would wade into the ocean. When they did, they would taste her.

Lavender's love, in a mouthful of salt.

10 Hours

You have seen rivers, and you have seen lakes, but you have seen the ocean only once.

The Massachusetts coast, years ago. You were driving to visit Jenny's grandparents, and she insisted you travel the extra miles—you were twenty-five years old and not yet married.

I can't believe you've never seen the water, Jenny said, bouncing in her seat. You pulled into an inlet at the first ocean view, and she coaxed you knee-high into the surf. Her hair thrashed in the wind. Her mouth opened wide in a gaping laugh, an obscene red that yawned to the hollow of her throat—you could see the crowns that lined Jenny's molars.

If you focus hard enough now, you can almost replace

the concrete wall of your cell with that giant, roaring blue. The gulls screeching, the car engine grumbling, the sand shifting beneath your bare feet. Despite it all, you are thankful for the memory—for the sight of the sea, tumbling in the distance.

It is possible, looking at the ocean, to believe it never ends.

•

The note from Shawna is in the front of your shoe, balled up against your big toe. A limping pressure when you walk. A bomb, blasting everything gloriously open.

•

You are rinsing your paintbrushes in the sink when two officers appear. They gesture for your hands, which you reach through the slats in the door. To be handcuffed, you have to turn your back to the entrance, hunch in half, and sink to your knees with your arms twisted behind. You are strip-searched every time.

A visitor, they say.

The visitation room is a long row of white concrete booths. You rub your wrists as you take your seat. On the other side of the glass, your lawyer looks how she always does.

Tina Nakamura sits with her hands clasped firmly atop a manila folder. Inmates are not usually allowed to see a lawyer in person today, but the warden has always liked you. Special approval. Tina's mauve lipstick is expertly applied, severe around the edges of her thin mouth, and her lashes have been tastefully lengthened with the kind of makeup meant to trick men into believing she isn't wearing any. You are not fooled. Tina is around your age, you would guess—mid-forties— and her hair is pulled into its usual clean ponytail, high and silky on the crown of her head. Today's pantsuit is navy, crisp, tailored. When she leaves, you will peek at her shoes. Tina's shoes always betray her; you suspect she has knee problems, or maybe bunions, because they are not the glossy heels you would expect, but instead those foamy flats with ergonomic soles, made for elderly diner waitresses.

My team filed another appeal this morning, Tina says. All we can do now is wait for the phone call. We should know by this afternoon whether the court will consider it.

Tina has never been afraid to look you in the eye. Her gaze is constant and austere. Usually, the pure strength of it makes you inexplicably furious, but today Tina is small. She is insignificant. You press your toe to the crumple of Shawna's note, a reminder of that blistering secret.

The warden tells me you've invited a witness, Tina says.

Witness? you ask, though you know perfectly well.

For the execution, Tina says.

The execution, you repeat.

You like the flinch. The tremble of Tina's nostril when she speaks the word.

You'll never forget the look on Tina's face when she saw what you had done. She met you at the Houston jail, before the trial and the sentencing. One of Tina's assistants handed her the folder—the crime scene photos. Her face went ashen, and her gaze liquified into a shocked sympathy. You have since become accustomed to this display. You saw it on the judge. You saw it on the jury. You saw it on the courtroom audience, when the prosecution blew up those photos on a projector, magnifying the details to ten times their size.

You don't like to look at the photos. They are not how you remember it.

Will you be there, Tina? you ask.

You use your nicest voice, the one that softens people. But Tina only looks at you with the expression you know well. Sometimes you stand in front of the metal mirror in your dark white cell and you practice this face, twisting your own brow into a furrow, your eyes melting and sad. The look is horror. It is confusion. It is the worst kind of pity, a pity that despises itself.

I'll be there, Tina says, and you cannot help the flicker of smile.

In just a few hours, you will be running. Your legs will be burning; your lungs will be gasping fresh oxygen. You twist your expression back into the face it is supposed to be (solemn acceptance), but the joy of your secret rises in your chest, ecstatic, a choke. When you swallow down the burst of laugh, it sears like smoke held too long in your throat.

•

It will happen on the transfer van at noon.

What if they see me? Shawna asked, pausing outside your cell late one stolen night. You'd spread the plan out on three days' worth of notes, slid beneath lunch trays—Shawna clenched one in her fist as she gnawed at her nails, an anxious, twittering mumble.

You fixed her with your best imitation of hurt.

Shawna, my love. Don't you trust me?

•

It has been done before. There was a hostage situation in the seventies: two inmates escaped from the Walls Unit with guns pressed to the prison librarians' heads. Just a few years ago, three men broke free from the Polunsky recreation yard. They were shot, hauled back. There is a rumor that a man once escaped by using a green highlighter to dye his white prison scrubs and walked out pretending to be a doctor. Given the circumstances, you would make like Ted Bundy and crawl through an air shaft. But you haven't been given an air shaft—only Shawna, and forty minutes in a van between Polunsky and the Walls Unit.

Back in your cell, you stand over the bulk of your notebooks, the red mesh bags sprawled taunting on the bed.

Five legal pads—seven incarcerated years of thinking and writing, transcribed onto yellow ruled paper. The stack on your cot looks like a pile of handwritten pages, not visibly the masterpiece you know it to be. You always imagined you'd sign copies by mail, you'd get letters from fans and reviews in newspapers. On the jacket, they'd use that photo from the courtroom, your gaze so stark in black and white.

You will leave your Theory here. Shawna knows to find it under the bed. When they are looking for you—when the panic erupts, and the search parties scatter, and helicopter lights beam down on the plains—she will point them to it.

So, like a manifesto? Shawna asked, when you described the basics. You twitched with a rushing annoyance. Shawna could tell she'd said something stupid; she turned a humiliated shade of magenta. Manifestos are for crazy people, you explained slowly. Manifestos are incoherent, scrawled hastily before pointless acts of terror. Your Theory is more an exploration of the most inherent human truth. No one is all bad. No one is all good. We live as equals in the murky gray between.

•

Here is what you remember of your mother.

She is tall, and she is mostly hair. She crouches in a garden, lazes in a rocking chair, sinks into a rusty claw-foot tub. Sometimes the tub is filled with water and your mother's long dress floats wet like a jelly-fish. Other times she is dry—she holds out a strand of her own hair, a gift, glistening orange. You remember nothing of your father. Not a sound, not a smell. Your father is a vague presence, looming in the distance; he is an inexplicable ache at the back of your skull. You do not know why they left or where they went or why your mother exists so alone in these recollections. You only remember a rusty chain, pooled in the dent of your collarbone, and how you felt wearing it, like nothing could touch you.

Your mother is the part of the Theory you have not yet figured out. We are all bad, and we are all good, and no one should be condemned to one or the other. But if good can be tainted with the bad that comes after, then where do you place it? How do you count it? How much is it really worth?

In most of your memories, your mother is gone. And before she is gone, always, she is leaving.

•

The memory summons it.

You try to focus on the physical. The familiarity: Clanging metal doors, the smell of canned meat. Dust, urine. Greasy hair. You slide to the floor, press your spine into concrete.

It comes anyway.

In the pit of your subconscious, Baby Packer starts to wail. If you could play a soundtrack of your life, this noise would be the loudest constant, the screeching misery of an infant. The silence of your own helplessness. The fading of that shriek into a slow, pathetic whimper.

•

There is only one place that keeps the screaming away. You arrived there on a Saturday morning, seven years ago.

A bright summer day. 2012. You'd woken before sunrise, too anxious to stay in that empty bed—months after Jenny left, and her absence still felt like a raw sore. You drove slowly, memorizing. It was late June, and the morning was a juicy blue, scented with spruce, wet from a long night's rain. Tupper Lake, New York, had one crumbling church, a small boxy library, a gas station. A smattering of houses, surrounding a foggy lake. The clouds rolled like steam over the water, curling gentle into the sky. Your memory bestows a fated filter on this drive, this morning, the dense humidity. Though you only spent those few short weeks in Tupper Lake, it took the entirety of your life to bring you there. A series of conspiring and intentional years, all leading to this.

At the gas station, a pimpled teenager was scraping bits of melted cheese off a pizza display case.

Yeah? she said, without looking up.

I'm looking for a restaurant.

There's only one, the clerk said, as she picked a fleck of burnt cheese from the spatula and popped it into her mouth. You wanted to hear her say it. The Blue House.

•

As the baby's screaming begins—as your hands clap fruitlessly over your ears—you make the promise.

It will not end here.

The first time you hurt someone, you were eleven years old, and you did not know the difference between pain and wanting. You lived in a crumbling mansion with nine other children: it started with a wink, nearly accidental, a test of your own sweetness. When the girl across the dining room blushed beneath the heat of your attention, you felt your own power, surging addictive. You could not have seen how that tiny decision would catapult you into the future, directly onto this concrete floor. How your actions would become a chain, marching purposefully into the present.

When you are free, you will walk the length of the

Texas desert. You will hitch rides on fast trains; you will wash your face in frigid lakes. Eventually, you will reach the Blue House.

You will not do it. You are certain of that. You will not hurt a single person again.

Saffy
1984

S affron Singh could tell you how many things she loved, and there were four of them.

One: the sound of Miss Gemma's house late at night. From the room she shared on the third floor, Saffy could hear everything. Sneeze, groan, whimper. At night, the mysteries of the house laid themselves bare. Saffy huddled beneath her scratchy pink comforter and reveled in the exquisite aloneness as the house shifted, exhaled.

Two: the picture frame she'd taken from her mother's dresser, before the social workers brought her to Miss Gemma's. Her mother had placed a sheet of notebook paper beneath the glass, with a line of chicken-scratch cursive scrawled hastily across. *Felix culpa.* Saffy did not know what these words meant, but her mother had written them, and so she loved them. She slept with the frame tucked beneath her pillow.

Three: her bottle of Teenie Bikini nail polish. The color was a pastel purple, creamy and comforting. Saffy used it sparingly, only allowing herself one coat at a time. She did not love the bottle itself, but instead how it made her feel, like someone fancy and grown-up, a girl with clean shiny fingers.

Four: the boy downstairs. He slept in the room directly below hers. Lying awake, Saffy imagined the oxygen traveling from her lungs and out her nose, across the hall, down the staircase, and into his open mouth.

And that night was different. Special. That night, Ansel Packer had winked at her across the dining room table.

"Liar," Kristen had said earlier, when Saffy came rollicking upstairs. Kristen was on the floor, practicing the moves she'd memorized from the VHS of *Jane Fonda's Workout*. "Ansel could have any girl in the house. Are you sure he wasn't winking at Bailey?"

Bailey was the prettiest girl in the house, maybe the prettiest girl Saffy had ever seen. Bailey was fourteen years old—Ansel was eleven, Saffy was twelve—and she had hair like drippy caramel. Kristen and Lila often practiced swishing their hips like Bailey, rolling their eyes like Bailey, chewing their nails like Bailey did. Kristen had once stolen Bailey's bra, a 32C, and they'd all taken turns trying it on in the bathroom, fumbling with the clasp and pulling down their shirts to see what they'd look like. But Bailey had been sitting two seats over from Ansel at dinner. He would've had to turn his head a completely different direction.

The other option was that Ansel had winked, on purpose, at Saffy herself.

The thought spread through her stomach, then cracked down her legs. Liquid hot, thrilling. Saffy played the moment over until she couldn't remember what he'd been wearing or how the wink had been shaped, until she couldn't picture Ansel's face at all. But the fact remained: he had caused this feeling. She was pinned to the mattress. Electric, aching. She did not dare move, in case this melting decided—like everything did—to leave her all alone.

The yard behind Miss Gemma's was a wide slope, an acre of rolling field that led down to a creek. After breakfast, Saffy spread her scratchy pink blanket on the dewy grass; she'd inherited the blanket from a now-grown girl named Carol, who had been born with only one arm. Miss Gemma's patch of land near the Adirondack mountain range was rich in the summer, a wet, ecstatic green, and Saffy sat with her gangly legs stretched out, her notes sprawled in her lap. She picked an aphid off her favorite polka-dot leggings and squinted down at the page.

Saffy was solving a mystery.

It had started with the mouse. Headless. Just a tiny pink body splayed on the kitchen floor. Lila had been the one to find it, and she'd screamed until everyone had come running—Saffy and Kristen had helped her bury it in the yard. They'd worn black and recited somber poems while Lila sobbed.

Then, there was the squirrel. Shoved beneath a bush near the driveway. Saffy caught Miss Gemma carrying it to the garbage with a shovel, her face scrunched in disgust. *Coyotes,* she said, as she deposited the pile of bones in the dumpster. A second squirrel, left in the same spot. Miss Gemma made one of the older boys clean it up, while she watched in her bathrobe from the lawn. *Didn't I tell you to stay inside?* Miss Gemma barked at Saffy, when she poked her head out the sliding back door, curious.

Saffy knew a mystery when she saw it. She'd been reading the Nancy Drew books, one by one. She'd since spent every day outside, scouring the edges of the property, looking for clues. She did not know what exactly to look for, but she desperately wanted to be the one to solve the crime. So far, she'd scrawled down the dates of the murders. Described how the bodies had looked. (Horrific!) She wished she had a George or a Bess, someone to help her with her theories, but Kristen and Lila would rather gossip about Susan Dey's haircut, lying upside down with their torsos hanging off Kristen's top bunk.

She hoped maybe Ansel would help.

Ansel had spent his summer wandering along the marshy creek at the edge of Miss Gemma's property. Saffy liked to watch from her blanket as he traversed the perimeter of the field, taking notes in the big yellow pad he kept tucked beneath his arm. She'd seen the books he took out from the library's adult section, encyclopedias and biology textbooks. She'd heard Ansel was so smart, he skipped the first grade. She hoped that by watching, she could memorize his every motion: the slope of his shoulders as he picked through the cattails, ballpoint pen tucked behind his ear. Saffy wondered if she could see the facts on him, written in the tragic swoop of his neck.

She'd heard the story.

Everyone had.

Lila had whispered it excitedly one of the first nights after Saffy arrived at Miss Gemma's, bouncing with the glorious drama. One of the older boys had stolen all the files from Miss Gemma's den, and the details had spread around the house, changing shape as they expanded. Ansel had been abandoned by his parents at four years old, Lila said. They had lived on a farm, or maybe a ranch. When the police found Ansel, he was nearly starved. But the worst part—Lila's eyes had bugged during the retelling, like this was the worst part but also maybe the best—there had been a baby. Only two months old. By the time the police arrived, Ansel had been trying to feed the baby for a whole day. But it was too late.

The baby had died.

Saffy would never forget the image. A real baby, no bigger than a doll. She'd since heard a half dozen other versions: the baby had been sent to a different foster home, Ansel had killed the baby on purpose, the baby had never existed at all. But that first image stayed with her, grounded itself as truth. A tiny, lolling neck. Saffy had never seen a dead person, not even her mother, and certainly not an infant.

She watched Ansel pick through the brambles, so

studious and intent, and she thought how sad it was that a single bad thing could turn you into a story, a matter to be whispered about. Tragedy was undiscerning and totally unfair. Saffy certainly understood that.

•

That night, Saffy watched him all through dinner. Thirty-second intervals, so no one could accuse her of staring. If Ansel winked again, Saffy missed it, her gaze trained on her mashed potatoes as she counted down from twenty-nine.

When everyone gathered around the television for the eight o'clock episode of *Family Ties*, Saffy stole down to the basement. Her chest was heavy with disappointment, and the basement felt like the right place to be, all concrete and spiders and randomly strewn carpet squares. Miss Gemma kept a dusty record player down there, along with a cardboard box of albums. Saffy liked to sift through them, to study the photographs on the covers. Joni Mitchell had such an inviting gaze— Saffy had practiced that expression in the mirror, but it never looked the same.

"Hey."

It was Ansel.

He stood at the base of the stairs, half in shadow.

His hands were stuffed in the pockets of his corduroys, shoulders hunched self-conscious.

"Can I take a look?" he asked.

Then Ansel was beside her, flipping through the box. Saffy studied his fingers as they flitted past ABBA, Elton John, Simon and Garfunkel. Ansel's hands were too big for his body, the hands of a boy much older than eleven, like a puppy not yet grown into its paws.

"Have you heard this one?" Ansel asked, pulling a record from the stack. Nina Simone. Saffy let out a stupid, embarrassing squeak and shook her head no.

"Let's sit," Ansel said, gesturing to a clump of carpet squares on the floor. When he smiled, Saffy shivered. Once, Ansel had aimed this exact smile at Miss Gemma, who had blushed scarlet and pulled her bathrobe tighter—the girls made fun of Miss Gemma for days afterward.

When the music started, the feeling was uncanny. Saffy was certain she'd lived this moment before, in some other life, the song reaching through her chest to touch a place she'd somehow forgotten. Ansel lay down next to her, flat on his back. His shoulder was close to Saffy's, and when she began to see stars, Saffy realized she was holding her breath. The song swelled, the singer rasped—*I put a spell on you*—and Saffy wished she could stop time right there, take a still shot and save it, just to prove it back to herself.

Then it was over. The record hummed a beat of silence before the next song started. Ansel did not move, so Saffy did not either. They lay there until the record had finished, until Saffy's spine was sore against the hard, cold floor, until the bedtime bell rang, and the other kids' feet pounded and thunked across the ceiling. None of it touched her, because she had this. It was magic. Maybe, even, it was love. Love was a thing that could move you and change you, Saffy knew, a mysterious force that made you different and better and warmer and whole. A delicious smell. Familiar, untraceable. It made her hungry.

•

Before Saffy's mother died, she liked to talk about love.

Saffy's favorite nights were those she'd spent sitting cross-legged in her mother's closet, picking through floral hippie skirts from her mother's time in Reno, pairing them with clunky jewelry. *You'll see, Saffy girl,* her mother used to say. *Real love is like fire.*

Is that how you loved Dad? Saffy asked, tentative. *Like fire?*

Let me show you something, her mother had said,

and she'd reached for a shoebox on the closet's highest shelf.

Saffy wondered often about her father. He'd left them before Saffy was born, with nothing but his last name—Singh, a name the kids on the playground mocked in an accent they'd learned from taxi drivers on television. At the grocery store, people stared, as if Saffy could not possibly belong to her own blond mother. Her dad was from a city called Jaipur, and he lived there now, a fact she used to report proudly, until she realized it meant he had not loved her enough to stay.

Inside the dusty shoebox, there was a photograph. The only evidence Saffy had seen of her father's real, tangible existence. He sat in a library, books splayed across the table in front of him. He was smiling, his hair proudly covered in a navy turban, which her mother explained was a part of his religion. In his gaze, Saffy saw herself for the first time, squinting back like a startle in the mirror.

Why did he leave? Saffy had asked, careful, like her mother was a bird she might frighten from a branch.

His family needed him back home.

But what about us?

Listen, her mother had sighed, and Saffy knew she'd pushed too far. *Do you remember why I named you Saffron?*

It's a flower.

The most rare and precious flower, her mother said. *The kind of flower that could start a war.*

She put the photograph back in the box, her green eyes focused somewhere else—Saffy desperately wanted to see that place. To touch it by herself. *You'll know it when you feel it,* her mother said then. *The right kind of love will eat you alive.*

•

Ansel held both hands out, to help Saffy off the basement floor. His palms were damp, his thumbs stained with ink from writing all day in that yellow notepad—as he followed her up the stairs, Saffy was conscious of how he moved behind her. It was thrilling, Ansel's closeness, almost frightening. She wanted that closeness in the same way she wanted to watch a scary movie, with a chattering sort of precariousness. She wanted the jump, the shiver. The unexpected bite.

By the time Saffy settled on Lila's bottom bunk, she was breathless with the story, even more exciting in recollection. They pored eagerly over Kristen's stolen copy of *Teen* magazine, huddled together, a flashlight rigged to the mattress above so Miss Gemma would not yell about bedtime. They'd practically memorized the issue, but they flipped the worn pages anyway, breezing straight past their favorite interview with John Stamos. The most important piece in the magazine was finally relevant: *You've Snagged the Perfect Guy: Here's How to Keep Him.*

"You should go with option three," Lila hissed through her retainer. She'd gotten the retainer before she came to Miss Gemma's, and her teeth had since shifted, leaving blank gaps around the plastic. Lila's fingers were always wet, hovering constantly near her mouth. On her middle finger, she wore a gigantic vintage ring, which Saffy didn't have the guts to ask her about—it was too big for Lila's hand, fortified with layers of Scotch tape so it didn't fall off. The ring had a brassy gold band, studded with a massive purple gemstone. Saffy guessed it was maybe amethyst, though she once heard Lila claim purple sapphire. The gem was always shiny with Lila's slobber, her lips caressing it obsessively. The ring was in Lila's mouth now, and a string of drool bridging from her finger. Saffy grimaced.

"Number three," Kristen said. "Show him how much you care."

It was decided. Lila slumped over her pillow, already drowsy, while Saffy had never felt more disastrously awake.

The next morning, Saffy pulled a stack of construction paper from the craft box in the basement and set up on the bedroom floor. Her sixth-grade art teacher had said she had *an affinity for the visual.* Saffy swelled with a ruffling pride at the memory.

Hours later, the result was half poem, half comic. She and Ansel were miniature stick figures, the record player drawn in realistic detail between them—*Put a Spell on You,* she'd titled it. In the next frame, they held hands down by the river, a magnifying glass in Saffy's other palm as a cheering crowd clapped in the distance. *Mystery Solved,* she'd called it. A coyote hung from a net, and a group of happy squirrels ran circles by her feet. Saffy drew a heart between her little pinpoint head and Ansel's, though she crossed it out on second thought and replaced it with a fat black musical note.

When she was finished, Saffy folded the paper carefully and wrote Ansel's name on the front in her best cursive. She flushed, imagining how it would wrinkle in the pocket of his corduroys.

•

A late-afternoon sun pricked the back of Saffy's neck as she walked down the hill in the yard. She'd changed into her favorite dress—inherited from Bailey, it was yellow cotton with puffed sleeves, and it still smelled, at random moments, like Bailey's aerosol deodorant. As she reached the tall weeds near the edge of the creek, Saffy smoothed down the ends of her swishing braid.

Ansel was crouched at the bank, scribbling in the yellow notebook he always carried. Saffy could see that he'd combed his hair that morning; the curls were still damp. She stood behind him, the construction paper turning soggy in her sweaty palm.

It happened in a single moment of confusion, horror.

Saffy tapped Ansel on the shoulder.

Ansel turned, surprised. He tried to shield her with his body, but it was too late. She was standing directly over them, the soles of her favorite glitter sandals inches away.

They were laid out long in the grass near her feet. One, two, three of them. Little arms stretched over their heads in surrender, too methodical to be any sort of accident. There were two squirrels, eyes open, tongues lolling. And between them, a fox. The fox was bigger and had been dead much longer. There were holes in its face where something had pecked out its eyes, and its intestines were spread haphazard on the grass—the fox was a jumble of bones covered in tufts of burnt orange fur, rearranged by human hands back into a sick attempt at its original shape.

"Don't—" Ansel growled.

The worst part wasn't even the animals, Saffy realized. Not their bared teeth, or their jellied eyes, or the way they'd been placed six measured inches apart, little dolls in a bed.

The worst part was Ansel's face. He twisted into something Saffy had never seen before, a startling combination of surprise and anger. Ansel held the notebook close to his chest, protective, lips snarling. It looked nothing like him.

Saffy's body decided for her: she ran. Before Ansel could say anything, she stumbled, panicked, back up the hill, the construction paper comic lost somewhere in the grass. A bug flew into her open mouth, a big black fly—she started to cry, panting as she tried to spit it onto the ground, waxy wings sticking stubborn to her tongue. There was a fact about life that Saffy hated, then: how it took the bad things and settled them inside you. It didn't matter that you were a person, and it didn't matter what you wanted. The bad lived insistently in your blood, a part of you always, calling out like a magnet to the horror of the world.

•

This was not Saffy Singh's first experience with the morbid.

In the weeks after her mother died, Saffy imagined a frightening series of alternate deaths. She pictured her mother, decapitated on the side of the road. Her mother's legs, poking out beneath the flaming torso of their Volvo, her mother impaled through the chest by the pole of a stop sign. Though she was only nine years old at the time of the accident, Saffy knew the police would lie to protect her. Head injury, they told her. Quick and painless. No, they said, when Saffy had asked, there had not been much blood. Saffy pictured her mother's body, a crumpled heap in the middle of the road, like a discarded tissue.

•

Saffy slammed the back door to Miss Gemma's with a shuddering crack, her legs trembling out of control.

Kristen and Lila were lounging on the bedroom floor with the bottle of Teenie Bikini nail polish. They jumped up when Saffy came in—usually, she'd be furious—but they quieted at the sight of her. Hair frizzed, static shock. They gathered Saffy onto the floor at the base of her bunk. What happened? they begged, crowding, as the acetone scent of the nail polish swam through Saffy's head. Was it something bad? Where was Ansel? Saffy hated how they relished the thrill of the drama, her own this time. She could not fathom how to tell. She had solved the mystery after all.

When the knock came at the door, all three girls froze.

Kristen stood, tiptoed bravely forward.

"It's Ansel," she mouthed, peeking through the crack. At Saffy's terrified expression, the violent shake of her head, Kristen shimmied halfway into the hall. Saffy and Lila waited, trying to decipher the vague whispers.

"What do you want?" Kristen demanded. The rest was muffled as she inched out of the room.

When Kristen came back in, she looked dazed. Stunned.

"What? What did he say?" Lila breathed.

In Kristen's outstretched palm, she held two old and crumbling oatmeal raisin cookies. The kind Miss Gemma bought for birthdays, from a plastic carton on discount at the grocery store. They were tinged white with age—it seemed Ansel had been storing them to use in a moment like this. The sugary chunks stuck to the sweat on Kristen's hand, a bizarre, mistaken gift.

An uneasy quiet.

"Um," Kristen said, hushed now. "Whatever this means, Ansel said not to tell."

Saffy turned to the trash can next to the bed, filled with used midnight Kleenex, and she gagged into the basin. Tentatively, Lila started to laugh. Kristen joined in, an anxious giggle. Still holding the trash can in her lap, Saffy was relieved by the stupid sound of Lila's snorting, and she began to laugh too, those crumbling old cookies the weirdest thing any of them had ever seen.

•

That night, Saffy was on dinner duty. Tuna casserole. She plugged her nose when the smell of canned fish wafted from the sink.

"Are you okay, Saff?" Bailey asked. Bailey looked beautiful, her eyelashes clumped with mascara, hair hanging in a silky sheet. Kristen and Lila stood on chairs next to the stove, bickering over a pot of noodles, as Bailey pressed a cold hand to Saffy's forehead. "You look kind of pale. You should go lie down. We can finish the casserole."

Saffy could have cried with the kindness.

Back upstairs, she reveled in the alone of her bedroom. So delicious, and rare. Saffy climbed the ladder to her bunk, ready to topple in and forget. The smell did not stop her. It was unobtrusive at first, a faint rotting sweet. Halfway up the ladder, Saffy paused. Crinkled her nose. She pulled back her bedsheets.

The fox.

It had been moved, in all its disconnected parts, onto her floral sheets. The fox was just a heap of globbing bones and decomposed tissue, not even shaped like an animal anymore, flies swarming around its toothy jaw. It looked so wrong, lumpen and congealing on Carol's pink blanket, that Saffy's vision went dusky. She knew better than to scream.

Instead, she held an inhale. Gathered her shock into a little ball. She squeezed that shock tight, let the oncoming tears harden into a mass she could control. *Look*, Saffy thought, in her mother's most demanding voice. *You have already lived through much worse.* And it was true. So she let out the slowest, longest breath as she pulled the corners of the sheet from the mattress and balled the fox inside. Ansel must have dumped it while she was cooking with the girls, because the liquid had barely soaked through to the mattress.

With the bundle held away from her body, Saffy snuck down the stairs and slipped out to the dumpster.

We take care of ourselves, her mother had repeated. That face was Saffy's favorite of her mother's. Jaw set. Eyes like steel. *Me and you, Saffy girl*, her mother would say. *We are warriors.*

At the dinner table, Saffy said grace like always. When Miss Gemma asked her to pass the Fanta, she did.

Across the wide mahogany, Ansel piled casserole calmly onto his plate. Saffy could feel him in her periphery, every tiny way he moved. When Ansel stood to clear the dishes, Saffy flinched so violently she knocked over Lila's water glass. She watched the liquid pool across the table, thinking how love was not at all what her mother had promised it would be.

•

Saffy did not eat dinner that night. She did not eat breakfast the next day, or lunch either. By the time a week had passed, she'd lost nearly ten of her eighty-seven pounds. Kristen and Lila brought cups of juice to the couch—Saffy refused to go back into that bedroom. It did smell kind of weird, Kristen noted, though Saffy could not tell her why.

Miss Gemma was worried. When she sat down, a puff of musty couch air blew up toward Saffy's face, along with the sharp chemicals of Miss Gemma's perfume.

"Saffron, honey," Miss Gemma said. "You have to tell us what's going on."

Miss Gemma looked so ridiculous, blue paint powdered across her eyelids, house slippers shuffling against the carpet. Saffy didn't say anything. She couldn't. For two more days, Miss Gemma visited Saffy on the couch, unable to coax even a shaky spoonful of soup into her mouth.

Finally, a pair of social workers came. They murmured with Miss Gemma in the kitchen, then sat across from Saffy, hands clasped in their laps, faces stern. It's harder for mixed kids, they told her earnestly. She knew she was different, in more ways than one. She would be transferred to a new foster home; a change of scene often helps, they said. When Saffy began to cry, even she could not tell if the feeling was sadness or relief.

While Saffy packed, Kristen and Lila hovered. Kristen gave her a parting gift: the tube of lip gloss they'd swiped from Bailey's nightstand, Maybelline Kissing Gloss. Their most prized shared possession.

"Are you sure?" Saffy asked, crying again at the gesture. The tears were constant now, unstoppable, and Saffy felt so weak and dumb for all of it—for not being able to eat, for not being strong enough to handle this like her mother would have wanted, for the way Lila looked at her, full of pity and curiosity as she suckled that purple ring between her chapped lips.

"You should have it," Kristen said, closing the sticky tube of lip gloss into Saffy's palm.

Saffy was packing the last of her clothes when Ansel came to say goodbye.

Kristen and Lila had gone downstairs to pick at the donuts the social workers brought. Saffy was alone. She smelled him first. Laundry detergent and summer sweat, slightly bitter, the same scent from his T-shirt that night on the basement floor. The smell that had intoxicated her before now sent a shiver of fear down her spine. It was the sort of fear that felt somehow enticing, a fear she wanted to chase.

"Can I come in?" Ansel asked.

He looked infuriatingly normal. Saffy had made a point of glancing away the past few days whenever he entered a room. He held himself like nothing had happened at all. He looked as handsome as always, if slightly apologetic, a fact that burned annoying in Saffy's chest.

"What do you want?" she asked.

"Saff," he said. He had never called her that before. His eyes were new, a forced sort of sad. "I'm really sorry."

"The fox," she said. "Why did you do it?"

"I said I'm sorry."

"But why?" she asked.

"I heard you laughing," he said. "You and the girls. I don't like when people laugh at me."

"We weren't laughing at you," Saffy said. The words sounded wooden, untrue.

"I shouldn't have done it," he said. "Sometimes I do things I can't explain."

"You can't explain it?"

He shrugged. "You know what I mean. You know what it's like, to be left all alone. The sound itself can make you want to hurt things."

"I'm not alone," Saffy said, too forceful.

A pause, like he didn't believe her.

"I'm sorry, okay?" Ansel's voice was soft, full of everything she'd been looking for in the first place.

"It's too late," Saffy said, with less conviction now. "I'm leaving."

She hated Ansel, for the way he bit his lip. The wanting that had captured her was awake again, stretching stiff limbs. It was foreign, intolerable—her desire. A force Saffy could not wrangle into any proper shape, a new dimension that snuck up on her in the dark. She did not dare look it in the eye.

"Come on, Saff," Ansel said, walking closer. "Before you go, please forgive me."

Inches away, his face was bright and open, tragic and lovely. Ansel reached out and pressed one finger to the jut of Saffy's collarbone. She thought of the baby, dead in that farmhouse, tiny toes and lips and eyes and fingers. What it meant, to be stolen from.

She nodded, reluctant. Yes. Forgiven.

Ansel stepped forward, engulfing Saffy in a hug. It did not feel how she had imagined, his warm body pressed against hers. She was numb and stupefied, giddy with his touch. For the first time, Saffy hated herself. She hated herself with a profound sense of awareness, less like a girl and more like a woman— with fury, desperation, shame. It was the sort of hatred that lurked in the shallows, gnashing its jaws, the ugliest thing about being herself. She reached, cradling, and welcomed it in.

8 Hours

The screaming drowns. The screaming consumes. The screaming is like a flood—once it begins, you are stuck here, waiting in the ruin. The baby shrieks, blinded by some pain you cannot soothe, and time is a standstill, the terror painted directly across the walls of your skull. You know, from a lifetime of this place, that the screaming is a sound no one else can hear, that it is meant for you alone.

Baby Packer has something to tell you, but he is too little for words.

•

You curl fetal on the concrete. From the gut of you, an anguished moan.

When you first arrived at Polunsky, they called a doctor. The doctor took your pulse, and your blood pressure, then listened to your heart. You were fine, the doctor said, and he never came again. When the officers walk by, they pretend not to see you, rocking on the floor with your hands over your ears like a child playing some stubborn game. The Execution Watch Log requires a visit every fifteen minutes—you dread the officers now, witness to your misery. You know how it looks. The weakness only sharpens the fury.

Shawna caught you like this. Just once. She appeared right as the screaming took over, holding your lunch tray, a worried blur at the door. Words were impossible, through the baby's wailing. Her presence loomed, degrading.

When Shawna returned the next day, she wore a softness you had never seen before. The paradox hit you with a bursting sort of amusement: your weakness had melted her. She was riveted, caught in the thrill of your vulnerability.

This, you could use.

You know how to turn Shawna to clay—when you said that her eyes were the color of an Adirondack spruce, the delight rippled eagerly across her face. Jenny used to be the same, shivering as you ran a thumb over the ridge of her nose. When you tried that with Shawna, she giggled like a child, high-pitched and annoying. You crammed a tender smile into the corners of your mouth. Most of the time, you understand women—often better than they understand themselves.

But every now and then, you are very, very wrong.

•

The detective was a woman. Of all the ironies that make up your fate, this one seems particularly sharp.

She had dark hair that snaked down her back. Hooded eyes, soft woman skin. She spoke calmly, trailing you along until your shoulders had lowered. You were in that questioning room for only a few hours, but by the end it was like she had the tip of an ice pick lodged in your brain. Before the detective convinced you to tell the story—before she revealed her sneakiness, her trickery—you had not thought about those Girls in a long time. They were from another life. A different world. They never haunted.

What were you thinking? the detective asked, after. You were so exhausted, you could feel the tears streaming down your cheeks, some delayed physiological reaction.

I'm curious, Ansel. You were young then, only seventeen. What was going through your head when you killed those Girls?

You wanted to tell her it wasn't like that. Not a thought process, or a thing that curved in any traceable way. You wanted to tell her about the screaming, your urgent need for quiet. You felt like your child self, standing helpless, trying to confess: Sometimes I do things I can't explain. The need was piercing, persistent. It didn't really matter that the act was wrong—this seemed like the most trivial and irrelevant detail.

Why those three Girls, that summer? the detective asked. Why did you stop, until Houston?

You crawl to the cold breakfast tray in the corner of your cell and pull the fork from beneath a pile of ant-swarmed eggs. You crush it beneath your shoe, gather the tines in your palm, examining for the sharpest one. When you press the plastic into the soft of your wrist, it does not break the skin and it does not stop the flood of memory.

What was going through your head? You genuinely don't have an answer. You would explain it, if you could. Have you ever hurt so badly, you wish you could ask. Have you ever hurt so badly you lose every last trace of yourself?

•

The first Girl was a stranger.

At seventeen years old, you lived alone. You were the only child in your last foster home, a small house near Plattsburgh owned by a woman in her seventies. After your high school graduation, she set you up in a trailer near the edge of the woods, fifty dollars a month. You had a summer job at the Dairy Queen down the highway and a car you'd bought with a wad of crumpled cash. Suddenly, you were emancipated. The solitude was a shock to the system. A dunk of frigid water.

Seventeen, and the world had new edges. The corners were cruel, too sharp, and you spent hours on the musty couch in that trailer, digging around in the stew of yourself. It was strange to be in school, where girls laughed and shrieked, where boys embarrassed one another and showed off their bigness. But it was even stranger to be alone in the heat. After hours of contemplation, when the screaming pressed, violent, nearly deafening, you swore you could see your mother's figure out the window, standing at the edge of the forest. She always vanished as soon as she'd arrived.

It happened in the middle of June. You had been chasing your coworker at the Dairy Queen all summer, a high school dropout with streaky dyed hair that flaked dandruff down her shoulders. You'd complimented her. You'd teased her like you'd seen the boys from school do. She had finally come back to your trailer, lay down on the couch, and unclasped her bra. It snuck up on you as you were quivering at the hilt: the screaming. The baby's endless wailing, so distracting you could hardly see. Your penis drooped. The frustration only made it worse—and before your coworker left, she laughed. The sound, like a hideous track layered over the baby's shrieking. You sat with the lights on until morning, the echo of your own agony ringing awful in your ears.

At work the next day, she wouldn't even look at you. By the time you closed up, took the trash out to the dumpsters, and locked the Dairy Queen, you were bent entirely into yourself. The highway pulsed all the way home—you maneuvered your clattering VW Bug carelessly, swerving over the yellow lines, the wind whipping a beat into your ear, that screaming endless, unbearable.

She materialized in the headlights.

In the moonlight, that first Girl was just a shadow at the end of a long driveway. A ripple of hair. The Girl squinted in the bright of your headlights—her face was perfectly animal, vulnerable and confused.

You braked. You opened the door. You stepped onto the gravel.

•

Now, time melts. You hear the scrawl of the officer's pen as he fills out the Watch Log. The thunk of his footsteps, lumbering uselessly away. You sink into the muck, the wild, furious dark, the cell widening and tightening until you are not a person, only a little ball. You press your forehead to the concrete, pleading with the baby. Please, stop crying.

If Jenny were here, she would know to gather your limbs. She would swaddle you tight, whisper consolations—It will pass, Jenny would hum, her skin like ripened fruit. It always does.

Jenny comes when you are weakest. When you most want to forget.

Her hair fanned out on the faded pillowcase.

Her footprints after a shower, dripping wet across the bathroom floor.

Hazel
1990

Hazel's first memory of herself was also a memory of her sister.

It was the sort of memory that lingered and haunted, lurking in the very marrow of her bones. It arrived when Hazel's pulse raced—every time she stepped onstage or drove too fast down the highway, she was transported. In the memory, Hazel was just a pumping mass of tissue, blurry and floating. Around her, a darkness that beat like a drum.

There was evidence of this time, in the ultrasound her mother kept balanced on the nightstand. Within the silver frame, Hazel and her sister were two little specks of molecule, growing together in this dark and primitive space. Her mother loved that photo, because you could see it even then, before either of them had ears or toenails. Two tiny webbed hands reaching out to each other, like deep-sea creatures in silent conversation.

In every important second of Hazel's life, she could hear the phantom sound of her sister's heartbeat layered over her own, as if they were still suspended together in the womb. It was a familiar syncopation. The most comforting thump. And no matter how far apart they were, how different or distant, Hazel's hand would lift, always, to meet Jenny's.

The morning Jenny came home from college, Hazel sat in the shower, letting the water beat scalding lashes onto the curve of her back. The seat her parents had installed in the corner of the tub was slippery beneath her bare thighs, and Hazel soaped her knee carefully, running the sponge over scar tissue. The place where the doctors had stitched up her skin was still a furious, blistering red—she could see the exact spot where her own ligament had been reconstructed, replaced with that of a stranger who had died right before surgery. Often, when Hazel looked at her knee, she thought of that nameless person, now just ash or bone.

She shampooed quickly, then turned off the water,

listening as her hair dripped onto the shower floor. Downstairs, Hazel's parents were frantic—her mother was banging idly around the kitchen, fussing with the marinade for the Christmas brisket. Her father's shovel scraped against the driveway as he cleared the snow for Jenny's car. They'd been in a blustery panic for days; her mother had wrapped the gifts weeks ago, and they'd been waiting stale beneath the tree ever since, dust gathering on glossy paper. Hazel's father worked from home, and her mother had transformed his office into a guest room for the occasion, returning from the department store one frigid afternoon, arms filled with curtains, sheets, a generic framed photograph of a beach at sunset. The frenzy, when she realized she'd forgotten the pillowcases at the checkout counter. *I don't think he'll care if you use the old ones*, Hazel had said, from her perpetual spot on the sunken couch.

Hazel stood gingerly, her right foot raised to keep the weight off her knee—she bent over the edge of the slippery porcelain, leaning for the towel. Her arm cramped with the stretch, the muscles limp, unused for months. As she hopped to sit on the lid of the toilet seat, Hazel twisted the towel around her hair, wondering exactly where Jenny was now.

It was a game they'd played as children. A Summoning, they called it.

I can tell when you're sick, Jenny had said, arriving in the elementary school nurse's office before their mother had even been called. *And I can tell when you're sad.* Jenny would shake Hazel awake in the dead of night, pulling her from the worst of her nightmares. *I can read your mind*, Jenny would say—and when Hazel startled with the fact of the intrusion, Jenny only looked confused. *What?* she would ask. *Can't you read mine, too?* Hazel would burrow deep into herself, trying to conjure the interior of Jenny's body the way she conjured her own. She never could read Jenny's mind, but this didn't stop her from trying, or from claiming that she had the same telepathic power. *You're lying*, she'd guess, when Jenny faked a stomachache. *You like that boy*, she'd tease, when Jenny crossed her arms over her chest at the middle-school locker. Hazel wouldn't call this a Summoning—not the kind of thing Jenny could do. It was just intuition, many years of noticing. Hazel knew her sister's face.

Jenny would be driving now. The route from Northern Vermont University to their suburb outside Burlington was just over an hour. A Nirvana song would be playing, humming crackly from the radio, Jenny's hands fluttering on the steering wheel. Jenny's new boyfriend would be sitting in the passenger's seat—here, the image faded, blurred.

Hazel gathered her crutches, wiped the steam from the mirror. In the dim winter light, she looked pale, grim, lifeless. She did not look like Jenny. She did not even look like herself.

Hazel's real self was not this bathroom ghost. Her real self had cheeks blushing pink beneath scorching bulb lights, hair sprayed back into a slick, glossy bun. She wore long black lashes, glued sticky to her eyelids. Her collarbone jutted out beneath the straps of a corset that tapered down into a custom-designed tutu, glitter dabbed subtly along the ridge of her chest, engineered to reflect the stage lights with a turn or a leap.

For a precious moment, Hazel was no longer leaning against the damp sink. Instead, she was following the sound of the orchestra into the velvet wings, as the instruments hummed the opening notes of Swan Lake. The smell, like elastic and rosin. She was rolling onto her pointe shoes, reveling in the ethereal stretch of her hamstring. The audience hushed, alert, awaiting her arrival. She was caught in that long, agonizing moment, before she stepped into the gold.

Hazel was her real self when she danced—but she was more than that. She was feather, she was breath.

She was an illusion, a mirage that answered only to music and memory. She flew.

•

Downstairs, the front door slammed. Gertie the basset hound erupted in a fit of barking as Hazel's mother cooed. Hazel's hair was still dripping cold—she climbed onto Jenny's twin bed to peer out the window. Jenny's old station wagon puffed in the driveway.

Jenny had come home twice since college started. Both times for dinner. She had refused to stay the night, packing herself back into her car after the leftovers had been scooped into plastic containers for the mini fridge in her dorm room. Hazel tried to picture the house through Jenny's new, worldly eyes: nearly identical to the homes that fanned around it, clustered at the edges of a sheltered little town. Burlington had never felt so quaint and silly as it did when Jenny came to visit, all ice cream shops and mountaineering stores. Both those dinners had been before Hazel's knee, and she had not been able to pinpoint exactly how Jenny had changed.

From the distance of Hazel's bedroom window, still framed by Jenny's John Hughes posters, the differences were obvious. She and Jenny had always looked as close to identical as you could get while still technically being fraternal, but Hazel could see, with an uncomfortable jolt, how age would separate them further.

She'd heard the story of their birth so many times, it felt like fable. Jenny had come out first, slick and easy, her exit dislodging Hazel's entire body from the birth canal—a nurse had massaged their mother's swollen belly until Hazel came out kicking, her face blue, the umbilical cord wrapped around her neck. *We thought we'd lost you*, Hazel's mother always said, and only recently did Hazel realize that her parents had lived entire minutes believing Jenny would be their only child. Hazel could imagine it, looking now at her sister. Jenny was growing even prettier, the dimple in her cheek more pronounced. Jenny had a heart-shaped face, supple and inviting, while Hazel's had always been gaunt and witchy. And, of course, there was the freckle. As their mother pulled Jenny into a hug, Hazel reached up instinctively to touch it.

The Twins. This was how they had learned to know themselves. At slumber parties and school events, field trips and family holidays, she and Jenny were a single unit. One name. One bedroom shellacked in pink wallpaper. As children, Hazel and Jenny took pleasure in switching clothes between class periods to confuse their teachers. They used to wear matching versions of the same outfit, Jenny in purple, Hazel in blue. *Does it ever bother you?* Hazel said to Jenny once, when one of the boys in middle school joked about asking the Twins to the spring dance. *You know, being the Twins?* Jenny had looked at her with a gaze so narrowed and cold, Hazel knew she wore it to veil her hurt. Hazel still remembered how her own tongue had flitted across her canine teeth, which were pointier than her sister's, more overlapped, how she'd bit down until she tasted a warm prick of blood. *Why would it bother me?* Jenny had asked, her voice like a woodland creature. Hazel still burned with the shame of this question. Only in the last four months—since Jenny had been at school—did Hazel respond to her own name alone. For the entirety of her life, Jenny's name would echo across a room, and Hazel would turn, ready to answer.

Now, the mole beneath Hazel's left eye felt the same as it always had, a raised and fleshy bump shaped vaguely like a teardrop. People loved to point it out. *Hazel,* they would say, tapping their own cheeks, distinguishing her, like Hazel needed a reminder of her own imperfection.

•

There Jenny was, at the bottom of the stairs. When Hazel looked up from the complicated math of her crutches, Jenny was grinning, soft and expectant, those same sister eyes, that same sister mouth, Jenny's whole sister self, waiting. She wore a pair of oversized combat boots, an army parka Hazel had never seen before, and a big studded belt like Courtney Love. As Jenny engulfed Hazel in a hug, the hall filled with her smell, hidden beneath something foreign. A new brand of soap, or maybe shampoo, fruity and sugared. Hazel itched for a sneeze.

"It's so good to be home," Jenny marveled, as she bent to soothe the dog, Gertie's fat little paws tugging at her jeans.

She turned to the boy behind her.

Jenny's new boyfriend was not what Hazel had expected. Hazel had known her sister to drift toward bulky shoulders and taut corded necks, boys who looked like tree trunks. By the end of high school, Jenny and Hazel had split the world evenly: Hazel had ballet, a rotating series of pointe shoes and wrap skirts and intricate rehearsal schedules to be negotiated with the car they shared. In turn, Jenny claimed school. Jenny had the test scores, the report cards, the Honor Society. Hazel could usually find her sister laughing near the trophy cases, Jenny's body propped naturally against the chest of a hockey player, a linebacker, the statewide shot-put champion. Hazel knew these boys only from the stories

Jenny told as she drove Hazel to the studio—she listened intently, both enthralled and repulsed.

The boy standing in the foyer was definitely not an athlete. He was lean and rigid, a pair of oversized glasses resting loose on the bridge of his nose. His pants were slightly too short at the ankle, a few wiry leg hairs curled beneath the cuffs.

"You must be Hazel," he said. "I'm Ansel."

When Ansel smiled, the grin spread across his face, like a runny egg cracked open. Of course, Hazel thought—of course Jenny would choose a person like this. A human magnet. Hazel blushed with the attention, conscious of her context in the frame of this moment. Her existence, simplified. She was Jenny's body double.

"Ansel," Hazel said. "I've heard so much about you."

This was not true, and Hazel regretted saying it. When Ansel stretched out his hand confidently, Hazel gathered the muscles in her abdomen—*the entire body revolves around the core.* She lifted one sweaty arm from the metal of her crutch and shook.

•

Jenny had not called after that night onstage.

After the three-hour surgery, after the cards and

flowers had flooded Hazel's bedside, after her arms had bulked from pushing the wheelchair down the hospital halls—no word from Jenny. Even after Hazel had been deposited onto her parents' couch, where she sat for the next six weeks, only dragging herself occasionally upstairs for a shower—nothing. Hazel tried the dorm phone twice, left messages with the perky RA. Jenny did not call her back.

She's thinking of you, Hazel's mother said, unconvincing, as she delivered another bowl of soup.

While she wasted away on the couch, Gertie's jowls slobbering into her lap, Hazel tried to conjure her sister. In the hydrocodone haze, she imagined that Jenny would be at a Friday night party, wearing the denim skirt they'd picked up at the thrift store that summer. On a Wednesday morning, Jenny would be in the dining hall picking the cantaloupe out of a wilting fruit salad or playing Pearl Jam on her Walkman as she ambled to class. Hazel couldn't picture Jenny's classes—she'd never been on a real college campus, her schedule already packed with rehearsals when Jenny and their dad drove out for the tour. She imagined tweed jackets, button-up shirts, her sister's fingers scrunched around a pencil. Those images felt manufactured to Hazel, less like a Summoning and instead a fantasy that likely had nothing to do with Jenny's reality. The effort only made her angry. *Where are you?* Hazel would beg, pathetic, her knee pounding like a gavel beneath her skin.

•

Hazel's father hefted the suitcases up the porch, frigid December air blowing into the house from the frosted cul-de-sac. For a long, tense instant, Hazel faced her sister, who looked undefinably different. As Jenny's eyes flicked down to Hazel's knee brace, then back up again, she said nothing—but Hazel saw the glint. There was something satisfied in Jenny's gaze. Shining and wise. Like Jenny knew what it meant, to be the sister standing.

•

While everyone prepared for dinner, Hazel sat at the table. Usually, she and Jenny would have set the place mats together, bickering over which napkins to use. But Hazel's crutches leaned against the sliding glass door, exempting her.

Their mother served the chicken as Jenny gestured with an open bottle of wine. Hazel shook her head no. She had never liked the taste of alcohol or the way it made her head swim, and besides, she still had a few painkillers left. Her mother had been counting them out every morning, as she insisted Hazel wean slowly off. *You have to be careful,* her mother had said. *Addiction runs in your blood. Just look at your grandfather.* Hazel chewed her chicken tepidly, the half capsule flooding her system, dulling the throb in her knee. Everyone's teeth had purpled with wine—her mother patted her hair anxiously as she asked Ansel questions about school, which he answered dutifully. He was a philosophy major, he said, aiming for graduate school. *I want to be an academic writer. Thought is the purest thing you can leave behind.* His voice was soft, lilting, seeping inky into Hazel's core. His skin was milky pale, the interior of his forearm like a blank sheet of paper. He really was handsome—the kind of handsome that solidified the longer you looked.

A startle, when he said her name.

"Hazel," Ansel said, a spotlight swiveling. "Jenny tells me you're a ballet dancer. How is your knee feeling?"

"She's almost healed," Hazel's mother jumped in. "Just a few more weeks on those crutches, then physical therapy. She'll be dancing again in no time."

Hazel nodded politely. Ansel idled on her, genuine, curious—no one had looked at her this way in months.

Without pity or discomfort. She recognized a flicker of awe in the moon of his smile, a sliver of the reverence she pulled out of the audience after a perfect series of fouettés.

"I have an announcement," Jenny said, tearing Ansel's attention away. Jenny's lips were flecked purple with sediment—a flare of hatred burst through Hazel, uncontrollable.

"I've been thinking about our birth story," Jenny said. "About the nurse who saved us. We never even learned her name, but she's the whole reason we're alive. Or at least the reason Hazel is, right? Anyway, I've decided on my major. I want to study nursing. Specifically, labor and delivery."

Hazel's parents beamed across the table, the pride spreading involuntary. Exaggerated, nearly obscene. The room felt cold, everyone drunker and sloppier than they had been only minutes before. The whole display, so abruptly pointless. As her father raised his whiskey for a toast, as Jenny lifted her smudgy wineglass, Hazel clutched her water and stared into the kitchen light until the bulb had sufficiently blinded her.

That night, Hazel fell asleep to a memory.

Come on, Jenny was saying, her gangly arms hanging from the farthest monkey bar as the sun beat down on the scorching playground. Jenny was wearing the costume they'd begged their mother to buy, a sparkly wedding dress that they shared, with sleeves like Princess Di's. Fear crystallized in Hazel's chest—her shoulders ached from the two monkey bars she'd already reached through careful assessment. Jenny looked very far away in the billowing white, her fingers slipping sweaty. *You have to believe you can do it,* Jenny said. *Put your body into it, Hazel, and swing.*

•

Christmas morning. A gentle film of white blanketed the neighborhood—dawn had just broken, the sun rising a supple orange over the snow-glittered suburb. Hazel lay in bed, thick and anxious. Jenny was staying in the guest room with Ansel, and the bare twin mattress across from her own looked singularly empty.

Since the accident, Hazel's body had taken on a shape her clothes did not recognize. Her stomach and thighs had thickened; the muscles in her calves had shrunk. The seam of her pajama pants felt too tight. Hazel stuck her hand beneath the elastic cord, stretching it away. Her body felt so foreign—it could have been someone else's hand, sliding into her underwear, beneath the tuft of hair and down into the wet. She thought of Ansel. The silky cream of his skin. How his smile leaked like a flood across his face. It played out like a film, lit in gauzy yellow—Ansel was hovering above, Hazel splayed out on her bed—his shoulders were tight, muscled beneath her fingers, the skin on his stomach tensing into the fine trail of hair that led into his waistband, his checkered boxer shorts sliding down over his hips. He was leaning, spreading her with two fingers, his smile lowering, riveting, contagious—

Hazel came before she was ready. She bent into her own fingers, shuddering a gasp that melted far too quickly, her legs trembling beneath the sheets, suffocatingly sticky. An accusation. When she pulled her hand back into the open air, her fingers were shiny and slicked, the skin wrinkled like she'd stayed too long underwater.

•

Hazel's parents were waiting downstairs. Her dad's old-man hair stuck up in every direction, an affront, and her mother was lumpy in the armchair, her pilled bathrobe pulled tight. Gertie snored from the couch, drool pooling on her favorite cushion. On television, the news was mumbling. Hazel craved a shower, but it was too difficult with the knee brace—she could smell her own sweat, the stale stench of her desire.

"Did they mention what time they'll be up?" Hazel's mother asked.

"I didn't hear anything," Hazel said.

It was another half hour before Jenny and Ansel appeared. Jenny's hair was wet from the shower, and Ansel wore a pair of tight-fitting corduroys. When Hazel noticed how they scrunched around his knees, she filled with a boiling shame.

They opened the gifts one at a time. Jenny had gotten a new backpack, made of real leather, ordered from a store that didn't exist in Burlington. Hazel's mother must have sent away for it. *For your textbooks*, her mother said, shining proud. Hazel mustered all her energy into an exclamation of delight; they'd gotten her a set of fantasy novels, a genre she'd liked as a child. Every gift before this year had been related to ballet, and everyone looked pointedly away as Hazel mumbled her thanks for the books, the sweater.

Ansel went next. He ripped the paper awkwardly while her parents beamed. Jenny had specifically instructed them not to get him anything. Ansel had a hard childhood—they shouldn't ask about it—and he disliked family holidays. Her mother had picked up a pair of pajama pants anyway, and a book about primates. Ansel thanked them, clearly uncomfortable, as Jenny glared, shooting daggers.

The last two gifts were the most predictable. Two identical packages lay lonely beneath the tree. Hazel caught Jenny's eye—they were kids again, their secret language communicated in one flickering glance.

It was tradition: twice a year, on Christmas and her birthday, Hazel received an outfit that matched Jenny's. They tore open the wrapping paper, Hazel's cheeks aching from the fake smile. It was a dress this time, cotton, long-sleeved, the kind of thing you'd wear to a dinner party or a nice restaurant. Hazel could not fathom what she'd wear it for, but she forced down a grimace as she held the dress up, modeling, heather gray to Jenny's olive green.

Her mother clapped, pleased.

"Okay," she said. "Pancakes. Your father got that special syrup—"

"Wait."

It was Ansel. His voice was raspy and frogged. He had barely spoken all morning. An odd tension radiated off him, scattered bolts of energy.

"I have something. A gift."

Hazel sat quiet, listening to Ansel's footsteps as he disappeared upstairs, the zip of his duffel bag. Her parents shifted uncomfortably, while Jenny picked little bits of carpet from the floor.

Ansel came back with his fists clenched, his angular features infused with a false excitement that felt stiff, almost cold.

"I'm sorry," Ansel said, uncurling his palm. "I didn't wrap it. But it's for you, Jenny."

Everyone gaped. Jenny's hand flew to her mouth.

It was a ring. Not an engagement ring, though Hazel was certain the thought crossed her parents' minds, as they exchanged apprehensive glances. The ring was chunky, vintage, the kind of jewelry that had clearly once belonged to someone else. It had a brassy band of unpolished gold, and the gem was large and purple, a size that would be garish if it weren't for the color. A soft, lovely lilac. Amethyst.

"Ansel," Jenny breathed. She seemed both thrilled and embarrassed—Hazel knew her sister. Jenny wanted to spin this narrative, to let it become something bigger and better as she retold it later, and she wished their parents were not sitting there, witnessing this lopsided truth. The halfhearted gesture, the ring's otherworldly shine. "You really didn't have to. Where did you get it?"

Ansel grinned, shrugging. "It made me think of you."

Hazel could not pinpoint the sinking, as Jenny

slipped the ring onto her finger, as her mother mumbled about resizing. She watched the stone glint in the early-morning light, refracted in the snowy bright—she did not know if the wrongness had to do with the ring, or the boy, or her sister, or maybe Hazel herself. *You are happy for her*, Hazel commanded, forceful. But the thickness spread anyway, gelling sickly across the back of her throat.

•

That Christmas dinner, Hazel tried to catch Jenny's eye. At their mother's urging, they'd both changed reluctantly into the matching dresses, though Jenny had already spilled a splotch of red wine down the front of hers. The purple ring glittered from Jenny's finger—Hazel's parents tried to feign normalcy, but her mother's gaze flitted constantly to Jenny's hand, which looked new and foreign, somehow older, as it reached for the platter of brisket.

Hazel and her parents had been firmly instructed not to ask about Ansel's family. *It's complicated*, Jenny had claimed. But Hazel's dad was drinking whiskey.

"So," her father said, his cheeks ruddy. "What does your family do for Christmas, Ansel?"

It was like the shock of bad news. A slow, fevered pause in the room, a dripping sort of dread. She could physically picture her father's question hovering above the table. She wanted to reach out and grab the words, shove them back into his mouth. Hazel trained her gaze steadily on her plate, the gnawed bones glaring morosely from a puddle of juice. At her feet, Gertie gazed up hopefully, eyes wet and droopy, blissfully ignorant.

"I grew up in foster care," Ansel said. Hazel watched her father's face twist, mortified, his mistake dawning. "We didn't really have traditions."

"I'm so sorry—" her mother stammered.

"It's okay."

The awkwardness lingered in the air, mixed with something else. Something Hazel recognized, from all those years onstage—how the audience used to need her. Ansel had them hooked. Mesmerized.

"My parents left when I was four years old," he said. "I don't remember holidays with them. I had a little brother, but he died."

It was horrifying, how little Hazel knew. She knew nothing about this person, or the endless moments Jenny had spent with him. She knew nothing about the world as a whole. Here Hazel was, in the boring cozy house she'd always taken for granted, full of socks for gifts and food they'd throw away when the leftovers turned. In this pretty little town, where nothing bad ever happened. Her parents were not wealthy, but they were comfortable. She had never wanted something she truly couldn't have.

"I've been reading a lot of philosophy lately," Ansel said. "Locke, in particular. He rejects the concept of bodily continuity, the idea that our physical beings make us who we are. Instead, he latches on to memory. Memory as the thing that makes us individual, as the thing that separates my human consciousness from yours. I have this idea. This theory, I guess. There is no such thing as good or evil. Instead, we have memory and choice, and we all live at various points on the spectrum between. We are created by what has happened to us, combined with who we choose to be. Anyway, I wanted to thank you. All of you, for allowing me into your home. Jenny, for everything. If I'm simply a series of choices, I'm glad they led me here."

Hazel understood it, then. A glimmer of the intrigue that had sucked Jenny in and was slowly stealing her away. Hazel herself was breathless, all stuttering adrenaline and stunned curiosity. Tragedy had a texture. A knot, begging to be unraveled. The things Hazel wanted were unspeakable, intangible, too blurry to touch—the things she wanted already belonged to her sister.

•

The bathroom was a cool black cave. Hazel stumbled in, her crutches clattering to the floor. She did not bother to turn on the lights—she did not want to see the beige paint, the crooked landscape on the wall, the little bowl of seashells her mother dusted every week. She hunched over the toilet and stuck her face right into the bowl, inches from the putrid water. Hazel gagged as the sound of clinking forks and polite voices came muffled through the door.

She hated Jenny. Actual hatred, stinging and aware. Hazel vomited, wishing she could expel everything from her body, all the grief and terror of such a bitter, selfish thing. But she knew it would linger regardless, dissipating until it transformed back into the boundless love she had always known. The love between sisters was not the sort of thing she'd read about in books or swooned over in movies. It embodied a category all in itself, a quiet knowing that swam in her veins, even when Jenny was miles away. Sister love was like food, or air, or memory itself. It was molecular. The very stuff of her. But it was not a love she chose, and for this, Hazel would always resent the part of herself that feared—maybe hoped—that she would never love anyone quite the way she loved Jenny.

•

A knock on the door.

Hazel lay flat on her twin bed, her Discman playing an old Springsteen CD she'd found at the record store downtown.

In the dim glow from the hall, Jenny was a shadow. She wore a pair of pajama pants and a faded, oversized T-shirt she'd left behind. Hazel was very familiar with this shirt. When she bored of her own clothes, she'd sometimes limp over to Jenny's dresser and rifle through the drawers, slipping Jenny's forgotten Nirvana concert tee over her own skinny ribs, wriggling her hips into the outdated jeans Jenny hadn't loved enough to take to school.

Now, Jenny climbed onto Hazel's bed, hugging her legs to her chest. Hazel pulled off her foamy headphones. Across the room, Jenny's mattress sat naked—their mother had stripped the bed, though she'd left Jenny's posters lined up along the wall.

"Are you feeling better?" Jenny asked, in the soft lamplight. "Mom wanted me to check."

"I'm fine," Hazel said, though the words came out serrated.

"You're mad," Jenny said.

"I'm not mad," Hazel told her, and this was true. She was tired. Lost and withering. Hazel almost wished she were angry—that would be easier than this wide and lonely nothing.

"I saw," Jenny said. "I saw how you looked at me at dinner."

"Oh, you noticed? You haven't looked me in the eye since you came home."

A long, tense pause.

"I'm sorry about your knee, Hazel," Jenny said finally.

The admission felt impossibly small. This was the first time Jenny had addressed the accident. Hazel understood, with a shock of clarity, why Jenny had been ignoring her knee. It was not because Jenny didn't care. No, Jenny knew exactly what Hazel's knee meant—what her failure meant—for both of them. It was easier not to look.

"Hard things will change you," Jenny said. "Ansel taught me that. I don't know real struggle, and neither do you."

Hazel was about to protest, to defend her own suffering, but Jenny continued.

"We've had everything handed to us, Hazel. This boring little house, three bedrooms, cream carpet. We have parents who love us."

Jenny paused, bit her lip.

"Ansel is different. He lived in four separate foster homes. And his little brother, the one he mentioned at dinner? I've never heard him say it aloud, before tonight. That his brother died. Ansel has never told me the story, but he screams in his sleep. *The baby,* he says. *The baby.*"

Jenny had always seemed older than Hazel—as kids, she reminded Hazel constantly of those three minutes. Sitting now in her childhood bed, a stuffed giraffe squashed beneath Hazel's thigh, the disparity felt stark. Drastic.

"Ansel is not like everyone else," Jenny said. "He doesn't feel things like other people. Sometimes I wonder if he feels anything at all."

"If he doesn't feel anything at all," Hazel asked slowly, "then how do you know he loves you?"

Jenny only shrugged.

"I guess I don't," she said.

The differences between them were loud, nearly deafening. Jenny, with her whiskey breath and smudged eyeliner, had been touched by someone else, shaped and formed by him. She was no longer the other half of Hazel's whole—instead, her own throbbing and vibrant thing. *Come back*, Hazel wanted to beg, though she knew it was fruitless. She was no longer the closest thing to her sister. They were no longer an *us*, but rather two separate people, growing at two separate paces, one awake and blazing, the other formless and grasping.

When Jenny stood, the imprint of the wall had mussed her hair. It stuck out straight in a static puff. She stopped at the door, melting back into silhouette.

"I'm sorry," Jenny said. "About your knee. I'm sorry I didn't come home. I'm sorry I didn't call."

The words felt useless. Far too light.

"Why didn't you?" Hazel asked.

"I could feel it," Jenny said. "Like back when we were kids. I was in the library, studying, and I could feel it the second it happened. Like my very own tendons were snapping. It hurt, Hazel. It was the first time I felt that power and wished I didn't have it."

When Jenny left, Hazel's room felt empty, changed. On the blanket, Jenny had left a single shiny hair. Hazel picked it up at the tip, watched the tail sashay gracefully through the air. She brought it to her lips. Rolled it into her mouth. The strand of hair tasted like nothing at all—she could only feel the shape of it, firmly existent, a spider on the pad of her tongue.

•

The performance had begun like any other. Swan Lake. The stage lights were hot, Hazel's shoes soft against the marley. They were on their last wear, before she'd sew the ribbons on a new pair. She didn't feel it in her toes, though perhaps she should have. She'd made it almost to the finale, her last solo sequence, and she felt edgeless, full of energy. When Hazel began her fouetté turns, the audience spun and righted itself, eight counts and again, her head flicking to keep up with the whip of her body.

She was fully inside the choreography when it happened. Remembering, Hazel felt grateful for those last few moments of herself. For the way her legs carried her into the preparation for the leap, the pas de bourrée, the two bounding steps before the grand jeté. In the infinite moment before the landing, before the twist and crack of her knee as it bent sideways, Hazel thought: *Love is adoration. Love is a gasp, love is a stretch, love is this.* A blinking glimpse of eternity, aflame beneath a golden spotlight. It was the only thing she had ever learned to want.

Hazel did not know how long she'd been asleep when she jolted awake to the sound of barking.

She was still wearing her Christmas dress, rumpled up around her waist, legs splayed uncomfortable on top of the covers. The room was dark, stale, and hushed, the quiet interrupted by Gertie's barking, which echoed insistently from the back door—they'd learned to ignore the dog until she lulled herself back to sleep. But as Gertie continued, frantic, Hazel heaved herself from the bed, hopping one-legged past the window.

The sudden motion stopped her. A flicker of movement, beyond the glass. Hazel rubbed the sleep from her eyes, blinked hard to be sure she wasn't dreaming.

It was Ansel, clear in the moonlight. He stood beneath the maple tree in her parents' backyard, flannel pajama pants tucked into winter boots. He leaned on the shovel from the garage, his jacket revealing his wrists as he scooped clumps of snow and wet dirt. A scoop, a whack. Hazel watched, bemused, as Ansel dug a hole. It was maybe a foot deep—he dug until his forearm disappeared into the depth of it. By the time he clapped the dirt from his hands, Gertie had gone quiet, and Hazel slipped back into bed, listening to the whoosh of the sliding glass door, to Ansel's footsteps shuffling up the stairs.

Her clock read 4:16 a.m.—surely, Jenny was asleep, unaware. Sleep would be impossible, Hazel's brain frenetic with the strangeness of what she had seen. Five o'clock passed, then six. By six thirty, the sky out the window had blanched to a sweet, unfettered blue, and a new sound revealed itself down the hall. So subtle at first, Hazel strained to listen.

Whispers. Rustling.

This time, Hazel reached through the dim for her crutches. Her bedroom door made no sound as it opened—she took soft steps across the carpet, her heart alert and listless. She knew before she reached the guest room exactly what she would find.

They were naked on top of the comforter, the door cracked slightly open. Exposed in the rising light, their eyes were closed—Jenny's back was pressed to Ansel's chest, and Ansel's massive hand cupped Jenny's breast as he pulsed into her, the shaft of him glinting wet. His hands had been washed, a pristine white, no sign now of the dirt or the shovel. Hazel wondered if she had dreamed the scene, imagined it altogether. Jenny's legs were spread, her head thrown back; her neck was so delicate in the winter dawn, unprotected. In the reticent strip of light, Jenny's body was not necessarily Jenny's.

She could have been Hazel, covered in this sheen of sweat, so loose and gasping. Hazel, lost to the kind of motion that made you wiser, the kind that made you separate, the kind that made you real.

Ansel opened his eyes.

Hazel did not have time to move from the door or to conceal herself. In that gut-dropping millisecond before the shock exploded and she stumbled back on her crutches, Ansel's gaze bore right into her. There was something new in him, something savage, like the damp, infested soil beneath an overturned rock. She had witnessed a secret in the yard, something meant to stay hidden. And now Hazel was watching Ansel's return, his transformation from single to double, his insertion back into Jenny. It was scary, his body's forceful wanting. Stark, what it told her.

The universe did not care how you loved. You could love like this—urgent and slippery, like a girlfriend, or a wife. You could love like a sister, or even a twin. It didn't matter.

Two connected things must always come apart.

7 Hours

Gravy, for lunch. The soggy mass slides into your cell, a gelatinous lump atop a meager portion of turkey, accompanied by half a cup of green beans, floating in water. No coffee today—a collective groan echoes down the row. A-Pod is organized so you cannot see anyone, but you know the distinctive sounds of each inmate. Today, they are hungry. As you spoon the formless substance into your mouth, you imagine you are eating a cheeseburger instead, biting into a patty of rare, simmering pink.

Joy is a cousin of love, you read once. If you cannot feel love, there is at least this weaker relative, tantalizing in memory: the relish of meat, perfectly cooked, melting on the tongue. You know how to swallow, to close your eyes and delight.

•

You recognize Shawna by her footsteps.

Shawna shuffles when she walks, so unlike the hefty stomping of the men. A limping drag, constantly unsure of herself. The baby's screaming has passed, and you sit on the edge of your cot, taking steady breaths. The baby is dead, you tell yourself. The baby is dead. You remember the social worker who sat you down as a child, her knuckles thick and gnarled: Your brother is in a better place now, she said, too busy or too pained to look you in the eye.

Shawna walks by, sent on some other errand, peering anxiously through your window. The inmates are constantly harassing her, masturbating against the glass as she walks by—gunning her down, they call it. But to Shawna, you are different. There is fear in her glance. Excitement. Before you ever saw her face, you heard the tentative scratch of her boots on the concrete and you knew: Shawna is a woman made up of other people's perceptions. The most malleable type. She shops at Costco, she bites her nails. She never learned how to properly apply makeup, so it runs in blue streaks beneath her eyes. Shawna is the kind of woman who likes to be told exactly who she is.

You have whispered with Shawna, you have schemed with Shawna, you have passed illicit notes. The two inmates on either side of you have likely heard it all—but Jackson and Dorito know not to mess with you. You are very good at chess, and for this reason, you have the most valuable collection of commissary items on all of 12 Building, the only bargaining power this place affords. When you win a chess game— sometimes twice a day, calling out a checkmate down the hall—the bettors kite the profits your way, tied to the ends of a bedsheet. You slide every other prize to Jackson or Dorito, extra garlic bagel chips or nutty wafer bars. They stay quiet.

Now, as Shawna shuffles away, you feel a swell of pride. Those eyes, lit up with fever. Shawna is scaring herself. You have forty-nine minutes until the transfer to the Walls Unit. Shawna is reaching a peak she did not know she could climb.

You understand the outline of Shawna. When she gets off work, she goes home to her double-wide, where her husband's shirts are still folded into sagging drawers, where his coats hang untouched above the vinyl welcome mat. He died less than a year ago: forklift accident. She makes Hamburger Helper for dinner, drinks a Bud Light in front of the static television.

It's a nice little place, she told you, as you hashed out the details of the plan.

What will we do when I'm out? you asked. Tell me about it.

Well, Shawna said, we'll make a big dinner. Steak grilled out on the porch. We'll have a bottle of wine.

It's insane, really, that Shawna believes you intend to stay at her house, twenty miles from Polunsky. That she hasn't considered the dogs, or the helicopters, or the interrogation she'll invariably undergo. It is possible that Shawna has considered these things and simply chosen to live inside her own fantasy—it doesn't matter either way. You need her. You need her for the plan, and after, you need her to make sure your Theory gets out to the world. She has agreed to leak your notebooks to the press, submit them to publishers. Nothing else matters, as long as she goes through with this.

Everyone tells me I'm too nice, Shawna whispered that night, as she dragged a trembling hand across her mouth.

She looked so fragile. Like she might break if you bent her too far.

My love, you breathed. My love. How could that possibly be a bad thing?

It will happen on the transfer van at noon.

Shawna slipped into the warden's office weeks ago. She found the stack of paperwork, detailing your transfer. The van number, the route. Her note this morning told you everything.

I did it.

This morning, Shawna swiped into the employee parking lot. She crowbarred the van door open, placed her husband's old pistol beneath the driver's seat.

Shawna has described the highway near her house, the surrounding area dense with woods. You will use your feet to pull the gun from beneath the driver's seat, and you will aim with cuffed hands as you list your demands. Shawna has drawn a crude map in pencil on the back of a visitation form, and you will zag through the trees. When you reach the stream she has described, you will shed your clothes. A half mile more, and you will reach her trailer, where a box of hair dye and color contacts will be waiting on the kitchen counter, along with a pair of construction coveralls that once belonged to her husband.

There is the possibility—even likelihood—that it will all go horribly awry. The transfer team will be armed with assault rifles. You'll take a bullet to the brain. You'll be ripped to shreds by a well-trained Rottweiler or smashed to a pulp by a truck as you're crossing the highway. But these options are all preferable to that room. The gurney.

•

Packer.

The warden is raspy, a graveled voice at your door.

The warden chews gum loudly, jaw pumping with the effort. The pores on his nose are the first thing you see, greasy and prominent, and his crew cut is even and flat. Some days he wears a wedding ring, but today he does not.

I wanna make sure you're ready, the warden says. You know what will happen next? The chaplain's gone over it all?

You nod. A subtle glance at your watch: thirty-five minutes until the transfer. In thirty-five minutes, you will be handcuffed and marched into the waiting van, which the warden believes will bring you to the Walls Unit. Inside that infamous building, there will be a holding cell. A chair, for the chaplain. A phone, for goodbye.

You flush with the knowledge: you will not see any

of it. You imagine how the warden's face will look in a few hours—embarrassed in front of the news cameras. His cheeks will be ruddy, the tendons tight in his neck.

Warden, you say. Can you do me one favor?

The man crosses his burly arms.

My witness, you say. Can you tell her I'm sorry?

You have heard the warden's cruelty. You've listened to him yell at the other men, pull the taser from his pocket, back them up against the wall. You've heard how they scream. But you are not stupid. You know how to handle women, and you know how to handle certain types of men. You understand men like the warden, standing with his feet spread wide in that manufactured power stance. You are careful to stay seated on the edge of your cot, to keep your head slightly bowed in deference. You have never once stood to reach the warden's height; always, you let the man be taller. For this reason, you have your jokes. You have even shared some of your Theory with the warden. You are his favorite prisoner, in the entirety of Polunsky Unit. Ansel P, he hollers, like you are two men on a couch watching a football game. He fist-bumps you through the slats in the recreation cage.

The warden loops his gum around his tongue and pops it. You smell saliva, cinnamon.

Make sure your stuff is ready by the door, the warden says.

You take this for a yes.

⦁

The warden only got to you once—once, in your seven years at Polunsky. He did not use a taser or the hulk of his arms. You are different. There is a ruffling pride, mixed with the shame of remembering. You require a special technique.

You'd been talking about the Theory.

Explain it to me, the warden said, leaning bored against the wall. It was the middle of a sweltering Texas summer, when the row stank constantly of sweat and slick feet, the air unbreathable at ninety-eight degrees.

Well, you said. It's a Theory about good and evil.

Written? he asked. Like a book?

Of course, you said. I work on it every night.

Okay, the warden said. So what's your thesis?

You pulled one of your notebooks from under the bed and slid it beneath the door.

Hypothesis 51A, the warden read aloud. On Infinity?

Yes, you said. On Infinity explores the concept of choice. We have billions of potential lives, thousands of alternate universes, running like streams beneath our current reality. If morality is determined by our choices, then we must also consider those other universes, in which we've made different ones.

Where are you in those? the warden asked.

Where am I?

In those other lives, the warden said. Where are you, if you're not here?

I don't know, you said. The options are infinite. Our alternate selves live in another dimension, multiplying, just outside our line of sight. I could be a writer, or a philosopher, or a baseball player. The possibilities are endless. They prove that who I am—my goodness or my badness—it's fluctuating. Morality is not fixed. It's fluid, ever-changing.

The warden seemed to ponder.

Then where would they be now? the warden asked.

Who?

Those Girls, Ansel. In an alternate world, a world in which you had not killed them, what would they be doing in this exact moment?

The question stunned. A blindside attack. It stung, this sudden turn of the warden. You stared at the veins in your hands until the man huffed a chuckle; he rapped on the steel door, as though to remind you of your own entrapment.

So you're a manifesto guy, huh?

It's not a manifesto, you said.

Show me one and I've seen them all, the warden said. They all look like this. Like justification. There is no justification for what you've done, Ansel P, but God knows you've got the time to keep searching.

With that, the warden walked away, leaving you alone with your furious breath. How dangerous, you thought. How futile. How senseless, to reveal even a corner of yourself—when that self, they say, is monster.

•

Now, the warden is gone. You wait. Nine minutes until the transfer. Sometimes you are certain this is all you are made of: a fleeting instant between action and inaction. Doing something, or not. Where is the difference, you wonder? Where is the choice. Where is the line, between stillness and motion?

•

The second Girl was a waitress at the diner.

That teenage summer progressed: 1990, Bon Jovi and Vanilla Ice. Weeks went by, and the search parties faltered. The missing posters faded, and the news programs died down, and only in the most random and surreal moments did you think about what you had done. You had killed someone. A Girl. You remembered only blips of the act itself: your belt undone and snaking, the calluses on your hands from the tugging. The fact felt completely detached from your being, something vaguely related to you but not quite urgent. You'd wake in the middle of the night to the regular sounds of the trailer park and you'd imagine footsteps. Sirens. Rattling chains. You'd huddle beneath your cheap scratchy sheets, certain this was it—finally, they were coming for you.

But they never did. June passed, then it was July, and still, they had not found her.

Late at night, you drove to the diner. Nestled in a dark corner off the highway, the diner closed at midnight, and you liked to spend those sleepy hours drinking coffee in a back booth, avoiding the gloom of your trailer. Your favorite waitress had a perky blond ponytail and freckles scattered across her cheeks—she chattered as she refilled your coffee. She was young, maybe sixteen, and easy to blush. Angela, read the tag on her apron. You repeated her name in the shower, on the road, in the walk-in freezer as you organized tubs of vanilla.

In truth: the screaming had started again.

There were a few days, after that first Girl, when you

were certain you had banished it for good. Everything had been lighter. Prettier. You wondered if this was the feeling people talked about, if this was happy. You still had your summer job at the Dairy Queen. You handed smiling children their ice cream cones, complimented your coworker on her haircut. She cocked her head, mumbled a confused thanks. Her words were tinged with suspicion, a quiet fear that made you angry—it was dripping slowly back into you, the sound of the baby's screaming. Like a leak in the ceiling.

That night was humid. Middle of July. You remember the sweat, how it soaked straight through your T-shirt. Through the glowing diner window, Angela stacked the chairs, mopped the floor, shut the lights. Finally, she came out of the restaurant, her purse clutched in her armpit—she fiddled with the keys, locked the door, and squinted across the pavement toward her car. She didn't see you at first, standing dead still in the center of the empty parking lot. A jolt, at the sound of your breathing. Right away, she recognized danger. Angela screamed, piercing, but you clapped a hand over her mouth.

After, it was different.

The relief was muted. A dilution. A weak, flaccid high. This Girl did not feel anything like the first. By the time you dragged her limp into your car, by the time you used the wheelbarrow behind your trailer to cut a path through the dense woods, by the time she'd joined the other Girl in the ground at the wild center of the abandoned forest, it was gone. The relief. Like it had never been there at all. Your body was streaked with dirt, and the sun threatened light above the canopy of trees. Your hands were stinging, blistered from where the belt had ripped your skin, the pearl bracelet from the Girl's wrist twisted between your fingers.

A memory surfaced, buried until now. Your mother, clasping a chain around your neck—this will always keep you safe. You pressed your face into your filthy palms. You wept.

·

They will be here any second. Shawna, and the transfer team.

You stand to pull Blue's letter down from the shelf. The letter is only one page: you fold it as small as you can, tuck it into the elastic waistband of your pants. This single sheet of paper will come with you, a corner poking into your thigh as you run into the wild.

But the photo. You do not know what to do with the photo.

The photograph feels dire—when you hold the Blue House up to your face, the image blurs. This close, you can almost see the salt and pepper shakers, the crusty ketchup bottles. You can almost hear the whining hum of the soda machine, Blue's cackling laugh from behind the kitchen door. But breathing in, you smell only glossy paper.

When you stick out your tongue, the surface of the photograph is bitter. Metallic. You taste ink, chemicals.

Wincing, you rip off a single corner: the edge of the lawn, Blue's parked car. You pop it into your mouth like a potato chip. The ink numbs in your throat, a sweet poisonous burn, as you realize what you need to do. You rip the precious photograph into strips your molars will understand. The ink is sickening between your teeth. You crunch down anyway, until the photo has evaporated sharp in your throat, until the Blue House is forever a part of you.

•

You do believe in the multiverse. The eternal possibility of it. There is a version of you out there—a child, unabandoned. A boy who came home from school to a mother who read you stories and kissed your forehead goodnight. There is a version of you who never put that fox in Saffy Singh's bed, who learned how to banish Baby Packer's screaming any other way. A man who never married Jenny. There is a version of yourself who lost only the things that everyone loses. You like to believe that every alternate self would have found the Blue House, too.

But the most bemusing version of you—the one you cannot reckon with—is the Ansel Packer who did everything the same and simply never got caught.

Saffy
1999

The day they found the missing girls, Saffy thought of the long, sloping yard behind Miss Gemma's house. The overgrown grass, the looming cattails— how she used to explore, hunting for secrets.

Saffy had now seen more dead things than she could count, and every time, they forced that sickening drop through her abdomen. She had hoped it would get better with age: Saffy was twenty-seven years old now, three weeks into her promotion to investigator with the New York State Police, and still, it felt like electrocution. Sergeant Moretti crouched by Saffy's boots, one hand cupped around a yellowing skull. Standing over the bodies, Saffy remembered how certain she had felt as a little girl, playing detective in the grass. How easily she had believed that every mystery could be solved.

"Singh," Moretti said, squinting up. "Bring CSI back here. Tell them there are three."

The skull was half buried, just an empty eye socket peering up from the dirt. The October sun was relentless, golden through the trees—flaming-red leaves cast shadows over the forest floor, where they'd found three femurs already. Saffy could see the stringy remnants of the girl's hair, patchy and thin, still clumped against the bone. She pulled the radio from her belt, an inkling of truth already nestling in the hollow of her throat; before the three femurs, a hiker had found the shredded remains of a backpack. Saffy had recognized it immediately—red nylon, with a patch hand-sewn onto the pocket, a denim square cut from an old pair of jeans. In the photo above Saffy's desk, that backpack was flung over the arm of a teenage girl, who looked momentarily over her shoulder for the click of the shutter before walking on, oblivious.

The bodies had been buried by a stream. In the years since, the ground had shifted, churned up with the rain and the rising creek, and the bones had scattered, resettled across the forest floor. As the forensic photographer crouched over that discolored skull, lonely in its patch of dirt, Moretti turned to Saffy, one hand propped to shield the sun from her eyes.

"Remind me what we have around here?" Moretti asked. "Homes, farms?"

Saffy tilted toward the canopy of trees, trying to banish the scent of decay. Moretti was an outsider, originally from Atlanta. She would never understand this land like Saffy did, would never know the subtleties of the forest at night.

"Mostly farmland," Saffy said. "There's a convenience store about a mile away and a trailer park with a dozen homes behind it. The rest is protected wilderness."

"These woods are too dense for a car, or even a bike."

"He could have used a wagon or something," Saffy said. "Or else he's a big man."

"Three separate trips, don't you think? He couldn't have brought them all here at once. That, or we've found our crime scene."

Saffy shook her head. "It's too tangled back here. The brambles are so thick. This feels like a spot for stashing, not for lingering."

Moretti sighed. "We'll confirm at the morgue, but it's them all right. The decomposition, that damn backpack. These are our missing girls from '90."

Saffy watched as the forensic team hunted through the dirt. If these bones belonged to the girls from 1990, they had been here over nine years now, and any chance of footprints or fibers, fingerprints or stray hairs, had long been degraded.

"Honestly, Singh?" Moretti sighed. "I didn't think we'd ever find them."

There was a plea in Sergeant Moretti's gaze—a cynical hope Saffy had come to recognize, the most honest expression of this inscrutable job. A perfect mirror of the fucked-up world, violence and tragedy mingling with a desperate sort of faith.

"I'll take care of the witness," Saffy offered, leaving Moretti to her own reflection.

The hiker sat on a mossy log, wrapped in a trauma blanket. He grimaced as Saffy approached—an older man, with a gash oozing up the back of his muddy calf. He'd tripped down the mountain in his rush to reach a pay phone.

"I've already answered all your questions," he said, exhausted, as he took in Saffy's curt smile, her tight ponytail, her fitted navy blazer.

"I'm sorry," Saffy said. "But we need a formal statement."

She sat gingerly on the log and turned toward the man, noting the tracks down his dirt-stained face where tears had rolled into his wiry beard. *Get a statement then take him home*, Moretti had murmured, as the man choked out his story. *He just got unlucky.* Saffy's instincts discerned the same. At its most fundamental level, detective work was a study in reading people, and Saffy had been perfecting the art all her life.

"Did you touch anything?" Saffy asked. "Maybe when you first discovered the scene?"

"No. I found the backpack first, and I reached to pick it up—I hate when people litter on the trails—and that's when I saw the skull. I ran right back down for the phone."

The hiker's story was short and uncomplicated, useless but necessary. *It's all about building a case,* Moretti liked to say. *Nothing counts until it counts in court.*

"You look awfully young for this job, don't you?" the man said, after the statement had been signed, as he chugged a paper cup of water from the CSI tent.

She did. Saffy knew her face still carried the narrow naivety of adolescence, along with the surprise of her brown skin, a constant questioning she read regularly in strangers' eyes. When she landed the promotion, her young features had not helped: at the record age of twenty-six, Saffy would be training under Emilia Moretti, the only female senior investigator in the state of New York. The other troopers had been livid. It was true that Saffy had only served the requisite four years as a state trooper, that Moretti had written a glowing recommendation directly to the superintendent, but it still stung when one pimply guy cornered her in the parking lot, a cop Saffy had known since Basic School in Albany. *Bitch*. He'd spat a wad of saliva right onto her chunky black boot. *Next time, try working for it.*

Saffy had almost reminded him of the Hunter case, though no one had forgotten. When the Hunter boy went missing, Saffy stayed late every night, holed up past midnight in her stiff wool uniform. *Tiny Tits*, the other troopers hooted, frat-boy loud. *Does she even speak English?* They busted into Saffy's locker and filled it with days-old takeout from the single Indian restaurant in town. They only stopped after Saffy convinced Moretti to drive out to the crumbling cabin where the Hunter boy's karate instructor had taken his monthly fishing trips. Sure enough. The child was traumatized but alive. Saffy had watched from the station window as the boy collapsed into his sobbing mother's arms.

"Come on," Saffy said, ignoring the man's question. She stood, brushed a pat of moss from her pants. "I'll drive you home."

She helped the hiker into the back seat of her Crown Victoria, which to this point had mostly carried drunken day laborers from the bar to the police station. As they pulled away from the trailhead, Saffy turned onto the service road she knew by heart, the mountain rising green in her rearview. The memories seemed to follow, kicked up like dust beneath her tires. She had known the underbelly of this land, smelled the rancid bloom of its decay, seen the ghosts that floated hazy through the night. She knew what this place was capable of.

The girls had disappeared nine years ago. 1990.

Saffy remembered that summer with a sluggish haze that bordered on blackout. Roaring bonfires in empty fields, gritty sleeping bags filled with sand. Needles, beer cans, unwashed hair. She had been eighteen years old when those girls went missing, and she remembered how her dropout friends had talked—like the missing girls were not just one town over, but another world over, like it could never happen to them.

But Saffy knew about catastrophe. It was arbitrary. A thing that descended from nowhere, pointed a bony finger, and smirked. As if to say: *I choose you.*

Saffy had been transferred, after Miss Gemma's, to a quiet home three towns north. Twelve years old by then, she had lived with one other foster child, a toddler with a runny nose and needy hands, their shared bedroom always stinking of diapers. Saffy watched the baby most nights while her foster parents drove to the casino across the Canadian border. She spent her middle school years lingering on the basketball courts just to avoid that house, shivering in sweatshirts too small at the wrists. The month Saffy turned sixteen, she was transferred to her last foster family, an elderly couple with an unsupervised basement. Saffy had her own entrance, a door with a key that dangled on a plastic lanyard, a microwave, and a camping stove. She lost herself.

Those teenage years passed in blurs and blips. She remembered the school counselor crying with frustration, the social workers threatening their useless disappointment, moldy beams creaking along the basement ceiling. Ages sixteen through eighteen were a fog, one long chain of mistakes that could have lasted forever. Until that summer, when everything changed.

The girls went missing.

Izzy Sanchez disappeared first. Saffy was eighteen years old, just released from the system and living with her boyfriend Travis, a weed dealer with missing molars and a reliable coke connect. Travis was into all the hard stuff, but Saffy stuck entirely to cocaine, preferring the way it energized her from the inside out. She heard about Izzy in a dim living room, heavy curtains crowding the windows, Salt-N-Pepa blaring from the stereo. One of Travis's friends had witnessed the scene. He told the story with a lazy glaze, smoke curling around his acne-scarred cheeks. Izzy had been sixteen years old, waiting for a ride outside a party like this one, last seen standing at the end of a long driveway. And then she was gone. Vanished, without a trace.

The second girl went missing a few weeks later. Saffy watched the news from the couch in Travis's trailer, surrounded by burrito wrappers and over-flowing ashtrays. Angela Meyer. Also sixteen years old—she'd worked the closing shift at the diner a few miles away. Saffy hugged her legs to her chest, sweaty on the fraying couch, a humid breeze wheezing from the box fan in the window. Travis was already passed out on the folding bed, the tracks up his arms like veins in the half-light.

Saffy did not have a high school diploma. She did not have friends, not really—the girls from the field hockey team had long abandoned her, and the only person who kept in touch was Kristen. Kristen had been transferred south after Miss Gemma's. She'd attended a much better high school, emancipated a year early, and now rented her own dingy apartment near a strip mall half an hour away. Kristen was bound for community college, a success story that made those same social workers proud. Kristen made an effort to call every few weeks, *just to say hi.* Most nights, Saffy sat alone after Travis descended into the ether, dropping ice cubes down her sports bra and trying not to think about the black hole of her future—when she heard about Angela, that hole seemed to expand, a supernova.

Then, the third girl went missing.

The third girl had been attending her boyfriend's punk show at a dive bar near Port Douglass. She'd stepped outside for a cigarette. Gone. The panic was escalating—number three, officially an epidemic—though that girl had the least public appeal. There was no crying mother on the news, no tragically normal home. The third girl was a high school dropout like Saffy, no family available for interviews. But she was third, so her name blared across the television.

Lila Maroney.

When Saffy heard about Lila, she remembered their old bedroom. Lila on the bottom bunk, the skin on her knees nicked and scabbed from an attempt at shaving with Bailey's razor. Over the years, she and Kristen spotted Lila occasionally, updating each other over the phone. *Lila's got blue hair now. Lila's got a nose ring, the kind like a bull. Lila dropped out, heard she's working at the Goodwill.* By the time Lila went missing, she and Saffy traveled in overlapping circles, sometimes appearing at the same parties, rarely speaking about anything substantial. So when Saffy saw the news, she thought of that little girl in an oversized T-shirt, her face lit up in the ghostly glow of a flashlight, breath whistling through a retainer that never seemed to fit her teeth.

"Yo," Travis said, dumb on the couch, the tip of his joint glowing orange. "What the fuck, Saff?"

Saffy realized she was crying—big, gulping sobs. The trailer pulsed, dizzy. She tugged on a pair of jeans and left, slamming the screen door shut behind her. Travis's Camry had a dented bumper and a quarter tank of gas, but Saffy wound up toward Plattsburgh, watching as the needle drifted toward empty.

The police station was mayhem, all news cameras and panicked parents, troopers scrawling statements in notepads. The lights in the parking lot blasted, a flood—the early-evening lines of coke still rippled through Saffy's system, brightening obnoxious. She swiped at her eyes with the heel of her hand.

It was pure luck. It was chance, or maybe it was fate. As Saffy entered the police station, tentative and self-conscious, the person she found was Emilia Moretti.

Moretti was a brand of woman Saffy hadn't previously known you could be. She surveilled the scene with sharp hawk eyes, glossy and firm, rigid, brilliant. Back then, Moretti had been in her early thirties, and her wedding ring glinted in the bright overheads, casting laser beams. She looked like the kind of woman who drank a single glass of tasteful white wine with dinner and used expensive skin creams that made the lines on her face look like streams cutting through soft soil. Approaching, Saffy felt shriveled and unkempt. Used up.

"Excuse me," Saffy had croaked. "I want to help."

Moretti had seen the bags under Saffy's eyes, the flaking skin beneath her nose, the crop top she'd cut with a blunt pair of kiddie scissors. And still, she had listened to Saffy's stories about Lila. When Saffy finished talking, Moretti handed her a business card. *Call me if you hear anything.* Saffy didn't hear anything, but she called Moretti the next morning anyway and volunteered for the citizen search effort.

And that was how Saffy found it: police work. She loved the brisk, efficient instructions, the lack of sentimentality, the stern tenderness of Moretti's gaze as they combed the grassy foothills.

There were so many ways her life could have turned. She could have lived one long basement party. She could have died alongside Travis in his overdose three years ago. She could very well have cleaned up some other way. Saffy did not like to question the forces that drove her to Moretti, to her GED, to community college and then to Candidate Processing Weekend with the New York State Police. When Saffy questioned these forces, she only became more aware of how precarious they really were.

•

By the time Saffy came home to the blinking light on her answering machine, it was nearly midnight. The day had passed in a frenzy, the evidence logged, the scene photographed meticulously. Tomorrow, the news would go public.

Saffy dropped her keys and gun on the counter, her apartment morose and frigid in shadow. She changed into an old NYSP sweatshirt, washed her face, pulled her shellacked ponytail from its rubber band. The few women in Basic School had recommended cutting it short, but Saffy could not bear to lose this release, her mass of hair tumbling free. An exhale, this unsheathing.

"Hey, it's me," Kristen sang through Saffy's dusty answering machine. "You still on for Saturday? Jake's gonna be at a conference, and I rented *You've Got Mail.*"

That hipbone.

Kristen would want to know about Lila. They had
been a trio, all those years ago at Miss Gemma's—
Saffy, Kristen, and Lila. They had braided friendship
bracelets, climbed trees, and made up games; they had
whispered secrets from top bunk to bottom. But Saffy
could not fathom returning Kristen's call, saying the
words. She stood frozen at the counter as the robot
droned: *No new messages.* Her apartment smelled
musty, like old carpet and dirty dishes. The studio was
nicer than any place she'd ever rented, a unit in a refurbished old Victorian a few blocks from the Saranac
River, a good deal from Kristen's boyfriend, the heir
to his family's real estate business. *You have to take
better care of yourself,* Kristen was always saying—
the sunflowers Saffy had bought last week drooped
in their vase, the water browned to a fuzzy swamp.
Saffy heated a can of soup on the stove and fell asleep
while it was cooling, collapsed in the blue light of the
television.

The medical examiner kept a dingy office in the basement of the local hospital. When Saffy arrived, fifteen
minutes early, Moretti was already waiting by the elevator. Her jaw was tight, clenching the spearmint gum

she always chewed, her hair blown glossy—beneath the dim glare, Saffy could see the bags puffing beneath her tired eyes.

"Singh," Moretti said, a sly grin breaking across her face. "It's official. Lieutenant took you off the Saranac robbery. You're working this case with me now."

That familiar glow, swelling warm from Saffy's chest. The sparkling halo of being chosen—being trusted—by Moretti.

"Lieutenant put Kensington on it too, but Kensington runs late." Moretti looked at her watch, pressed the elevator button. "We'll start without him."

Kensington was a slick, cocky detective with unnaturally white teeth. He was a mediocre cop for the most part, but he could charm even the coldest suspects in an interrogation, pooling confessions regularly at his feet. And the lieutenant made no secret of his reasoning: they could not work a team of only women. Bad for optics.

As the coroner ushered them into the morgue, Saffy tried not to inhale; the smell engulfed her anyway, a chilly rush of formaldehyde. The bones had been laid out on plastic tarps across three separate tables, like an excavation from an archaeological dig—ancient artifacts, uncovered from some forgotten era. The coroner had logged each fragment, marked them with little white flags.

"We're still waiting on dental records," the coroner said, running a hand through his froth of white hair. "But decomposition looks right. Between eight and nine years. These are your girls."

"Cause of death?" Moretti asked.

"Hard to say. Two of the spinal cords show some damage, but with this level of erosion, I can't make any definitive conclusions."

"Strangulation?" Saffy asked.

"Probably," the coroner said. "No trauma to the skulls or any of the other bones. One of the girls had a fracture in her arm, but it healed premortem."

"Angela Meyer," Saffy said. "She broke her arm earlier in the spring on an ATV, had to take a few weeks off waitressing. Her boss said she'd just returned to work when she was murdered."

The coroner raised his eyebrows.

"She's got a good memory," Moretti explained, winking as Saffy flushed.

"Then you can tell your captain we have ID," the coroner said.

As he detailed the rest of his report, the bones they had uncovered, the many still missing, Saffy tried not to wonder. Which femur belonged to Lila, which incomplete set of ribs. The room was dank and sterile, everything tinted a noxious shade of green. Laid out on the tables, the girls looked more animal than human.

When Kensington finally rushed in, the coroner had already signed the report, tucked safely into Moretti's briefcase. Kensington panted, breathless, his suit wrinkled, hair greased back with a wet fistful of gel.

"Well," Moretti said, clapping her hands together decisively as Kensington spluttered. "I think we're done here. Kensington, you get to notify the families."

•

Back at the station, Saffy let the buzz expand. Until then, her rotation had included robberies and domestic incidents, nothing especially contentious—it was a new exhilaration, the thrill of catching a good case, and as she followed Moretti through the bullpen, even the troopers could not bring her down. She ignored the usual, a whispered joke concealed behind a hand, a laugh so muffled she could not track it to the source. All her life, strangers and teachers and peers and colleagues had made her feel acutely aware of her dark skin. It never seemed to matter that she had grown up here, that she had never been to India, a place she yearned for idly—as a child she had traced the country's shape, a reverent finger on the map, outlining its careful borders. Next to the hordes of tobacco-chewing boys, muddy boots propped on their desks, Saffy would always feel outcast.

"We'll set up here," Moretti directed. The backroom conference table was littered with the half-solved cases still in rotation: the Saranac robbery, a series of Y2K conspiracy threats, a child abduction Kensington had been working for months.

"I'm putting you on the old files," Moretti said. "Kensington and I remember too much. You're completely fresh—I want you reading through everything."

"What exactly am I looking for?"

"Anything that puts us near that forest."

On the television in the corner of the room, the press conference blared. The captain's face was somber as he monotoned a careful statement, glancing only sparingly at the audience of reporters. When the camera panned to the photographs, the girls looked younger than ever. Izzy and Angela smiled in front of blue backdrops in staged high school portraits—Angela wore a shirt embroidered with yellow polka dots, and Izzy had a spattering of acne across her cheeks. Lila didn't have a school photo; her boyfriend had provided that single known photograph, back when she'd gone missing. Lila stood on a sidewalk overgrown with weeds, red backpack flung over her shoulder, head twisted back to smile at the photographer.

"You'll be okay?" Moretti asked, a half question. Moretti had not forgotten. Lila had been a beacon, that night in Travis's trailer, guiding Saffy directly here. This very case, pulling her into the light.

The old files appeared then, a distraction and a relief—four dusty boxes, lugged in by a disgruntled trooper, sweat stains blooming in the pits of his uniform.

"I take it these are mine now?" Saffy said.

Moretti winced, apologetic. "I'll grab us lunch."

When Moretti had gone, Saffy lined the bulletin board with new photographs from the crime scene. The forensics team had uncovered the girls' belongings, in various states of decay. Shoes, earrings. Lila's backpack, Angela's purse. Izzy's mother had been the first to notice—a beaded barrette was missing, Izzy's favorite. Her mother was certain she'd been wearing it that night. Angela's mother mentioned a pearl bracelet, a family heirloom her daughter never took off. Moretti was convinced the jewelry had gotten lost in the brush, and besides, nothing of Lila's had been taken. But, Saffy pointed out, Lila didn't have parents. No one had been watching. *Trinkets,* Saffy had suggested to a tight-lipped Morettti. *Maybe he took souvenirs.*

Saffy crouched on the fraying carpet. The first of the four cardboard boxes contained the witness interviews—the base had collapsed, sagging with the sheer number of reports. She would have to track them all down again, take new statements.

At the very bottom of the stack, Saffy found the original print: Lila's photo. It had been shot on a disposable camera, dusty and faded, Lila's smile bleached and pallid. Saffy thought of Kristen then—Kristen, with her stable job at the salon, where her clients told her she looked like Jennifer Aniston, how her clothes hung easily on her thin, lithe frame. Kristen, who had always known she was bound for something better, who had worked for stability and then accepted it without question. Saffy studied the photo of Lila, a girl reduced to a discolored snapshot, and wondered if she would always feel like this: a pendulum swinging between the two of them, never sure of what she might have become.

Beneath Lila's photo, there was a bag. A hunk of dark hair lay limp in the clear plastic, evidence an officer had found at the bottom of the driveway where Izzy disappeared. As Saffy leaned against the backroom wall, Izzy's hair in her lap, she was transported into a hallucination that had stalked her for years now, a parallel universe that felt sickening, nearly fatal in its limitlessness.

A highway, dusk. A flicker of long black ponytail. Izzy had died at sixteen, but she was older here: nineteen, maybe twenty. Windows open, air whipping hard, an old bluegrass song twanging from the radio. There would have been a boy, sitting in the passenger's seat— Izzy would not have loved him, not here, maybe not ever, but this wouldn't have mattered, in the hot flush of youth, his calloused fingers creeping up her thigh, the horizon bleeding behind the Adirondack peaks.

In this almost-world—the substitute reality that lingered like a daydream—Izzy was never a pile of bones on a table. She was bright and golden, a blazing instant of mundane and perfect glory.

•

Saffy tracked down a handful of the witnesses from the initial case—Angela's boss from the diner, the kids from Izzy's party, the friend Lila had gone out with that night. The locals were confused, wary, oddly giddy to find her waiting on their stoops. As Saffy perched on sinking couches and politely declined tepid cups of tea, Moretti kept the captain at bay, while Kensington handled the never-ending tip line. Most witnesses couldn't remember much. She had gathered no new information.

Her last witness of the long, parched day was a young woman named Olympia Fitzgerald. Saffy pulled up in front of an unfinished house, a single-story ranch perched on a wide swath of field, pieces of construction equipment scattered across the browning grass. October in the Adirondacks looked like a postcard; Saffy sat in her car, skimming the transcript, the details fading off the page. Olympia had been twenty years old in 1990, and her interview had lasted all of seven minutes before the lead investigator dismissed her. The sun slouched over the horizon, the sky a magnetic blue, and Saffy closed the file, too tired to finish.

A woman in a tattered velvet tracksuit answered the door, her gray hair like a thinning mane. Inside, a grandfather clock spilled its guts onto the living room floor. A younger woman—Olympia, the daughter— had propped her bare feet on the coffee table next to an open bottle of neon orange nail polish.

"What's up," Olympia said, disinterested, even as Saffy flashed her badge. Saffy yearned for Moretti's voice, silky and exacting, so naturally competent.

"Back in 1990, you talked to Sergeant Albright about the disappearances of three local girls."

Finally, Olympia looked up, shifting as she sat up straight. Her mother loped into the room and stood behind the couch, hands protective on Olympia's shoulders. They had not invited Saffy to sit. She hovered awkwardly next to a fraying armchair.

"I know," Olympia said. She used her palms to push back a greasy strand of hair, her fingernails still glistening wet. "I saw the news. You found those bodies."

"Yes," Saffy said.

"I told him everything." Olympia's voice cracked, a hint of panic. "The detective, back then. I told him everything I know."

"We're reopening the investigation, Olympia. I'd like to hear exactly what you remember."

Mrs. Fitzgerald nodded her daughter forward— Olympia hesitated as her mother's fingers massaged her neck.

"The summer those girls went missing, I worked at the Dairy Queen off the highway. I had this coworker, this boy. He was a little younger than me, just graduated high school."

"Go on."

"I remember the night Izzy Sanchez went missing," Olympia said. "I remember it really clearly, because it was also the night after he and I—well, we'd been flirting all summer. I went over to his place, in that trailer park by the forest where you found the bodies. One thing led to another, and . . . we tried to, you know. But he couldn't. So, I left. And the next day at work, he seemed strange, completely off. When I tried to talk to him, he had this look in his eye. Like he wanted to hurt me. It was so many years ago, but I'll never forget it. I let him close the store alone. That was the same night Izzy disappeared."

"What was his name?" Saffy asked.

"Ansel," Olympia said simply. "Ansel Packer."

That name.

Saffy's jaw filled with saliva, the sulfuric rush before a spew of vomit.

"Did you notice anything else?" Saffy asked, quaking.

"I'm sorry," Olympia said. "I don't remember much, not like that. I spent a long time just trying to forget."

Memory, Saffy thought, was unreliable. Memory was a thing to be savored or reviled, never to be trusted.

"Did you laugh at him?"

The women gaped. An endless pause.

"Please," Saffy said. "Do you remember, Olympia? It's important. It sounds like he felt threatened, embarrassed. Do you remember if you laughed at him?"

Olympia's expression was a cracked veneer of shame. Saffy had her answer. The room smelled like Christmas candles and smoked meat. A sudden wave of understanding broke over Saffy's body, the recognition simmering. A patch of orange fur, stuck bloody to

Saffy's palm; Lila's giant eleven-year-old eyes, a handful of crumbling oatmeal raisin cookies. The way the squirrels laid in death, one, two, three with the fox, arms stretched deliberately above their heads in surrender. Moretti's finger hooked through the eye socket of that skull. Fur, skin. The way death peeled itself deliberately from a bone.

•

The Fitzgeralds' bathroom was papered in peeling pink. Mrs. Fitzgerald had lined the counter with little figurines—angels and shepherds, porcelain cherubs. A bowl of potpourri sat by the faucet, old and crunchy, a layer of dust gathered on the petals. Saffy ran the water cold, splashed it onto her face.

As the years faded, Saffy remembered less and less about her mother. The tiny things had slipped away without saying goodbye. Her mother's favorite shoes were red patent leather. Saffy could not recall the shape. She remembered dark lipstick, but not the slope of her mother's canine teeth. These tiny reckonings seemed unfair, as Saffy leaned both hands against the faux marble counter. In the mirror, she still saw bits of her mother, except her mother had been white, and for that reason, Saffy would always resemble her father to everyone else. When people asked where she was from—no, where she was *really* from—Saffy would tell them. *My father is from India. No, I've never been. Yes, I'd like to go someday.* And every time, she would feel an exhaustion that reached her very bones.

Saffy wished her mother were here now. She would have words for this change, riling ferocious from Saffy's gut. A monster, roaring the sound of that name: Ansel Packer.

Saffy still kept the photo frame, with her mother's handwriting inside. It sat now on her nightstand—the glass polished clean. *Felix culpa,* her mother had written. The happy fault. The horrible thing that leads to the good. As Saffy fled the Fitzgeralds' house without goodbye or explanation, she wondered about her father; if he had grown up learning religious phrases similar to those she'd been forced to study in the Bible as a foster child. *For God judged it better to bring good out of evil than not to permit evil to exist at all.*

•

"We have a lead," Saffy said, breathless.

Moretti looked worn, her hair uncharacteristically mussed as they sat in the late-night hush of the station. The bullpen was blissfully abandoned. Moretti had sent

Kensington home, after he'd sulked over and plopped the day's reports onto the conference room table. The tip lines had exploded since the press conference, and Kensington had spent the day listening to a series of unhinged townie theories. The girls were kidnapped by a serial killer from the seventies, the girls were members of a Satanic cult, the girls had fought, then murdered one another. The tip line was necessary, Moretti had lectured to a cranky Kensington, who'd taken a flask from his jacket and swigged it blatantly. They had to check every box.

But now, Saffy had this. Something real.

Ansel Packer.

Saffy's clothes still carried the mildew stench of the Fitzgeralds' house. Beneath the glow of the desk lamp, she detailed Olympia's statement, explaining what she knew of Ansel Packer as a boy.

"He exhibits all the traits of our perpetrator. Explosive, but not consistently so. Fragile with his masculinity, always trying to prove it. Socially competent enough to avoid calling attention to himself. It makes sense—I've seen him before, humiliated. Those animals in the yard, also buried by a creek. He kills in threes, Sergeant."

Moretti eyed Saffy with a doubt that felt horribly akin to pity.

"So you had personal relationships with them both," she said slowly. "The victim and the suspect."

"Yes," Saffy admitted. There were very few cases in their department that did not carry similar conflicts—the Adirondacks were small.

"There is a difference," Moretti said gently, "between believing something is true and having the facts to prove that it's true. It doesn't matter what you suspect. It doesn't matter what you think, unless you build a case that can stand up in court."

Even as the surety rushed through her veins, Saffy could not speak of the fox. She had never told anyone what Ansel had done, how that corpse had globbed onto her bedsheets—it felt too raw, too personal to divulge. The incident lived inside her, a private bubble of shame that she poked on her worst days, just to see if it had changed shape. It never did.

"What about the trailer park?" Saffy asked. "What if he's still there?"

Olympia had given a detailed description of Ansel's trailer, inside and out. She'd described his strange behavior, his paranoid ramblings. *He was always going on about the universe,* Olympia had said. *About multiple realities or something.*

"Unlikely. Didn't your witness say he was going to college? She didn't have any evidence, Singh."

"What about the trinkets? The jewelry? What if he has them?"

"It's a stretch."

The night felt heavy. Out the window, a brisk autumn wind battered the trees, the summer critters retreated and gone. Saffy let the chill creep up her spine.

"Look," Moretti said, with an unbearable sort of tenderness. "I know what it's like, to want something to be true. That does not make it so, and you can't let that cloud your judgment or close your eyes to other leads. Things are different for us here, okay? It's important that we don't let our emotions get in the way of our reasoning. Sometimes—sometimes it's our job *not* to feel however we do. Do you understand what I'm saying?"

•

Kristen's house looked like a movie set. It was rustic, cabin-pretty, with big windows overlooking the hills and centralized heat. Even from the stoop, it smelled like air freshener and expensive candles. It was a Saturday evening, nearly Halloween, the sun setting over the treetops in ghostly rays. Saffy had done her face up using the makeup samples Kristen had gifted, which the salon received for free—the foundation was

184 • DANYA KUKAFKA

always two shades too light for Saffy's skin, but this was not something she could tell Kristen without embarrassing her.

"Hi, hi, come in," Kristen said. "I just popped the pizza in the oven. I hope you're not starving."

Saffy shed her shoes while Kristen chattered. Kristen's house had been Jake's until six months ago, when he'd asked her to move in—already, Saffy could see where her friend had taken over. Little calligraphy signs and pillows with needlepoint catchphrases like *Laughter Is the Best Medicine* and *It's 5 O'Clock Somewhere!* Kristen's technician's apron had its own hook in the front hall, glitter smeared across the fabric. Kristen was obsessed with the impending Y2K disaster, and as they crept closer to the New Year, her fixation only grew. She had lined every shelf in the house with stores of canned food and tubs of bottled water.

"Do you mind?" Kristen asked, sheepish, as she pulled half a bottle of chardonnay from the fridge.

Saffy shook her head. Moretti had a set of unbreakable rules—no substances, however casual. By the time Saffy applied to the NYSP, she had gotten entirely clean, with no proof of her past, no arrest records or criminal charges.

"Are you okay?" Saffy asked, as they settled on

NOTES ON AN EXECUTION · 185

the couch, Kristen's fingers fidgeting the stem of her
wineglass.

"I'm fine," Kristen said.

A long quiet.

"Lila," Saffy said finally.

She and Kristen rarely talked about those years, in which Saffy had drifted through the underbelly of this unforgiving town, mirroring Lila's downward spiral. Now, Saffy wanted to tell Kristen how the drugs had felt, melting through her veins, how she'd passed entire days lying on a dusty mattress. How she'd known Lila's life and then grown out of it—how Lila had not gotten the chance to do the same.

"Kristen," Saffy started. "Do you remember Ansel Packer?"

"Of course," she said. "That kid was so weird. He was transferred too, when Miss Gemma got sick. Aren't you working that robbery case?"

"Moretti got me transferred to this one. To Lila's."

"God, that woman loves you."

"I don't know why she—"

"Oh, shut up," Kristen said. "You're the best young investigator they've seen in decades. And besides, you make a good story, Saff. Wayward teen turns her life around. You're like a detective from a TV show, the poor little orphan haunted by her past. Plus, you found that missing boy all on your own—"

"Ansel Packer," Saffy interrupted. "Do you remember anything strange about him? Anything worrying?"

"I remember he had this way of staring. Like he was trying to figure out how useful you'd be."

"Anything else?"

"Come on, Saff. He was just a kid. It's not healthy to go back like this."

But what else was there? There was only going back. Tracing the lines, there to here. Self to self.

"You know," Kristen said. Her chin quivered. "For a detective, you're not very observant, are you?"

Her grin was celestial as she held up her hand. On her left ring finger, Kristen wore a small band studded with twinkling diamonds.

Saffy could not name the despair. It was shallow, crude, the sour taste of milk gone bad. She registered it only long enough to twist herself, arrange her face into the appropriate expression of joy. Kristen let out an excited, shrieking squeal, and the bitterness cracked and fled as Saffy pulled her friend in for a hug. She let the smell of Kristen's hair products engulf her, with the knowledge she'd harbored for a while now—Kristen was Saffy's only family, and soon Kristen would not belong to her.

They talked through the evening. They forgot about

the movie and about the pizza; it burned so badly that the kitchen filled with smoke and they could only eat the blackened pepperonis off the top. They fell asleep like they used to, head to toe, Kristen's foot nestled warm beneath Saffy's shoulder.

The obsession burrowed sometime in the night. Saffy woke up still wearing her jeans, her hand wedged between the couch cushions, that old smell lingering noxious in her throat. Marshy grass, sunscreen. Decomposing skin. The decay of those squirrels, little arms splayed helpless. Kristen was gone—at some point, Jake must have come home. As Saffy studied the detritus of their night, the bloody pizza stripped of its cheesy skin, Kristen's wineglass greasy with fingerprints, she felt queasy.

Early Sunday morning, and the country roads were empty. Saffy rolled down the window of her patrol car, let the fresh air kiss her oncoming headache. The autumn sun blasted through the trees, dancing shadows along the pavement.

Finally, she reached the trailer park.

It was farther out from the rest of them, Olympia had told her. *Like, all the way back. It didn't look like there should be anything over there.*

A mile from where they'd found the bodies, Saffy counted twelve mobile homes. They loomed in the morning mist, arranged in the vague shape of a V. She could hear a small dog yapping, a television murmuring. A phlegmy cough. Saffy climbed out of her car, creeping past a Rottweiler on a chain, its nose twitching at the crunch of her boots.

Olympia was right. At the very edge of the property, there was a single trailer, set fifty feet back from the rest, nearly invisible in the thicket of ruby red trees. Saffy walked circles around the plot, her badge clutched loose in her palm, still wearing her jeans and wrinkled top from the day before.

She took the creaky steps one by one. She cleared her throat. Rapped on the door.

It opened to a middle-aged man. He wore a pair of ripped boxer shorts and the scabbed face of an addict. She could see a television in the background, playing static noise, a table covered in old beer bottles, a cat that looked like it hadn't been fed in weeks.

"Yeah?"

For an excruciating instant, Saffy inhaled stale smoke, sour breath. She did not know what she thought she'd find. Evidence of Ansel's life, maybe. Something, anything. Her own cluelessness now felt distinctly dangerous.

"Hey," the man called to Saffy's back as she turned away. "What do you want?"

She ran.

When Saffy cracked the Hunter case, the captain had been thrilled. *You've got something special here*, he'd said to Moretti, congratulating. But Saffy had not felt special. She'd wanted to ask Moretti if every case would feel like this: the dizzying rush of surety, followed by a gnawing, feral fear. A fear that felt oddly addictive. There was something alive in Saffy's cells, feeding hungry on such doubt—it was sick, tainted, and it had grown like a tree, curious as it twisted upward. It had driven her to the edge of ruin, all those years ago. It had driven her to police work; it had driven her right to this trailer park.

By the time she reached the highway, Saffy's headache had turned splitting. She stepped on the gas, her hair falling in her face as the engine revved faster, until she had reached a hundred miles an hour and she was certain she had nothing left inside, until she opened her mouth to the blank highway and let out the deepest darkest blackest scream.

●

In the days that followed, Saffy lost control of her desk. The case swallowed her up, sucked her into its undertow. It had been a week since they'd found the bodies, and Saffy could not remember the last real meal she'd eaten. Drive-through fast food, days ago— she'd been subsisting otherwise on coffee and granola bars, her stomach growling at her desk late into the night. She'd returned to her apartment only twice, to shower and pack a duffel bag of clothes.

The captain was pushing his favorite suspect: a homeless man named Nicholas Richards, who had evaded multiple drug charges. A personal vendetta, maybe, but they'd all been ordered to prioritize the lead. The surface of Saffy's desk was a mess of phone logs and witness transcripts—beneath it all, her suspicion pulsed, impossible to ignore.

Ansel Packer's transcript showed he'd gone to Northern Vermont University, where he dropped out right before getting his diploma. He'd applied for a philosophy fellowship his last semester. The records contained a mixed recommendation from a Professor May Brown. Saffy had left four messages on the professor's machine. She had no idea where Ansel was now. He paid taxes from an address that no longer existed, an apartment building near the university, demolished years ago. Ansel had no police record. Not even a speeding ticket.

When Moretti walked by, Saffy hid her work beneath a nondescript file box. *Drop everything else, Singh*, Moretti had warned, firm. *We need more on the captain's suspect. That's an order.* They were closing in on arrest—Nicholas Richards had camped illegally near the burial site. If the ranger could place him on all three dates, they would move in. Moretti had relayed this information with a smug surety that made Saffy's pulse jump with exhausted frustration.

So when her phone rang, minutes before Moretti packed up for the night, Saffy answered with premature disappointment.

"Saffron Singh."

"Hello? This is Professor Brown, returning your call."

Saffy pressed the receiver close, trying to muffle the hoot of the troopers. On the other side of the backroom window, they had inexplicably filled a condom with shaving cream and were whacking one another with it, waiting for it to pop. A few feet away, Moretti was bent over a stack of phone logs, tapping a highlighter against the bow of her lips in concentration. Saffy spoke low into the receiver.

"You recommended a student named Ansel Packer for a philosophy fellowship," Saffy said.

"Ah, yes. He didn't get the fellowship in the end. From what I remember, he was—how do I put this? An average student who believed he deserved more. One of his female classmates got the award instead, and I don't think he took it well. He dropped out shortly after."

"Anything else you can tell me about him?" Saffy asked. "Do you know where he is now?"

"I have no idea." Professor Brown paused. "Have you already spoken with the girlfriend?"

"Girlfriend?"

"The one he had in college. They were quite serious at the time, if I remember correctly. She was always waiting outside his classes. I had her for Intro to Physics, I think. Jenny. Jenny Fisk. She was in the nursing program. Or maybe psychology? Sweet girl. You could try her."

Saffy hung up the phone, adrenaline zapping her gloriously awake. Moretti stood, dug out her car keys, slipped on her sleek, designer parka.

"You look like you found something," Moretti said, stifling a yawn.

Saffy shook her head. "It's nothing."

She waited until Moretti's taillights had disappeared from the parking lot. There were four Jenny Fisks in the old dial-up system, and three Jennifers—half were too old, one was deceased, and one was in prison for drug charges. But there was a Jenny Fisk living in a small town in Vermont, just a few miles from the university Ansel Packer had attended.

As she dialed, Saffy noted the tremble of her own fingers, the jump of excitement ballooning in her throat.

"Hello?"

A woman's voice. Saffy could hear water running in the background.

"Am I speaking with Jenny Fisk?"

"Who is this?"

"Saffron Singh, New York State Police. Do you have a moment to talk? I'd like to ask you a few questions."

"Sorry, what—?"

"I'm looking for a man named Ansel Packer."

A stuttering pause, frozen. In the background, Saffy could hear the murmur of a television, heavy footsteps.

"What—what is this about? I'm sorry, I—I can't talk now."

"Is there a better time?"

"I mean—well, I'll be at the hospital tomorrow. Northeast Regional, around noon."

And Jenny hung up. As the empty station pulsed around her, Saffy remembered how it felt to snort lines of energy straight into her bloodstream. This was something more. This was irresistible.

•

The emergency room lights glowed neon. When Saffy flashed her badge, the girl behind the reception desk fluttered.

"Jenny Fisk?" Eyes wide. "I'll get her. You can have a seat if you want."

Saffy settled into one of the scratchy chairs. She'd gone home the night before, pulled on a pair of pajama pants, and lain atop her neatly made bed until the clock proved it was almost morning. As Saffy drove around Lake Champlain and into Vermont, she'd chugged cold coffee from a Styrofoam cup and tried to talk herself down. It was the same feeling that led her to the Hunter boy, only magnified now, a nagging sense of dread. Fever, or some twisted version of memory. Moretti's orders had been firm: drop everything and focus on the captain's suspect, until he'd been arrested or cleared. Saffy had not answered her pager all morning. Moretti would be furious. But as she sat in the waiting room three hours east of the Plattsburgh police station, Saffy felt crazed, electric.

The ER was hushed, slow on a Friday, the smell of sterile chemicals lingering. The beeper on Saffy's belt buzzed twice, three times. She silenced it without looking.

"Hi."

A woman in pink scrubs stood, hesitant, at the entrance to the surgical wing. Jenny Fisk had freckled arms and long hair parted in the middle, pulled from her face with two butterfly clips. Mid-twenties, Saffy guessed. She recognized Jenny's type on instinct: high school pretty. She would have been popular the way Kristen was, all easy lines and midriff. Her face was a symmetrical, unremarkable lovely.

"Hello." Saffy stretched out a firm hand. "Thank you so much for agreeing to talk. Do you mind stepping outside?"

It happened when Jenny reached for the handshake. The shock of recognition, flooding—a shimmer, winking, from Jenny's thin finger.

The flash of amethyst, unmistakable.

Lila's ring.

It was a specific feeling, a case breaking open. A heady rush, like water surging through a dam, or ripe fruit splitting juicy down the middle.

But as Saffy took Jenny's hand, dizzy, stunned, the sensation was different. There was no ecstatic swell. Only a burst of memory: Lila's chapped lips, how they'd suckled that purple gem. *Gross*, Kristen had whined, as slobber coated Lila's fingers. *Why do you put it in your mouth like that?* Lila had only shrugged, her hair constant in its tangle. *It tastes good*, she'd said, like that was a reason. Lila's smile, gap-toothed and dreamy. Lila's skinny finger, loose beneath the brass.

"What's all this about?"

Jenny leaned against the brick wall outside the ER,

purple ring glinting. Saffy had quit smoking when she quit everything else, but she took the cigarette when Jenny offered it, if only to hide the quiver of her hands. Jenny hadn't brought a jacket, and goose bumps formed on her bare arms, frigid in the autumn chill. Saffy felt a celestial sense of knowing, a cosmic certainty. She wanted to cry.

"I'm looking for someone you used to date. Ansel Packer."

Jenny leaned in with the lighter, tightening alert. She blew a cloud of smoke from the corner of her mouth. "What do you want with him?"

"You know where he is?"

Jenny squinted, assessing. She lifted her hand, a gesture to the ring.

"You're—married?" Saffy stammered.

"Engaged."

A wide, angry lump formed in Saffy's throat. Her own incompetence, like a sudden choke hold; she had not imagined, had not even considered, an outcome like this. Those footsteps, echoing last night through the phone.

"You're still—" Saffy spluttered. "I'm sorry. That ring. Ansel gave it to you?"

Jenny's thumb caressed the gem. "Why does that matter?"

"It matters. We're looking into an old case."

"You don't look like a detective."

Saffy didn't feel like a detective either. An abrupt nakedness overwhelmed her, like Jenny had seen something private.

"What did he do?" Jenny asked. She heaved a long sigh, laced with precarity. "Something bad?"

And there it was. The very thing Saffy had come for. She wished she could bottle up this moment, save it for later, use it as proof. The slant of Jenny's gaze. The shiver of her lip. Jenny was not surprised by this question. It was how she said those words: *something bad.* Jenny had been waiting.

"We're looking into a homicide case," Saffy said gently. "Three girls were murdered, over in New York."

The pause that followed was sharp, penetrating. The automatic doors swished open, then closed again. Jenny mashed her cigarette against the wall, leaving a sooty streak across the brick. She cupped the butt carefully in her palm—not the kind of person to litter on the sidewalk—and shuddered. Saffy realized, too late, that it was over. Jenny had shut down. A curtain of hair fell across her cheek, obstructive, as she turned away.

"Don't go," Saffy said. "I just want to talk—"

"You've got it wrong," Jenny mumbled, as she

backed toward the swishing doors. "Please, just leave us alone."

And then she was gone. An ambulance screamed past as Saffy stood abandoned, her cigarette flaking ash onto the sidewalk.

What was it like? Kristen had asked, once. *You know, with Travis and his friends?*

Saffy couldn't describe those years—though on the surface, she tried. She told Kristen about the underground parties, the makeshift campsites, dens draped in smoky curtains. Their crew had moved from house to house, party to party, indifferent and impulsive. Saffy had felt safe, swaddled in such recklessness: it was easy to self-destruct when you had nothing, really, at stake. When Saffy yearned now, she did not yearn for the drugs themselves or the high they provided, cheap and flimsy—she yearned instead for the freedom. The knowledge that though she walked a tightrope between life and death, it hadn't really mattered which way she fell.

Now, Saffy trudged back to her car, glistening in the parking lot sun. She knew she should return to the precinct; she'd missed half a day of work already. But as her pager buzzed incessantly, she recognized a sliver of that old self, desire ticking like an activated bomb. She threw the pager beneath a sweatshirt in her trunk and pulled the scribbled address from her pocket.

As Saffy sped down the highway, she felt manic. She passed a stretch of boutiques and restaurants, then wound into a suburb—the houses scattered awkwardly, like Monopoly pieces thrown onto a board. Vermont looked like New York, Saffy thought, only with an extra layer of polish. Saffy pulled up to a single-story home with peeling paint and a cluttered porch, braked at the curb.

And there he was.

Ansel.

He crouched at the top of the driveway in the midday light, wearing a pair of plastic goggles. He looked vaguely the same, distended with age but still handsome in a conventional, nondescript way. He was sawing the legs off an old chair, the sound buzzing hostile through the car window. Saffy watched as he handled the chain saw, flecking dust in a cloud around his head. There was Lila's ring, the only evidence she really needed—but there was also this. The way Ansel held himself, like he was above it all.

One, two, three with the fox.

One, two, Lila.

For a thrilling instant, Saffy considered approaching. She could do it. She could walk right up to him, one hand threatening the gun on her hip.

Ansel would squint, remembering.

Saff, he would say. This time, she would have the power. She would be the one to fear. *Please, forgive me?*

Saffy did not approach. She'd only have one chance, and this was too important. She needed Moretti, confidence, experience, that needling expertise. Saffy tore out of the cul-de-sac, toward the border of Vermont and back around the lake. She left the radio off and let the highway cocoon her, savoring the vitality that only this work could give. It was a feeling no person had ever managed to match.

There had been flings, fizzling and temporary. There had been boys behind bleachers and men in dusky bars. One real relationship: Mikey Sullivan, a trooper from Unit C, whom she'd met in Basic School. Saffy still missed Mikey's smell after a shower, all aftershave and steam. As farmland melted into mountain, Saffy remembered their last night together. They'd slipped into bed after a lazy dinner of spaghetti and Corona, Mikey's hand sliding into the waistband of her jeans. He'd wriggled on top of her, same as always, his breath like red sauce, arms like a cage. As he pressed into her, Saffy swelled with a sudden emptiness, a void that needed urgent filling. She had reached for Mikey's hand, pressed his palm to her throat.

Squeeze, she'd ordered.

And for the tiniest instant, he had. As Saffy's vision blurred and the room began to spin, she glimpsed a shadow of the thing she did not realize she'd been chasing. It felt like a breath of oxygen, even as she gasped for air—it felt like a younger, freer self, one who cared significantly less about survival. She had missed that danger. She had missed that liberation.

Mikey had pitched away, panting. The yellow lamp had flicked on, his disgust evident in the bright. As he grabbed his keys and stormed out, his discomfort hurling the shame onto her, Saffy recognized the monster in her own body. A wild creature, reaching out hungry, starving for annihilation.

She glimpsed that same craving in Jenny Fisk—an ask, for suffering. It was the scariest thing about being a woman. It was hardwired, ageless, the part that knew you could have the good without the hurt, but it wouldn't be nearly as exquisite.

•

When Saffy finally reached the station, the sun had set, and she'd missed a full day of work. She straightened her blazer, familiar with this feeling from her days ditching class. A determined uncaring, laced with dread around the edges.

The station was oddly busy, the troopers humming with collective excitement. They hushed when they saw her, shirt wrinkled and untucked, jacket stained with coffee down the front. Saffy headed straight for the captain's office door and pushed it open without knocking.

"Sergeant—"

The scene materialized, zooming slowly into focus: Moretti stumbled in her heels, gripping the mahogany desk for balance. She and the captain had sprung apart at Saffy's entrance, awkward, red, and rattled.

"Where the hell have you been all day?" Moretti began.

"I found him," Saffy said, a stammer, her resolve teetering. She had never seen Moretti like this, bumbling, embarrassed. The pieces of the scene were clicking into place. The shrewd slip of the captain's hand when Saffy first walked in. His knuckles, cupping the curve of Moretti's back pocket.

"Ansel Packer," Saffy stuttered. "I found him. His fiancée was wearing Lila's ring. The trinkets, Sergeant. He took them."

A slow, blinking pause. The captain's voice was low and raspy, his gaze leering as it stripped her down.

"Moretti, get a hold of your subordinate."

"Wait," Saffy said. "I found evidence. Actual evidence—"

"Singh," Moretti interrupted, "if you had attended your own job today, or answered any of my pages, you would know that an arrest has been made. Nicholas Richards will be arraigned in the morning."

The homeless man. The captain's favorite suspect. The flood of the lights was oppressive, the room turned gauzy—Saffy's exhaustion arrived, a single swoop landing heavy on her shoulders. Her own recklessness seemed to seep, wet from her body, chastising, like bloodstained underwear.

"You disobeyed me," Moretti said. "My instructions were clear, and you explicitly ignored them. Kensington got us everything we needed."

"I'm sorry, but I found—"

"This is not about you, Singh. This is not about some childhood grudge. This is police work. It's about truth, about fact, and at the end of the day, it's about this department."

"So that's it, then? That's what you're calling this?" She gestured to Moretti, the captain, both their faces still flushed raw. "The *department*?"

A vicious wind, shifting. Saffy had never before talked back to Moretti.

"Probation," the captain said dismissively, stepping past them both. "Two weeks without pay. Singh, you're dismissed."

When he was gone, Moretti only stared at the tattered carpet. The shock of what she had just seen—what she'd just interrupted—whooshed through Saffy's gut, delayed, like a punch. What had Moretti always told her? *Less than ten percent of law enforcement is made up of women. You cannot succeed without sacrifice.*

Saffy slunk from the office, disgraced. The troopers snickered as she slipped back into the crisp autumn night, certain she had witnessed a truth she was already supposed to know.

The nightmares came. Saffy woke, drenched and trembling, piles of laundry looming from the floor like childhood monsters as she gulped down the stale water on her nightstand.

Sometimes the nightmares featured the fox, hovering sickly around the corners of Saffy's vision, a cloud of rotting flesh. More often, they featured Lila, standing in the door of Saffy's studio apartment. Eleven-year-old Lila with her retainer, or teenage Lila with her nose ring, decomposed Lila with those clumps of hair still attached to her scalp. But on the worst nights, Lila was alive.

She would have been twenty-six years old. A yellow sundress, a green backyard. The Fourth of July. Lila would have glowed, all pollen and sunscreen, a crowd of friends in plastic chairs on the porch—she would have clasped her hands along her middle, that purple ring twinkling on the hump of her bulging stomach. Thirty-two weeks. Nauseous and anticipating, the morning sickness replaced with an ache in her spine. She would have been hungry, her giant belly growling with the smell of hickory meat; she would have been tired and ecstatic and anxious and thrilled. The pale ghost of the moon, the zap of a firefly. Her bare heels, sinking into the soft of the earth.

Near the end of her probation, Saffy went to the tavern alone.

She had not left her apartment in days. Twice, she'd driven out to Ansel Packer's, sat in her car, and watched the house for any sign of movement. She knew it was not healthy. She knew it was not reasonable. But her failure with Moretti had only hardened her resolve.

She chose the man at the end of the bar. He was a traveling salesman, he told her, as he blinked at his own good fortune. Only in town for a few days. *What do you sell?* Saffy asked. *Fishing rods.* Saffy had planned to say she worked as a waitress, but the question never came. *Are you Arab?* he asked instead. He pronounced it like A-Rab.

Back at Saffy's apartment, she did not turn on the lights. She didn't want to see the dirty dishes stacked in the sink or dilute the vodka tonic coursing through her bloodstream. She pushed the salesman onto the couch, flung off his tie, bit the flesh of his neck. She pulled his erection from his pants, stiff and unimpressive in the glow of the streetlamp out the window—she shoved it into her mouth. She gagged as the smell of her couch cushions wafted up and thought about what she deserved. It was an ambitious concept, justice. The idea that your lot in life could be based on your own choices. That you could work for things or ruin them for yourself. For a flashing instant, she considered biting down, but the salt of him tasted like some sort of wanting. Saffy shimmied out of her jeans and pushed him inside. He grunted. She purred. She felt very little. She fucked him harder, until he was gasping and stuttering, his fingers twisting her nipples, until Saffy thought, *Okay.* The warmth of the salesman shot up inside her. Okay. This, at least, was an explosion she had asked for. She knew how to live in the wreck.

•

Kristen married on a Sunday in April.

Saffy stood at the altar with three of Kristen's friends from the salon, wearing a silky purple dress she couldn't really afford. Kristen's spine looked so delicate in her intricate white gown, Saffy wanted to fling herself across the vertebrae, to protect them from the harsh of the world. Over Kristen's shoulder, Jake looked like the heavens had opened up. Saffy had to give the man some credit. He was not one of the bad ones.

She had been reinstated at work. The winter had been long and dark, and things felt different now. Moretti was icy, distant. She still gave Saffy advice under her breath as they approached a scene, still came in with an extra cup of coffee, but there was a layer of coolness that hadn't been there before. Moretti was more untouchable, more unknowable, more inimitable than ever, and most days Saffy tried not to let it break her heart.

The trial for Izzy, Angela, and Lila was coming up soon, and everyone knew they'd lose. The homeless guy they arrested had become the center of a newfound wrongful-conviction campaign, and the committee had pooled the funds for his bail and a fancy lawyer. The captain, so keen on the arrest, hadn't prepared for this. The case was shaky, the evidence even shakier. Saffy knew, with a grim and somewhat smug acceptance, that they'd been wrong, and the jury would see it. Nicholas Richards was innocent, and he would walk free.

Saffy told no one about her drives, though she thought of them now, as Kristen's bridal veil whipped in the wind. The long weekends she spent winding through Vermont, only to park in front of Ansel Packer's house, waiting for something to give him away. She'd watched as he unloaded groceries from the bed of his pickup, as he hunched over the workbench in the garage, as he washed dishes in front of the kitchen window. It was not obsession, and it was not addiction, though the hours she spent trailing Ansel filled some of the cravings of both.

It was only a matter of time. Saffy knew you could not hide your real self forever, no matter how normal you looked; the truth would come out eventually.

"In sickness and in health," Kristen was saying. Goose bumps prickled Saffy's arms as the wind picked up. A storm had gathered in the distance, hovering over the mountains in a looming black cloud, though the sun still shone flaxen over the wedding guests. Saffy begged the rain closer.

This day was about love, but Saffy had always been more interested in power. The black and pulsing heart of it. Power was the clink of her badge against the kitchen counter. It was the heft of the gun at her waist. As she stood at the altar, wind blowing her carefully pinned hair from its bun, as the bride and groom kissed and thunder rumbled in the distance, Saffy wondered about her own internal compass, the needle that kept her on this path, stopped her from wandering or regressing or giving up entirely. It scared her to realize there was no compass. There were only days and the choices she made within them.

6 Hours

Goodbye to every crack in the wall. Goodbye library books, goodbye radio. Goodbye to the toilet's sour stench and filmy rot. Goodbye, you say, to the elephant on the ceiling.

Goodbye, old friend.

•

You reach back for the handcuffs.

They clink, snap.

Shawna stands behind the rest of the group. Her head is bowed to her shoes—you cannot catch her eye. She hunches between two familiar guards, pasty men with jiggling bellies, all of whom have gathered to see you out. One pudgy guard steps forward, slings your red mesh bag over his shoulder. You have left your Theory where Shawna has agreed to retrieve it later, a stack of pages tucked beneath the bed. Shawna will make copies in Huntsville. She will send them to the news stations, the talk shows, the big book publishers.

Do you have everything, Packer? the warden asks, with a sadness that ages him. A jowly, sagging pity. In it, you see the hundreds of other men the warden has walked down this stretch of concrete, the murderers and pedophiles and gang members and drunk drivers, indistinguishable in those fifty traveling feet.

Yes, you say. I'm ready.

As they lead you from your cell into the narrow white hall, you steal one last fleeting glance at Shawna. She cannot come along, but you try to say it with your eyes: We can do this. She is sweaty with nerves, her skin shining. A single tear travels down her cheek, delicate. You know, from years of practice with Jenny, how to shape your expression in a way that reassures her. You know how it's supposed to look. Love. You slip it on, aim it at Shawna. Visibly, she softens.

As you make the fated march down the hall, the men in the surrounding cages are silent. This is the tradition: a blank, unnerving quiet. It is alarming to see their faces, a solemn procession behind the streaky glass. This farewell feels sad, deranged, aimed wrongly at you. You want to reassure them—you have a plan. You are not like the rest of them.

You step forward, through the crash gates. Metal detectors. Reception area.

A gasp.

You are outside.

The things you have forgotten. Clouds. The cotton candy puff of them, lethargic and easy, half asleep. The recreation cage only gets slats of light through the roof, and you have forgotten this texture, this detail. The smell of pavement, baking in the sun. Car exhaust. The trees on the other side of the parking lot stand still in the rancid heat, green leaves barely fluttering in the wind. You have forgotten the sun, tickling the skin on your arms, and you stop for a sweet breath before the warden yanks you forward.

The world is bristling, magic. And soon it will be yours again.

•

The van is waiting by the chain link fence.

You expected a flock of correctional officers, dopey and power-drunk. Instead, you find half a dozen men in business attire—you recognize the senior warden, and the deputy executive director. They are flanked by a mass of sanctioned peace officers, sent by the Office of the Inspector General: a small herd of hulking men in fatigues, armed with assault rifles. You think of the little pistol Shawna has described, her husband's old Smith & Wesson revolver, and something shifts uncomfortable in the pit of your stomach.

You approach the grumbling vehicle, surrounded on all sides. The warden slides the door open, and a lingering second of utter panic engulfs you—the gun will be waiting on the floor beneath the front seat. The anxiety eases slightly as they push you toward the far window of the van, right where Shawna has promised, just behind the driver. The van smells like rubber boots and old vinyl. You knew that these officers would ride along, that the armored cars would follow, a police motorcade, but you did not expect it to feel so menacing.

Gravel crunches. As the van bumbles from the parking lot, you take a long exhale, extend your legs beneath the seat, where Shawna has planted the pistol. Your shoe brushes something hard. Metal. But the reassurance does not come. You picture Shawna's face, the self-conscious blush of her flaky skin, and it occurs to you that the plan is not perfect.

The plan is hardly a plan at all.

Soon, you will reach the river. The highway will take you past scattered homes and dry plots of land, swampy ponds and old manufacturing plants. Eventually, you will pass the Sam Houston Monument. The signal.

Until then, you wait. The driver's window is cracked slightly open. Outside smells like April—the scent filters through the inch-wide slit, a promiscuous hint of floral summer. Teasing, fresh.

It brings you back.

•

The third Girl came right after the second. A test, that bottomless summer.

You went alone to a bar, where you ordered a Coke and scanned the crowd. The disappointment hovered, looming. You suspected you would not find that stunning relief again, but you had to try, just one more time. You did not care what it meant, that peace came only after violence, and then only sometimes. It felt less like a choice and more like a need—you had to chase the quiet.

There was a punk band playing, a shrill screech that distracted everything, sweaty bodies grinding through the heat. When you noticed the top of her bobbing head, retreating through the side door for a cigarette, you followed, asked if you could bum one. The third Girl looked obscurely familiar—she had hair dyed blue, a ring like a bull through the cartilage of her nose. Don't you remember me? she said. Her eyes were inquisitive, a joke and a dare. You nodded. You lunged.

The music played on in the bar, a deafening squall that drowned out her wheezing. You hoped maybe the danger would heighten it, the possibility of capture, the fact that she gasped only feet from the door. But no. This last one was a bad idea; she fought back, kicking you so hard in the eye you saw stars. A scuffle, a shriek. At one point, she had you pinned against the wall. But in the end, you were bigger—it took so long to tighten the belt around her neck, you dragged her to the car still twitching, afraid someone would see. Pure luck: no one did.

As you shoveled the dirt over her limp and useless form, you felt a wide, furious nothing. She was dead, and you were the same, and nothing mattered at all.

In the sour moonlight, you examined the ring you'd plucked from her finger.

You knew this ring. Miss Gemma's. You remembered how those girls had laughed through the door, when you gifted those cookies. It seemed impossible that the same Girl splayed limp before you, that the world had served her back to you like this. The recognition felt like a slap from a parent—standing over all three of those Girls, you wished you could take it back.

You shouldn't have done it. You were sick and wrong. Most devastatingly, you were unchanged.

Your Theory grew then, expanding, a truth proven as the moonlight jumped off purple amethyst. You can do the vilest thing. It's not so hard, to be bad. Evil isn't something you can pinpoint or hold, cradle or banish. Evil hides, sly and invisible, in the corners of everything else.

After, you stumbled through the thicket of trees. You got into your car, hands trembling deranged, the ring in your pocket poking jagged against your thigh. Four in the morning, and furious tears flew down your cheeks as you swerved onto the highway. You drove, resigned, to the hospital.

You have never told this part of the story. You don't know where it came from. Maybe it came from that little girl's smile, laughing in the glow of Miss Gemma's television. Or maybe from the fact that it did not even feel good anymore—and if it did not feel good, then you had no idea why you'd killed them.

You left the car running in front of the emergency

room. The hospital was lit up bright, all whites and blues, daunting and sterile. You walked, stunned, into the searing light. You knew how you must look, shaking and covered in soil, the welt of your black eye already swollen to a soft oozing purple.

Can I help you? a woman called from the reception desk. The waiting room was empty, and it smelled like latex and disinfectant.

Please, you whispered.

Sir?

Please, you said. I don't want to be like this.

The woman stood. She was wearing pastel scrubs patterned with smiling teddy bears. She gaped at you with the confused and vaguely alarmed eyes of everyone you'd ever known, all the social workers and foster parents and concerned teachers. You realized it then. If you could be helped, they would have done it long ago. The singular truth of your life seemed to rise from your chest, unignorable, as you backed out through the ER's sliding doors. You were impossible. Beyond help. You would never be more than your own creature self.

•

The breeze calls you back. A smack to the face, whistling through the window of the transfer van. You surface from the memory to find that you have already passed the lake, that the Sam Houston Monument is rising in the distance, towering over the border of Huntsville. This is Shawna's cue. As the van speeds closer, the statue reveals itself, gigantic in sculpted marble.

The world seems to slow, sinking into the molasses of the moment. The importance builds into an anxious thrill, and your ears start to ring, blood thudding through your body like a drum.

The future expands before you. It will be scary, to run. It will be exciting and dangerous and hungry and hard. You don't have a plan, beyond basic survival. You will hide in drainage pipes. You will scale the roofs of train cars. And even if you never see the Blue House again, the fact of that place will push you forward. A reminder, a testament: You are capable of being better. You are capable of living on.

•

It's time.

The seconds stretch into eternity. The whole of the weeks spent planning and the years spent waiting converge into a span of three crucial seconds. In one graceless motion, you lean as far as your handcuffs will allow—you extend one leg beneath the driver's seat, your foot brushing metal.

You pull, as hard as you can.

What slides out is not a pistol. It is not a gun. It is the metal tip to a pair of broken jumper cables.

•

What if I had done it?

You asked Shawna this question last night, your forehead pressed up against the streaky window.

Done what?

You know. Everything they say I did.

Why? Shawna had asked. Why would you ever do something so awful?

I wouldn't, you told her. But say I did. Just for a second. Would you still love me?

You had been certain. You had been sure you'd pulled Shawna far enough, that she was ready for the possibility—that she'd been feigning delusion until now, that deep down, she knew the truth. The distaste in her eyes felt like a punch. It was a fascinated repulsion, laced with an unfamiliar suspicion. You had been certain of Shawna's fawning laugh, her bashful longing. You had been certain of an easy yes.

I didn't do it, of course, you said, too quickly.

A long pause. You wondered, briefly, if you had blown it. If all the work you'd put into Shawna could implode with this tiny mistake. You tried to backpedal, but her face had already crashed.

It's all in my Theory, you said, grasping. You'll see, when you read it. Good and evil are simply stories that we tell ourselves, narratives we've created to justify being alive. No person is wholly good, and no person is wholly evil. Everyone deserves the chance to keep living, don't you think?

The fluorescents were a blinding white. The pimples around Shawna's mouth made her face look like a bruise.

I have to go, she'd stuttered, stepping away. I'll have an answer for you in the morning.

•

The officers stiffen at the surprise of your lunge, draw their guns in apprehension, growl their warnings. You stare at the jumper cables, all rusted metal and peeling wire.

You know now what has happened.

The options: You could smash your own head against the window. You could stretch your legs, kick your feet against the driver's seat. You could start screaming, demand the things you've planned for; you could reach, cuffed and stunted, for the jumper cables. The truth is overwhelming, a staggering fact. You are one hundred and eighty pounds of flesh, handcuffed to a vinyl seat, surrounded by five armed officers with military training. You have placed your trust in Shawna, a person you severely overestimated—a person who proves the only thing you've ever known about women.

Always, they leave you alone.

Lavender

2002

Lavender spoke to the redwoods, and sometimes they spoke back.

There was a language special for the trees. A whispered understanding. The sound was clearest early in the morning, when the mist curled between rustling leaves and Lavender could still smell the night, lingering smoky in the redwoods' bark.

Though Lavender did not believe in God, she did believe in time. She had been coming here every morning for the past twenty-three years, and the trees had seen her evolution. They had welcomed her as a girl, broken and wandering in dirty jeans—and they soothed her now, forty-six years old and a different person entirely. The scent always brought her back: to the deck behind the farmhouse, all cedar breeze and alpine sigh. Sometimes Lavender caught a whiff of milky breath, puckered baby lips, tiny hands flailing, and in these moments, she pressed her forehead to the mottled bark and prayed.

Lavender crunched through the morning dim. She slipped past the Spruce building, then past Aspen, Magnolia, and Fern. The main house, Sequoia, stood towering on its hill, a single light aglow in the belly of the kitchen, where Sunshine was already kneading the day's bread, rolling the dough beneath her scarred red fingers. She slipped past the laundry lines, flapping like clean white ghosts, past the horses, dreaming in their stables. As she entered the forest, Lavender focused on her breath, measuring like she'd learned in group workshop. The fresh cold moved up through her sinuses, igniting her groggy mind.

When Lavender reached the clearing, she knelt at the base of the tree.

Sequoiadendron giganteum—a redwood, massive and existentially untouchable. When she rested her brow against the splintered wood, a wide generosity overcame her. The tree loved her back; Lavender did not take this for granted.

Today, though, she had questions. Today, she

thought of Johnny and the farmhouse, her baby boys, a scene now decades in the past but still lingering in her bones. As the breeze sighed through the forest leaves, Lavender asked the question she'd tucked so carefully away—to murmur it still felt like whispering a secret.

What have I done?

The tree never answered to desperation. Lavender pressed her mouth to the bark, the sap stinging raw against her lips.

•

By the time Lavender slipped back into the valley, the sun had risen entirely, bathing the hills in a milky orange glow. Gentle Valley split open at her feet, lush and imposing. The vegetable gardens and fruit trees rose from the center field, lines of organized chaos. The women were awake: steam chugged from Sequoia's chimney, and Lavender could hear their distant laughter, echoing over the clink of breakfast dishes.

After the redwoods, Lavender often felt small. Mortal, flimsy. It was always disappointing: the sun would rise, and again, the truth. No matter how far

Lavender traveled, that girl from the farmhouse followed on her heels, a wispy shadow, starving for relief.

But today, she would have an answer: she was going to San Francisco. Today, she would find out what that girl had created.

•

Harmony sat with Lavender while she packed.

"It's okay to feel anxious," Harmony said. She was using the voice she saved for group sessions, a manufactured soft. When Harmony was drunk, she sounded like a completely different person, her voice blazing with the affectations of whatever world she'd left behind. A shrieking snort, a nasal laugh—so unlike this honeyed calm. After many political disputes within the hierarchies of the commune, Harmony had finally been elected workshop leader, and now she seemed desperate to prove herself.

"You're sure you don't mind driving?" Lavender asked, for the third time.

It was fruitless. Harmony was not backing out. The women had voted to set aside the van for Lavender's trip, and Harmony had arranged an overnight with a friend in the Mission. It was a three-hour drive into the city, but in the past two decades, Lavender had only occasionally left Gentle Valley, accompanying Sunshine into Mendocino, where they stopped at the hardware store, the wholesale market, the bank.

Lavender tucked a pouch of balsam into her duffel. Harmony handed over a balled-up pair of socks, her expression transforming into a focused sort of sympathy.

Things had been different, since Lavender told the women. The truth had come out six months ago, in a group therapy session that went long into the night. Her whole story. She'd kept her secrets tucked tight for so many years, she had thought expulsion might feel like relief. But so far, the endeavor had only resulted in a recognizable ache, a pooling unease in the pit of Lavender's gut, a tamping down of something poisonous. It lived inside her now, a writhing virus. When the idea for the trip came up, Lavender regretted telling them at all. She was grateful, of course, that the women were so supportive, that they'd put so much thought and effort into her healing, but gratitude did not make the anxiety any lighter. *We want to help you find your center,* Harmony had said, while everyone nodded from the circle on the floor. *We cannot be whole until we face what has broken us.* Even Juniper had gotten behind it, her weathered face crinkling as she nodded her approval. So Lavender had not protested when they hired the private investigator, sent those emails, RSVPed yes on her behalf. *It's time*, Harmony had said. *Time to face your demons.*

Lavender wanted to tell them what she had learned about demons. Often, they were not demons at all—only the jagged parts of herself she'd hidden from the sun.

•

Lavender found Gentle Valley twenty-three years ago.

She had been on a bus, traveling up the coast. The sign had flashed, a vision from the side of the road—finger-painted words adorned with bright flowers, primitive and friendly. There was something distinctly feminine about the red and yellow cursive, something vital. Lavender stood, asked the bus driver to pull over.

She'd been in San Diego for two long years: 1977 to 1979. There had been motel rooms bathed in faded green light, camps beneath highways and men who smiled with rotting teeth, thumbs outstretched for rides across the desert. A brief stint at a club off the interstate, where Lavender strutted lazily across a raised platform in a gold bikini, swiping singles from truckers who told her she looked like Patty Hearst. On every curve of every freeway, she searched for Julie. Often she spotted Julie at a distance: a woman laughing in the window of a coffee shop, a tangle of long hair whizzing past in a pickup. She never did find her friend, but Lavender pushed forward those years on the road with a surprising sense of infallibility—the world felt bearable, knowing Julie had survived it first.

There were men. Men with tattoos, men with ponytails, men with dead eyes, just back from Vietnam. And to Lavender's surprise, there were women, too. Another dancer at the club, her fingers like honey as they slipped beneath Lavender's skirt. She'd spent a few intoxicating months with that woman, an art student who danced to support her sick mother, loved Led Zeppelin, and kept an apartment full of potted plants. *So what's your deal, exactly?* she had asked one morning in bed, thumb roving Lavender's bare hip. Lavender knew she was waiting for an answer: lesbian, bisexual, maybe neither, maybe both. But she'd only shrugged. Most days she barely felt like a person.

The dancer told Lavender about the communes. *Take a drive up the coast, and you'll find them.* The area was littered with self-sustaining homesteads like Gentle Valley, havens that promised healing and togetherness. It was pure luck that Lavender had not stumbled into one of the communities that had turned quickly feral or cult-like—in the last twenty years, nearly all the others had imploded. Leadership flaws. Male ego. It was dumb, beautiful luck that of all the communes Lavender could have found, she stopped at Gentle Valley: a group of thirty women that had since grown to sixty, established by a pair of psychologists, Juniper and Rose. Their mission statement aligned vaguely with second-wave feminism, a small-scale dismantling of the patriarchy and its many accoutrements, with a focus specifically on behavioral therapy for traumatized women. Rose had since died, but Juniper still ran sessions from the Sequoia building. The women of Gentle Valley lived entirely off the land, supplemented with income from the hammocks they wove from natural materials and sold to health goods and tchotchke stores across the country. Lavender loved Gentle Valley's motto, so inarguably appealing: *Eyes wide, heart open.*

Lavender still missed men, sometimes. The gruff of them. Their unruliness. Occasionally, Juniper allowed a man to stay for a while, a brother or a son or a husband, as long as it was clear the mountain still belonged to women. During these periods, the energy shifted, tensed. Lavender thought sometimes about that question—*so what's your deal, exactly?*—and she loved Gentle Valley for the fact that here, it didn't matter.

On that day twenty-three years ago, Lavender had stepped off the whining bus and onto the gravel road that led into the valley. When she saw the Sequoia building for the first time, glistening statuesque with its solar-paneled roof, Lavender burned with weariness, and awe at the natural perfection of the place. The trees, gigantic and swaying, like soldier guardians. The smell, like fresh grass and wildflowers. In one hand, she clutched the small duffel of her belongings, and in the other, she clutched her stomach. Her body had never gelled back into its own shape—it wrinkled and folded in ways that reminded her constantly of where she'd been. What she'd left behind. Lavender grabbed a fistful of skin from her belly, clutching the flesh, proof of a past life, as she walked into the dust.

•

Now, Lavender buckled herself into the front seat of the van. The women from therapy were lined up at the edge of the valley path—one by one, they approached, whispering lines of poetry through the open window. Rilke from Lemon, Yeats from Brooke, and some Joni Mitchell lyrics from Pony. Faced with the prospect of the outside world, Lavender considered how strange they looked, lined up in their home-made clothing, hair shorn identically to reveal sturdy, stubbled scalps (Juniper encouraged them to embrace the unfeminine). When it was Sunshine's turn, she uncurled Lavender's fingers to place a figurine in the center: the lucky Buddha that sat on Sunshine's nightstand.

The day was bright, crisp, cloudless. A perfect California autumn. As Harmony maneuvered the van down the long dirt road, Lavender examined the translucent jade Buddha. It looked graceless in her palm, hokey and small. She tucked the figurine into the pocket of her shirt, then took a quavering breath as she traced the edges of the manila folder.

She did not need to open it. She'd memorized most of the pages. They were comforting, in the van's distinct claustrophobia—reports Lavender knew by heart, phone numbers she'd copied mindlessly, printed emails she'd labored over in the back office of the Sequoia building. It all culminated now in a nauseous sense of understanding, as Lavender fiddled with the folder in her lap: she had lost control. She didn't want this. She had let the women's kindness obscure everything, and now she was careening into her own nightmare.

Still, there was the name. Once she heard that name, Lavender knew she would never forget it.

Ellis Harrison.

•

What's the worst that could happen? Harmony had asked, as she convinced Lavender to hire the private investigator. *What's the worst thing you could find?*

Lavender liked to imagine that her children were happy. That her boys had found their own ways to exist in the world, that they were soft and satisfied. This was as far as she would go. This was the reason she'd swaddled herself so forcefully in the isolation of Gentle Valley—here, she did not have to look. She did not have to wonder about the long tentacles of a choice she'd made when she was a different person, practically still a child. She did not have to see how the arms of that choice had reached into the world, the infinite number of realities they might have sculpted.

•

The private investigator found Baby Packer first.

It was easy, from the records. He had been adopted

back in 1977, after only a few days in the hospital. A two-month-old baby with a case of malnutrition. When Lavender closed her eyes, she could still remember how he had looked, that last day on the farmhouse floor, his infant limbs squirming spastic.

Cheryl and Denny Harrison had filled out the proper paperwork, still available in the state records. They had given Baby Packer a starchy new name. Ellis. According to the investigator, Ellis Harrison no longer lived in New York City, but he'd grown up there. When Lavender tried to picture that skinny infant as a twenty-four-year-old man, her heart beat so slowly, so exaggeratedly, she wondered if it had liquified.

What about Ansel? Lavender had asked, tentative.

Ansel would be twenty-nine years old now. According to the investigator, he lived in a small town in Vermont—he had studied philosophy in college and now worked at a furniture store. At this, Lavender beamed with pride. College. Of course. He'd been such a smart little boy. Harmony had printed Ansel's address on a folded sheet of paper, which Lavender had purposefully let slip through the dusty crack behind her dresser.

The women had spent the following weeks in therapy discussing Lavender's options. Harmony urged Lavender to write Ansel a letter—wasn't she always writing letters in her head? But even the remote prospect felt impossible. The thought of meeting her children again made Lavender so queasy, they often had to end their sessions early so she could lie down.

Ansel, especially. Ansel would remember.

Eventually, they settled on a compromise. She would start with the furthest point of contact, a level of interaction distant enough that Lavender could gather some information without crushing herself entirely.

Dear Lavender, Cheryl Harrison had written, in response to the letter she and Harmony had crafted. *I'm glad you reached out. I have a photography show opening in San Francisco next month—would you like to meet then? I don't know what you're hoping for, and I'm not sure I can help, but I'm happy to talk. If you want to come to the gallery, my assistant can arrange it. With warmth, Cheryl.*

Now, as the van merged onto the highway, Lavender thought of Johnny. His ghost was a devil, whispering constantly on her shoulder, persistent even after all these years. *Jesus, Lav. What a stupid idea.*

The investigator included it at the very end of the report, an afterthought. Johnny was dead. He had never returned to the farmhouse, had dodged child protective services, started a new half-life in a redneck town just an hour's drive south. Fifteen years ago, he had driven drunk down the interstate and collided with a semi-truck, killing himself as the car exploded on impact.

When Lavender thought of Johnny now, she could only see the flames.

•

The city emerged, restless, before them. Harmony hummed along to the radio as skyscrapers rose from the fog—Lavender gripped Sunshine's Buddha so tightly it indented a print in the center of her palm. She had been so many people in this short life. It seemed remarkable that the girl from the farmhouse had evolved into such a ripened self. Lavender had learned to meditate. She could do a headstand. She could bake enough apple pie to feed sixty people. She had cocooned herself so definitively in the warmth of other women, in the rhythms of Gentle Valley—the therapy sessions and dinnertime poetry and afternoons in the garden—she had almost forgotten the sharpness of the world outside. She'd stopped reading the newspaper last year: 9/11 was too raw, too tragic. As San Francisco uncurled itself in the distance, a glittering menace against the overcast sky, Lavender felt unmoored, like a weightless body hurtling through space. She tried to summon the girl she'd been at twenty-one, traveling alone for months, breasts heavy with milk—that now seemed like a disparate universe. *Sometimes I feel like I'm shedding myself,* she told Sunshine once, the only person who understood. *Sometimes it's like I'm stuck on the floor, searching for the cast of my own skin.*

Sunshine had come to Gentle Valley pregnant, with hands covered in red blistering burns and a mouth that refused to speak. Not a single word. Lavender had been there nearly a year when she arrived, and she recognized something visceral in the way Sunshine jolted at every heavy footstep.

Sunshine's baby was born a few months later. Lavender was wordlessly appointed godmother—Sunshine panted as the nurse held a cool washcloth to her forehead, unspeaking as always when it came time for a name. When Sunshine handed the baby over, Lavender felt a spasm of love, devastating and familiar, so extreme she nearly burst into a wail. Most of the women in Gentle Valley had taken on the names of flowers, trees, colors. But another person came to her, as she examined the infant's red, flaky skin—the reason Lavender stood, alive, this tiny heart beating into her palm.

Minnie, she'd said, recalling the woman from the convenience store all those years ago. Sunshine had nodded her agreement. *Let's name her Minnie.*

As godmother, Lavender made it her job to witness. Minnie grew, from a squealing toddler, to an eight-year-old with blackened knees, to a sullen teenager who refused to cut her hair. Finally, to a young woman, who packed a single bag one morning and walked out of the valley. When Minnie left, Lavender spent days tracing the forest paths with Sunshine, arms crossed against the chill, their boots crinkling dried leaves into the dirt.

So Sunshine understood how time could be a knife. Lodged already, just waiting to twist. As the van slowed onto a crowded city block, Lavender stroked the Buddha in her slick, nervous palm, imagining Sunshine in the back seat. Sunshine would shake her prickly head, a question without judgment, a genuine wondering: *Why didn't you ever go back for them?*

•

"Are you ready?" Harmony asked.

They idled outside the coffee shop where she would be meeting Cheryl. The gallery was across the street—the opening did not begin for another hour, but the block seemed charged already, buzzing with anticipation.

"Not really," Lavender said.

"It will be okay," Harmony said, though her voice was shaky and uncertain. "I'll be at Deena's, a few blocks away. You're strong, Lavender. So incredibly strong."

Lavender had no patience for Harmony's platitudes. She grabbed her backpack, checked her teeth in the rearview, and opened the door. Her hair felt greasy, even buzzed as it was, and a nervous sweat had soaked through her shirt, dried cold. The cardigan she'd brought was not heavy enough for the salty breeze that whistled between the low, bright buildings. Without another word, Lavender slid from the car, her body surging with a shot of adrenaline.

The city was a monster. She stepped into the mouth of it.

•

The coffee shop was young and trendy, with succulents lining every windowsill. When Lavender ordered a green tea, the barista took in her appearance: bald head, beaded earrings, dirt-caked clogs. She fumbled clumsily with the cash, overtipping as she took stock of the place—a few tables were occupied by fashionable young people reading books or chatting quietly. Lavender's throat felt gravelly. Anxious, full of regret. There was only one other woman her age, perched at a table in the corner.

Cheryl Harrison.

When she stood to wave, Lavender saw that Cheryl was tall. Nearly six feet. She had a shock of chestnut hair, bundled elegantly beneath a knotted scarf, and wore delicate hoop earrings with a dress that billowed at the elbows. The dress was made of a flowing satin, silky and deliberate. Liquid brown eyes roved up and down as Lavender slid into the empty seat. Cheryl had ordered a black coffee, and a perfect kiss of lipstick circled the rim of the mug.

"Well," Cheryl said. "You must be Lavender."

Cheryl's back was narrow and straight, perched at the edge of her chair. Like a cat, Lavender thought. Regal, elegant. Cheryl was probably in her early sixties, though there was a texture to her skin that made Lavender feel baggy—when she smiled, her face showed no wrinkles, only laugh lines refined around the eyes. She wore a pair of high-heeled sandals, and her toes were painted red, like clean little cherries.

When Cheryl lifted her coffee cup, Lavender noticed a streak of yellow paint across the belly of her palm.

"Congratulations," Lavender said, awkward. "On the gallery, I mean."

"Oh, thank you. It's rather exciting, isn't it? Denny, my husband, encouraged me to get into photography before he died, and I only wish I'd done it sooner."

The barista delivered Lavender's tea—an empty mug, accompanied by a complicated contraption of a teapot. There was a certain hardness to Cheryl, Lavender thought, but it was not unkindness. Instead, a wisdom. The sort of self-assurance that seemed to shrink Lavender inside her own skin. Just a year ago, this woman had presumably lived through September 11. Yet here she sat, her trauma enviably invisible.

Cheryl squinted, appraising. "Have you ever been painted?"

"Uh," Lavender stumbled. "No."

"Really," Cheryl said. "I mean, your face. There are whole worlds in it."

Lavender had no idea what to do with that, and Cheryl seemed to acquiesce, because she shifted, the satin of her dress pooling in her lap. Lavender could picture Cheryl's apartment, a sudden vision in perfect clarity: high ceilings, gilded windows, art all over the walls. Everything would be vivid and intentional. A modern sofa, a refurbished oak table, trinkets from foreign countries displayed next to first-edition poetry books. The kind of alternate, moneyed life Lavender sometimes imagined for herself—a fantasy in which things had been different from the start.

"So," Cheryl said. "You wanted to talk."

"I wanted to ask," Lavender said. "What his life has been like."

"I'm glad you came to me," Cheryl said. "And not— well, not to Ellis."

"Does he know?"

"He's always known he's adopted, yes. But he doesn't know we're meeting. I didn't want to add anything more to his plate."

A thick ball appeared in Lavender's throat, looming unwelcome.

"Is he happy?" Lavender asked.

"Oh yes," Cheryl said. A sliver of genuine smile. "I've hardly met someone happier."

"He grew up in New York City?" Lavender said.

Cheryl nodded. "He lives upstate now. We used to rent a cabin in the Adirondacks every summer—we thought it would be nice to keep him connected to his roots, and Ellis has always loved the mountains. He's lived up there since high school graduation. He'd been accepted at NYU, but Denny and I could see he wasn't happy. Ellis wanted something else, something beyond what the city could give him, beyond what everyone expected. He met Rachel that June. We learned in August that she was pregnant. Sometimes life has a way of telling you where you belong, don't you think? Anyway, they opened a restaurant. Ellis bakes the most incredible sourdough."

The heaviness built in Lavender's glands, a suffocation. She wished, with a feverish desperation, that she'd never let Harmony talk her into this. It was too big. Too much.

"So there's—a grandchild?"

Cheryl nodded. She leaned in, her scent lingering, expensive and tasteful, like sunflowers.

"I have an idea," Cheryl said. "Why don't we go over to the gallery? The opening isn't for another hour, but everything is already set up. I can give you a private tour."

The offer felt like a sort of generosity. A hand, outstretched. Lavender followed Cheryl from the coffee shop, her tea steaming untouched on the table.

The afternoon had grown dense, the sky a stormy gray. The street bustled and brayed—Lavender felt a distinct relief when they reached the storefront at the end of the block.

The gallery itself was just a small white room. Four

walls, barren and spare. A beggar was curled on the stoop in front of the door, but Cheryl stepped confidently over him and ushered Lavender inside. In the corner of the room, two young women in button-up shirts were organizing bottles of wine, stacking glasses across a crisp tablecloth.

"I've titled it *Homeland*," Cheryl said amiably, gesturing to the far wall, where a series of frames were lined up evenly. "It's meant to show how we are always reinventing ourselves, creating new homes to accompany our various evolutions. The family pictured here is both evolving and permanent. I wanted to explore that paradox."

Lavender stepped close to the photo in the center.

It was unmistakable.

Baby Packer. No longer a baby. Grown now.

Ellis Harrison looked nothing like the child she remembered. Of course, Lavender chastised herself, he had been too young then, just a blob of squishy infant. But the photograph proved it, beyond doubt. It was her son. The portrait was taken in blinding color: Ellis stood against a paneled wall, painted a vibrant shade of blue. He peered sagely into the camera, a smudge of something dark streaking across his cheek. Charcoal, or maybe kitchen grease. His freckles spattered in patterns she recognized—the Big Dipper

stretched across his nose in a constellation that perfectly mirrored Lavender's own. His eyes belonged to
Lavender too, heavy-lidded, with lashes so light they
were nearly transparent. She understood why Cheryl
watched her, hawkish and curious. The boy was so
obviously Lavender's. Johnny had only made the
smallest appearance, in the set of Ellis's jaw.

Lavender did not want to cry, but the intensity of
the day had compounded. It reverberated, an ache in
her jaw.

The next photo featured a little girl, maybe six years
old. She reached one hand up toward Ellis, while the
other stretched to examine something on the sidewalk.
A dandelion.

"Her name is Blue," Cheryl said from behind.

"Blue," Lavender said.

Cheryl rolled her eyes. "Her name is Beatrice, actually, but the locals nicknamed her. She's a precocious
little girl, very empathetic. Last month they found an
injured garden snake in a box under her bed—she'd
been nursing it back to health." Cheryl chuckled.
"That's the restaurant. The Blue House."

The following photographs were set inside the restaurant. Blue perched on the kitchen counter while a
pretty brunette chopped a large bowl of scallions. Ellis
and the woman, his wife, attended to different tasks

at the industrial stove—the camera captured a glint of spatula, a curl of steam, a garbage can overflowing with corn husks. There was a shot of Blue, her lips clasped around a straw as she suckled soda from a plastic cup. Blue, sitting in a booth with French fries up her nose, playing walrus. The last photo in the collection felt, to Lavender, like hyperventilation. Ellis and his wife hunched at a long oak bar, seemingly blind to the camera. Little Blue was tucked between them, her parents' cheeks resting on either side of her head. Looking, Lavender could almost smell the girl's scalp. That child scent, sticky and sweet.

"Please," Cheryl said.

Lavender's heart was an orchestra, crashing delirious.

"Please, Lavender. Promise you won't go to him. Ellis knows himself, his world, his life. He has been perfectly happy without you for a long time now."

Cheryl faced the photographs with her arms crossed, a familiar expression written along her cheeks. Lavender recognized it instinctually. She had felt such a thing herself, many years ago, for the very same child. Protection and love, desperation and sacrifice.

"Okay," Lavender breathed. She turned away from the photos, unable to look any longer. She was crying now, so terribly unraveled. "I should go. Thank you, Cheryl. Thank you for showing me."

"Won't you stay for the opening?"

"I don't think so," Lavender said. She pushed past Cheryl, toward the exit. The sky outside had darkened to a ripe evening purple. "Just one last thing. My other son, Ansel. Does Ellis know about him?"

"No," Cheryl said quietly. "Ellis never knew about the brother. We only saw him once. In the hospital, when we went to pick up Ellis. The social worker took me from the NICU to the pediatric ward. He was in a little room, reading a book in a beanbag chair. He looked okay, through the glass. Healthy. Fine."

"What happened after that?"

"I don't know. They asked, of course. But we couldn't take him, too."

It was startling, the envy. Like a slap. Cheryl seemed so at ease in this tasteful room, wearing her beautiful clothes as her staff bustled around. Cheryl was graceful. Cheryl was assured. Cheryl was confident enough in her understanding of the world to tamper with its colors, to turn darks to lights and brights to empties. She had been kind to Lavender, for no reason at all. In another life, Lavender thought, all this would have been hers—color and solace, a clean sense of conviction. A good mother, satisfied.

"You just left Ansel there?" Lavender asked, surprised by the blame in her own voice.

Cheryl's gaze softened, like she could see straight through Lavender's body and down into the raw.

"Oh, Lavender," Cheryl said. "Ansel was never our child. He was yours."

•

Dark, now.

The gallery spat Lavender unceremoniously back onto the street. She stumbled down the sidewalk on jelly trembling legs, her body shocked into numbness, as the swell of memory rushed up from her rib cage, clouding everything. She walked until the buildings all looked different, until she'd lost Cheryl's photographs in the maze and chaos.

Eventually, she reached the waterfront. Lavender glided to the edge of the sidewalk, where concrete met the sea, grateful for the relative abandonment. If she plugged her ears and looked up, the blank and starless night could almost be home. Lavender staggered forward, the motions of the city beating like capillaries against the stun of the day.

The memories swamped. Filled her mouth to choking. That dusty yellow mattress, huddling her boys. Dried blood beneath her fingernails. She could still smell Ansel's hair, his stiff dirty curls, could still feel the gummy melt of his palms after a day in the yard. She could still see the baby, soft in the fortress of sheets, a trickle of drool forming a bridge from chin to chest.

Her molecules. Her very soul. Safe, beneath the blankets.

Lavender reached into the pocket of her hemp shirt. She had sewn a pocket on the interior of every garment she owned, for exactly this purpose. Inside, she kept the locket. The charm she'd promised to her child then accidentally stolen away. In the dim city light, it looked worn, haunted. She did not know why she carried it still—she could not bear to clasp it around her neck, but she also could not bear to set it down.

Over the years, Lavender had learned many different ways to love. There was the love of a friend, good conversation late at night. The love of a party, whiskey in the moonlight. The love of sex, tinged magenta—for a few years, there had been a woman named Joy. And Lavender had finally learned how to love the stretch of her own limbs, first thing in the morning. But it was clear now, in the devastating narrow of her memory. There was nothing like the love you had for your own child. It was biological. Primal and evolutionary. It was chronic, unbanishable. It had been living inside her all this time. Bone-deep.

Lavender let the night blacken. This journey was

over. A hideous mistake. The past was a thing you could open like a box, gaze down on with starry eyes. But it was too dangerous to step inside.

The bay pooled velvet at her feet. They flashed before her like a film reel—every precious instant Cheryl had captured. Someday, Lavender knew, she would either regret this trip or move further into it, but for now, she could only revel in the strangeness. The brutality. How cruel it felt, to create something then let it go, with only snapshot evidence of how it had grown.

•

When Harmony rolled up in the van, Lavender spoke with a palpable heaviness: *Take me home.* Harmony did not ask questions, didn't even argue to spend the night like they'd planned. As they sat in traffic at the foot of the bridge, the silence of the van's interior felt accusatory. The city beat like a drum out the window, and Lavender had the miserable thought that if she passed her children on the sidewalk, she would not recognize either of them. She wondered about Ansel, now twenty-nine years old—if he was married, if he loved his work, if he had any children. If there was a world in which he needed her, still.

For the first time, Lavender let herself question. What

if she had gone back. What if she had traveled north, instead of three thousand miles west, if she had scooped those boys from the hardwood floor and held them tight, promised never to let them go. Would Blue still exist? Would Lavender? How would the universe look now, if she had saved her children instead of herself?

Dear Ansel.

I hope that you can smell the trees. They talk, did you know? If you ever feel lost, just whisper to the bark.

Dear Ansel.

I hope the world has been good to you. I hope you have been good to it.

Dear Ansel.

My love. My heart. My little boy.

I—

Home. The smell of leaves, trampled into the ground. Damp oak, the smoky char of Sequoia's cooking stove.

When Lavender creaked open the door to her room, her patterned quilt sat folded on the edge of the bed, gentle and welcoming, just how she'd left it.

The next morning, the women recited a poem. Juniper herself had requested printed copies of Lavender's favorite Mary Oliver and placed a sheet on each clean breakfast plate. Harmony was sheepish—when she laid a hand on Lavender's shoulder to excuse her from dish duty, Harmony's fingers trembled like she knew she'd made a mistake. It wasn't Harmony's fault; Lavender could only blame her for the idea. Lavender herself had stepped into that gallery.

After dinner, she and Sunshine took a walk around the valley. They sank into the evening glimmer, the vague insect clatter, the sleepy rustle of birds in their nests. When the campfires had been extinguished, when the lights flickered one by one and Gentle Valley was blanketed in sleep, Sunshine followed Lavender back to her bedroom. They left the lights off, clamored fully clothed beneath Lavender's sheets. Lavender shook with the grief of it all, as Sunshine wrapped herself tenderly around, the shape of her body a reassurance against Lavender's heaving spine. In another life, maybe, Lavender would have turned to face Sunshine, would have let her tongue ask about its own wanting. But this was Lavender's life, and Sunshine was simply a good friend who knew what she needed—a swaddle, a rocking, the sweet lullaby of skin.

When Sunshine fell asleep, Lavender stood in the generous dark. She pulled the chair from the desk beneath her window, settled her aching hips into the frame. In the moonlight, the blank sheet of paper was luminescent. The pen in her hand a glistening dagger.

Dear Ansel, she thought, as she pressed the ink to the sheet. A missive she would write but knew she'd never send, another addition to a universe of what-ifs.

Dear Ansel. Tell me. Show me. Let me see what you've become.

4 Hours

B end, the officer says. Pants off.
   The new prison smells different. Like the paste
that holds old bricks together, like wet concrete and
steam, which rises from the building next door—the
factory, where the low-security prisoners make lumpy
mattresses for college dorms.

Pants off, the officer repeats.

The sheet of notebook paper is still folded against
your hip, a sharp edge pressed into elastic. Blue's letter.
As you fiddle with your waistband, you try to tuck the
paper into your palm, but a corner of white flutters inevitably into sight. The officers move fast: in a matter
of seconds, your cheek is pressed to the dusty floor,
wind pummeled from your chest, pants tangled around

your feet. The officers cackle as they unfold the note, taunting.

What do we have here?

Dear Ansel, one of them begins to read aloud in a high, false woman's voice. My answer is yes. I'll be there, to witness. I don't want to—

You struggle to stand, pain flooding your ribs as you wriggle obediently out of your underwear. Your penis curls into its nest of hair, small and soft and unprotected. One officer checks your rectum while the other hovers, mocking. He reads Blue's words in a nasally mimic:

I don't want to see you, and I don't want to talk—

Stop. Please.

The officer gestures like maybe he'll give the paper back—squatting naked, you reach. The officer grins, holding the page by one delicate corner. Slowly, he rips it in half. He rips again, then again, until the long white strips break down into confetti. Something internal shreds along with the words, but you stay crouched until your knees quake. Blue's handwriting drifts to the floor. Graceful, like falling snow.

•

The officers pull you violently down the hall.

Please, no—

You did not expect to beg. They only tug harder, a warning. Don't fight. Your legs are sludgy now with a panicked hesitation, but they prod you forward anyway, ignoring the weak dig of your heels.

Right now, you should be reaching the river. You should be listening to the grumble of water, flowing over smooth rocks. You should be putting one foot into the stream—a shiver, then the other. You imagine how the cold would feel on your ankles, the icy water slapping you gloriously awake.

The shock spreads. It thrums, then collapses, rolling in waves of bewilderment. Until this instant, you did not realize how wholly you had believed it. You had believed that you would escape, or at least that you would die trying. You had believed this for so long—so fully—that the truth now seems ridiculous. Impossible.

There is no sky. There is no grass. There is no getting out.

•

You are a fingerprint.

A thumb, pressed firm to an electronic pad. No question: it is you, wiping dust from your eyes with the back of your hand, it is you, tugged forward by the link of your handcuffs, it is you, wearing new white scrubs that smell inexplicably like meat. It is you, stepping across the threshold. It is you, now, in this place they call the Death House.

The holding cell is small. Back on 12 Building, descriptions of this famed place always varied in shape and size, depending on who came back to tell the story. When you reach the door, you clock the difference immediately: your old cell at Polunsky had a window built into steel. The Walls Unit keeps open bars.

It would be so easy with Shawna, to touch through these bars. But Shawna does not work at the Death House. Shawna is back at Polunsky, walking Jackson down the hall for his shower, her fleshy arms jiggling as she shuffles through the gray. You picture her face, guilty and stupefied, as you walked out of 12 Building for the last time—how Shawna stood, watching useless, knowing she had lied.

There was no gun. There was never any gun.

All those chunks of wasted time. The stolen moments, sappy love notes, grazing touch, all for nothing. Shawna is nothing, with her rolling hips and the sores across her mouth, a stutter forming on her chapped and cracking lips. Shawna is weak. So very woman. Her future will be empty without you—Shawna will complete her morning rounds, she will drink watery coffee from her old stained thermos, she will serve hundreds of meals to other bad men, and eventually she will forget these weeks, in which she was nearly significant, a part of something important. Almost, you feel sorry for her.

But then you see the room.

It is only a glimpse, taken in the tiny second before they shove you into the holding cell. Fifteen feet away, down the hall to the right, the door is propped open. You catch just a sliver of that halfway place, a fleeting flash, the stuff of lore. The execution room. In that millisecond glance, you see the walls, a noxious shade of mint green. You see the window, a curtain shrouding. The two rear wheels of a gurney.

You stumble into the cell, wishing you had not looked. That room is like heaven, or hell, or the moment of death itself: a place you should not see until your name is called.

•

Three hours, fifty-four minutes.

The world goes sideways, all wrong with the change. You sit on the edge of the new cot, hands firm on the mattress, trying to figure how you have arrived here.

You have had months—years—to consider this outcome. In all that time, you never imagined you might actually see the Death House. The future always managed to twist itself, expanding into pliant and inscrutable shapes. The future was a mystery, unknowable. You honestly never considered that the future might come to this. It feels too small, too helpless, for a person like you.

You remember that man back at Polunsky—the inmate who famously gouged his own eye out and ate it. You recognize some obscure corner of that feeling, a desire that makes some raw sense to you now. The desperation is intentional, maybe the most important part of this exercise. It is why they made you wait for years, then months, now hours and minutes, the whole of your life transformed into a countdown. The point is this. The waiting, the knowing, the not wanting to die.

•

How do you work this job?

You asked the question one noontime shift—Shawna looked tired, purple bags sinking beneath her eyes. Big Bear had been taken to the Walls Unit that morning. He'd sobbed as they marched him out to the van, heaving, wracking, two hundred and fifty pounds of utter devastation. Big Bear, a Black man with a singing voice like God. Big Bear, the only person you are absolutely certain did not deserve the Death House. Twenty years ago, Big Bear had been watching TV in his living room when a team of police officers burst in with a no-knock warrant, meant for the man in the apartment one floor above. Big Bear kept a gun beneath the couch cushions. The room was dark.

That day, the row went silent in mourning. The only sound was your whispering rage as Shawna grasped vaguely for comfort, twirling her hair anxiously between her fingers.

How do you wake up every morning? you had asked, unable to keep the anger from your voice. How do you get out of bed, knowing you work in a system like this?

My dad had this job, she said with a shrug. My brother, too.

But don't you ever think about what you're participating in?

Not really, Shawna had said, disinterested.

You wanted to tell Shawna that she was a cog in a deplorable machine, that prisons are also companies, maximizing profit, staying afloat on a pile of bodies like Big Bear's. You have been watching the news. You have been reading the paper. It is not your problem, not your concern, but still no coincidence that you are one of only three white men on A-Pod. You wouldn't care much about all that, if you were not subject to the same psychotic system.

You wanted to push Shawna, but it wasn't worth the risk. You needed her too badly. She wiped a sheen of sweat from her forehead with the back of her hand—you both listened to the sound of the row, muted for once, a group of men grieving over something more despicable than themselves.

•

The new warden appears. He has a crew cut and a boxy jaw—his gaze makes you feel like an earthworm, crushed soggy along the bottom of his shoe.

Do you understand today's procedure?

Yes.

Here is your Execution Summary, your Religious Orientation Statement, a copy of your Offender's Travel Card, your Current Visitation List, your Execution Watch Notification, your Execution Watch Log, your Offender Property Inventory, your medical records. Do you have any questions?

No.

He slides the paperwork beneath the steel bars. You cannot speak, those first rigid questions echoing.

Do you know who you are?

Yes.

Do you know why you are here?

You had no choice.

The answer was yes.

•

Into a new visitation room.

Tina wears the same outfit as this morning, which feels like a thousand years ago. Sitting behind the glass, you recall the smug surety of your last meeting—the fact jumps angry in your throat. Impossible.

Hello, Ansel, Tina says through the phone. I'm afraid I don't have the best news.

You know what is coming. You clench your jaw until it aches—you have given very little thought to the appeal. It was supposed to be irrelevant.

The appeal, Tina says. The court decided not to consider it.

What do you mean? you ask. They can't just ignore it entirely.

Yes, Tina says, they can. It's not uncommon.

But didn't you tell them? Didn't you tell them I'm—

You cannot say the word. Innocent. Tina knows better.

Didn't you tell them I don't want to die?

As soon as the phrase leaves your mouth, you regret it. It sounds childish, too hopeless.

We filed, Tina says, not answering the question. I'm sorry. We did everything we could.

You hate her for this lie. This glossy woman, who clicks her nails against the table like little hard candies, flicking her tongue between white Chiclet teeth. It occurs to you then, a burst of clarity: Tina believes you deserve this punishment.

I'm sorry, Tina says. I'm—

You don't let her finish. You consider the weight of the telephone in your hand, then rear your arm back. You hurl the phone against the glass, which does not shatter, only bounces the phone off with a loud, unsatisfying crack. Tina does not move, does not even flinch.

The guards come running, like you knew they would. You don't fight, but they handle you hard anyway, twisting your arms so far back that your shoulders will be sore tomorrow. Tomorrow. The last you see of Tina is the top of her head, bowed in reverence or disdain or indifference or sorrow, you cannot tell which.

•

A violent push, back into your cell. The door slams shut. You lie flat on the lumpy cot, arm flung over your eyes. You try to think of Blue—usually, she brings you comfort. But it's this room. It's this cell, new and alien. When you conjure Blue now, she is looking at you with that familiar question.

What happened with Jenny? Blue had asked.

It was your second week at the Blue House. A sunny day, humid and fragrant. You had spent all morning in the yard sawing lumber, and a trail of sweat trickled slow down your back.

Sometimes things just don't work out, you said.

Why not? Blue asked.

She held a can of Coke with the tab flicked off, her head tilted hopeful and curious.

Marriage isn't easy, you said simply.

Do you still love her? Blue asked.

You wiped your forehead with your shirtsleeve, considering. As Blue waited for an answer, innocent and quizzical, there came a swelling fondness. For Blue, and for this place. For the breeze that soothed your salty skin.

Of course I still love her, you said. But the good parts of the story are nowhere near the end.

You decided, then, to go back to the beginning.

•

You first saw Jenny on a warm evening in October.

Freshman year of college, first semester. You were seventeen years old, standing on the quad, unsure as always what to do with your body. You'd arrived at Northern Vermont University on a full scholarship— the principal at your high school had cried with the news. The kids at school had never liked you much, but you had always been good with teachers, counselors, social workers. You knew how to let them feel useful.

It was the same with your professors; you were quiet, hardworking, charming when you needed to be. You buried yourself in lectures and late study sessions, ignored your beefy roommate when he came home puking drunk. You avoided the squawking girls on your dorm hall and the other work-study students at the cafeteria. You bought a pair of glasses at the drug- store, lenses blurry with a prescription you did not need. You examined yourself in the bathroom mirror. You tried to conjure someone new.

The rest of that awful summer had passed in a haze. The baby screamed constantly, background noise, as you scooped cones and listened to the radio next to the cash register. No leads on the missing Girls. You carried those Girls with you at first: they lived and died in your memory as you waited in line at the dining hall, as you raised your hand in philosophy class. They lived and died in the shadows of the trees, as you walked from the library to your dorm in the middle of the night. You wondered if people could see those Girls on you, if you wore them visibly or just internally, like any other secret.

Everything changed, when you saw her.

Jenny sat in the grass on the quad, the late-autumn light glowing everything orange. She wore a pair of nylon pants and tall white socks—her friends cheered as she did a confident backbend, hands planted in the grass. You watched from across the yawning lawn as Jenny's belly button arched toward the sky, the curve of her like a monument to something holy.

Right then, you made the promise. You would be normal. You would be good. You took the memories of that summer, and you balled them up, shoving them deep into the crevasse of your unruly body. The sight of her arching back would dissolve those Girls, somehow erase them. You would offer yourself up to her sly, teasing grin, her soft fawn eyes—you would hand her the microscope.

You picked up your notebook, took the first step toward her. That was the great power of Jenny: not love at first sight, but some kind of un-haunting.

This would be it. Your last and only Girl.

Hazel

2011

The night before everything changed, Hazel woke to a squeezing in her chest.

The pain was searing, clenched like an angry fist beneath her ribs. She sat up, shrieking a gasp—it was a September midnight, the sort of humid that still felt like summer, and Hazel panted into the empty vacuum of the bedroom, clutching at her chest, the flame already fading.

"Hazel?"

Luis blinked up from the pillow. The room was lit only by the baby monitor crackling from her nightstand, and Luis's breath was stale, like sour toothpaste and the garlic chicken she'd cooked for dinner. From the street, Hazel heard nothing—their cul-de-sac was still. She'd become used to the epic hush, but nights like this, the quiet inhabited a personality of its own. Nights like this, it mocked her.

"It's nothing," Hazel said, massaging her sternum. "Go back to sleep."

The feeling had already gone. It did not leave a trace—not even a lingering spasm. It was a pain that could have been imagined, the tail of a dream flicking briefly as it whipped out of sight.

•

Hazel didn't hear her phone, buzzing from the kitchen counter.

Alma had just come home from the bus stop, and she was singing softly to herself as she untied her shoes, the tune drowned out by the tantrum Mattie was throwing from his high chair. Hazel crouched on the floor, wiping a splat of applesauce with a paper towel.

"Mattie, honey," she begged. "Please just eat your snack."

But Mattie only shrieked, scattering a handful of saliva-damp Cheerios onto the floor, pudgy fists banging against the plastic tray. Alma plucked a wet Cheerio from the hardwood and popped it into her mouth, grinning as she sang the tune intended to help her adapt to the first grade. The song was so catchy, Hazel had caught Luis humming it that morning as he swiped shaving cream across his jaw. *We love to learn, we love to play, that's how we do it at Parkwood Day!*

"Mama," Alma whined. "Your phone is ringing."

Hazel strained against Mattie's hollering, listening for the vibration. When she finally found her phone, facedown next to the stove in a puddle of water, it was still buzzing. JENNY, it blinked.

"Hey." Hazel clamped the phone between her ear and her shoulder as she lifted Mattie by the armpits out of his high chair. Content on the floor, Mattie picked up Alma's discarded shoe and lifted the dirty sole to his slobbering mouth.

"The job," Jenny was saying.

"What? I can't hear—"

"I got the job," Jenny said. "I did it, Hazel. I left him. But it was bad, really bad. I didn't have time to do any of the things we talked about. Ansel read my email, he woke me up late last night. I left, I checked into the hotel, but I don't have any of my things. Can you come?"

Jenny was crying, choked through the speaker, a siren wailing vaguely in the background. Hazel looked down at Alma, always far too perceptive for her age, an expression of concern painted across her little fox face. Hazel wrapped her fingers in Alma's silky hair and gazed out at the flat expanse of the neighborhood.

It was placid as ever, the sky a blank autumn blue. The calm seemed unfair, nearly taunting.

She remembered only after she made the plan, hung up the phone. Late last night. The squeeze in her chest, that phantom fist. At thirty-nine years old, Hazel had experienced her first Summoning.

•

No one could tell Hazel, now, that she had nothing.

She had Barbie dolls and board books. Baby formula, playdates, macaroni art. She had rice pudding smeared into the carpet and sticky hands early in the morning. A tantrum in the shampoo aisle at Target, a tantrum at the Italian restaurant downtown, a tantrum at her parents' anniversary party. In the rare moment she found time to reflect, Hazel tried to revel in the chaos and motion, the fierce existence of the world she had so deliberately created.

So when Jenny called with the news, Hazel hunched over the kitchen table, shaking with the calibration. A younger self came flooding in, an annihilating rush: she was eighteen years old again, and Jenny was the whitest sun, the sharpest sound. The refrain from those withering teenage years echoed suddenly back. *Be happy for her.* In the cave of Hazel's head, the phrase took on an old wounded tone, the words limp and defeated.

Alma reached out, her face like a worried little psychiatrist—she stroked Hazel's hair, tender, her palm covered in half-peeled Winnie the Pooh stickers.

•

The change had happened slowly, almost imperceptibly. Hazel could trace the start of it back to Jenny's wedding day.

Their parents had rented a tent on a golf course, with a partially obscured view of Lake Champlain. There were only thirty guests, mostly aunts, cousins, and Jenny's high school friends. Hazel had only been dating Luis a few months by then, and it was the sort of new and giggling love that could be fractured by the politics of an event like this. She had not invited him. Standing behind Jenny as she pinned up loose tendrils of hair, Hazel ached for Luis's presence— Luis was the kind of man who could not handle sad movies, or scary ones either. He cooked his mother's tamale recipe on Sunday nights, kneading the dough with his knuckles.

Luis was the only person Hazel had told about Jenny's secret.

Ansel hadn't graduated from college. He didn't show up for any of his finals, that last semester—Jenny mentioned a fellowship he didn't get, a professor who had written a bad recommendation. *He's too smart for them,* she told Hazel, Ansel's voice layered beneath the words. Jenny lied at the graduation ceremony, told their parents the philosophy program did something separate, while Ansel sulked in his dorm room. Ansel had worked at a furniture store ever since, where he polished handmade chairs and artisan tables and delivered them to wealthy families across Lake Champlain and the Adirondacks. He was writing a book, Jenny said proudly. That part was true. Hazel had seen the pages, stacked on a makeshift desk in the garage when she'd gone to visit. She found it difficult to picture him sitting there, committing his thoughts to paper—it seemed more like a show than a genuine endeavor, a way for Ansel to remind himself of his own middling intellectualism. And there were other things she'd noticed, in that small rental house. The recycling bin, filled with empty wine bottles, a cheap chardonnay Ansel would never touch.

In the bridal tent before the wedding, Hazel tried to talk to Jenny. But she had waited too long. Jenny's breath was sour with champagne, her eyes glassy as Hazel handed over a tube of lipstick.

Hey, Hazel had said. *Are you sure this is what you want?*

Don't be stupid, Jenny had answered. She cupped a condescending hand to Hazel's cheek, that purple ring glinting from her finger. *I know what I'm doing.*

At the reception, Ansel was perfectly charming. He complimented her aunt's jewelry, joked with her dad as they cut the cake. But Hazel caught him so many times that night, looking dead-eyed over Jenny's shoulder. His smile melted instantaneously off his face the second he did not need it—he held Jenny with a rigid back and a shallow happiness, impermanent as wet paint. After the ceremony, Hazel escaped to the bathroom, where she stared herself down in the mirror. She remembered that night on her twin bed, the question she had posed to Jenny. *If he doesn't feel anything at all, then how do you know he loves you?* In her ugly silk bridesmaid dress, Hazel pressed a finger to the mole beneath her eye. With a jolt of surprise, she felt thankful for it. One day, she would wear a white dress, too. She would stand across from a very different man, a good man who felt everything in vivid color—and she would know exactly how he loved her. For the first time, Hazel felt bigger than her sister. The feeling was so sick, so addictive, she knew she could never let it go.

•

Hazel parked behind the studio, in the spot reserved by the dumpsters. Luis had come home early to take the kids—he'd been working the Arts and Entertainment desk the last few weeks, and the news was slower, his schedule easier. Hazel had left a box of mac and cheese on the counter, which Luis would let them eat with ketchup squirted over it.

Through the sheer studio curtains, the Level 4s marked a jump sequence across the floor, a wave of forest green leotards. Hazel kept her head down as she pushed through the horde of parents in the lobby, chattering and sewing ribbons as they waited. At the reception desk, Sara bent over a pile of paperwork. When the students didn't pass their quarterly assessments, when the costume fees came in and the cast lists were posted, Sara took the shiny-haired complaints, the weightless threats. *I swear we will pull her from this studio*, a glossy mother would say, and Sara would serve her easy, blameless smile. As if to say: *Go right ahead.*

"I need a favor," Hazel said. "It's an emergency."

"Your sister?" Sara squinted up. "Did she finally leave the psychopath?"

A wince, at the word. It felt suddenly like something

private. Jenny's darkest heart, not a thing to be gossiped about.

"She got the nursing job in Texas. She has a flight on Wednesday," Hazel said. "Can you hold down the fort until then? Log your overtime, of course."

Always, the studio was busy. But at a certain point—once classes were scheduled, tuition bills paid, directors hired for the seasonal showcases—the studio moved like choreography. Hazel's anxiety was something more. She'd miss her Tuesday night. Tuesdays, Luis did baths and bedtime. Tuesdays, Hazel sent Sara home early and locked the front door. Alone, she queued up her favorite Bach CD, reveling in the high studio ceilings as she led herself through a barre warm-up. She let her body say the rest. She stretched, she leapt. She hurled herself against the floor. For that hour every Tuesday, Hazel did not have children, or medical bills, or debt from the business degree she probably didn't need, no tummy-aches or broccoli on the floor or screaming for dessert. She only had her joints, rapt and unbetraying. Her muscles, exalted.

When Hazel first purchased the studio, using a loan from her parents and the majority of Luis's inheritance, the building was decrepit. She and Luis had done most of the work themselves—hung the drywall, covered the concrete with soft marley, bulldozed and paved a parking lot. Hazel was not yet pregnant with Alma, and she spent her evenings with Luis on the unfinished floor, drinking beer with their tools scattered around.

Rarely, during this time, did Hazel think of Jenny. She remembered that period tenderly—a stretch of months during which she did not feel Jenny and Jenny did not feel her, when they spoke intermittently on the phone, grazing only the surface details.

They were the best months of Hazel's life.

When can we see it? Hazel's mother had pestered. *Soon,* Hazel had promised. *Just wait until it's ready.* When her parents finally came over in the minivan they'd driven since Hazel was in high school, she paced the wide, empty space, satisfied. Her parents stood at the entrance to the gleaming studio, looking small and frumpy in the spacious wall of mirrors. They examined the mahogany reception desk and the hanging light fixtures, the shiny stereo and the ample dressing room. Her mother's face was awed, ecstatic. Unraveled proud. It was exactly the way she used to look at Jenny.

•

Hazel left in the pink blush of sunset. She cracked the car window open, let the autumn air rush in as she pulled onto the highway.

I don't know what to do at night, Jenny had said over the phone just last week. *I've been drinking so much tea.* She'd said it spitefully, like the cups of chamomile were to blame for the nervous tremble, her racing thoughts. *What does Tricia think?* Hazel had asked. Jenny's sponsor had been sober nearly twenty years. Hazel had never met Tricia, but Tricia met Jenny every morning at the café across the street from the hospital. It was Tricia who urged Jenny to call Hazel in the first place, to start these nightly confessions. Tricia, whose voice Hazel heard in the background as Jenny cried into the speaker. *I always wanted kids,* Jenny said during one long sniffling call. *But I never thought I could go nine months without it.* Ansel claimed ambivalence about fatherhood, though he seemed distinctly put off by the rowdiness of Hazel's children—she could never picture him as a father, and Jenny had always shrugged off the question. Only now did Hazel understand the extent of her sister's disentangling.

Hazel did not have advice. She couldn't tell Jenny about the fairy tales whispered in the glow of Alma's night-light or how it felt to stand over Mattie's crib at naptime, his lashes fluttering delicate. Jenny adored Alma and Mattie, but Hazel knew the longing she saw in Jenny's eyes. It was envy. She was mortified by how good it felt, to hand that feeling finally over to her sister.

She passed wide fields, outlet malls. The evening dimmed to a lilting, satin blue.

•

Jenny stood over the pastries. The café was closing, the chairs already stacked on their heads as a barista skirted the corners with a mop. The light from the pastry case glowed Jenny's scrubs gold—her face was bloated and puffy, ponytail mussed from a busy shift. Aside from their hair, which had always been a similarly wavy chestnut length, Hazel realized: she and Jenny looked nothing alike. Jenny had gained weight the past few years, and Hazel felt guilty for noticing. Her sister was wide around the middle, veering viscerally toward middle age. For the first time in her life, Hazel looked at Jenny and did not see herself at all. A stranger would never stop to ask: *Are you twins?* The fact struck Hazel with an acidic devastation, her mouth already unbearably sour from the highway.

Jenny turned.

"You're here."

Hazel gathered her sister up, held her shoulders close. It was still there, beneath the scent of croissants and coffee grounds. That Jenny smell: fruity hair, cigarettes, generic laundry detergent.

"Maybe we should come back later," Jenny said from the passenger's seat.

Hazel's car idled on the curb—the squat, single-story rental looked definitively menacing. It was Jenny's last day at the hospital, and Ansel was supposed to be at work. But when they pulled up on Jenny's lunch break, Rihanna crooning from the car radio, Hazel's gut dropped: Ansel's white pickup truck was parked around the side. Looming, waiting.

"We have our list," Hazel said, unconvincing.

They'd been talking it over for months. They'd made the plan carefully: load the car while Ansel was at work, drop everything at the hotel, come back to tell him right before the flight. The plan had not included a midnight screaming match or Jenny's email pulled up on the computer in the corner of the living room, now cracked across the dusty screen.

"Come on," Hazel said. "We'll be quick."

Hazel stepped from the car, hands clammy. She tried to tamp down the terror, to stand a little taller as Jenny followed her to the door. The scent of Jenny's house hit her right away, remembered instinctually from visits years ago. Unwashed sheets, garbage sitting too long in the bag. Musty carpet, thrift-store furniture.

"Hello?" Hazel called.

Ansel sat on the flaking leather couch. He had his cell phone in his hand, like he'd been waiting for a call, or maybe just for this. Hazel had not seen him in nearly two years, and she was surprised by what time had done to him. Ansel had always been handsome, a prize Jenny could drag to work functions, flushing while the other nurses whispered jealous. But he was getting older. Gravity had begun its work. Ansel's stomach folded over his jeans in the faint shape of a beer belly, and his skin looked sallow, tinged a sunless yellow. His glasses were smudged with greasy finger-prints, and his face had rounded out, sagging beneath the chin. For the first time, Hazel could picture exactly how he'd look as an old man. Gruff, gnarled. Devoid of any surface-level charm.

A sneer curled across his stubbled mouth—Hazel stepped back instinctively, surprised by her own cur-rent of fear.

"Oh," Ansel said, his face rearranging itself instan-taneously back into a veneer of calm. It seemed he had mistaken her shadow for Jenny's. "Hazel. I didn't expect you."

He stood. For a terrifying second, Hazel thought he might lean in for a hug. She tensed, bracing, the fear mixed with something else now: a dripping, metallic guilt. In that single glance, she saw a sliver of the complexity Jenny had been living. The sharp corners, the chilling subtleties. Hazel knew only the outline of her sister's reality, and it was shocking to stand now in the depths of it.

Ansel brushed past her to find Jenny, who lingered paralyzed on the front porch, the door hanging open like a jaw.

"You fucking serious?" he called.

"We're just here to get her things," Hazel said. "Jenny, show me where the suitcase is?"

While Hazel fished the suitcase from the closet, Ansel hovered—he looked almost amused, hands shoved casually into his paint-spattered pockets. They tore down the list hastily, throwing everything sloppily into the bag: Jenny's bras, her shirts, her shoes. A box of high school mementos, a tin of earrings that had once belonged to their grandmother. Jenny would leave her cast-iron pots and pans, she would leave the sheets she'd picked out years ago to match the shag carpet, she would leave her hair products in the bathroom cabinet. Hazel dumped a wad of dresses into the suitcase, still on their hangers, as she listened to Ansel's breath. A whistle, loitering too close.

"You're proving it, Jenny," he kept saying, a repetition that grew louder. "You're proving me right."

The bedroom was alive with electricity, intimate and ugly. Jenny dumped an armful of T-shirts into the bag, shaking with a restrained sob.

"It's just like my Theory," Ansel said. Hazel pried the suitcase from Jenny's tight white grip and lugged it back across the hall, beckoning her forward. "Like Sartre said. The very nature of love's suffering makes the concept impossible. No one thing can be wholly good, can it?"

"I'm sorry," Jenny croaked, a half whisper.

"It's ironic, isn't it?" he said, almost laughing. "Love cannot exist as something pure—the spectrum will always infiltrate. The badness will always sneak in."

"Come on," Hazel urged, so close to the car now. She tried to tune out Ansel's rambling, so faux-philosophical it sounded psychotic.

"I'm sorry," Jenny said from the stoop, snot running shiny from her nose as she stumbled down the front steps. "I'm sorry."

Finally, they were outside, and Ansel was just a following mass. Toxic shadow. Hazel's steps were heavy, panicked, and when she was certain she heard Jenny behind her, she broke into an involuntary run.

Ansel stood on the porch, so tense he looked like he might burst. Hazel hefted the suitcase down the sidewalk—when they finally slammed the car doors shut, Jenny burst into a frantic sob.

"Don't look," Hazel said. "Just don't look." While Jenny buried her face in her hands, Hazel took one last hesitant glance: framed in the door, utterly still, Ansel stood straight and tall, his face twisted into the purest expression of rage Hazel had ever seen. He was a wolf, gnashing teeth. Inhuman. She pulled away from the curb in stuttered spurts, her legs shaking so hard the car jerked, her gaze transfixed on the rearview mirror. Hazel knew she would forever think of him like this, a menacing form in reflection, the shape of a furious man on a porch, getting smaller and smaller until he was nothing at all. A pinprick, a thing of the past. As Hazel's hands trembled on the steering wheel, she had the naive, comforting thought: she would never have to see Ansel Packer again.

•

The hotel room was faceless, with matching twin beds made up neat. It reminded Hazel of the vacations they used to take as kids, to vague affordable cities like Cleveland and Pittsburgh—she and Jenny would share one bed, their parents would share the other, and during the day they'd drag their feet through museums. Hazel and Jenny would play Go Fish on the floor of the lobby while their parents took photos of art they didn't understand.

Hazel was thankful now for the anonymity of the pleated lampshades, the bars of soap wrapped in plastic. Jenny came out of the bathroom wearing sweatpants and a thin cotton shirt, a towel wrapped around her head. Outside, the sun had set—car doors slammed in the parking lot, suitcases rolled over gravel. A child shrieked, the sound setting off a pang in Hazel's core. She wished to conjure the smell of Alma's hair. Mattie's milky breath.

"Room service?" Hazel suggested, tossing Jenny a menu.

"Ansel never did that." Jenny snorted, flipping through the laminated booklet. "Too expensive. When we traveled we'd always go to McDonald's. Ooh, look, they have Alfredo."

They ordered extravagantly. Linguine Alfredo, Caesar salads, mashed potatoes, and a chocolate lava cake for dessert. The air was wobbly as they waited— shell-shocked, like they'd just survived an earthquake. Jenny sat on the bed, confirming her flight on Hazel's laptop, emailing her new landlord, booking the rental car for when she landed. The divorce papers would wait, sent later in an envelope stamped with a lawyer's name. The plan had formed years ago, Jenny admitted—a clean break—but it had taken the new job to escalate the process. It didn't feel real, she said, now that the time had come.

When the food arrived, they set up on the floor between the two beds, cross-legged around the plates. The mashed potatoes had been scooped into an undeniably phallic shape, and when Jenny pointed it out, they both burst into laughter—the heaviness of the day seemed to shrug and skulk away.

Jenny ate ravenously, grease coating her lips.

"You think he'll call?" she asked. "Before I change my number?"

"If he does, you won't answer," Hazel said.

"Right."

A pause.

"It wasn't always like that," Jenny said. "We had some good nights, after I started going to the meetings. He's the one who suggested AA in the first place. I know what it looked like today, but . . . you should know that Ansel never hurt me. Not physically."

"What's the deal with the philosophy stuff?" Hazel said.

"What do you mean?"

"I mean, his 'theory' or whatever. He sounds like a

freshman philosophy student. Like, he really wants to be smart but he's maybe not that smart."

Jenny laughed, breathy and barbed. "I don't know. I've only read bits and pieces of the manuscript. It's more like a list of questions than a book, if I'm being honest. And you're right—none of his ideas are particularly new or interesting. But I think he's trying to make meaning, and that's admirable enough. He's trying to figure out who he is and how to exist. He's trying to justify himself. Aren't we all doing some version of that?"

She stabbed a piece of lettuce with her fork.

"There were so many things he never told me," she said. "About his family, his childhood. He got so quiet when I asked. He'd ice me out for days. After I let go of the drinking, I woke up one morning, looked over, and realized he was practically a stranger. Did I ever tell you . . . did I ever tell you about the detective?"

Hazel shook her head no. The pasta lurched in her stomach, oily and dense.

"It was years ago," Jenny said. She put down her fork. Pulled her knees to her chest. "I mean, years. I was still in training at the hospital; we weren't even married yet. This detective, this woman, found my number. I didn't believe she was a cop at first. She seemed too young. She came to the hospital, showed me her badge, asked if I would answer some questions.

She wanted to know about Ansel. I'll never forget her name, because I'd never heard it before. Saffron. Like the flower. Anyway, I've noticed her since, Hazel. For years now, though I never told Ansel. She'll pop up every few months, sitting in her car on our street. Just watching. I even saw her a few weeks ago. She's like a shadow."

"What was she looking for?" Hazel asked. "Did she tell you?"

Jenny mustered her fake smile. It was the smile she used to direct at less popular girls in the locker room, the one Hazel recognized from when teenage Jenny lied to their mother. It was an alarm, bursting. It didn't feel right.

"It's so dumb," Jenny said. "I mean, he would never."

"What was it?"

"I can't even say it," Jenny said. "It seems so . . . I don't know. I found the case online, when I Googled her. She's been investigating the deaths of three girls. They died over in New York, before I even met Ansel, when he was in high school. *Homicide.* How ridiculous is that?"

In the dim greenish light, Jenny was baring an approximation of a smile, her teeth intentionally exposed. Hazel knew that she too was thinking of Ansel's face this afternoon. The word was a knife, slashing violently

between them. Homicide. Hazel did not think she had
ever spoken it aloud; the very possibility felt like a foreign creature, thrashing uncomfortable on her tongue.

"How can you be sure?" Hazel asked slowly. "I
mean . . . how do you know he didn't?"

The false smile melted down. A storm rolled across
Jenny's face, so sudden that Hazel filled with a liquid
regret.

"Oh my God," Jenny said. "This is so classic."

"What?"

Jenny smirked. Let out a phony little laugh.

"Come on, Hazel," Jenny said, her tone incredulous
now, almost amused. "You love this."

"I don't understand," Hazel said, cheeks burning
like panic.

"You're actually enjoying this, aren't you? You cling
to anything that makes me weaker than you."

"That's not fair, Jenny."

"You know it's true. Ansel would never do anything
like that—but you actually wish that he had, don't
you? You would go as far as wishing my husband had
murdered people, because it would make you better
than me."

"Jenny, please."

"I remember how it used to be. How you used to
look at me, at Ansel, at everything I had." Jenny ges-

tured to the starched hotel sheets, the sloppy plates, the puddles of grease. "I know a part of you is happy. You only feel content, Hazel, because I've ended up here."

"That's not true," Hazel said. Meek, shamed.

"You won, okay?" Jenny said. "You got everything you wanted."

Jenny's words hovered in the air. An infection. As the tears bubbled, scorching in Hazel's throat, as Jenny rolled her eyes and flicked on the television, Hazel felt like a human swamp, stewing in her own vulgarity. The TV played a rerun of *Real Housewives*—Hazel did not look at Jenny, and Jenny did not speak again. They passed an hour like that before Hazel noticed that her sister had slumped against the bed, her head nodding along her chest, that Jenny had fallen asleep.

•

Hazel stacked the plates as quietly as she could, then kicked the door open, depositing the detritus of their meal onto the floor of the hall. The air smelled different, outside that stifling room. Sterile and new. Hazel exhaled, a great relief flooding—she wedged a towel into the doorframe, let it creak heavily shut behind her.

It had never been more obvious or more embarrassing: Hazel was sheltered, privileged, ignorant by default. Luis often poked fun at her for it. *You white girls always have it good.* It seemed impossible that a concept as violent as that word—homicide— had latched on to Jenny, her own sister. Things like this did not happen in Burlington. Hazel had always felt confident in her vision of right and wrong, good versus evil. She had voted for Obama. She believed she would have been the kind of German to hide a family of Jews in her attic (though of course this theory had never been tested). For the first time, Hazel felt close to something that scared her. She wanted to be brave.

Hazel slid to the scratchy carpet in the musty dim hall, her head pounding fogged. She peered down the corridor of endless identical rooms, then pulled her cell phone from her pocket. The hotel's Wi-Fi was slow—she waited anxious as the search engine buffered.

Saffron Singh appeared right away. A search for *Saffron police New York* produced an article from the *Adirondack Daily Enterprise*: NY STATE INVESTIGATOR PROMOTED TO BCI CAPTAIN. It was accompanied by a photo of a woman, standing rigid on a stage in a military-style cap. She looked competent, capable, her face delicate and angular. Hazel navigated to the state police website, where Saffron Singh's office information appeared immediately, a phone number blinking beneath an email address.

She dialed.

The first ring felt like a dunk in a frigid pool—shocking, harsh. Hazel pulled the phone from her cheek, nearly hurling it in surprise at her own nerve, as a tinny whoosh of static came through the other end. A breath.

"Captain Singh."

The adrenaline rushed as Hazel's own idiocy pulsed, taunting.

"Hello?" the voice said. "Is anyone there?"

Hazel smashed her thumb down, ending the call. The silence that followed was interrupted only by her panting, jagged breath. She sat with the shock, praying that Saffron Singh would not look up her number or try to call her back. She was reacting to the gravity of the question Jenny had refused to pose—Hazel knew it would sit in her gut, a niggling suspicion she would not be able to answer or expel. She couldn't consider it, in any complex way. It was too heinous, too unfathomable. And, most obviously, unprovable.

So she navigated back to her phone's home screen, fingers quaking. She counted four breaths in, all cleaning supplies and vacuumed carpet. Luis answered after three rings—he'd been asleep. His voice was low, creaky. Hazel cried at the very soft of it.

The airport was fluttering busy. Jenny had dressed up for the flight—she'd coated her lashes in a careful layer of mascara, pulled on a pair of low-heeled boots. Back in the hotel room, Hazel had braced for an explosion, an acknowledgment of those ugly vulnerable truths, but Jenny had only hummed idly as she ran a brush through her tangled hair. Hazel hadn't slept all night, Jenny's light snores mingling with her accusation in the dank pit of Hazel's mind.

They walked together to security.

"I guess this is it," Jenny said, stopped in front of a store that sold luxury backpacks.

People flooded around, jostling.

"Don't cry, Hazel." Jenny rolled her eyes. "You're starting to look like Mom."

They hugged, and Hazel swayed. *You are the strong sister*, she wanted to say. *You are the brave.* But all that came out was a whisper, muffled into Jenny's hair. *I'm sorry.* As they broke apart, a snag caught on Hazel's sweater. A long moment as they both looked at it, the gem tangled in a loose thread: the ring.

"I guess that's a sign." Jenny laughed.

She twisted the ring from her finger, placed it in Hazel's open palm.

"You don't want to take it?" Hazel asked.

"Hang on to it for me, will you? It's time to start new. I don't need to carry any reminders."

The ring was heavy, morose, sliding into Hazel's pocket. She wondered how Jenny had worn it all those years, dragging such weight.

"Okay," Jenny said. "See you on the other side."

Hazel watched Jenny's bobbing head disappear into the crowd—she had never, in her entire life, felt further from her sister. On the airplane, Jenny would order a Sprite with a wedge of lime, she'd flip through a tabloid magazine, folding down the corner of the horoscope page. Hazel would always know these things about Jenny—the details, the habits, the tiny gravitations. But details did not make a person. And in the days and weeks and months to follow, Jenny's details would change. She'd live in a city Hazel had never seen, feel a southern sun that had never scalded Hazel's skin. Jenny would create a new iteration of her half of the whole, shaping herself intentionally into something fresh. All the while, Hazel would be here. Here Hazel was, paralyzed in the shiny terminal, all linoleum floors and rushing bodies. Here Hazel was, burning with the familiar urge to follow, to keep up, and, eventually, to surpass. Here Hazel was, always the same.

The parking garage was midnight dark. In the concrete dim, Hazel examined the ring—an object from a different universe. Amethyst and brass. It did not belong here. Before starting for home, Hazel opened the glove compartment and let the ring drop unceremoniously in. A clink, a tumble. She would let it sit there, forgotten, until it was like it had never existed at all.

•

"Are you sure?" the woman asked, two hours later. "All of it?"

"All of it," Hazel said.

She sat in a swiveling chair at the fanciest salon in Burlington. Her clothes still smelled starchy, like the hotel room—when she texted Luis that she'd be late, he replied with a photo of Alma's gums, a bloody hole where her first baby tooth had wriggled free.

The stylist snipped, admired, held out a hunk of hair. *Take a look at that.* Hazel's lank ponytail hung severed in the woman's hand, still clumped in its rubber band. With an inch of hair left—*just like Emma Watson*, the stylist exclaimed—Hazel looked like a little boy. Like a nymph, or a fairy from one of Alma's bedtime stories. A bit, yes, like Emma Watson. Transfixed by her reflection, Hazel imagined she had lived her entire life as this unrecognizable human, that she had always known this slim stranger face. Hazel lifted a hand from beneath the damp smock, to touch the teardrop freckle on her cheek. It seemed much larger than it had before. Less like a blemish, and more like a signal, the very thing that made Hazel herself. The feeling was so utterly delicious—Hazel watched, euphoric, as the twin in the mirror opened her mouth to a laugh that looked like waking, like becoming, like salvation.

2 Hours

Two hours, four minutes.

Jenny used to say that everything happens for a reason—you always teased her for the cliché. If everything happens for a reason, then what about war? What about cancer, school shootings? Jenny would only shake her head, wise and wistful, so resigned in her faith. There has to be a purpose, she would say. Pointless pain isn't human instinct. We'll always find meaning in it.

Optimistic, you'd say.

It's not optimism, Jenny would tell you. Just survival.

•

There is a guard standing outside your cell. He coughs into his arm, phlegmy and wet. You know why this guard is here: the Watch Log has resumed. He will walk past your cell every few minutes to ensure that you do not kill yourself. You don't really want to kill yourself, but you would do it if you could—this situation might have a point, if you were to control it. But you have searched, and there is nothing. No shoelace to wrap around your neck. No shard of glass to slit your wrists. No meaning to find in the long, cruel wait.

•

Ansel?

The chaplain has arrived. A red mesh bag from Polunsky is tucked beneath his arm. The bald of his head shines with sweat—from where you lie on the cot, the chaplain looks bigger than he ever has. He drags a clanking metal chair across the concrete, sits up close to the bars that separate you. The Walls Unit employs a different full-time chaplain, but you requested this man come from Polunsky—you like to picture him maneuvering an old station wagon down the highway, windows open, radio humming softly.

The warden gave me this, the chaplain says, handing you the bag. Officer Billings passed it along.

You know the shape immediately. Your Theory. It has only been two hours since you arrived at the Walls

Unit, barely enough time to hand the bag off to the chaplain. Not enough time to make copies at the FedEx in Huntsville, not enough time to mail those copies out to publishers, and certainly not enough time to drop a stack at the local news station. You pull the notebooks from the bag, the truth sickening in your chest. The despair blossoms slow, a leaking sore.

Your Theory—your legacy—is not going anywhere.

Bailing on the plan was one thing. You'd half expected this of Shawna. But it seems nearly barbaric, returning the Theory to you this way. You don't have the time or the resources to send it out yourself. Shawna knows this. It would be fruitless, anyway, without her part in the plan. The irony is sharp, acidic. What you've done is bad, but not bad enough to warrant the attention that was supposed to come along with your escape. You could send the Theory out, sure. But at this point, it's useless.

No one will care.

•

Why all the writing?

Shawna asked you this once, near the beginning. You were sitting on the floor with your notebooks spread around, your hands stained black with ink.

It's the only way to be permanent, you told her. It's like I'm leaving a piece of myself behind.

What exactly are you trying to leave? Shawna asked.

I don't know, you said, irritated. My thoughts. My beliefs. Don't you think it's important to know that something of yourself exists beyond your own body? Something that can outlive death?

Shawna only shrugged and said: I think some people have left enough already.

•

You send the chaplain away. You spread the pages of your Theory in a circle on the floor, where they grimace like missing teeth. Cross-legged in the fray, you study the proof of your brilliance—it looks so small and scrawling, spread out disorganized. Notes for something bigger, notes for something better.

So. This is it. Your Theory will disappear after you're gone, relegated to a back office at best, a dumpster at worst. A life's worth of thinking and writing, faded into oblivion. Your eye catches a random page, lying haphazard on the concrete. Morality is not finite, it reads. Morality is not permanent. There is always the potential for change. It seems impossible that such a basic thing—potential—can be taken away.

What about the Blue House?

You whisper it, gentle at first. The pages on the floor do not move, do not rustle, only stare up at you. So you say it louder. The words echo back, bouncing hollow off the walls.

What about the Blue House?

Even if it ends right here—even if no one listens—there is always the Blue House. The Blue House is your Theory, standing steadfast. The Blue House is proof. You are expansive, like everyone else. You are complex. You are more than just the wicked.

•

The Blue House surfaced in the hot crux of summer. Almost a year after Jenny left for Texas. You were decaying, alone in Vermont; Jenny was gone, and your days were gray and silent. You had been eating hot dogs every night, cold from the plastic—after dinner you lugged Jenny's favorite pieces of furniture to the garage, where you hacked them to bits with a chain saw.

The letter arrived in the mail one June morning. You ripped the envelope carelessly, the screen door still hanging open, confused by the bubbly handwriting on the lined notebook sheet. Her first letter was simple, only a few sentences.

Dear Ansel. My name is Blue Harrison. Before my father was adopted from a hospital near Essex, New York, he had an older brother. I think that brother might be you.

You staggered to the kitchen, let the letter float to the scratched oak table. It seemed, then, that the universe was both cruel and miraculous. Spiteful and forgiving. Baby Packer had not been screaming all those years to punish you. He had been screaming like all babies did: to tell you something.

The very next weekend, you went to the Blue House. You had driven through Tupper Lake on furniture deliveries, but your arrival felt alive this time, buoyed with meaning. The sky unfurled, a canopy over the lake, the sun sparkled the water a lustrous blue. The restaurant sat a few blocks up from the beach, a house perched on a small plot of land. It winked at you, beckoning.

The bell at the entrance tinkled when you walked in.

You recognized her immediately. Blue Harrison was waiting at a table in the corner, hunched and self-conscious, so very sixteen as she fiddled with a plastic straw. The sight of her was visceral, astounding. Until you saw Blue Harrison, you did not realize how constant that sound had been. A silence settled in the darkest cave of your head, the place where the baby had been softly mewling for years—the relief was nearly crippling in its totality.

Blue Harrison looked almost exactly like your mother.

In that instant, Baby Packer seemed to look up. Calm now, sweet and blinking. As if to say: Finally. You found me.

Saffy
2012

Saffy knew how to solve a mystery.

She knew that itch. The restless tingling at the tips of her fingers—the hunt and the capture, the rush and release. She knew how to twist and fray each morsel of information, tugging tiny threads until the whole thing dissolved. A mystery, Saffy could unravel then study, an exact and unequivocal science. But some cases evolved beyond mystery, into something more crooked, more complex; the worst kind of mystery transcended its own body, transformed into a brand-new sort of monster. Some cases turned cannibal, devouring themselves until there was nothing left but gristle.

•

Saffy stood at the front of the chattering crowd, her hands steady on the podium. The fluorescent back-room was packed full, the troopers rowdy in plastic chairs, the investigators slouching coolly along the far wall. Lieutenant Kensington leaned against the door, half inside the room, like he was planning his immi-nent escape.

Saffy cleared her throat, authoritative. She threw her shoulders back, let her voice boom low.

"As many of you know, we have received a date for the Lawson retrial," she said. The room quieted. "Two weeks from Monday. Considering the high pro-file of this case, the DA is asking for our help—they want our eyes, our ears, our best efforts. Until the trial date, I want you all breathing, sleeping, and shit-ting this case."

She had them now. How little it took: the brash, fa-miliar cadence of their own machismo, gruff for the sake of it. In the months since her promotion to captain, Saffy had been careful to pepper her orders with these phrases—she needed their trust. She had been prac-ticing some version of this speech for years, in the six she'd served as sergeant, then four as lieutenant. Saffy was forty years old now, the only female captain in the history of Troop B, and she had long ago accepted that to lead them, she'd have to speak like them.

"Sergeant Caldwell, why don't you handle the briefing."

Corinne leaned against the backroom wall, arms crossed over her beat leather jacket, her voice rasping soft and even.

"Marjorie Lawson was murdered two years ago in her own kitchen. Bashed in the back of the head with a frying pan. Her husband, Greg Lawson, assistant butcher at Painter and Sons, was the only suspect, and by every standard, it looks like he did it. But thanks to a leak in our own department, the defense filed for a mistrial."

With this, Saffy gazed pointedly at Lieutenant Kensington, who was studying his expensive Italian shoes. Years before, Kensington had been careless at the local tavern, talking drunkenly to a juror about Lawson's obvious guilt, and now it was Saffy who would pay the price. Saffy had inherited this shitshow from their old captain, nudged into retirement by this very case, and now she would have to find an untouched piece of evidence, a new investigative angle. She would need to build something fresh from a pile of dust.

"Thank you, Sergeant," Saffy said. "Lewis and

Taminsky, I want you on the witnesses. Interview everyone again, push them hard. Hartford, you take the victim's family, find anything you can about the Lawsons' marriage. Benny and Mugs, you're on forensics. And, Kensington, you get to deal with the DA and the attorneys. The verdict is on the prosecution, but for the next two weeks we put everything we have into helping them make a case. Let's get to work."

As the troopers filed out, Saffy turned to the bulletin board. She'd memorized the photographs, but there was something about a crime scene. When she'd been sitting on a case too long, when all her leads had dwindled to nothing, Saffy returned to the physical: Marjorie Lawson, sprawled on her own kitchen floor, blood pooling from the back of her head, seeping across the freshly scrubbed tile. The oven light was on, the room hazy with smoke, cornbread burnt to a blackened log.

"Captain."

It was Corinne. Her only female investigator, the best of the bunch. Corinne had been Saffy's first hire as lieutenant, after Moretti decamped back to Atlanta. Corinne had solved dozens of homicide cases under Saffy's direction, had used her father-in-law's pull with the superintendent to help with the promotion to captain. Now, she lingered at Saffy's shoulder, all slouching gait and low, slick ponytail. Corinne was both subtle and savvy, with a dry sense of humor that had pulled Saffy through many long nights.

"We fucked this up," Saffy said quietly, small in the shadow of the photographs.

"It wasn't *you*," Corinne said.

"You know that doesn't matter," Saffy sighed. Corinne did not argue.

The day crept on. Saffy reviewed witness statements with Lewis and Taminsky, shuffled overtime forms, coughed down a frozen burrito as she approved a surveillance van for a narcotics operation. By the time the summer sun set, most of her team had gone home or out to the field, and the station was quiet. Saffy knew she should get some rest before she came back in tomorrow—a Saturday, her one supposed day off—but the air was a suffocating sort of humid and her chest had filled with a familiar longing.

She shouldn't do this. It was not healthy. It was not particularly sane. But Saffy was alone, blissfully alone, and the night would not judge. It had been months since she'd succumbed to this urge—April last time, a gray evening in the pouring rain.

Saffy pulled the filing cabinet from beneath her

desk. The folder was exactly where she'd left it, alongside the other cold cases, closed and forgotten. Saffy told no one. This was her dumbest secret, her sweetest shame.

The girls from 1990 gave her nothing in return. Still, Saffy tucked their file beneath her arm as she trudged out to the stale, empty parking lot. The girls always slipped out in moments like this, when she felt stuck or frustrated, when she had a dead end like the Lawson case. Izzy, Angela, Lila. They would slither from that folder, whispering conspiratorially. They would appear in the back seat of her unmarked Ford Explorer or behind a suspect in the interrogation room, a taunting nudge, a constant reminder. Saffy was captain, yes. But once, she'd been a girl. Every mystery was a story, and sometimes, to see the whole thing, you had to go all the way back to the beginning.

•

Izzy came, that night. A specter in a dream. The girls drove Saffy forward, then pulled her temptingly back—the girls, as they would have been. Izzy, on a porch at sunrise. Late thirties, smudged glasses, her favorite tattered flannel. A cup of coffee on a clean glass table. Her fingers, working at the shell of a hard-boiled egg, chipped nail polish bright against the white. The slimy skin of the egg, revealing itself, vulnerable and helpless, slick as a newborn.

•

When Saffy woke the next morning, she knew what she would do.

A layer of June had settled like a film in the night—dawn was rising, lonely out her bedroom window, and her sweaty sheets smelled sour, in need of a wash. Her phone was already pinging.

Reviewing the Lawson transcripts this morning, Corinne had texted. *Anything specific you want me to flag?*

Saffy wiped the crust from her eyes, tapped out a quick response.

Go back to the witnesses for the defense, look for any holes. Call LT for help. I'm off today.

By the time the sun had risen, Saffy was in the car, her mind still blurry as the air conditioner blasted, musty and stinking of plastic. She merged onto the highway as she unwrapped a granola bar, raving yellow lines already rippling with heat.

After thirteen years of driving this route, Saffy knew the turns of road by heart. She reached the state line and crossed into Vermont, Lake Champlain growing smaller in her rearview as fields melded into strip malls. As she sped down the empty road, Saffy pulled the carton of cigarettes from her glove box. She had not been a smoker since her teenage years, not normally, not technically. But on these drives, she allowed herself as many cigarettes as she wanted. She was already breaking her own rules. The guilt had arrived, along with the shame, and it seemed pointless to deny herself this tiny satisfaction.

She did not need anything specific from Ansel Packer. She never approached him, never announced her presence. Her wanting had no logic, no reason—she only needed to see. To watch. As strip malls turned to rows of old, crumbling houses, Saffy flicked a cloud of ash out the window and pictured her desire like a playground carousel, rusty and aging, turning endlessly.

When she arrived at the little yellow house, the morning had bloomed into a hot summer day. Saffy parked at the curb. She flipped open her notebook, took a long inhale, and squinted out at the scene.

Everything looked different now that Jenny had left. The grass was too long, the potted plants were dead, the porch held a scattering of muddy men's shoes. It had taken three visits, over the last nine months, before Saffy called the hospital, discovering the obvious.

Texas, the receptionist said. *She got a new job down there.*

Jenny was gone.

Saffy had only spoken to Jenny that one time outside the hospital, thirteen years ago—when she remembered that botched interview, the way she'd bumbled, she filled with a tenderness for her younger self. She had been a baby investigator then, so hopeful, so tactless. Over the following decade, on days off and empty weekends, Saffy had watched Jenny grow in increments. She'd seen bottles of wine overflowing the recycling bin, reality shows blaring from the television, how Jenny and Ansel spent their nights separately, Jenny in the living room, Ansel in the garage. She had once seen Jenny's sister—uncanny, the similarity—visiting with two children. Jenny had laughed as she buckled the little boy into his car seat.

Now, the house looked distinctly abandoned, though Ansel's truck was parked diagonally in the driveway. The string lights had fallen from the porch, drooping across the fence, and the cherry-print curtains hung lopsided in the kitchen window. The car engine grumbled as a familiar frustration washed through Saffy's gut. Stupid, to have come. There was nothing here. Saffy wanted to cry, her own impracticality like a bad glance in the mirror. She was about to turn around, to force herself home, when she heard the creak of the screen door.

Ansel stepped outside in a pair of heavy work boots, his jeans spattered with plaster. He wore a thinning T-shirt, yellow in the armpits, rising with the faint outline of a beer belly. Ansel's hair was receding, horn-rimmed glasses perched sweaty on his nose. Saffy sat straighter, curious, as he hefted his body into the cab of his pickup.

Saffy waited a beat, as he backed out of the driveway. She wished for a pack of gum—the cigarettes had turned bitter in her throat, dry and scratchy.

If there was one thing Saffy had learned on the job, it was this: Men like Ansel did not abide vulnerability. They could not stand it.

•

There were patterns, of course. There were tendencies, similarities, character profiles sketched by the FBI. Saffy and her investigators had pigeonholed many of their suspects this way—the gymnastics coach who groomed the quiet girls, the rapist who attended every town hall to hear his own crimes repeated, the ex-marine who beat his first wife, beat his second wife, killed his third. But Saffy credited her success to the knowledge: for every criminal who fit a stereotype, there were dozens who didn't. Every brain was different in its deviance—human hurt manifested in select, mysterious ways. It was a matter of finding the trigger point, the place where pain had landed and festered, the soft spot in every hard person that pushed them to violence. Saffy knew it was a matter of learning those intricacies, of trying to understand, an act that felt intolerably intimate. Unbearably human. Sometimes, like a twisted form of love.

•

In the decade Saffy had been tailing Ansel Packer, she had never seen him leave that little Vermont town. She had followed him to the supermarket. She'd shadowed him to work at the furniture store, to the bar down the block. Once, she'd followed him to a backyard barbecue, where he'd sat at a picnic table, nursing a beer while Jenny chattered with her friends.

Now, Saffy waited for a turn signal or a brake light—but Ansel drove on. He steered north, around Lake Champlain and across the New York border, past Miss Gemma's house and up toward Lake Placid. By the time Ansel finally turned off the highway, hours had passed and Saffy's bladder felt near to bursting.

318 · DANYA KUKAFKA

They had landed back in Troop B territory—a little town Saffy knew peripherally. Tupper Lake, New York.

Finally, a weekend off, Kristen had teased over the phone a few nights ago. *What are you getting up to, Captain?* Kristen's son's soccer game was this morning, the championship play-offs, and Saffy would be missing it without explanation. She thought of the Saturday she should have wanted: orange slices at halftime, a pile of toy trucks on a picnic blanket, ice cream on the way home.

Instead, she was here, shifting uncomfortable as they reached the north edge of Tupper Lake. Ansel's truck stopped briefly at a gas station, then pulled up in front of a residence: a house painted a bright bubblegum blue. As Ansel lumbered from his car, Saffy squinted closer.

It was a restaurant. A laminated menu sat in the window, and a little wrought-iron sign hung over the door, rusted red, barely visible.

The Blue House.

It was nearly noon, and Saffy desperately needed to pee. She shouldn't do this—it wasn't smart, it wasn't reasonable, and it certainly wasn't good police work. But Saffy knew that she would follow him inside. She had staked her career on this concept, had proven herself right time and again: Everyone had secrets. Everyone lived in some form of hiding.

Saffy, too. She was seeing a therapist now, a woman named Laurie who worked from the second floor of an outdated office building. Laurie kept a box of tissues on the coffee table and a soothing collection of potted plants on the windowsill. They talked mostly about Saffy's work, the horrors she witnessed every day: women beaten to death in their beds, children starved and chained in basements, overdose after overdose. Often, Saffy tried to change the subject, to discuss her new home renovation—she'd recently gutted her kitchen, with Kristen's help—or her dating woes, the men who flitted in and out of her life, rarely holding her interest. She told Laurie about the folder of recipes she kept propped on the kitchen windowsill; Rajasthani dishes she'd spent hours Googling, laal maas and dal baati, ordering the ingredients to be delivered in the mail. But Laurie always circled back to the job. The atrocity of Saffy's every day. *What draws you to this work?* Laurie liked to ask, her brow crinkled with good intention. *What part of your child self feels at home in trauma?*

Saffy always fought the urge to roll her eyes. She considered quitting therapy altogether, but she wanted to set an example for her young investigators, men who hid behind the manufactured masculinity of police work, making halfhearted gay jokes as they spit their tobacco. She was captain now. She knew how carefully they watched her.

As Saffy studied Ansel, his boots thunking up the stairs toward the Blue House, she remembered Laurie's words, the wise, infuriating tilt of Laurie's head. *What about your child self?*

Fine, Saffy thought, acquiescing, as Ansel approached the door. *What about her?*

Saffy still missed that little girl sometimes, alert in the top bunk as midnight rolled toward morning. Her desire had been so clear: she had wanted her mother back from the dead. She'd wondered so constantly about her father, he'd taken on a mythical sort of importance, like justice or truth, forever unknowable. Though her childhood was steeped in grief, things had been easier at Miss Gemma's, when she knew exactly what to wish for, when that simple wanting ran beneath everything, a constant streaming current.

But it was gone now. Saffy had shed that sense of longing, had shrugged it off during her rebel teen years or her bumbling twenties. She had replaced it with case reports filed at three in the morning, backroom interrogations that made her suspects cry, seven-hour drives just to interview a witness. Saffy examined the back of Ansel's head as he disappeared into the restaurant.

She wondered what of that yearning he'd managed to shed—or maybe, more importantly, what he had held on to.

•

The interior of the Blue House was homey and bright, dingy and decaying, a family establishment that had clearly passed its peak. A tinkle came from the bell above the door, announcing Saffy's entrance, inciting a minor pang of panic—this was a bad idea. She should drive home, catch the pizza dinner in Kristen's backyard, a tradition after soccer games.

But it also felt necessary. Surprisingly right.

"What can I do for you?"

The woman at the hostess stand was smiling warmly. Her hair frizzed behind an elastic headband and her apron was stained with ketchup and grease. Mid-thirties, Saffy guessed. A name tag had been pinned, lopsided, to her apron. *Rachel.*

"Just an iced tea," Saffy said, nodding toward the bar. She tried to sound more like herself and less like police, though the line between the two had determinedly blurred. "And where can I find your bathroom?"

As Rachel pointed her toward the back of the restaurant, Saffy scanned quickly for Ansel. It didn't take long. He sat at a table by the window, in a rickety chair that faced a young girl. A teenager. Her hair was braided and flung over one shoulder—she looked shy, nervous.

When Saffy reached the bathroom, she locked the door, breathing through the unfamiliar sensation. Terror, new and sharp. With her underwear around her knees, Saffy exhaled into her palms, bleach and urine and fried food engulfing her in a noxious cloud. She felt foolish, paranoid. But as Saffy ran the tap water hot, rinsed her trembling hands, she could not unsee it. The longing in Ansel's gaze. That girl was young. Too young.

Back in the dining room, a glass of iced tea waited at the end of the bar, sweating a pool of condensation onto the peeling vinyl.

"Any food today?"

Saffy shook her head, tongue thick. As Rachel disappeared back into the kitchen, the door swung shut, and Saffy saw the photograph. It was tacked to the kitchen door, printed in high quality, blown up in a frame. A small altar had sprouted up around the photo, dried flowers pinned around handwritten notes. The man in the photo smiled out from a blue-paneled wall— this very house—with a little girl on his hip, her arms twined around his neck. The image jolted Saffy into a heightened discomfort. It was not his name—Ellis Harrison—or the dates, 1977–2003, he had died at age twenty-six—or even the little girl, clearly a younger version of the teenager who sat in the corner now. It was the shape of the man's face. The tilt of his smile. He looked very much like Ansel Packer.

"Actually," Saffy said, when Rachel returned, "I'll take a tuna melt."

Saffy forced bits of sandwich into her mouth, listened hard. The placement of the bar kept her back to Ansel's table, but she caught select words, echoing phrases. The girl's voice. *Foreclosure notice from the bank. I don't know what we'll do.*

"How long have you been open?" Saffy asked Rachel, when the check appeared in a greasy plastic folder.

"My husband and I bought the place in '97. Been running it ever since."

Saffy nodded to the memorial on the kitchen door. "You run it all alone?"

Rachel leaned against the bar, exhaustion appearing in the crinkle of her eyes. "I'm not alone. I have my daughter."

They both turned to watch. Ansel was running a hand absently through his thinning hair. The girl blushed, swirling a plastic straw around the dregs of ice in an empty cup of Coke. A stark, unreasonable fear bubbled up Saffy's throat. *Run*, she wanted to scream. *Get away from that man.*

"How old is she?" Saffy asked instead.

"Sixteen." Rachel rolled her eyes, brightening. "Though Blue seems to think she's thirty."

Saffy left a twenty on the table, floated back out to her car on quavering legs. The sun beat along the pavement, furious. Ansel and that girl.

Sixteen.

Just the age he liked them.

•

It was an accident, what happened to the girls from 1990. It was a moment of passion, it was meticulously planned, it was a serial killer passing through town. It was someone's father, someone's uncle, someone's wayward brother. Maybe—just maybe—it was Ansel Packer. At a certain point, the *why* of it ceased to matter, lost in the crucial question of *who*. The injustice felt brutal, unnecessarily savage. The years of thinking and watching, then the world's inevitable forgetting. At a certain point, they all became Marjorie Lawson, spread-eagled on the floor, demanding something better.

•

Monday morning at the station, and the bullpen was bustling. Lieutenant Kensington rapped on Saffy's office door, jaunty with two knuckles, his uniform freshly pressed, hair slicked back. His wedding ring glinted dully from his finger. Kensington's wife had always hated Saffy—the troopers loved to spread rumors about Saffy and Kensington, rivals working side by side. She shook them off, along with her annoyance. Kensington was a prick, and a middling detective, but he glided up the ranks on the clean, easy strength of his charisma.

"The DA is asking for an update," Kensington said, rocking onto his heels.

"We don't have one," Saffy said.

"What can I do?" he asked, his voice gurgling with empathy. Saffy marveled at the guts of him, standing there chastely, like he had not created this problem in the first place. Kensington had gotten drunk one night, recognized a member of the jury, approached the man on his barstool, and started talking. He'd been saved by his uncle, the long-standing and well-respected captain of Troop C. If Saffy had made Kensington's mistakes, she would have been fired immediately.

"Get me Corinne," Saffy said. She had perfected this tone, both warm and dismissive. She made a point to keep herself level at work—nothing like the previous captain, who had once punched straight through a car window.

Two days had passed since Saffy tailed Ansel to the Blue House, and the images haunted, clouding her focus. Even as she led that morning's debrief, answered rambling questions, and assigned a list of tasks, Saffy pictured them. Ansel and that girl, calm at the diner's table. The meeting had carried the blushing tension of a first date, a concept Saffy could not reckon with the fact of the girl's mother, standing casual behind the bar. She hadn't been able to sleep, remembering how Blue had looked at Ansel, so clearly yearning. She could not parse exactly what she had witnessed.

When Corinne poked her head into Saffy's office, Saffy was massaging her temples, a headache looming. Corinne insisted on her first name—for this reason she evaded much of the troopers' ribbing and leering, the address too feminine, brash and awkward on their tongues.

"Sit," Saffy said.

"I've been reviewing the defense," Corinne said, letting out a sigh. "It's not good, Captain. If the DA can't get the witnesses to talk again, I don't think we can either."

"We're missing something," Saffy said.

"Probably," Corinne told her. "If so, it's buried deep."

Out in the bullpen, Saffy could hear the familiar hoot and holler of the boys, rowdy as always. Things had surely been different for Corinne in the NYPD, where Saffy had plucked her from the lower ranks—back in the Bronx, Corinne wasn't nearly so isolated as a Black woman. Sometimes Saffy wondered if Corinne regretted moving here, accepting Saffy's mentorship. Saffy had long been grappling with the contradictions of her job: the privileges her badge allowed, the fact that prisons were filled almost entirely with Black and brown people. She had felt the constant sting of ignorant people, the malicious and the well-meaning alike—she knew what it meant, to keep a gun on her hip. With Corinne here, Saffy felt distinctly less alone.

"We could go for intent this time around," Corinne suggested. "All those calls Marjorie made to the police, the domestic incidents. We could lean harder on that, try to dig up more. But prosecution knows it's shaky."

Saffy pictured Greg Lawson's face. Pale and pudgy, swollen alcoholic. Just another bad man, his head hung morose as he pled with the jury. This job was getting to her. Not the bodies, or the missing children, or the rampant opioids. It was this. Men like Lawson, who

believed their very existences afforded them lawless-
ness. Men who had been handed the world, trashed it,
and still demanded more.

"Are you okay?" Corinne asked, standing to leave.

Some nights after work, Saffy and Corinne drove
to the diner down the highway for cheesecake and
coffee—the same diner where Angela Meyer had gone
missing. They speculated new suspects; they belabored
old hunches. The case for Izzy, Angela, and Lila was
still open, though no one had touched it in years; Saffy
had outlined the basics for Corinne, painting Ansel
Packer as one promising suspect in a pool of cold leads.

"I need your help with something else," Saffy said,
before Corinne could leave. "Shut the door."

Saffy's house felt particularly empty that night. She
kicked off her shoes, locked her badge and gun in the
front hall cabinet. The silence was oppressive—in
the half-light of dusk, her living room looked sparse
and lifeless, furniture looming in twilight shadow.
She flopped onto the couch, pulled her phone from
her pocket, and opened her personal email, the room
glowing blue as her inbox refreshed.

Nothing.

The woman said it could take a while, Kristen had told her, attempting reassurance. The agency had been Kristen's idea—she'd first mentioned it as they opened the box of decorative pillows they'd ordered from India. Saffy was renovating, with Kristen's help, relying on her friend's impeccable eye for color. A few years ago, when Saffy first started researching Indian culture—religion and art, geography and food, the basics that might have been passed on by her father—she had commissioned a framed painting of Jaipur, done by a Rajasthani artist. She'd hung it on the wall in her bedroom, an instinctual comfort she often studied as she fell asleep.

Saffy knew very little about her father. Only that he'd been a visiting student in the same University of Vermont sociology program as her mother, a young man from Jaipur who'd returned before she was born. Shaurya Singh. A recent cursory search had pulled up hundreds of men—the name, she read, translated roughly to *bravery*, and she pictured that strength coursing through her own bloodstream.

She refreshed her inbox now, more anxious than she'd ever admit. The agency had warned it could take months, even years, to locate a birth parent. Saffy didn't know if her mother had shared the news of her pregnancy—if that was why he left—or whether her father was aware she existed at all. She should prepare for bad news. But none had come. She scrolled her inbox first thing every morning, all scattered hope as she scanned for the agency's logo. It had been over six weeks.

Saffy knew she should make dinner. A frozen pizza. She should change out of her rumpled work clothes, run a comb through her hair. Instead, she texted Corinne, who would be home by now, eating dinner or watching TV or jogging through the fields behind her wife's family farm.

Find anything?

She waited.

•

"They're related," Corinne said, breathless, the next afternoon. "Ansel Packer and the Harrisons."

They'd escaped to their favorite diner, Saffy's coffee cooling in a stained yellow mug. The station had felt too oppressive, everyone looking to Saffy for direction.

"Ansel doesn't have any family," Saffy said, too quickly.

Corinne raised her eyebrows. The many times they'd sat in this very booth, escaping into cold cases when they needed an outlet, spinning theories and re-working motives, Saffy had painted Ansel as a suspect.

Nothing more. But Corinne's bullshit detector was unflappable—the primary reason Saffy had hired her. Corinne's eagle eye extended beyond detective work and into a person's very essence. *She's like a human polygraph*, Corinne's wife, Melissa, had joked, at the late-summer bonfire they'd hosted on Melissa's family's property. Saffy hadn't told Corinne about Miss Gemma's house or the weekends she'd spent camped out in Vermont, spattering the last decade of her life, but she would not be surprised if, somehow, Corinne knew.

"Rachel Harrison was married to Ellis Harrison. They bought the restaurant and had the girl, Blue, when they were really young. He died in 2003. Cancer. I found his school files, a private academy in the city—a guidance counselor noted that Ellis was adopted, so I called the county, checked the records. And guess who had an older brother, from the same case report?"

"The baby," Saffy murmured.

"Ellis and Ansel were abandoned on a farm just outside of town. Here's the address, if you want it."

Corinne slipped a corner of notebook paper across the table, which Saffy shoved quickly into her pocket.

"So why is Ansel there? At the Blue House?"

"That's what I can't figure," Corinne said. "Blue is about to start her junior year at Tupper Lake High

School. Rachel runs the restaurant. They only have two employees, a cook and a dishwasher. But the finances look bad, really bad. They owe back on a huge loan, and it looks like the bank will come calling soon."

"So maybe she wants help. Money?"

"Maybe." Corinne shrugged. "Doesn't look like Ansel has much money, though."

Saffy pressed two fingers to the bridge of her nose, let the pressure alleviate the rising swell. "Blue wouldn't necessarily know that. Maybe she invited him there, to ask for help. But how did she find him? And why now?"

"I could ask you the same thing."

Corinne was watching her with a hapless sort of pity. Saffy gazed out the window, where the empty parking lot blistered in the sun.

"Why this case, Captain? With the Lawson trial coming up, why are we here?"

"I have a feeling." Somewhere in the back of Saffy's mind, Moretti rolled her eyes. The most important lesson Moretti had imparted: feelings meant nothing, until they became facts.

"Feelings won't—"

"I know," Saffy interrupted. "I need this, Corinne. Stay with me on this one."

Corinne took a sip of her coffee, then shrugged. "It does seem a long way for Packer to drive. You might be right. There might be something there."

The waitress arrived with the check. She was young, maybe twenty, freckles tossed carelessly along the ridge of her chest. Saffy wondered if this diner remembered Angela Meyer—if they talked about her still, or if she'd disappeared from the collective memory of this place. Saffy recognized, with an electric zap of surprise, that for the first time in many years, she felt wary, cautious. She felt afraid.

●

When Saffy pictured Angela, she saw her on a beach. California, or maybe Miami. Wide blue sky above a jutting balcony. Angela would have become a real estate agent or a pharmaceutical rep, the owner of a one-bedroom condo on the coast. She would have spent her Sundays making homemade face masks, she would have learned to cook risotto—she would have become bored, like Saffy, with most of the men she dated. Saffy pictured her often, standing on that balcony in her favorite silk pajamas, savoring her solitude, the sun dipping down over gentle rushing waves.

•

Seven days before the Lawson trial, Saffy returned to the Blue House.

A weekday morning. Only Corinne knew where she'd gone—when Saffy promised she'd be quick, Corinne had served a worried, sideways glance. This was an avoidance tactic, sure, but Saffy was burning out on the Lawson case. She needed to find something, anything. When Rachel delivered the plate of eggs, over easy with a side of pancakes, Saffy noted the blisters along her knuckles, where her skin had nicked the rim of an oven.

"Good to see you back here," Rachel said, wiping her hands on her apron.

A stereo in the corner played a stream of classic rock. Saffy studied the room: ten tables with four chairs each, napkins and silverware laid out hopefully. She was the only customer. The Blue House was shaped like a regular middle-class home, once aspirational, now slightly unkempt. The downstairs had been gutted and transformed to fit an industrial kitchen—a staircase near the back led to a second level. The residence, Saffy guessed. As she burst the yolk with her fork, a low, grumbling laugh echoed from the backyard.

Out the window, Blue was climbing the splintered

steps up the deck. She carried a toolbox, heavy in her arms, and she wore a T-shirt that read *Tupper Lake Track & Field*, her hair pulled into a messy ponytail. A pair of tiny denim shorts, plastic flip-flops clacking.

Behind her: a man. He was chuckling, voice low like thunder.

Ansel.

It was stunning, the moment of disbelief. Astonishment followed immediately by a roiling confusion. Saffy blinked hard, trying to understand—Ansel was not supposed to be here. He was supposed to be back in Vermont, reporting to work at the furniture store, sleeping in the sheets Jenny had left behind. He should not be here, pulling a tape measure from his pocket, running it along the dilapidated banister. He tugged a pencil from behind his ear, said something to Blue. Saffy could not hear their words, only the din of their conversation, relaxed and unworried.

That old, fluttering fear. Its wings, beating frantic.

"Everything okay?"

Rachel eyed Saffy's plate of untouched eggs, a layer of film crusting over the goop.

"You're doing construction?" Saffy asked, straining casual as she dug the side of her fork into the pancakes.

"Sort of," Rachel said. "We've had a rough few

years. We've got a friend helping out. We'll have outdoor seating again soon."

"Your daughter," Saffy said. "She's helping, too?"

A polite smile. A barely perceptible glint of suspicion.

"Remind me where you're from?" Rachel set the
coffeepot down on the table.

"Essex," Saffy said, too quickly. "I'm here to hike."

"Well," Rachel said. "You've come to the right place."

As Rachel launched into a description of the most
popular hiking trails in the area, Saffy nodded along,
one ear attuned to the sounds outside. Blue's and Ansel's laughter, humming easy through the glass.

"I'll be back soon," Saffy promised as she paid the
bill. Rachel nodded, studying Saffy just a moment too
long before she swiped the plate away, eggs congealed
along the porcelain.

•

Tupper Lake was small. Pretty. It looked similar to the
other half dozen towns that surrounded Lake Placid—
Saffy drove slowly, studying the quaint, threadbare
streets. The lake was a murky shade of algae-logged
green, crumbling docks sinking into the water. There
was a little library with a slanted roof, a middle school

and high school combined. A museum, a McDonald's, a Stewart's gas station. A defunct ski mountain dotted with abandoned chairlifts. A squat little motel sat a few blocks from the Blue House—when she saw the truck, parked lazy in the lot, Saffy's stomach dipped.

A muddy white pickup.

Ansel was staying.

There was more to this, Saffy knew, as she turned up the air conditioner, pulled her sweaty hair from her neck. Tupper Lake was part of the story that had obsessed her for years, haunting, inexplicable. It was Ansel's story, it was Lila's story—it was the story of Saffy's own heart, that tangly, knotted thing.

·

What do you want, Saffron? Laurie had asked, in their session the week before.

The question was plain and direct. Saffy had blanched as Laurie peered out from beneath her low-perched glasses—a series of landscapes hung above her desk, sweeping fields and marshy ponds. They had been discussing Phillip, a pilot Saffy had dated the previous year. She'd broken it off when things got too serious, when he started grunting disappointed if her work phone rang after dinner.

You crave success at work, Laurie said, when the question had curdled. *That much is obvious. But I'm interested in the things that live beneath that craving. A desire for acceptance? Admiration? Love?*

I have plenty of love, Saffy had snapped. And it was true. She had Kristen and the boys, who flung themselves at Saffy's waist when she arrived late on weeknights, toting boxes of Entenmann's donuts. She had men like Phillip, or Brian, or Ramón from the Counterterrorism Unit, who came along occasionally, and did the things she asked. She had Corinne and her team of investigators. She had long nights solving puzzles. The sludge of police work felt bearable, through this lens: a love affair between herself and the truth. But that concept was becoming increasingly elusive. Saffy could not fathom the purpose of truth, if she could not trust it to prevail. It had started out so simple: Saffy wanted to catch bad men and put them away. But this was not love either. It was something hard, something angry—it was also the thing Saffy knew most intimately about herself.

Laurie stared her down so long, Saffy squirmed, the boil of hurt rising until it bubbled up, a choke. She stung. She seethed. She did not say another word. Halfway through the session, Saffy stood and walked out.

•

The farmhouse sat ten miles outside Essex. A stretch of rural wilderness, chaotic, untamed. Saffy's GPS led her down a dirt road cratered with potholes, her tires bumbling over fallen branches and abandoned construction equipment as the tentacles of greenery loomed above. When she finally reached an opening, the voice on her phone crooned their arrival.

The land was abandoned. Long empty. The remnants of a house sat ruined in the clearing. The structure had collapsed on itself. Flecks of yellow paint dotted the exterior. Saffy imagined it might have been pretty once— the back porch was still intact, the beams sagging and splintered, overlooking the mountains. The farmhouse had been discovered by squatters, or teenagers looking for a spot to party; it was the kind of place Travis's old crew would have loved, heedless and spooky, safe for the wrecking. Garbage littered the rolling field beyond the house, and graffiti snaked up the boarded windows.

Saffy crunched through the debris, the sound of her footsteps lost to the breeze. As she approached, the house seemed to sigh. The closer she came, the more uncomfortable she felt—the house radiated an ailing, ghostly energy.

Saffy would not go inside. The front steps creaked beneath her weight, and from the entry she could see a smattering of old furniture, torn apart by people or animals. The fireplace was filled with trash. The windows had been broken, and afternoon sun streamed through shards of shattered glass.

She did not like to picture them here. Two little boys, playing games on the unfinished hardwood. A child, a baby. No mother had been good here. No father had been kind. Saffy knew abandonment, she knew tragedy, she knew loneliness. She knew violence, from the lifetime she had spent chasing it—she knew how it lingered, how it stained. Violence always left a fingerprint.

•

When Saffy finally returned to the station, the afternoon was tense, subdued. The troopers were hunched over their paperwork, worryingly well-behaved—they'd been blasting a terrible combination of Tim McGraw and Flo Rida from their desks for weeks, but all was quiet now. When Saffy arrived, Jamie eyed her from reception.

"The superintendent is here. Corinne brought him to the backroom."

The superintendent was a burly man from Albany, whom Saffy had only met twice. When she solved a serial rape case that had dogged Moretti for years, the superintendent drove up to shake Saffy's hand, take a photo, congratulate her. And when everything spiraled with the previous BCI captain, with Kensington and the Lawson case, the state had sent the superintendent to suggest a voluntary retirement.

There was nothing to congratulate now. Saffy felt a singular sense of doom as she entered the backroom. The superintendent sat in a creaky chair across from Corinne, holding a paper cup of water, miniature in the thick of his hands. Lewis and Taminsky looked particularly unkempt today, sheepish, their ill-fitting shirts awkward and untucked.

"Captain Singh." He stood for a handshake—Saffy had perfected the motion, spine straight, grip firm. "Sergeant Caldwell was filling me in about the Lawson case."

Corinne glanced up, apologetic.

"You'll continue investigating until the retrial? The DA has been in touch with our office, too. They're not happy."

"Of course, sir." Saffy blistered beneath the severity of his gaze.

"I'm very curious what you'll find," the man said.

"This case is getting a lot of press, and our image as an institution has suffered. We took a chance on you, Singh. I'd hate for this whole diversity initiative to flounder over one bad case."

Diversity initiative. This was the first Saffy had heard of such a thing. It was true that, at thirty-nine, she was the youngest BCI captain appointed in years, that she was the only woman, and the only person of color, ever to hold the position within Troop B. But her stats had gotten her the title. By the time she'd risen to lieutenant, Saffy had the highest arrest record in the state.

Still, she withered under the superintendent's stare. After reviewing the case and issuing another cryptic warning, the superintendent finally took his leave— when he had gone, the room seemed to deflate with his absence. A buzzing paranoia nipped at the edges of Saffy's consciousness, a fly too subtle to swat.

•

Kristen's house was beautiful in the summer. A jumbo-sized Craftsman perched in a cluster of vacation homes, with a yard that opened directly onto the shores of Lake Champlain. Saffy entered without knocking and followed the boys' laughter down the front hall. "I want to be the ninja!" one of them yelled, as the other shrieked with delight.

"You look like shit," Kristen said, handing Saffy a glass of chardonnay. Kristen had just renovated her kitchen, and everything was gleaming bright. Jake nodded hello as he stirred a pot of red sauce, a pile of LEGOs abandoned at his feet. "Bad day at work?"

The story spooled out in skeleton. The Lawson case, the superintendent, the condescension of his threat. She did not mention the diversity initiative— Kristen wouldn't understand. Kristen listened attentively, manicured nails tapping along the counter as the boys zoomed in and out. They were five and eight years old now, raucous as they elbowed past Saffy to chase the dog under the table, a purebred miniature poodle.

"I don't know," Saffy said. "Sometimes I wonder if this job even makes a difference. Or if I'm going to spend the rest of my life drowning in bureaucratic bullshit."

"This is about more than detective work," Kristen said. "What have you always said? The system needs changing from the inside. Well, you're here now. You're inside."

As Kristen clucked her consolations, a sense of tragedy loomed above, like a cloud threatening to burst.

This happened sometimes, when Saffy looked at Kristen's life. When she retreated upstairs to read the boys a bedtime story, their hair wet from the bath as they snuggled up against her in their racecar pajamas. She did not want what Kristen had. She could not imagine having children—she'd never felt the tug Kristen described, that primal need for a baby. But there was something to be said for this brightness. This sweetness. The heft of Jake's hand as he tousled the boys' hair, the scent of cooked basil wafting through the air. As Saffy tried to ingest Kristen's words, the feeling swarmed, dire, devastating. She wondered if it might kill her. Laurie's words came back, too cruel in that immaculate kitchen. *What do you want?*

•

And then there was Lila. A shadow in the glow of Kristen's glory. Lila never would have joined them, here in Kristen's kitchen. She would have inhabited her own crystalline world, a few miles down the road, or maybe a few towns over. Never far from home. Her own snacks in the cabinet, her own overflowing trash cans, her own windows streaked with greasy fingerprints. Saffy could see her clearly, a silhouette on a well-worn couch, the television muted as she unbuttoned her shirt. The baby would have latched, suckling. The hot release of milk. Her house would have murmured, ordinary, as a garbage truck idled gently on the street. A regular Tuesday. Lila would have been a woman by now, leaning down to inhale the milky sweet of her baby's scalp—a mother, no longer a girl at all. Grown, transformed, spectacularly new.

·

Four days before the trial, Kensington cornered her in the parking lot. It had been two weeks since Saffy discovered the Blue House, and though her team had been working tirelessly, the Lawson case had not budged. Two of the troopers had been caught dealing weed behind the Bullseye tavern, and Saffy had been forced to fire them. It was a long summer evening, the kind Saffy might have once spent drinking beers out by the river in a crowd of camping chairs, fishing poles dunked into the water, smoke swirling from fat, lazy joints.

"Captain," Kensington said, a grumbling voice from behind.

One of Kensington's strengths as an investigator: his ability to blend in anywhere. Saffy was consistently astonished by Kensington's mediocrity, how his

346 · DANYA KUKAFKA

performance did not matter as long as he flashed that smile, clapped the superintendent on the back like a fraternity brother.

"Do you have a second?" he asked.

"Sure." Saffy set her coffee cup on the roof of her car, crossed her arms, and waited.

"I—I wanted to say I'm . . ."

"Spit it out, Lieutenant."

"I'm sorry."

Saffy studied him, square-jawed and hollow in the sunset parking lot. It was audacious, and so like him, to throw her to the wolves then demand her forgiveness for it.

"I didn't mean to put you in this position. The investigation, I made a big mistake. It was lazy, and I'm sorry."

"Thanks for that," Saffy said.

"How about a beer?" he said, sheepish. "It's been a while. Lion's Head shouldn't be too crowded yet."

"Just go home, Kensington," Saffy said, filling with a frustration she could not name. With Kensington, with this job, this town—with the beauty of the pink sky, deteriorating over the parking lot, a saturated fuchsia she was too jaded to enjoy.

It was only later, as the sugary dusk lulled her home, that Saffy recognized the scene. Kensington, that practiced penitence. Ansel Packer framed in her bedroom door at Miss Gemma's. *I'm sorry, Saff. Please, forgive me?*

That night, Saffy dreamed of the Blue House—she was walking barefoot through the restaurant. When she lifted her heels, they were slippery with crimson. Blood. Rachel held a pot of coffee, her face drooping like the fox, her eyes pecked out, skin half-decomposed. Blue sat on the dilapidated deck, cross-legged with Lila. Lila was alive, and they giggled as they braided daisy chains on the splintered wood. Lila was dead, and Blue looked up at Saffy, confused and ravaged, cradling the bones.

Two days until the retrial. Saffy's desk felt like a cage, emails blaring from her inbox, sleeplessness crashing in a series of waves. The visit from the superintendent had sent the station into a spiral, circling rumors about layoffs—the troopers were stressed, bitchy, low on morale. When Saffy's phone pinged, she checked it idly, expecting more spam from Kristen's favorite furniture store. The name jumped out instead, the address she'd been waiting for.

The agency.

We regret to inform you—
A fog, descending.
We have located your father, Shaurya Singh.
Deceased, since 2004.

Her office rushed, zooming out of focus. Saffy stumbled from her chair and out into the bullpen, Corinne calling after—*Captain? Are you okay?* No oxygen. As the parking lot materialized, as the blazing summer evening curled pink into the horizon, as Saffy gasped in the humidity, she knew where she would go.

Back to the very start.

•

The Blue House was a beacon in the night. Light flooded the interior of the restaurant, like a stage with no curtains. From her spot at the curb, headlights off, Saffy could see Blue and Rachel, working together behind the counter. Ansel sat at the bar, his fingers relaxed around the neck of a beer bottle.

Saffy watched, bruising. A summer moth clambered gently across the windshield. Blue skirted around her mother to wipe down the counter. Rachel held a wineglass up to the light. Ansel crossed his arms, hunched over the barstool. Saffy might have been watching two parents and a daughter, closing their restaurant late on a Saturday. They seemed comfortable. They moved with grace, the easy elegance of family.

The thought was heartbreaking, even in consideration: maybe this was nothing sinister. So simple after all. Maybe Ansel only wanted the same things Saffy did. To know, finally, where he belonged.

Her father was dead. *Deceased.* The only photograph she'd ever seen of him had disappeared after her mother's death—she ached for it now. There were so many things she would never know. Her father's childhood home, the God he had worshipped, his favorite pair of worn-out pants. The exact shade of his eyes, the inflection of his voice. This loss, a part of Saffy herself.

As Blue pantomimed something with her hands, Ansel laughed, his head thrown back. Their joy, palpable.

She hated him for it.

•

Saffy woke up in her car, dawn cracking misty over the lake. Fog swirled up from the water, a buggy cloud, already warm with July. She had not meant to stay, couldn't remember dozing off—the exhaustion of the past few weeks had caught her unaware. She remembered Ansel's truck pulling out from the driveway, the restaurant lights flickering off, Blue's silhouette moving behind the upstairs curtain. Saffy's mouth was thick and sour, her eyelashes caked shut with the makeup she'd applied before work the previous day. Her back twitched, spasmed.

It was early. Barely seven o'clock. Saffy drove, aimless, toward the mountains.

The trailhead was completely empty. Cathedral Rock, one of the hikes Rachel had mentioned. Saffy had never understood the appeal of hiking, but this was one of the most popular mountains in the Adirondacks, famous for the sweeping views from the fire tower at the top. Saffy grabbed her purse, packed with a plastic water bottle and the protein bars she kept tucked away for long nights at the station. She wore jeans and a pair of work flats, already layered with dust as she trudged toward the opening in the trees.

She walked. Saffy wound her way up the trail as the sun climbed parallel, a soft hand caressing her gently awake. She walked for minutes or hours she did not count—she had turned off her phone to save the battery—pushing until her thighs burned, until a pool of sweat had soaked her pants along her lower back.

She walked until she reached the tree line, then along a ridge, where she could see the mountains spanning out below, offered up vulnerable.

The fire tower was perched on the summit, delicate and creaky. Beneath, the Adirondacks were indifferent, rolling hills painted a vivid summer green. When Saffy reached the landing, she peered out from the railing, letting the wind tangle her hair, chilling the sweat that dripped down her spine.

There was something about that girl. Blue. A feeling that dogged Saffy, relentless. It was envy, she realized, as the wind rippled the trees, miniature in the distance. It took a certain privilege to invite a man like Ansel into your world. To trust so freely. In the entirety of her life, Saffy had never once felt that sort of safety. As the world splayed beneath her, obscene in its beauty, Saffy marveled. She had known from a young age that everyone had darkness inside—some just controlled it better than others. Very few people believed that they were bad, and this was the scariest part. Human nature could be so hideous, but it persisted in this ugliness by insisting it was good.

By the time Saffy hiked back to the trailhead, the sun was high and sizzling. Her stomach grumbled and her shoulders had burned red—when she turned on her phone, she had eleven voicemails from Corinne.

Captain, call me.

It's Lawson.

He's dead.

•

Suicide, Corinne explained, as Saffy sped through town. The warden found him hanging from a bedsheet in his jail cell.

As Saffy wound through Tupper Lake, she let the anger flood. It was fury, yes—but it was more. She wasn't even surprised. Men like Lawson always found a way out. She'd seen it so many times—how they squirmed through the cracks in a system that favored them. How, even after they'd committed the most violent crimes, they felt entitled to their freedom, however that might look. Stopped at a red light three blocks past the Blue House, Saffy pictured Marjorie, her hair matted with blood against the kitchen tile, the room swirling with smoke. She pictured Lawson himself, feet spinning above a jailhouse cot.

The cycle was ruthless. Inoperable. Saffy pulled a U-turn in the middle of the road, remembering what she had once told Kristen—she wanted to change the system from the inside. She was inside now, holding a microscope, watching the virus swallow everything whole.

·

When Saffy walked into the Blue House, she found the girl, standing alone behind the counter. Blue tapped at her phone as she sipped a glass of ice water, just back from a run, her face flushed, cheeks rimmed with salt. She startled at the sound of the door, then reached for a menu.

"How many?"

"Just me."

Saffy took a stool at the bar, studying. Strawberry blond in a pair of running shoes. Blue's hair was pulled back into a damp messy ponytail, flecks of mud spattering up her calves. In Blue's profile, she could see flickering bits of Ansel—the rigid slant of her nose, something feline in the shape of her eyes.

Saffy held up her badge, a confession. "New York State Police. Can you go get your mother?"

By the time Rachel came out of the kitchen, Saffy had filled with a sickening doubt. Rachel wrapped an arm protectively around her daughter's shoulders, confused, afraid. This was unprofessional, Saffy knew—not illegal, but certainly not wise. But when Blue bit her lip, anxious, she looked exactly how she had in Saffy's dream, holding that pile of bones on the porch.

"Can you tell me about your relationship with Ansel Packer?"

"What's this about?" Rachel asked.

"Please, it's important. Why is he here?"

"He's my uncle," Blue said. "My dad's brother. We didn't even know he existed until last month, when my grandmother let it slip. My dad died without knowing he had any biological family, so I reached out. I thought we should know him."

"What do you want from him?" Saffy asked.

"Nothing," Blue said slowly. "He's building a new deck for the back. He's . . . well, he's family."

Saffy's own paranoia deflated, a wheezing exhale. It was stupidly simple. Uncomplicated all along. But that didn't mean the danger had disappeared. Saffy thought of the bedsheet, tight around Lawson's neck, bruised and battered blue.

The story came out then, a spew of excess detail. Saffy told them about the bodies—the way the girls had scattered, as though reaching for escape. She told them about the ring, glinting from Jenny's finger. She even told them about the fox, congealing on her bedsheets. Rachel's face hardened as she listened, while Blue's crumpled into unmistakable devastation. When Saffy finished talking, there was a long, throbbing pause. Her own regret seemed to wait, pregnant in the ravaged humidity.

"I don't understand," Rachel said. "Why isn't he in jail? Why hasn't he been arrested?"

It occurred to Saffy that there were many ways to hurt—not all of them physical. An ice machine grumbled in the distance.

"The short version is that the evidence didn't hold," Saffy said. "I'm giving you this information for your own safety. Please, just stay away from him."

And Saffy left them like that, stunned behind the bar, her phone number clutched in Rachel's hand. *Call me if you need anything.* As Saffy walked out of the restaurant, she memorized their shapes—two women, hurt but not fatally—and she knew that she was done. All these years, she had been watching Ansel Packer to see how his pain compared to her own. But it seemed Ansel had learned how to bury the past; it was time for Saffy to start her own digging.

•

That night, Saffy let herself into the station. Two o'clock in the morning, and the building was dead empty. The computers loomed, blinking asleep, her office pitch-dark. Saffy groped for her desk chair, calming with the immediate sense of authority as she sank into the leather. It was unprofessional, what she'd done. But if she couldn't make a difference in this job—the job that had vacuumed everything else in her life into extinction, the job that seesawed between nightmare and rhapsody—then at least she could make a difference somewhere. The lump in Saffy's throat cracked then burst. That old refrain echoed, inexhaustible. *What do you want?*

She wanted to be good, whatever that meant. As Saffy gazed up at the ceiling, hot tears burning down her cheeks, she prayed that the difference between good and evil was simply a matter of trying.

There would be no retrial. On the Monday they'd spent so long preparing for, Saffy gave her investigators the day off. Instead of clocking in at the station, instead of answering the many calls from the superintendent's office, from Lawson's defense attorney, from the hungry reporters, Saffy visited the cemetery.

Her mother's grave was unkempt. Saffy brought flowers, but she hated how they looked, alive against the mossy gray headstone. As she crouched in the grass and placed the flowers against her mother's name, etched permanent in granite, her mother's voice returned to her, a rare and precious moment of clarity. *You'll see, Saffy girl. The right kind of love will eat you alive.*

Rachel had called, her voice shaky but certain: She had sent Ansel away from the Blue House. His truck had disappeared from Tupper Lake. *Where did he go?* Saffy had asked. *I don't know*, Rachel had told her. That would have to be enough. This obsession had held her in its grasp far too long. This case would remain open, a permanent mystery.

But Saffy knew her mother had been right—this had to count as some form of love. The kind that stalked, the kind that hunted. A love startled like a sound in the night. As Saffy knelt at her mother's grave, forehead pressed to the gritty stone, the realization felt almost like a molting. Self to self. There to here. A wonder, a burden, this endless growing.

1 Hour

Your witness is here, the chaplain says.

Fifty-six minutes, and the dread is a sieve. A sluggishness has arrived, but it lifts with these words—everything lightens, your muscles stretching alert.

Blue, you say. She came.

She is older now. She does not want to see you. She does not want to talk. You will not lay eyes on her until she appears in the witness box—seven years have passed since that Blue House summer. She must be different. But it does not matter how Blue has grown. To you, she is eternally sixteen. To you, Blue will always be that teenager at the hostess stand, thumbs poked through the holes in her sweatshirt sleeves.

•

There was no big event. No life-changing reveal. When you think about the Blue House now, the simplicity brings a sort of devastation: there was only comfort.

There was only you, in the tall grass with Blue. She asked you questions about work, about school, about your favorite food as a child. She told you stories about her father, a man you came to know during those short bright weeks, a series of recounted memories. You could not believe that this girl was a result of the infant on the farmhouse floor, of the tragedy that had dogged you all these years. In her face, you found absolution.

It was easy, at the Blue House. You sat at the bar while Rachel and Blue closed up, telling stories about foster care, about Jenny, about the book you were writing. Your Theory. Blue fixed you a plate of homemade pie—the apple melted sweet on your tongue.

The truth feels stupid, in the shadow of tonight. Heartbreakingly simple. You had not known, until the Blue House, what you were capable of becoming. It was fleeting, ethereal. It was tragically uncomplicated.

At the Blue House, you were free.

•

Now, your last meal arrives.

You sit on the floor with your back resting against the bedframe, holding the tray in your lap: a slippery hunk of pork chop, a lump of mashed potato, a cube of neon green Jell-O. You cut into the meat with the side of your fork—it is the same meat they serve to the low-security prisoners at the rest of the Walls Unit. Nothing special. The infamous Last Meal is no longer a thing, banished years ago when requests got too outlandish and a new warden took charge. The meat splits easily. You stab a chunk, bring it to your mouth. It tastes rubbery, salty, unreal—you swallow, imagining how it will travel down your throat then into your intestines, how it will dissolve slowly along with the photograph. Whatever you eat now will not have the time to pass through you. It will decompose along with your skin and your internal organs, in a cheap cedar box paid for by the state, four and a half feet below the ground in an unmarked plot at the graveyard down the road.

You heave. That was it, you realize. It's already over.

You missed your own last bite.

•

The chaplain returns. He sits outside your cell, his chair flipped backward, like a teacher trying to be cool. He holds a leather-bound copy of the Holy Bible, and his thumb circles the cover in repetitive strokes.

I can pass a message along to Blue, the chaplain says. Is there anything you'd like to say?

You have nothing more to tell her. Blue has seen it already—the stickiest proof of your own humanity. Your Theory, compounded. There exists inside you a galaxy of possibility, a universe of promise.

How can they do it? you ask.

The chaplain grimaces, sheepish.

How can they go through with this, Chaplain?

I don't know.

That girl out there, you say. Blue. She is living proof. I can be normal. I can be good.

Of course you can be good, the chaplain says. Everyone can be good. That's not the question.

The chaplain looks unbearably paunchy. Fleshy, weak. You want to reach through the bars, take fistfuls of his potato face in your hands. There are practiced ways you could still gain control: You could embarrass him. You could outwit him. You could hurl yourself against the bars, intimidate him with pure physical force. But these options require too much inertia. You have forty-four minutes left, and the game feels pointless.

The question is how we face what you have done, the chaplain continues. The question is how we ask forgiveness.

Forgiveness is flimsy. Forgiveness is like a square of warm sun on the carpet. You'd like to curl up in it, feel its temporary comfort—but forgiveness will not change you. Forgiveness will not bring you back.

•

Jenny comes to you then. A ghost, an accusation. The softest thing.

She exists now in pure distillation—in minuscule details, daily routines, mundane remembrances of a life before this place. An ache, for that old house. The flannel bedsheets Jenny chose at the department store, the curtains over the sink, embroidered with lace. The beige carpet, which never seemed to look clean, the TV sitting dusty on its stand. You can picture her there, still. Jenny, coming through the front door in her nurse's scrubs, stomping the salt from her winter boots.

Love? she calls. I'm home.

The texture of Jenny. Fruit shampoo, hangover breath. You remember how she used to tease you, hands on your cheeks. It's okay to feel things, she liked to say with a laugh, and this always irritated you. But if you could go back now, you would clap your hands over hers, relish in the knobby warmth of Jenny's fingers—the only person who dared to stand between the world and yourself.

Please, you would beg. I'll feel anything.

Just show me how.

•

You can see the line now, in the spotlight of retrospect. The direct link, from the Blue House to Jenny.

The Harrisons sent you away on a Sunday morning. Blue and Rachel stood in the restaurant parking lot, their arms crossed, a palpable unease in their eyes. Don't come back, they said. We don't want you here anymore. You'd heard those words many times over the course of your life, but they felt different, coming from the Harrisons. The Blue House had brightened you, softened you, proven so much—finally, you were a part of something. A family.

But Rachel's voice was determined. You did not know what they'd learned or how they'd learned it, only that it was too much.

As you climbed into your truck and pulled out of

the parking lot, a furious itch rose in your fingertips. Everything fuzzed, slanted. You watched Blue and Rachel disappear in the rearview, their gazes searing permanent: they were afraid of you.

You drove to Texas. It took four days. You could not imagine going back to Vermont; you could not even go back to the motel. You left everything in that damp little room, your clothes and your cash, your razor and your toothbrush, the photograph Blue had gifted of the Blue House, shot on an overcast morning. You drove, blank and fuming, wondering how much more hurt your human body could sustain. The desperation was a parasite.

There was only one certainty, and that was Jenny. Her shape. Her smell. Her breath, sour on the pillow first thing in the morning. You needed it like you needed oxygen. How naive, how foolish you had been, to think that the Blue House could ever take her place.

So you slept in the bed of your truck. You tossed and twitched through each gusty night, until the air turned humid and leafy highways shifted into desert plains.

Jenny had blocked your number. She had only called once, since she left ten months earlier, to make sure you signed the divorce papers, her lawyer breathing heavy on the conference line.

When you finally reached Houston, you checked

into a seedy motel and found a public library. On a computer between the musty stacks, you typed her name—Facebook surfaced right away. In her profile photo, Jenny wore a pair of plastic sunglasses, her shoulders tan and surprisingly toned. She had been tagged, a few days earlier, in a photo of three women standing in a parking lot. *Last day of work for Bethany!* the caption read. Behind them, a sign bared the first four letters of the hospital's name. Google proved it— the hospital was in the suburbs. Not far from here. Your chest thrummed. Your body shaped itself momentarily back into something you understood.

Hope, like a blade.

The next morning, you waited in your car, patient outside the emergency room. You knew from Facebook that Jenny had cut her hair into a stylish bob, but you had not imagined it would suit her so well. It thinned out her face, lengthened her. Jenny looked good. She held a coffee cup in one hand and her phone in the other—when she laughed into the speaker, the echo drifted through your windshield. Maybe things would have been different if you'd just done it then, talked to her in the shock of day, as people streamed through the revolving doors. But you were too curious.

The hours passed, your story expanding as it smothered in the heat. You would fix things—a second chance.

You would go back to that house with the cherry red curtains, to nights fossilized on the couch. By the time Jenny came out, the sun was glowing pink over the asphalt, and she was walking with a man. The man wore a pair of sky-blue scrubs, his jaw scruffy and angular. He leaned to plant a slow kiss on Jenny's cheek.

A flush of rage, lightning hot.

After a long goodnight that made you queasy, after the man had gotten into his own car and driven away, you followed Jenny through a neighborhood of sprawling gingerbread-style mansions, then into a smaller subdivision. She stopped in front of a bland modern condo, which looked the same as all the condos around it, painted pastel, lined up like crayons. Jenny stood on the stoop, digging through her purse for her house keys. It was the same purse she always carried, the fake leather flaking off in chunks. Inside, you knew, there would be a pile of crinkled receipts and ChapStick tubes with crumbs stuck to their rims.

The lights in the apartment clicked on. Darkness had fallen like a sheet from the rafters, and everything solidified in those long throbbing minutes, before you slid from your car. The man's thumb, knuckling Jenny's cheek. The hurt, the crave, the shame—it all congealed, rancid.

You turned the knob. Locked.

So you kicked until the door flung open. Louder, more violent than you'd planned. This would be a point of contention, later—the felony charge, the prosecution claiming burglary, making you eligible for the death penalty.

But in that moment, there was only Jenny. She stood in the open marble kitchen, her back to the stove—Jenny's house was clean, gleaming. She had bought a fancy new espresso machine, shining against the granite counter-top, and there were fresh flowers bathing in a vase by the windowsill. Gas clicked beneath the teakettle, as one of her favorite old Sheryl Crow songs trilled from the speakers. The song was Jenny in her clearest form, so basic, so wanting, so sentimental. A cataclysm. In that moment, she was more than Jenny—she was all of them. Every woman who had left you behind.

Ansel, she said, trembling afraid. As you kicked down the door, Jenny had lunged in fear for a kitchen knife, shiny and stark, too big for her hands.

This was not how you'd pictured it.

Jenny, you wanted to plead. Jenny, it's me. You wanted the Jenny you had chosen for her patience and her comfort, the Jenny who'd rolled over in bed to press her lips to your shoulder blade. You wanted the Jenny who had believed you could be more than yourself. The Jenny who had given you a life worth surviving.

But there was only terror, in that kitchen.

There was a split second, where it could have gone differently. Maybe there were millions of those alternate seconds—if the kitchen knife had not glinted in her grasp—if, if, if—things could have been different. Even as you lunged, as Jenny raised her hands in a defense that looked like surrender, you ached for those substitute lives, the milliseconds that held endless possibility.

She was just a Girl. You were only you.

•

Thirty-one minutes.

You stand rigid in the far corner of your cell. The chaplain is gone, and the tip of your nose mashes into the wall. Cool, gritty. Your body feels sensitive to every touch, a walking fever.

No one seems to care. No one seems to understand how intent can change things. Of all the facts that brought you here, this one feels most important: that night came from your very core. You did not plan it or fantasize it. You only moved on the force of what you knew yourself to be. It should matter, the distance between your desire and your actions. It should matter that you wanted to love Jenny, or at least to learn how. You did not want to kill her.

Hazel
2012

There was no Summoning.

No lightning bolt zapped down her spine.

When it happened, Hazel was sorting laundry with the TV on mute. As she folded Alma's school uniform, Luis's boxer shorts, her own tattered bras, Hazel felt nothing. No heart-stopping pain, no flare of worry. She tucked Mattie's socks into colorful little bundles as the television played an ad for a stationary bike. A sponge that washed itself. Auto insurance.

•

Hazel was crouched in the garden the next morning, her hands full of milkweed stems, when Luis appeared on the back porch. He was wearing his Saturday sweatpants and waving her phone in the air.

"Hazel," he said. "Your mom's called like six times."

The dread was acerbic, her body's primitive preparation. Her mother never called more than once—usually, she left a cheery voicemail. Her parents were getting old. Maybe someone had taken a fall. As she dialed her mother back, Hazel wiped her sweaty brow with a forearm. The ringing clicked into a gasping sob.

"Mom," she begged, gut plunging. "Mom, please, what happened?"

"Oh, honey," her mother heaved. "It's Jenny. She's dead."

Hazel's vision, half gone.

"Ansel. They have him in custody. She was at the apartment—a kitchen knife—"

Hazel did not recognize the wail that came from her own throat. It broke up and through her, visceral, a level of pain that had been waiting in her depths, unpossessed. Luis hovered as Hazel slumped to the burning wood of the porch. Her mother's voice echoed tinny from the phone, which she'd hurled across the deck, now splayed ten feet away. Hazel stared at a spiderweb on the leg of the porch chair, grasping; the web was silky and translucent, a single fly swaddled motionless in the center.

Time warped. It stretched, faded. Morning churned into afternoon, stammering spurts of surreal minutes that constricted in Hazel's throat like balloons. *The body*, Luis was saying on the phone with her father. *An arrest.* The hours passed, shell-shocked, incoherent.

The only person Hazel wished to call with the news was Jenny herself. Jenny would answer with a perky hello, chipper as she had been these last months in Texas. *I met someone*, she'd told Hazel, giddy. *He's a surgical nurse, and he's so sweet. He cooks me dinner, we watch TV. You'll meet him when you're here.* Hazel had been planning to visit with Alma for Thanksgiving—she'd booked the flights already. Now, she thought of Jenny's earlobes, fuzzed and smooth. Her sister's fingernails, ragged at the cuticles.

•

Grief was a hole. A portal to nothing. Grief was a walk so long Hazel forgot her own legs. It was a shock of blinding sun. A burst of remembering: sandals on pavement, a sleepy back seat, nails painted on the bathroom floor. Grief was a loneliness that felt like a planet.

•

Four days later, Hazel stood in her parents' kitchen, surrounded by cold casserole dishes and distant voices. The afternoon had faded to a gloomy night, and the post-funeral reception was cast in the haze that had spread across everything, a scrim of white filmed over a pond.

Hazel had refused to wear black. She'd dug through the back of her closet instead, until she found the cotton dress she'd been gifted that long-ago Christmas. Heather gray to Jenny's olive green. The service had been impersonal, almost offensively forgettable: Hazel had sat with her parents in the front pew of the church they'd attended maybe twice, while a priest made vague concessions to Jenny's excellent character. Hazel had marched dutifully to the cemetery, where the coffin had been lowered slowly into the ground as the sky threatened release. Hours later, she still clenched the memorial program in her sweaty palm—a folded sheet of paper with Jenny's photo plastered across the front, printed cheap in grayscale. Jenny perched on the edge of the living room couch, hands cupping her chin, her smile luminous, young and hopeful. On Jenny's finger, that awful purple ring, winking coy at the camera.

"We can leave, if you want," Luis said, a hand pressed to Hazel's back as he passed her another paper cup of coffee.

Around them, neighbors gawked. Aunts and uncles hugged Hazel with spidery arms, murmuring apology. Most of these people had come purely for the spectacle—Hazel knew this was the worst and most interesting thing that had ever happened to their cul-de-sac, to her father's colleagues, to the women from her mother's swim aerobics class. They approached Hazel warily, a steady line. *I'm sorry for your loss.* The phrase felt blank and lifeless, like her loss was a cell phone left on the seat of a taxi.

"Soon," Hazel said. "Give me a minute."

In the muted chaos, no one noticed Hazel slipping out the front door.

Her ears rang with the sudden silence of the outside world. Hazel slid into her car, parked across the street because the driveway was full. The empty block was dim. A buggy, navy blue. From out here, the house looked like a television screen, playing a sad movie. A relief, to be alone. Hazel did not turn on the engine, only sat in the quiet, reveling, before she leaned over and opened the glove compartment.

It was still there. Just as heavy as she remembered. That cursed and miserable ring.

Just ten months ago, Hazel had dropped Jenny off at the airport—had seen her sister for the very last time. Now, she held the jewel in her palm as a simmering rage arrived, along with a memory she'd stowed away years ago: Ansel, the day he gifted Jenny this ring. Ansel, out in the moonlight, digging.

Hazel stumbled through her parents' back gate, the purple ring glistening, beckoning her forward. The maple tree was just as Hazel had always known it, the branches like fatherly arms, reaching to comfort. Hazel paced circles around it—all those winters ago, she had seen Ansel from her bedroom, holding her dad's shovel. She had convinced her teenage self that it had been a dream, but as Hazel trailed the base of the tree, it seemed crucial that she find the spot.

She crouched, squinted. Alert for the first time in days, Hazel stood over a patch of earth where the grass had been flattened, turned up bare. As Hazel pulled her father's shovel off the wall of the garage, the plastic handle cold beneath her fingers, she knew it had not been a dream. She had seen Ansel out here, in the glow of the winter moon. He had been digging.

By the time Hazel's shovel hit the little box, her nails were black with dirt. She flicked on her cell phone light, aimed it into the pit—she'd hit an old jewelry box of Jenny's, plastic and unsentimental. The sort of clutter Jenny would never miss. Hazel brushed the soil away and tucked the box awkwardly beneath her dress, before pushing discreetly back into the house. Head down, she ducked for the stairs.

Her parents had recently renovated—they'd turned Hazel and Jenny's old bedroom into a gym. When Hazel creaked the door open, she almost expected to see her ballet shoes hanging from hooks on the wall, makeup scattered across the surface of Jenny's dresser. The smell of exercise equipment hit her instead, the metallic tang of the dumbbells her father never used. A treadmill sat in the center of the room and a series of workout DVDs were lined up beneath the static television. In the corner, Hazel could still see the imprints in the carpet where the feet of Jenny's bed had dug in.

She sat on the edge of the treadmill, ran a hand along the track of unmoving vinyl. She let a wave of grief engulf her, then pass. Like when they were little, playing in the surf on the Nantucket shore. *When you see a wave, you have to make a choice,* Jenny had instructed, bossy as always. *Either swim against it or ride it home.*

The box in Hazel's lap was caked in a sheet of dirt.

She cleared it away, flecking soil onto the carpet as she clicked open the lid. There was no wave of recognition. No crush of nostalgia. The jewelry inside did not belong to Jenny. Hazel had never seen it before. A beaded barrette, and a small pearl bracelet.

Disappointment crashed down, a foamy burst. Luis would know what to do with the jewelry, the hole in the ground, the unanswerable questions. Hazel could only revel in the unfairness. The inescapability.

This was her story now. It would always be something that had happened to Jenny, and to Hazel, and she would be rewriting the narrative for the rest of her life, shaping it, defining it, hurling it against the wall. It would be years before she learned to inhabit a world without her sister, if such a thing were even possible. The magnitude of what she'd lost felt reckless, inexhaustible. She had not yet considered Ansel in any real way—she pushed the anger away when it nudged at her ribs, too immersed in the long swim through shock. This was not about him. It never had been. It seemed insane, almost laughable, that one person—Ansel, a single man, so deeply average—had created a chasm so colossal.

Hazel closed her eyes and wished the gym equipment away. She prayed desperately for a Summoning, but all she got was this: the reception clattering on downstairs, the pattering unfairness of her own ragged breath. It seemed that from now on, nothing would be a Summoning, or everything would be, depending how she saw it. Hazel was no longer one half of a whole, but instead the whole itself—a Summoning was not magic, or telepathy, or some freaky twin thing. Jenny was gone, and now their connection was as primal and elusive as the fluid in which they'd both been formed. It was cellular. It was infinite. Simply, it was memory.

Saffy

2012

When Saffy heard the news, she pictured Jenny's collarbone. The hollow of Jenny's throat, contracting as she inhaled, cigarette between her lips. How Jenny had looked, all those years ago outside the emergency room—like she'd known, somehow, where all of this was going.

Corinne called late on a Tuesday. Saffy was slumped on her living room couch, case files splayed obscene on the coffee table. In the time since Lawson's suicide, the slog was insistent, pushing relentlessly on—more overdoses along the border, a body they'd caught from Troop C. The job didn't care that her case had crumbled. The morning after Lawson's trial date, Saffy picked up an extra-large coffee and got back to work.

Saffy answered the phone, swiping a trail of popcorn crumbs from the folds of her T-shirt.

"Captain." Corinne's voice was steady, efficient. "You should sit down for this."

"Just tell me."

"Jenny Fisk, from the 1990 case. The homicide squad down in Houston found her a few days ago. Multiple stab wounds. They brought the ex-husband in, but they didn't have enough evidence to hold him. It's your guy, Captain. Ansel Packer."

The scent of burnt popcorn was suddenly nauseating, chemical and repulsive.

"I'm sorry," Corinne said. "I know this isn't a good time for—"

"Thank you, Sergeant."

Saffy hung up.

Just a week ago, she had slept outside the Blue House. A week ago, she stood across from Blue and Rachel, told them things she'd never admitted to anyone. It had provided an easy relief, a cozy sense of pride—here was Blue, the same age as the others, alive and sunburnt in her faded plastic flip-flops. Guilt came, then horror. A drip, then a flood.

Saffy had not saved anyone.

•

The woman appeared on her stoop the next evening.

Saffy's fingers were slick with marinade, from the chicken cutlets Kristen had adamantly delivered. A dusky forest haze filtered in through the window. The cicadas hummed, restless. Saffy wiped her hands on a paper towel and padded in her socks to the door.

The woman on the porch had hair cut short. A large mole dotted her cheek. Her face was like a wound, open, smarting. Saffy recognized her immediately: in the photo from the news reports, Jenny Fisk leaned forward on a couch, smiling easy. The obituary had run in the Burlington paper—*survived by her parents and her twin sister.*

"I'm sorry to bother you at home," the woman said. "My name is Hazel Fisk. I, um, I found something. Sergeant Caldwell sent me, she said you'd want to see."

Saffy led Hazel to the living room, where twilight seeped in mellow rays across the rug. Saffy did not realize how attentively, unconsciously, she had studied Jenny's face—Hazel was the shadow imprint of her sister, warped in grief.

Hazel pulled a plastic bag from her purse and handed it over, explaining. Saffy clicked open the dirt-lined box, careful not to fingerprint—when she peered inside, her throat rushed with a melancholic regret. She should have felt relief. She should have felt satisfaction. She had been right all along. But as Saffy studied the trinkets, she felt only a long, stretching sorrow, the kind of probing sadness that seemed to seep, then absorb. It looked so small, so helpless, at the bottom of the plastic bag. Lila's purple ring.

"That ring," Hazel said. "He gave it to Jenny the same night I saw him digging in the yard. It's connected to this jewelry, isn't it?"

Saffy almost told her the truth. The trinkets, what they signified. It made a crooked sort of sense: Ansel had given Jenny the ring, then realized his own incrimination. He'd linked himself to the girls—he had to get rid of the rest. Or maybe it was something else, some psychological complexity Saffy couldn't bother to guess. It didn't matter. The shame burned up Saffy's throat, and the words would not come.

She had known all along. For so many years, she had watched Jenny put on lipstick in the rearview, unload shopping bags from the trunk. She had known what Ansel was capable of, and she'd done nothing but observe. Saffy could not tell Hazel about the depth of her failure—already, Hazel looked at her with a blame that could be misread as heartbreak, particularly raw. Saffy knew this expression. Her mistakes lived between them, too permanent to acknowledge.

Saffy walked Hazel back out to her car, with thanks and a promise. She would do her best for Jenny. As the headlights bumped away, Saffy stood in the driveway, a cloud of evening bugs hovering over the pavement. The implications felt heavy, a shadow Saffy could not shake. That paralyzing what-if. What if she had never followed Ansel? If she had never meddled, if she had let him stay at the Blue House? What if Ansel's time with the Harrisons had been simple, if his intentions had been pure all along? There was a world Saffy could not bear to consider—a world that was quickly consuming her own—in which Saffy had turned Ansel into exactly the monster she needed him to be.

•

They still came, the girls. They were older now, grown into themselves. They were mothers, travelers, amateur bakers. Fans of trashy television, fans of the Mets, regional women's pinball champions. They were avid hikers and Sunday brunchers, a trio of karaoke queens, ice cream lovers, morning masturbators, hosts of legendary Halloween parties.

The possibilities stalked and haunted—the infinite number of lives they had not lived. Often, Saffy pictured Lila, stroking her swollen belly, pregnant for the third time, praying for a girl. A girl would be more vulnerable and also more cavernous. Imagine, Lila seemed to say, from the depths of Saffy's subconscious. There were so many things a girl could be.

When Hazel's headlights disappeared from the window, Saffy put the chicken back in the fridge and poured herself a bowl of Frosted Flakes. The trinkets sat in their box, looming from the counter. She flipped open her laptop, a beacon in the blackening kitchen. There was a flight to Houston early in the morning—she booked it quickly, then dialed Detective Rollins.

Detective Andrea Rollins was one of twelve women who made up the informal group, formed after the magazine profile published. *Women in Blue: The Female Rise in Law Enforcement.* Saffy had been photographed alongside Rollins and the others in an embarrassingly glossy spread—in the months that followed the article, they began a sardonic email chain where they riffed and complained, bounced the theories no one else would hear. Andrea Rollins was a senior detective with Houston homicide.

"Captain Singh," Rollins sighed into the receiver. "It's not looking good."

"Who found her?"

"A nosy neighbor, just a few hours postmortem. The condo's front door was hanging open. Neighbor saw a white pickup truck lingering on the street, CCTV turned up the license plate. By the time we tracked Ansel Packer down, he'd wiped the car seats clean and driven halfway across the state."

"You couldn't hold him?"

"The murder weapon is long gone. He could have ditched it anywhere. We tried fingerprinting, but he wiped down the doorknobs, everything. We threatened him pretty good. I don't think he'll leave the state. We've got his motel room under constant surveillance just in case."

"Rollins, I'm coming down tomorrow. Packer is a suspect in an old case of mine, and I just found new evidence."

Rollins let out a long, whistling breath. "Let me talk to my commander. I'll see what we can do."

"Send me your file," Saffy said. "I want a confession."

Detective Rollins was waiting at baggage claim—an elegant woman with curly hair, no makeup, and a ripened fatigue lurking in the round of her shoulders. As they sped down the scorching Texas highway, sirens blaring, Rollins filled Saffy in. Ansel Packer wouldn't talk; he'd shut down completely. Her commander was skeptical but desperate. Saffy could have an hour with him.

Saffy studied the plains as they flicked by, parched and withering. A memory had arrived that morning, a relief in its innocence: Miss Gemma's house, those oatmeal raisin cookies. Saffy recalled that day with painful lucidity—how the sugar had crumbled, white and aging in Kristen's palm. How Ansel had believed those cookies could somehow equalize him, make up for the harm he'd done. Saffy thought about the cookies as Rollins toured her through the Houston Police Department, as she shook the commander's hand. She thought about those cookies as she promised, once more, that New York would not interfere with their investigation, that Texas could have him, that she only wanted a confession for the girls, and their families. She thought about those cookies as she stepped into the blank, gloomy room.

The cookies were proof, breathing in the void of Saffy's memory: Ansel Packer was capable of feeling sorry. They were a testament to how the brain could skew itself. The many intricate ways that people could be wrong.

•

The interrogation room was gray and anonymous. Ansel sat at the table, his arms hanging limp. Saffy could smell his breath from the door, stagnant and sour—he'd been sitting in this room for over three hours, and the detectives had been carefully wearing him down. A cold metal chair, lopsided in the legs, plus a low buzzing sound, set to an irritating frequency. A series of endless and degrading questions. Good cop, then bad cop, then good cop again. According to Rollins, Ansel had only asked for water. He had used the bathroom once. He was not interested in talking. Saffy had expected Ansel to argue his own innocence, to rage at the unfairness; apparently, he'd done exactly this at first, insisting he did not need a lawyer. But he was tired now, bleary and spent. She had expected to feel hurt, or rage, or hate, upon seeing him. But there was only a lagging sort of pity.

Saffy adjusted the chair, straightened her jacket.

She clasped her hands atop the cool metal, a sign of patience, a subtle comfort. Ansel's expression was barren, utterly empty. She was not surprised: he didn't recognize her.

"So," Saffy said. "Let's talk about Jenny."

Saffy wished he would fight, or sneer, or laugh at her. She wanted Ansel to flip the game, to argue his own brilliance. *Prove it*, Saffy dared. A challenge. *Prove to me that you are worth all this.* His silence was dumb and disappointing. She thought about those TV shows, addictive and misleading—in scenes like these, glossy lawyers hovered over handsome men. Evil geniuses, masterminds who planned horror for the sake of it, angular faces that hid some unmatched cleverness beneath the veneer of their devilry. It was almost pathetic, this distance from reality: Ansel was no evil genius. He did not even seem particularly smart. From across the table, the brilliant psychopath she'd hounded all these years looked to Saffy like an unremarkable man, aging and apathetic, bloated and dull. Some men, Saffy knew, killed from a place of anger. Others killed from humiliation, or hatred, or depraved sexual need. Ansel was not rare or mystifying. He was the least nuanced of them all, a murky combination of all the above. A small and boring man who killed because he felt like it.

"Who are you, anyway?" Ansel asked.

"New York State Police," Saffy said.

She flashed her badge, let his gaze flicker.

"Why are you here?"

"Why do you think?"

"I can leave whenever I want," he said.

"Yes," Saffy said. "But I brought something I think you'll want to see."

She lifted her briefcase into her lap, placed a coy hand on the latch.

"You're playing games with me," Ansel said.

"I didn't come all this way to play games," Saffy said. "Why don't you tell me about Jenny? She seemed like a good wife."

Ansel looked down at his hands, an approximation of apology. He was still in control—the anger had burrowed deep. He would make Saffy dig.

"She was a great wife," he said.

"Until she left you."

"It was a mutual separation," he said. "She found a new job in Texas. I told her to take it."

"That's not what her sister said."

Ansel snorted. "Hazel's always been jealous."

"Jealous of what?"

"Of me and Jenny, everything we had. I would never hurt her, you have to understand."

"I understand. Jenny was the only girl for you. The only one you loved."

"Yes."

"But there were other girls, too."

She let him sit with this.

"Blue Harrison," Saffy offered.

A sudden sharpness, as Ansel folded his arms across his chest.

"How do you know about that?"

"I stopped by the Blue House for lunch. I know Rachel, and I know Blue. I know you were in Tupper Lake, staying in the motel down the road."

"They needed help. The restaurant was going under. I was fixing up their deck."

"What I can't understand," Saffy said slowly, "is what you really wanted from the Harrisons."

"They were family," he said simply.

"That's it?"

"That's it."

And there it was: the flash of realization, angling across his exhausted face.

"It was you," Ansel breathed. "You're the reason they sent me away. What did you tell them?"

"You didn't hurt her." Saffy ignored him. "You didn't hurt Blue."

"Why would I hurt her?"

"She's the right age."

This close, Saffy could see every pore on Ansel's nose. The lines around his eyes seemed to squint, then narrow.

"I spent a long time looking for those girls, you know," Saffy said. "Izzy. Angela. Lila. They were our age in school. You remember Lila, don't you? You remember how she used to sing along to the *Jeffersons* theme song?"

A dazed confusion, as he puzzled her.

"Ah," Saffy said. "You really don't recognize me, do you?"

Saffy's phone lay on the table between them, queued and ready. When she hit play, the opening notes of the song brought a bursting life into the concrete space. They whined, they drifted. As Nina Simone's rasping voice filled every corner of the room, Saffy waited for the transfiguration. The saxophone moaned, stuttered—*I put a spell on you.* Ansel blinked fast, his focus captured.

"We were young. Eleven or twelve," Saffy said.

It landed. A visible unrest. Ansel shifted like he wanted to stand, or run, and Saffy knew that she had snagged something. Whatever substance Ansel was made of, finally, she had touched it.

"The fox came first," she said. "Those animals, at Miss Gemma's house, down along the creek. Can you describe it to me, Ansel? I want to know how it felt, to hurt them."

"It felt like nothing," he said.

"That seems unfair," Saffy said. "I mean, I imagine it feels good to kill something. The release. The relief. It must feel good, right? Otherwise, what's the point?"

"It feels like nothing," Ansel said. "Like nothing at all."

The song accelerated into climax, ethereal and uncanny. Saffy reached into her briefcase.

"You know what these are."

First, the barrette. Then, the bracelet. Little bits of dirt were caught in the barrette's clip, between the bracelet's milky pearls. A sheen of sweat had broken across Ansel's forehead—he appraised the trinkets like an archaeologist, uncovering lost artifacts.

"I'm curious, Ansel," Saffy said. "Why did you take these? What purpose did they serve?"

"I don't know what you're—"

"Wait, you don't have to explain. I can tell you the story. You were at Jenny's house for Christmas that year. You were what, seventeen or eighteen, right? Hazel told me all about it. Her parents got you those nice gifts, even after Jenny promised they wouldn't, and you felt small and poor and insecure. You'd been carrying these trinkets for months, because you liked the memory, a reminder of a moment where you were big and important. You gave the ring to Jenny that day to feel a little taste of that power again. But then you realized what you'd done. You'd incriminated yourself—if anyone recognized the ring, you'd be in deep shit. So you got up in the middle of the night and buried the rest in the yard."

"It wasn't like that."

"What was it like, then?"

"I gave her the ring because it was beautiful. I wanted her to have it."

"But you took this jewelry off those girls. When you left their bodies in the woods. You took these trinkets to remember. To relive all the sick things you'd done."

"No," he said, louder now. "No. Stop."

"You got high off remembering. You relished in it. You loved—"

"Stop!" A bark of a yell. He heaved, his breath fading ragged. "I never relished in anything."

It was like a crack of lightning. The breaking was physical, a massive shudder, the sign Saffy recognized from her many years in interrogation rooms like this one—his walls were crumbling. One more nudge, and he would shatter.

"Then why?" Saffy asked gently. "Why did you need to take these trinkets?"

Ansel reached for the bracelet, his fingers shaking wild. He could not stop himself. He slipped the delicate strand of pearl onto his hairy wrist, admiring the ivory beads, elegant and feminine.

"They were supposed to keep me safe."

"You killed those girls for the same reason you killed Jenny. Because you felt small."

"No," Ansel said, remarkably calm. "You're wrong. I don't know why I killed them. I don't know why I killed any of them."

Ansel stroked the pearls affectionately as he spoke, as if in a trance. His voice, distinctly childlike in its recounting. The story formed, the details fused. The recording device clicked forward, forward.

He confessed.

•

As the story spooled from Ansel's mouth, Saffy saw her perfectly. Jenny, that night, as she should have been.

She would have been tired. She would have set her purse on the counter, flicked on the lights, turned a Sheryl Crow album loud on the speaker. There would have been no banging at the door—the kitchen knife would have sat, untouched in its plain wooden stand.

Jenny would have microwaved a bowl of leftovers, then eaten them standing up over the kitchen counter.

After, she'd have run a bath. A splash of eucalyptus oil. Jenny would have stripped off her scrubs and lowered herself in; submerged in steaming warmth, her muscles would have released, exhaling the ordinary day. She'd have lowered herself farther, farther, until her head went fully under, the glassy pulse of water like an echo, or the thoughtless slip into a dream. The sound of her heartbeat, miraculous in its magnification, expanding along the porcelain walls. This quiet, exquisite—this being, a wonder. Time stoppered, sublime.

•

The detectives swarmed. They wrenched Ansel from the chair, cuffed his wrists harsh. Standing with his arms twisted behind, Ansel looked weary and puny, vaguely apologetic.

Saffy remembered how it felt to walk up Miss Gemma's basement steps, with Ansel's presence close on her heels. His lumbering gait, her own hammering nausea. She had craved that fleeting sense of danger. Love, she had been told, was both thrilling and noxious, an addictive threat that defied all logic—love was footsteps on the bottom stair, a pair of hands at the base of her throat. But love did not have to be tainted with hurt. She thought of Kristen and her kids, splashing in the backyard pool, singing along to some pop song Saffy didn't know. She thought of Corinne and her wife, hands clasped proudly at the station's Christmas party. Saffy had spent her life so steeped in this examination of pain, what it meant, why it persisted. She had spent her years chasing pointless violence, if only to prove it could not touch her. What a waste this hunt had been. What a disappointment. She had finally solved this epic mystery—touched the place where Ansel's hurt had congealed—only to find his pain looked just like everyone else's. The difference lay in what he chose to do with it.

"Saffy, wait."

Her own name was like a wound, oozing from his mouth.

"Do you ever wonder about an alternate universe?" Ansel's voice cracked, desperate, as the officers tugged him forward. "Another world out there, where we both live different lives? Where maybe we've made different choices?"

"I wonder all the time," Saffy said, nearly a whisper. "But there's only this world, Ansel. Just this one."

They marched him away.

Alone, the interrogation room was deathly still, the walls frigid and impersonal. A gritty disappointment settled beneath Saffy's skin—there was no surge of victory. No swell of triumph. It was impossible to think about the lives she could have lived without thinking of those she could have saved. So Saffy decided not to consider them at all. From that moment forward, she would forget that tempting almost-world; there was only this, a brief and imperfect and singular reality. She would have to find a way to live it.

Lavender

2019

The locket was old. Rusty, burnt orange with age. When Lavender reached into the pocket of her sweater, the shape of the charm felt soothing, an enduring ridge across the pad of her thumb. Today, the pooling chain felt less like accusation and more like possibility. Or maybe just a reminder of history.

"Milk and sugar?" the girl asked.

The girl looked, to Lavender, like the best kind of poem. Standing over the table, holding a pot of coffee, her every gesture was a series of letters, melding into one graceful sentence. The fact of her existence still seemed shaky, like the vastness of the universe might swallow her back up again.

Blue, a girl with freckled cheeks. Blue, a name in

vivid color. Blue, a feeling not quite sorrow—a blooming like grief, with its petals curled open.

•

The restaurant was special. Lavender knew it the moment she walked in. There was a coziness to the place, a stimulating sort of energy—Harmony had been talking about auras for years, and Lavender had always chalked it up to hippie nonsense. But it felt reasonable now, as she stirred a sugar cube into her coffee, fingers twitching nervous. The Blue House seemed to pulse with a warm, hazy light.

Lavender sipped at the coffee, perfectly bitter, as Blue untied her apron and hung it on the back of the rickety chair. Her heart roared, a rioting beast. Lavender had imagined this scene so many times, it was almost like she'd lived it already—but Blue's face had been hazy in her abstractions, a combination of the photos she'd seen of Ellis, the photos she'd seen of Blue, now twenty-three years old, and the memory of herself at that age. Vaguely a woman, vaguely a girl. She'd stared openly this morning when Blue met her at the airport in Albany, stolen careful glances as they made small talk through the drive upstate. Blue was both exactly how Lavender had imagined and also completely different. Where Lavender was gaunt and inelegant, Blue was round and inviting. Lips plump, cheekbones high. She wore a pair of jeans, snug on the hips and ripped at the knee, and her hair was braided long over one shoulder. Her knuckles were stacked with silver rings, the kind purchased from street vendors and thrift stores, and she had a small tattoo of a humming-bird cresting the inside of her wrist. Lavender knew from the photos they'd exchanged that Blue's hair was exactly the color of her own—a shade of strawberry nearly translucent in the sun. The sight in person was like a fist to the gut. As they wound up the mountain road and into Tupper Lake, a lump of amazement had lodged firm in Lavender's throat.

Now, Blue sat across the café table, so close and so real that Lavender could see each of her granddaugh-ter's willowy eyelashes. She could not help it. When Lavender began to cry, it felt like a split of thunder, a cloud breaking over a summer afternoon.

●

It started with a letter.

The first envelope had arrived nearly a year ago. Lavender and Sunshine had just moved into Magnolia house, the family unit with the best kitchen in all of

Gentle Valley—the women had unanimously agreed that Sunshine should have the glossy, capable stove. Sunshine, with her blistered red hands, which Lavender often traced in her sleep. Sunshine, who spoke entire conversations through a zap of cinnamon in a pan of flaxseed muffins. Sunshine, who cupped a gentle palm around Lavender's hip when the letter arrived, her presence an instinctual comfort.

Dear Lavender,

You don't know me, but hello. My name is Blue Harrison.

Blue had gotten the address from her grandmother Cheryl. Cheryl had been holding it for years; she'd handed it over reluctantly after a conversation about Ellis's origins. If Lavender was interested, Blue would like to be in touch. She had left a phone number and an email address at the bottom of the page.

Lavender had tucked the letter beneath her pillow, where she let it simmer for nearly a month. There was a landline in the Sequoia building, but Lavender was awkward over the phone, stilted with lack of experience. Sunshine sometimes pulled her laptop out before bed, and they flicked through photos of Minnie's life online. Sunshine's daughter ran a bakery in Mendocino, with a baby of her own. But the internet seemed like a foreign, complicated place.

So Lavender sat down with a sheet of paper and her favorite felt-tip pen. All those years, crafting letters in her head.

Practice, just for this.

She wrote about Gentle Valley. About the sun, glowing orange over the hills at daybreak, about the rosemary sprouting in Sunshine's herb garden. She and Sunshine had taken a trip to the Grand Canyon, Lavender's first time on an airplane, and she told Blue about the red-clay cliffs, the way the chasms had curved, like bends in a river. Blue sent warm anecdotes in return. By the time months had passed, dozens of letters had been exchanged, and Lavender could picture Ellis's beard, the heft of his shoulders as he bounced along to the radio in the Blue House kitchen.

Lavender brought it up herself. She couched the question in the middle of a paragraph, so discreet it could be easily ignored. Just writing the words brought back the old sludge of guilt, flooding inexorable.

Do you know anything about my other son, Ansel?

Blue's response took weeks to arrive. When it did,

Lavender understood that her granddaughter had taken care to be particularly gentle. *Ansel spent some time in the Blue House, seven years ago,* she wrote. *I can tell you more, if you're sure you want to hear. But I'll warn you, it's painful.*

The feeling was wider than curiosity—Lavender knew that to scratch at the truth would bring her peace, no matter the hurt. She had never before hungered for information. It was a sign. Her wounds had scarred. Her days had rooted. She was ready.

It's not the kind of thing you should read in a letter, Blue had replied, when Lavender pressed for more. *But I have an idea. Why don't you come out to the Blue House?* The women of Gentle Valley had thrilled at the idea, put the funds together without question.

Now, Lavender watched as Blue talked, unselfconscious, a charming lilt to her voice. An extrovert. Blue unknotted her braid and ran her fingers through her hair, wafting the scent of young-girl deodorant as she chattered idly about her apartment in Brooklyn, the restaurant she worked at in the city, her volunteer work with the animal shelter. Lavender nodded along, awestruck. *I made this person,* she thought, as Blue's hands fluttered unencumbered. It seemed miraculous, such cosmic grace. Like the first peep of green after a long gray winter.

After dinner, they sat on the deck. String lights had been woven through the slats in the polished wood, and the night was humid, gusting a floral breeze as the dishwasher whirred. Rachel had excused herself with a warm goodnight; Blue's mother was both generous and reserved, patient with her daughter's curiosity.

"Is it weird to be here?" Blue asked.

Lavender leaned forward in the plastic deck chair. She peered into the shadowy yard—the land shifted, stilled into night.

"It's easier than I imagined," Lavender said.

"I can still feel him here, sometimes. My dad."

"I think I can, too." It was true. Lavender could feel Ellis in strange, glimpsing slivers. He was in the carefully framed maps of the Adirondack peaks, in the blinding blue of the house's exterior paint. He was in the arc and slant of Blue's pale cheek.

"Ansel was here, too?" Lavender asked. "He found you?"

The question inflated, metastasized.

"I found him, actually." Blue picked at her nails, a chipped periwinkle. "I invited him here."

"I'm ready, sweetheart. Whatever it is, you can tell me."

"Before I say anything," Blue said, "you should know that I was happy to meet him. He was happy to be here. He helped us around the house, didn't ask anything in return. We closed up the restaurant with my mom, laughed into the night. It was easy, with him. Almost like having my dad back again. Sometimes, when I think about what he did, who he is, I still don't want to believe it."

"Go on," Lavender said.

An anguish arrived on Blue's face, sweet and pained, pleading apologetic.

"I'm sorry," Blue said. "I'm so sorry to tell you this."

•

The night was an open sore. The heart was an organ that beat on and on. The trees creaked their unanimous sorrow.

•

Lavender slept fitfully. She dreamed episodically of women she did not know, strangers in the distance, naked and screaming. Downstairs, the industrial refrigerator grumbled like a starving belly. Blue's words hovered, menacing little ghosts over the unfamiliar bed—she had only told Lavender the outline of the story, no real details, but it ballooned monstrous.

She could not picture it. Lavender could not picture the little boy she had known doing any of the things Blue described. She could not imagine him waiting in a prison cell, counting down his days. She could not fathom that word. Execution. The man who had grown from her child felt as distant as the cucumbers she'd planted last summer and failed to bring to fruit.

When the bed became a cage, Lavender crept into the hall. Early morning, still black. Blue's bedroom door was cracked open—a beam of moonlight shone onto the lump of her, illuminating. Her face was peaceful in sleep, so devastatingly young.

Give yourself a moment every day, Harmony had suggested once in group therapy. *A single moment in which you are absolved of all responsibility.*

How much responsibility could a person hold, Lavender wondered. How much, before the overflow?

Lavender slid to the floor outside Blue's bedroom, her knees cracking like gunshots all the way down. There were people who could look atrocity in the eye and keep marching forward—people who did such things by choice. But atrocity was not a thing Lavender could afford to consider. Blue's breath came steady and even through the door, like the flow of some earth-bound tide. It seemed, then, that mothering did not have to be so rigid. There was no arc to it, no frame through which it ended or began. Mothering could be as simple as this: a woman and her very own blood, breathing in tandem through the darkest heart of night.

The rest of Lavender's visit passed quickly, brimming with novelty. Blue twined a steady arm through Lavender's—they took walks around the lake, naming the trees. Blue showed Lavender her collection of little treasures: a perfectly round acorn, a tiny glass-blown statue of a sheep, a diamond earring with a broken setting she'd found in Central Park. In these objects, Lavender could see her granddaughter's softness, her pristine strangeness. Blue promised she would come to Gentle Valley soon, where Lavender guaranteed a pan of Sunshine's famous cinnamon rolls. They posed for a selfie, Blue's phone outstretched as they pressed their temples together, grinning against the backdrop of the mountains.

On Lavender's last night in the Blue House, Rachel joined them at the bar for a whiskey. Glazed and sleepy, tipsy with laughter, Lavender began to talk. Blue and Rachel listened attentively, silhouettes perched curious.

As she told them everything she could remember—the sparkling and the hideous, the fond and the searing—a fraction of her life's weight seemed to lift with the words. This was the gift of the young, Lavender thought. They had the strength to carry.

"Ansel had this idea," Blue said, after Rachel had gone to bed. Lavender leaned back against the bar's pocked mahogany, her glass empty. "He talked about it a lot: the other worlds that might exist, if you changed just one tiny choice. The infinite universe, or whatever. I still think about it sometimes—how things might have been different, if I'd never found Ansel. If I'd never invited him here."

"I ask those questions, too," Lavender said.

And it was true: Lavender no longer wondered about the farmhouse, or California, or any of the choices she made to save herself. Those had been necessary. But she would always wonder about the letters, the hundreds or thousands she'd written in her head. Dear Ansel. What would have happened, if she'd sent just one? Lavender wondered if she could have made the difference. If her child had only needed his mother.

"When is it happening?" Lavender asked, choking a bit. "The execution?"

"Next month," Blue said. "We've kept in touch a bit. He asked me to witness."

"Will you go?"

"I think so," Blue said. She glanced around the dining room, the tables streaked with bleach, the looming chairs. She seemed to ponder. "I wrote back last week. I told him yes."

"Why?" Lavender asked.

"I only knew the good person," Blue said. "The person he could have been. Those other universes—I guess I want to honor them."

"That's generous," Lavender said.

Blue only shrugged. "He's family. Someone should be there, I think."

"Wait, I'm sorry," Lavender said. A sudden suffocation. "Don't tell me any more. I don't want to know the date. I don't want to be waiting."

Lavender reached into the pocket of her sweater: it was there like always, that tiny weight. In the yeasty dim, her mother's locket looked shabby. Decrepit. In a matter of hours, Lavender would be home. She would let this quell, then fade. She would sink back into her days with Sunshine, and she would not ask Blue for any more details—Lavender would do the only thing possible to ensure her own survival. She would refuse to take custody.

"Will you take this with you?" Lavender asked.

Blue reached for the locket. She clasped it easy

around her neck, the chain glistening along her collar-bone. It was like sinking backward in time, Lavender thought. Like looking in a mirror at a younger self, glittering, golden. So blessedly unbroken.

"He won't be alone?" Lavender said.

"He won't be alone," Blue told her. "I promise."

Lavender knew, then, that the world was a forgiving place. That every horror she had lived or caused could be balanced with such gutting kindness. It would be a tragedy, she thought—inhumane—if we were defined only by the things we left behind.

18 Minutes

E very second is a year. Every second is your failure, every second is your lifeline. Every second goes to waste.

When you think of your confession now, you feel a burning incredulity—you cannot believe you said those things aloud.

Your lawyer tried vaguely to argue coercion, but your confession felt more physiological than that. A force, expelled. Saffron Singh was a bridge. A line drawn, an arrow pointed. When she took the pearl bracelet out of its evidence bag, when she slid the beaded barrette across the table, she took you back to those nights on the forest floor. Back to the Girls. Throughout those long teenage months, you carried the jewelry with you, loose in your pockets or on the dashboard of your car. It calmed you. The day you gave Jenny that ring—a thoughtless whim—you'd buried the rest in a panic. It was a shock to see those trinkets again, laid out like cadavers on a table.

Then, the song. Your old favorite. You remembered a fox, half decomposed. The irony: your child self led you here.

So it was not you who told the story—instead, that little boy. He possessed you, in the indignity of the interrogation room, eleven years old with sorry doleful eyes. You spoke to make the little boy happy. You spoke to set him free. As you sealed your own fate, there seemed an exquisite pain in the knowledge. There would be no release.

•

You have asked the chaplain not to return. You will see him in the execution room, and you cannot bear to spend your last sixteen minutes looking at his droopy, benevolent face. Alone, you pull your Theory from the floor. Gritty with dust, you reassemble the manuscript page by page—it looks unfinished in your hands, a disconnected series of digressions.

You wanted to talk about good and evil. You wanted to talk about the spectrum of morality. You wanted to talk, and you wanted someone to listen. You think of the men back at Polunsky—their hopeful chess moves, their hoarded photos, their sobs and moans in the middle of the night. A wash of embarrassment roils over you: Your Theory was supposed to make you different. It was supposed to make you special, better, more.

Now, the irony feels intolerably sharp. If you believe in the multiverse, you have to look at this:

You are seventeen years old, at the end of a long driveway. The first Girl appears, a doe in your headlights. You ease on the brakes, open the door. Do you need a ride? You wait at the curb until she's safely inside. You are seventeen years old, sitting in that diner booth, nursing one last cup of coffee, working up the nerve to ask the waitress for her number. You are seventeen years old, in the crowd at that concert—when the last Girl offers you a cigarette, you take it. You smoke it down to the butt. You thank her. You go home.

•

Twelve minutes. The walls shrink, condense. You pull your knees to your chest, and weakly, you pray. You have never believed in God, but you address him now, last-ditch, halfhearted. God, if you are out there. God, if you can hear me. God—

•

You remember a meteor shower. You were small, maybe three. Grass poked through the thick wool blanket, and you gazed up with a child's awe. Your mother's breath was sour and sweet, like a dream in-terrupted halfway through. She held you by the ribs as comets shot across the sky. It is a comfort to know that once, you were little enough to be cradled. Once, there was only wheatgrass and wonder, the earth turn-ing ordinary beneath the train of your spine.

•

You begin to cry.

Thoughtless, wordless. You cry like it is the last thing you will ever do, which maybe it is. You cry until you are not yourself anymore, until the sob has overtaken your body and transformed you mercifully into someone, anyone else. You cry for your Theory. For the person you were when you woke up this morning. You cry for the number of breaths you will not take, for the mornings you will not squint into the sun, the long drives you will not steer down mountain roads, the whiskey that will not sting your throat. Forty-six years you have lived, and all of it, for what. For this.

When it's over, you straighten. You wipe your eyes, blow your nose onto the floor in a gleaming puddle. Though you refuse to look at the clock on the wall, you can feel them ticking by, slipping effortlessly from the room. Those seconds. You want to hold on to each one, to feel the texture of your life as it slinks regretfully away.

•

It is a surprise, but the inevitable kind, when you hear the footsteps ascending from the mouth of the hall.

It is time.

Vaguely, you want to fight. You want to kick and scream in the name of the things you will lose, but that sounds grueling, and painful, and useless. Down the hall, the footsteps shuffle louder. The tie-down team. Six trained prison officials will come for you, and they will come now. You have known, of course, that this moment would arrive, but you did not expect it to feel so trivial, just another second blending with the millions that make up your insignificant little life.

You hear the approach. The patter of fate, arriving to sweep you away.

You lift your chin to the sound.

Lavender

Now

Lavender bends over the laundry tub. Her knees are bare and dusty, sore from crouching in the dirt. Afternoon brightens over the Sequoia building. Inside, the women are washing the lunch dishes, bickering over the clang of pots and pans. Beyond the laundry basin, Lavender can see the silhouetting crest of the mountains, hazy wild citrus in the full day's light. At the bottom of the hill, Sunshine bends over the vegetable garden in her wide straw hat. Lavender is sixty-three years old now, and she does not believe in happiness, not as a pure or categoric thing. But she does believe in the future, and she can see it now, stretching luxurious down the mountain, across the rippling grass. Sunshine pulls a zucchini from the vine, her body like a map, the ridges and peaks so carefully charted.

The sound begins soft at first, barely discernible. Lavender sits straight, wondering if she's imagined it. She stretches to make it out—there. A whine, a gasp. An animal, dying in the gut of the woods. Lavender goes still, hovering with sudsy arms over the basin. The whimper deepens.

Something is in pain.

She tilts her head.

She listens.

Saffy
Now

S affy steps from the shower. The mirror is cloudy—even through the condensation, the weight of this night sits heavy on her shoulders. Her funeral outfit is laid out on the bed, like a weary person flopped down exhausted. Saffy has worn this black dress to hundreds of funerals, her hair pulled into an authoritative bun. It feels too crisp tonight, too formal.

She wonders, vaguely, what Ansel is doing now. Eating his last meal or staring up at a blank gray ceiling. She hopes the cell is cold, she hopes his thoughts are haunting—she hopes, of course, that he is sorry. That he is afraid. As the sun sinks through the blinds, Saffy is grateful that Texas is so far away, that soon he will be somewhere else entirely, or maybe nowhere at all.

•

Saffy's phone pings as she's drying her hair.

Blue Harrison.

I'm here, the text reads. *It's happening soon.*

Saffy still stops by the Blue House occasionally. She orders a tuna melt, chats with Rachel at the bar. When Ansel wrote to invite her to the execution, Blue called the station—*I think I want to go*, she'd said, almost a whisper. *I think I want to be there.* Saffy wasn't sure exactly why Blue had dialed her, but she could hear a quaking in the girl's voice. Blue was asking for permission. For some kind of acknowledgment. Saffy remembered how Ansel had looked as a boy, vulnerable and unstable, broken but not yet gone, his choices still his own to make. Ansel was bad, and he would die for it—but Saffy knew, along with Blue, that he was other things, too.

You should go, Saffy had told her. She could hear the Blue House espresso machine grinding in the background.

Will you come with me? Blue had asked.

The answer was easy. No.

•

The vigil is in the park by the high school.

When Saffy arrives, night has fallen in a velvet blanket, and she sees only the flicker of candles at the far edge of the lawn. She wades across the field toward the huddled, shadowy figures. There are maybe twenty people, a sprinkling crowd, heads bent in the dim candlelight. Saffy has abandoned her funeral dress, swapped it for a long blue skirt, dotted with daisies. She sees Kristen on the fringe, her arms crossed against the April chill—by the time Saffy reaches the spot, her sandals are slick beneath her toes, dewy from the grass.

"You made it," Kristen says.

"We got these for you, Captain." Kristen's older son hands Saffy a bouquet of lilies—he is fifteen years old now, lanky and awkward. Saffy thanks him and takes the bundle, plastic wrap crinkling.

The photographs are blown up huge. Izzy, Angela, and Lila lie propped in a sea of flowers. Saffy recognizes many of the glowing faces surrounding the fountain: Izzy's parents are here, along with her sister. Izzy's little brother was only five years old when she went missing, and now he holds an infant, swaddled in the crook of his arm. Angela's mother stands folded into their group, and she gives Saffy a small wave, stooped, withered. Twenty years have passed since they found the bodies—twenty-nine since the girls went missing—and still, a news camera hovers at the edge of the vigil, determined to make a story. Saffy feels slimy, the truth prickling. There would be no story, for these girls alone. There would be no vigil, no attention at all. They are relevant because of Ansel and the fascination the world has for men like him.

Kristen hands Saffy a candle. The wax drips down, melting onto her fingers.

It is almost time. A thousand miles away, justice is being served—but justice, Saffy thinks, is supposed to feel like more. Justice is supposed to be an anchor, an answer. She wonders how a concept like justice made it into the human psyche, how she ever believed that something so abstract could be labeled, meted out. Justice does not feel like compensation. It does not even feel like satisfaction. As Saffy takes a long breath of alpine air, she pictures the needle, pressing into Ansel's arm. The blue pop of vein. How unnecessary, she thinks. How pointless. The system has failed them all.

•

"Come over tonight," Kristen says, as the crowd disperses. "You shouldn't be alone."

Her son is already in the car, adjusting the mirrors. He has thirty more hours of supervised driving before he can test for his license. Kristen's earrings glint in the rearview, a gifted souvenir from Saffy's trip last year to Rajasthan, gold tasseled droplets with stones that match the warm turquoise of her friend's eyes.

"I can't tonight," Saffy says. "Work."

Kristen smirks, warm, sarcastic. It occurs to Saffy how long they have grown together, how far they have walked, the things they have outlasted. "The parking brake, honey," Kristen says to her son, as she sinks into the passenger's seat. Her voice is like a lullaby, carrying through the night.

•

It's late by the time Saffy reaches the station. A Friday night, and most everyone is gone. Only Corinne remains, bent in the spotlight of her desk lamp.

"Captain," she says. "What are you doing here?"

Corinne glances at the clock. She knows what is happening tonight—Corinne is observant as always, meticulous. Once a month, Saffy has Corinne and Melissa over for dinner, where they sit in her kitchen, chatting as the smell of baked salmon or homemade pizza wafts from the oven. Corinne's wife declined the wine; they have been trying through IVF for a baby. Saffy is grateful for her crow's-feet now, for the lines wrinkling around her mouth. *See?* she wants to tell Corinne. *You don't need to have it all. You only need to figure out how much is enough.*

Saffy almost sits. She almost collapses, rests her head on the cool surface of Corinne's desk. Almost, she confesses the truth: she cannot go home, to that blissfully empty house. Most nights, Saffy is thankful for her solitude, but tonight that gift feels empty. *Why don't you find yourself a good man? You're still pretty, and young enough.* Kensington's wife had looked so sincere as she'd said it, cubic zirconia glinting from her ears. Saffy had smiled politely, wondering what this woman thought she could possibly gain from such a thing.

This, right here, is all she needs. A good fight. The only one.

"The Jackson case," Saffy says to Corinne. A feeling like hope pricks the base of her throat.

Saffy keeps her files stacked on the desk. They waver in piles, messy reminders—when she leans back in the rolling chair, shaking her computer's mouse awake, the white light is comforting, an accusation she knows intimately.

The Jackson case waits, impatient, on her keyboard.

In the photo clipped to the top of the report, Tanisha Jackson is smiling. She is fourteen, her hair in braids, purple beads dangling. She stands in an overgrown backyard—elbows jostle for paper plates in the background. Tanisha has been missing for six days. They have a few promising leads: a teacher at her middle school with a sketchy alibi, a strange man with a scar on his cheek, passing through town. It is a matter, now, of sifting through facts until the truth comes winking to the surface, like gold in a pan. She studies the freckles that span Tanisha's cheeks—Saffy believes that Tanisha is still alive. That vitality is possible even after trauma, that the path does not always lead to devastation. That not every girl must become a Girl.

The minutes stretch, blinking into hours. Saffy jots down notes, chips at the information. She will sit here until dawn. She will sit here until something shakes loose. She will sit here.

Hazel
Now

Hazel stands at the edge of the motel pool. The pool is drained and full of dead leaves, a smattering of plastic lawn chairs lying haphazard around the perimeter.

Hazel's mother appears, fumbling with the key to her room. She has dressed up for the occasion. She wears a pantsuit dug straight out of the eighties, the shoulders too wide for her shrinking frame. She edges around the derelict swimming pool in a pair of chunky black pumps. As her mother comes closer, Hazel feels a mild suffocation—it could be the humidity, or that ill-fitting suit, or the thing her mother's eyes do when they first catch sight of Hazel. They snag, widen. A brief flicker of hope cools into disappointment. In that bottomless millisecond, her mother sees two daughters. Hazel is always the wrong one.

A beige sedan pulls into the motel parking lot, and a woman with a haircut like a poodle approaches them. Linda, she says, as she shakes their hands, her French manicure crisp and bawdy. Linda is a representative from the Texas Department of Criminal Justice Victim Services—she will drive them to the prison, but first, they have paperwork to review.

For months, Hazel's mother has been feigning excitement. *I can't sleep, Hazel, not until I watch him fry.* It has been seven years since Jenny's death. Their father died of a heart attack just six months later, and her mother often refers to them as a unit, like they are together by choice, simply living elsewhere. *They'll be glad to hear it*, she muttered, when Ansel's sentence rippled through the courtroom. But it appears her mother's bravado has evaporated—as Linda sits them down around a water-stained table, as she fans out the stack of paperwork, Hazel's mother looks like she might blow away in the wind.

Linda reviews each page slowly. A description of the offender's crime—*As if we forgot*, Hazel nearly spits—and an overview of the execution process. The evening's schedule, like they are attending the theater. Ansel has invited two witnesses: his lawyer, and a name Hazel has never heard before. Beatrice Harrison.

What is the point of all this? Hazel wants to ask. Ostensibly, today is occurring for her own benefit. For Jenny, for their family, for some twisted form of recompense. But it feels backward. Almost like a gift to Ansel.

He gets the attention. He gets the media, the discourse, the carefully regulated procedure. Real punishment would look different, Hazel knows—like a lonely, epic nothing. A life sentence in a men's prison, the years rotting as they pass. The long forgetting of his name. A heart attack or a slip in the shower, the sort of faceless death he deserves. Instead, Ansel has been given this noble sacrifice. Martyr status. Hazel feels guilty, complicit in the process. She sees the constant stream of Black men on the evening news, shot by police as they're stopped for broken taillights, hauled into prison for carrying a pocketful of weed, and she tries feebly to teach her children about inequity, about institutional prejudice, about the poisonous history of this country's justice system. She makes cardboard signs and marches through Burlington's downtown, chanting for equality. She repeats these phrases to Alma, even as she knows: it is a privilege, to stand in front of the cameras. It is a privilege to be seen, to speak your last words into a microphone. Ansel gets the glorified title of *serial killer*, a phrase that seems to inspire a bizarre, primitive lust. Books and documentaries and dark tunnels on the internet. Crowds of women, captivated.

As Hazel helps her mother into Linda's car, which smells like saltine crackers and air freshener, she feels a magnified sense of helplessness. The dread curls in her gut, a dozing animal.

●

The building is made of stately red brick. Colonial, grandiose. It looks to Hazel like a courthouse or a suburban high school. She helps her mother through the imposing front door.

They are greeted by a somber crowd. The trauma support team, the emergency action staff, titles that flow through Hazel's consciousness like water. The warden is square and stocky, his handshake clammy.

"How was your trip?" he asks.

Hazel's throat is empty of answer. He gestures to the tub where she should place her shoes—the concrete is frigid beneath Hazel's bare feet. The prison smells like linoleum, like dust and metal. They pass through the security scanner, Hazel's mother's hair puffing out of its bun in a wiry frizz, then down the hall to the support room, a dismal parade. Brightly colored office chairs surround a sterile wooden table.

"Water?" the warden asks. "Coffee?"

Hazel shakes her head no. The room echoes when the warden is gone, exaggerating her mother's every shuddering breath. *It will be okay*, Hazel wants to reassure. *It will be better, once all this is over.* But such promises would feel false coming from her mouth, so Hazel only listens to the buzz of the overhead lights, the prison clatter muted through the heavy steel door. She hears the faint din of men. A far whoop, a husky laugh. She waits.

•

Alma woke up early this morning, to say goodbye before the flight. She padded downstairs in her pajamas and perched at the kitchen island while Hazel prepared her coffee for the car. Alma's cheeks were imprinted in the pattern of her pillow, her dark hair pulled into a sloppy bun, tangled and spilling down her shoulders. Alma is fourteen now—she has a mouth full of shiny braces and constantly adjusts the straps of the training bra she doesn't need. Before school, she spends twenty minutes in the bathroom trying to wrangle herself into some unnatural shape. When she laughs, her hand flies self-conscious to her mouth.

Are you going to be okay, Mom? Alma asked, handing over the sugar bowl.

I'll be fine, sweetpea.

Aunt Jenny would be proud. Alma reddened, embarrassed by her own sentimentality. *She'd be proud of how brave you are.*

Hazel cupped her daughter's cheek.

Hazel does not know if Jenny would be proud. In one version of the universe, Jenny's grin is sardonic. *Classic Hazel,* Jenny says, with her signature eye roll. *Making this all about you.* In another, Jenny is relieved to have Hazel there, a body double, a stand-in duplicate. In yet another, Jenny is still alive, and she and Hazel wait in line for coffee—when Jenny turns to take Hazel's order, she looks very much like someone new.

•

The warden returns to the conference room, followed by two men in button-up shirts. They take seats in the far corner, nodding vaguely in acknowledgment—they wear lanyards clipped to plastic badges.

Reporters.

Hazel does not like journalists. In the weeks after Ansel's confession, they parked their vans on her curb, lingered on her lawn. They showed up at Luis's office, at the ballet studio, and they even went once to Mattie's daycare, cameras hefted onto their shoulders. They cornered Hazel outside the playground—*Go away,* she shrieked, as the other mothers ushered their toddlers away. *Please, just leave us alone.*

It has never been about Jenny. Jenny is not interesting. Men kill their ex-wives all the time.

It's about the other girls.

The question, of course, is why. This is the reason the reporters still appear, shoving microphones in Hazel's face, the reason Ansel is granted space in the newspapers. He is captivating. Fascinating. A national phenomenon. It is shocking—*intriguing,* someone told her once—to be so unpredictably bad. Why did he kill those girls as a teenager, then no one until Jenny, twenty years later? Why them? Why then?

Hazel cannot fathom a less interesting question. Of course, she is sorry for those girls, for their families. But the attention, that big question: it baffles her. It does not matter how Ansel felt. His pain is irrelevant, beyond the horizon of her consideration. It does not matter why he killed those girls, or Jenny. Hazel believes that a person can be evil, and nothing more.

There are millions of men out there who want to hurt women—people seem to think that Ansel Packer is extraordinary, because he actually did.

•

The bathroom is lit fluorescent green.

Hazel curls over the sink, wheezing. She exhales, waits for the panic to slink away. The bathroom accosts. A mistake—she should not have come in here. Today, the mirror will not be kind.

It happens in flickers, flashes. When Hazel looks inevitably up from the porcelain, she catches her own reflection, her short hair, that teardrop freckle. But Hazel will never be just herself again: Jenny reveals herself in a flare, a lurch. Jenny smirks in the curve of Hazel's jaw. She hides in the crease of Hazel's eyelid, lingers in the divot above Hazel's lip.

A toilet flushes. Hazel breaks from her trance, startling backward into the sharp corner of the paper towel dispenser. When the stall door creaks open, a girl appears in the frame. She appraises Hazel, confused, the silence curdling.

"I'm sorry, I—" the girl finally stammers. "It's just, you look exactly like her."

"Excuse me?"

She reaches out, passive, as though to shake Hazel's hand, her arm hanging limp between them. A flash of tattoo, a little bird on the inside of her wrist. She is dishwater blond, mid-twenties and notably unsettled, though her eyes flame with a distinct curiosity.

"Um, I'm Blue," she says, like a question. "I'm really sorry, I should have known. He told me Jenny had a twin, I should have—"

"You knew my sister?" Hazel asks.

Blue shakes her head. "I never met her."

The girl's eyes are Ansel's. A faint shade of light green, like early-summer moss.

"You're here for Ansel, aren't you?" Hazel asks. "His witness. You're not—you can't be his daughter."

"Oh," Blue says quickly. "No. I'm his niece."

"Ansel doesn't have any family," Hazel says.

"His brother," Blue says. "My dad."

Hazel remembers that Christmas, so many years ago. How Ansel's face had softened when he'd talked about his baby brother. A mask, she has since assumed, an intentional show of tragedy, engineered specifically for sympathy. Blue steps tentatively past—she flicks the faucet on, pumps soap from the dispenser. Hazel can see bits of Ansel in the slump of her shoulders. The pitch of her nose. It all seems so fallible, the things she once took for truth.

"Why are you here?" Hazel asks. "Why would you come, for someone like him?"

"If I'm being honest, I don't really know." The girl's voice collapses. "I think—well, bad people feel pain, too."

Blue's hands drip into the basin. The bathroom echoes, cavernous. In the long wait, Hazel sees hurt. It is different from Hazel's own, but it is hurt nonetheless. With soapy fingers, Blue reaches up. She says nothing more as she watches Hazel leave, her fingers playing at a locket, rusted red, dangling graceless around her neck.

•

When Hazel imagines death, she pictures a long, yawning sleep. More than a few times, she has yearned for it. She does not believe in heaven or hell, though faith would certainly be easier. As she stumbles back down the hall, abandoning Blue to the mirror, Hazel thinks how stupid it is. How absurd. A death like this—sterile, regulated, watched from a box—is just death. She has no idea to what extent it serves as punishment. The futility comes barreling down, a crumbling house. Hazel itches in the rubble. The utter pointlessness. The pure waste.

Back in the conference room, Hazel's mother sips a paper cup of water. The warden paces by the door—when he sees Hazel, he nods toward the exit. The reporters gather their things, as Hazel takes her mother's feathery hand.

"Are you ready?" the warden asks.

•

The memory comes with the first reluctant step. As Hazel follows the procession down the blank and empty hall, ribs thrumming, the enormity brings her back.

Come on, Hazel. I swear, the view is worth it.

Hazel is eight years old. She stands near the back-yard fence, blinking up at Jenny, who straddles the highest branch of the maple tree. They are not sup-posed to climb this tree—too dangerous, their mother has warned. From below, Hazel can see the soles of Jenny's bare feet, black from playing on the asphalt. Jenny leans down, offering a slippery hand, so con-fident, so easy to trust. Hazel kicks panicked at the trunk, fear twisting through her abdomen as Jenny grips her wrist, pulls her onto the creaking branch. Hazel balances, her legs dangling down toward the lawn, savoring the rush of fearlessness.

Look, Jenny says, beaming.

The neighborhood fans out through the speckled leaves. Hazel can see into neighbors' yards, over fences and onto roofs, through shiny windows. The horizon is wide, and for the first time, endless. Jenny seems to know what she has gifted, because she pats Hazel on the shoulder, abundantly wise.

You can see everything, Jenny says, as the world folds open. *From the beginning, all the way to the end.*

The witness room is a tiny theater. The window is paneled with bars, the beige curtains drawn shut. There are no seats. Hazel leads her mother inside—they stand awkwardly in the center of the concrete box, the reporters lingering respectfully behind. From the other side of the curtain, Hazel can hear a faint, shuffling murmur. The glug of an IV bag. A heart monitor's persistent beep.

Jenny arrives then, hovering. As the curtains slide open, as Hazel squints onto the stage, Jenny is here.

She is a scent, fleeting. A whiff. A glimmer. Jenny is in the oxygen that fills Hazel's lungs, she is in the stubborn clench of Hazel's fist. As Hazel peers through the glass and into the execution room, Jenny winks out from her own reflection. This, Hazel knows, is the miracle of sisterhood. Of love itself. Death is cruel, and infinite, and inevitable, but it is not the end. Jenny exists in every room Hazel walks through. She fills, she shivers. She spreads, dispersing, until she is nowhere—until she is everywhere—until she lives wherever Hazel carries her.

0

It is now.

As the footsteps arrive, you press a hand to your cheek. Stubble, jutting bone. You try to memorize the curve of your own jaw, the shape of the self you have lived with all your life. You do not know whether you hate your own body or if you will miss it when it's gone.

•

The officers wait in front of your cell. Six of them, faceless, plus the chaplain, the Death House warden, and a balding man from the Office of the Inspector General. His voice is muffled, far away, like you are listening from underwater. They reach through the bars with a pair of handcuffs.

Your heart is a stick of dynamite. Waiting, useless, for the explosion. The guards unlock the door and beckon you forward.

One step, then another. You walk through.

The march from the cell to the execution chamber is cruelly short. Fifteen feet. You count each pace as it passes, the officers flanking like you are the president of the United States. Each second stretches, incalculable.

Too soon, you are in the room.

The execution chamber looks exactly how you imagined. The walls are green, the brick painted in a sickly shade of mint, like a stick of spearmint gum. There is a new smell here: medical equipment, the sharp zing of chemicals. In the center of the space, there is a gurney. The gurney has straps along the sides for each of your limbs, like some medieval device, and a microphone hangs on a cord from the ceiling.

How insane, you think. How deranged. The government paid money for this glorified table and placed it in this room. These twelve people woke up this morning, put on their uniforms, and drove to work, just to perform this demented exercise. The citizens of your very own country pay taxes to keep this operation running, to supply the three drugs that will flow through the IV. Your own neighbors—your mailman, your grocery store clerk, the single mother across the street—pay money to make sure your government can kill you in exactly this way.

They do not give you time. It moves too fast: you are ushered forward, and your own traitor legs propel you thoughtlessly onto the gurney. A flurry of activity, as the officers strap you down, a practiced choreography.

When the process is done, you stare up at the ceiling, arms stretched to the sides like a child flopped down to make a snow angel. The ceiling has no cracks. The ceiling has no stains. You miss your elephant.

•

A memory. You are nine years old. You are on the living room floor at Miss Gemma's, fingers tangled in the brown shag carpet. You sit in a circle with the other children, a copy of the Holy Bible open in your lap. A pretty older girl reads from Corinthians—you watch her lips, not hearing the words.

What do we know about Jesus's crucifix? Miss

Gemma asks. Miss Gemma's eyes are lidded heavy, her hair a chemical dyed halo. She fingers a dainty cross, glinting across her sunspotted chest.

The crucifix helps us understand Jesus's suffering, she says. It also helps us understand his love.

The warden's cologne is oppressive, filling the space in a noxious cloud. He checks the straps on the gurney. The medical team bustles around you, preoccupied, indifferent to your discomfort. The chaplain is the only one who gravitates to your center—the chaplain understands that you do not want to speak, because he only stands there, like a dog with its head nestled against your leg.

You look away as the IVs are inserted. Both arms. You feel the tiny pricks of pain, hear the fluid gulping through the bag. The medical technician adjusts the settings—you can smell the specific of her, not a perfume or a deodorant, but the way her house must smell when you first walk inside. Like cucumber soap, with something mustier beneath it. A strand of her hair has wafted onto your shirt, landed just beneath your armpit, and it lifts into the air with the force of your breath. Delicate, feminine, floating adrift.

The names come to you then—a surprise. You so rarely think of them as separate people, those Girls, but they feel different in this instant. Distinct and exacting. Izzy, Angela, Lila. Jenny.

Are you comfortable? the technician asks.

No, you say.

Is it the IV? she asks.

No, you say.

She clicks out of the room.

•

A sound, behind the curtains. Shuffling feet, soft murmur.

The witnesses.

Before you can prepare yourself, the curtains shimmy open, and you are no longer alone.

•

Through the window on the right, Jenny's mother appears.

She is stooped now, elderly. Her face is wrecked—

even through the trial, through the sentencing, she never looked quite like this. Above the collar of her suit jacket, Jenny's mother looks devastated, tears falling rapidly and silently down her papery cheeks. You can tell from how her brow knits: she is crying for Jenny, but there is more. This woman has known you for nearly thirty years, and you recognize her shattered pity. Jenny's mother is also crying for you.

By her side, Hazel stands rigid. She watches you, intent, without fear or hesitation. You remember how Hazel used to steal glances from across the living room—how she used to want you. Now, she does not smile. She does not cry. She only blames her gaze right onto your helplessness. Unsettled, you realize it is exactly how Jenny used to look at you. From the angled gurney, Hazel is just as implacable as Jenny herself. Just as perplexing. Your arm jerks against the gurney's strap, your body's instinct a cruelty in itself—you want to touch her one last time.

And there she is. Through the window on the left.

Blue stands next to Tina, strawberry hair pulled back from her neck. The corners of her have filled out, grown. Blue looks like a summer evening. Like a dusk spent wading through fields of bluegrass, like gentle hands brushing your hair from your eyes. At the sight of Blue's freckled nose, you hear your mother's voice, clearer than ever before.

•

The seconds tick down. You catch your own reflection in the glass, an accident. You are transparent in the crowd of their faces. A ghost already, halfway gone. Your cheekbones look hollow, your glasses sit too big on your face. You are horrified to see that in these last waiting minutes, you only look like yourself.

You are certain, then. Within all the despicable things you have done—here, in the last two minutes of your life—here is the proof. You do not feel the same love that everyone else does. Yours is muted, damp, not bursting or breaking. But there is a place for you, in the category of personhood. There has to be. Humanity can discard you, but they cannot deny it. Your heart pounds. Your palms sweat. Your body wants and wants. It seems abundantly clear now, the opportunity you've wasted. There is good and there is evil, and the contradiction lives in everyone. The good is simply the stuff worth remembering. The good is the point of it all. The slippery thing you have always been chasing.

It arrives, at first, tingling small. Fleeting, a lump at the base of your throat. Something fragile and birdlike is trapped in your body, fluttering inconsolable.

Fear.

You swallow it in.

Last words, the warden says. The medical staff and the chaplain have all gone now—you suspect they wait somewhere behind the smudgy glass mirror. The room feels smaller, just you and the warden.

A boom mic is lowered from the ceiling. You have not prepared. Ten seconds pass by, unbearably thick. For once, there is no game to play. No power to withhold, nobody to trick or impress. You have lived your years in careful imitation, mimicking the things someone else would say, think, feel, and now you are tired. The microphone is too far from the gurney—you struggle against the straps, trying to reach.

I promise I'll be better, you say, your voice booming sorry. Give me one more chance.

There is no answer. Only the shifting eyes of the witnesses behind the glass, averted uncomfortable.

You wish for touch, in this moment, for the feeling of someone else's hand in yours. Your whole body shudders, grasping for something more meaningful than tears.

The warden removes his glasses.

The infamous signal.

Now.

You pray. In the next life, you hope you will be reincarnated as something softer—something that understands the innate sort of longing that makes a being whole. A graceful creature. Hummingbird. A dove.

They swore you would not feel it. They swore it would not hurt. But there is pain in this kind of fear—blistering, primal. It hurts, the chemicals bursting through your veins, your limbs twitching wild against the straps.

No, you beg.

A consuming panic, as the poison floods your body.

Don't. Please.

Outside this room, the beating world continues. The sun is low and pinking. Tall grass splays across endless fields. The air smells, out there, like spruce and river, like salt and hydrangea. You see it all, a flash of perfect omniscience: the whole of the planet, orbiting carelessly, indifferent and vivid and stunning and cruel. It blinks at you, briefly, before moving on.

•

As your hands lose sensation, as the edges of your vision water and dissolve, something seems to rise. A mass. It lifts from your chest and into the air, hovering above the blurry room. You want to reach out and touch—but you are immobile. The mass is the dark of you, the thing that tugs. In this last half-second, the very end of yourself, you understand both the tragedy and the mercy. You look it dead in the eye, the center of that raging storm. Cleaved from you, it seems so small. Powerless.

There is a millisecond of glory, in which you exist without it, in which you are bright, erupting. Full of love. This is it, you know. The sensation you've been

missing. In this fading instant, it fills you to bursting—
your life's great and singular generosity.

One last shuddering exhale, one last rattling whoosh
of breath.

A wide and awful lunge. Sweeping, wrecking.
Blazing, glorious.

At last.

Elsewhere

In another world, they are sleeping. They are setting the table, or jogging through the park, they are watching the news or helping with math homework, they are working late, walking the dog, pulling clogs of hair from the shower drain. In another world, this is a regular evening for Izzy, Angela, Lila, Jenny. But they do not live in that world—and they do not live in this one.

•

Here is how Izzy Sanchez would like to be remembered:

She is lying on her grandfather's sailboat, stretched long on a purple towel. The Tampa day is cartoon sunny. Her sister, Selena, is slathered in tanning spray, coconut-scented oil pooled in the dent of her belly button. Izzy's fingers are sticky, her nails yellow from the tangerine she just peeled—she throws the skin off the side of the boat, watches it float behind in the wake. A manatee! her little brother shouts. Her mother holds him by the ribs to keep him from falling overboard— ten cuidado, pequeño. Izzy's hipbones protrude like jutting jaws from her bikini bottom, and her fingers smell like orange and sunscreen.

No one remembers Izzy like this. Her sister, Selena, does, but only when she makes herself think past the horror. Usually Izzy—the real Izzy—is invisible beneath the shadow of what happened to her. The tragedy is that she is dead, but the tragedy is also that she belongs to him. The bad man, who did the bad thing. There are millions of other moments Izzy has lived, but he has eaten them up one by one, until she exists in most memories as a summation of that awful second, distilled constantly in her fear, her pain, the brutal fact.

From wherever Izzy is now, she wishes she could say: Before all this, my shoulders burned scarlet. I peeled off the flakes, flicked them into the sink. There were things I felt, before the fear.

I ate an orange in the sun. Let me tell you how it tasted.

Angela Meyer would have traveled to twenty-seven countries. Her favorite would have been Italy—not nearly as exotic as Malaysia or Botswana or Uruguay, but she would have loved the ancient heart of that country, entrenched proudly in tradition. She would have walked the cobblestones of Florence, Siena, Sorrento, licking plastic spoons of gelato, head buzzing from the wine. Angela would have taken her mother on vacation to the Amalfi Coast. They would have ordered vongole pasta on the balcony of their seaside hotel, the air tinged lavish with lemon trees and salt.

At the end of the trip, Angela would have tipped the housekeepers twenty percent. Those women, local teenagers, would have used the bills on shots of tequila at the nightclub across the street, not thinking of Angela, only thinking of the heat, their young sweating bodies, the pulse of the lights and the sound of the music, beating everything into oblivion.

Lila's third child would have been a girl after all.

They would have named her Grace.

She does not exist, but if she did, Grace would have

become the executive director of the Columbus Zoo. She would have managed eight hundred employees, ten thousand animals, and a five-hundred-acre property.

Grace's favorite charge would have been the snow leopard: a lean, dignified animal with a lush coat of spotted white. After closing one night, a sweltering June, Grace would have found herself alone in the feline wing, the cleaning staff already gone home. She would have walked down to the leopard's terrarium, intent on admiring before she said goodnight. She'd have stood at the entrance to the leopard's high cage, stunned by the elegance of the animal—giant yellow eyes would have met hers. An invitation. She'd have unlocked the feeding door, her heart warning a patter as she inched forward, two steps. Forward, two more. The leopard would have watched as Grace slid to the floor against the interior wall, a smile snarling at its jaw. The leopard would have stalked slowly up to her, sniffed Grace's outstretched hand in a whoosh of meaty breath. The animal would have unfurled its limbs, curled its long body into the nook where Grace's armpit met her ribs. Together, they'd have slept.

At dawn, Grace would have woken to a mouthful of fur, the leopard's head resting gigantic on her knee. She would have thought: How gentle, this world. How tender, this mercy.

•

There would have been 6,552 babies. Over a span of eighteen years, 6,552 hearts would have beat unconscious, cocooned in the blank swim of their mothers' wombs. 204 of those babies would have been born blue, then slapped awake. 81 would have died. But 6,471 infants would have taken their first gasps of oxygen as they slid from echoing caves—they'd have stretched their thrashing limbs into Jenny's waiting hands.

Jenny would have been a blur. Their eyes, still so new, would not have been able to track her face. But 6,471 newborns would have felt the soothing capability of Jenny's gloved palms, the humility of her fingertips as she checked their vitals, wiped them clean. They'd have heard Jenny's voice, rumbling the same words every time she passed them into their mothers' sticky arms.

Welcome, little one, Jenny would have whispered into each precious seashell ear.

You'll see. It's good here.

Acknowledgments

This book is dedicated to my literary agent, Dana
Murphy, because I owe its existence to her pro-
foundly generous mind. Dana held faith in my work
through moments of existential fear and self-doubt—
she provided wise counsel, a level voice, necessary hon-
esty, and a tender understanding of the novel's aim. I
am lucky to call her my artistic soul mate and a dear,
invaluable friend.

In my editor, Jessica Williams, I've found a warm
creative home. Jessica saw straight down to the heart of
this book, pulled out its best parts, and held them up
to the light. I'm grateful to Jessica, and to Julia Elliott,
for making this publishing experience feel dynamic,
delightful, and extraordinarily rewarding.

Thank you to Liate Stehlik for her support, to Brittani Hilles and the William Morrow publicity team for their dedication, and to the HarperCollins sales force for their stunning show of enthusiasm. Thank you to production editor Jessica Rozler, copyeditor Andrea Monagle, and sensitivity reader Neha Patel. For his incisive help with detailed research, many thanks to Dylan Simburger. I'm grateful to the lovely ladies of the Book Group, and to Jenny Meyer for her belief in this novel's life abroad; thank you to Darian Lanzetta, Austin Denesuk, Dana Spector, and the rest of the team at CAA. Thank you to Francesca Main and Phoenix Books for providing this novel a loving home in the UK.

I am forever indebted to Michelle Brower, who gave me a career as a literary agent—a job I didn't know I needed, which has enriched my world so fully. Thank you to my colleagues at Aevitas Creative Management, and to my clients for trusting me with their words.

Thank you to my inimitable writing group here in Seattle: Kim Fu, Danielle Mohlman, and Lucy Tan, thank you for listening over coffee all these years. Thank you to Caitlin Flynn, for her steady friendship and passion for all things crime. Thank you to Mary Rourke and Janet Charbonnier, for providing an outlet and a source of comfort at Acorn Street Shop (also, lots of yarn). Thank you to Dominick Scavelli and Janelle Chandler for their help behind the scenes.

I'm overwhelmed with gratitude for the crowd of friends that lifted me up along this particular winding path: Jenessa Abrams, Carla Bruce-Eddings, Al Guillen, Maggie Honig, Abi Inman, Zack Knoll, Ida Knox, Ellen Kobori, Danielle Lazarin, Emily McDermott, Kaitlyn Lundeby Miller, Karthika Raja, and many more. You know who you are.

I would not be here without my beloved family. Thank you to Arielle Kukafka, David Kukafka, Laurel Kukafka, and Joshua Kukafka. Thank you to Avi Rocklin, Talia Zalesne, and Zach Zalesne. Thank you to Shannon Duffy, Pete Weiland, and Maddy Weiland. Lisa Kaye, Aiden Kaye, and the whole extended crew. I love you all so much.

Thank you to Tory Kamen, because of course. To Hannah Neff, my oldest and always. To Remy-Bear, smallest of pups, sweetest of baby boys, source of constant and unbridled joy. Thank you to Liam Weiland, my love, for this astonishing life.

About the Author

DANYA KUKAFKA is the internationally bestselling author of *Girl in Snow*. She is a graduate of New York University's Gallatin School of Individualized Study. She works as a literary agent.

HARPER
LARGE PRINT

We hope you enjoyed reading
our new, comfortable print size and found it
an experience you would like to repeat.

Well – you're in luck!

Harper Large Print offers the finest in
fiction and nonfiction books in this same larger
print size and paperback format. Light and easy to read,
Harper Large Print paperbacks are for the book lovers
who want to see what they are reading without strain.

For a full listing of titles and
new releases to come, please visit our website:
www.hc.com

HARPER LARGE PRINT